D1497968

# BENEATH THE WIDE SILK SKY

# BENEATH THE WIDE SILK SKY

## EMILY INOUYE HUEY

SCHOLASTIC PRESS / *New York*

*A Note to Readers: The transliterations of Japanese words and phrases are italicized throughout the book in order to avoid any confusion with English words.*

Library of Congress Cataloging-in-Publication Data available

ISBN 978-1-338-78994-2

1 2022

Printed in the U.S.A. 23

First edition, October 2022

Book design by Elizabeth B. Parisi

Cherry blossoms art © Getty Images (Diane Labombarbe and Pingwin)

*In memory of Charles and Bessie Inouye*

"The dignity of man must always be preserved."
—Charles Ichiro Inouye

# CHAPTER 1

# TWO SURPRISES

*December 4, 1941*

I jumped as the rat streaked across the edge of the chicken pen. Feathers whirled around Clark Gable, our rooster, as he half ran, half flew at the rat. Head down and outstretched, Clark aimed for the rat with his sharp beak.

The rat dashed through the wire fencing of the chicken pen, then scuttled across the barn, out of Clark's reach. Its long tail disappeared through a crack in the barn's wood wall. Clark ruffled his gold and black feathers, somehow managing to look embarrassed.

I stood holding my rake, heart thumping. Rats were common on the farm, but still, each time . . .

"Sam? You in here?" Beau's voice rang, confident as the boy himself, through the open barn door.

I dropped my rake, and it clattered to the floor, sending up a cloud of straw and chicken feathers. Coughing, I used my hands to comb my bangs, shaking golden bits of hay out of my black hair. "Don't come in!" I called. "I'll come to you."

But Beau had already stepped inside. Through the doorway, cold December light silhouetted his round-shouldered frame. His hair spilled in a strawberry-blond halo around his head—an angel in suede. I stared, conscious of the difference between us.

"I—I'm just doing some chores." I pulled open the wire door that kept the chickens on their side of the barn and stumbled out of the pen.

Beau grinned. "You okay there?"

I straightened, trying to look as if I weren't ruffled. Beau was my best friend, but he lived on the other side of Linley Island—the "good" side. He would never have to rake chicken manure in a rat-infested barn, and his arrival in the middle of my chores felt like a clashing of worlds. "I'm fine," I said, swiping at my bangs again.

"Beau, we'll be late, and it's starting to snow." I stiffened at the nasal voice. SueAnn Clark stepped into the barn behind Beau. Her blond curls glowed gold with the light behind them. "And the smell in here!" She covered her nose with her handkerchief. "Are you sure we couldn't just—" She stopped. "Oh. Hello, Samantha." She said my name as if it tasted sour and edged closer to Beau.

I stared at the narrow gap between them—their hands might touch at any moment. Had they finally become an item? My stomach clenched, but I kept my voice light. "What brings you out?" I pivoted to face only Beau.

Beau fished a folded paper from his trouser pocket. "We're on our way to study chemistry at Hank's." My mouth twitched. I was in the same class and ate lunch with Hank, Beau, and SueAnn nearly every day—why hadn't I been invited? "But I had to stop by to give you this." Beau handed me the paper. "Saw it in one of Mother's magazines."

I unfolded what appeared to be some sort of entry form. Across the top, bold type read, "Call for amateur photographers! Statewide contest. Cash prizes in every category." I glanced at SueAnn and tilted the paper so she couldn't see. I scanned the subheading. "Wha—" My eyes darted to Beau, who was almost bouncing. I whispered, "Grand prize of fifty dollars?"

A smile rounded Beau's rosy cheeks. "You have to enter."

I rocked on my heels. Fifty dollars. It was more than I'd ever seen, let alone owned. My mind reeled at the thought of what I could buy. I could get a new camera. My current camera, an ancient Brownie, was taped together and sometimes leaked light.

I skim ed the rest of the form: "Top photos to be published in leading m gazine." My heart leapt. I had never had a photo published. It h d always seemed like something that was such a reach, only *maybe* possible, and only in the very far future.

"What's fifty dollars?" SueAnn stepped forward, her gray eyes sharp above the handkerchief.

"Never mind," I said, refolding the paper.

But Beau was already answering. "It's a photo contest."

"That's what you had to rush over to give her?" SueAnn asked. Her eyes narrowed and slid to me. "You take photos?"

My tongue felt fat. "Yes. Sometimes."

Beau's chest swelled with confidence I couldn't imagine. "Sam's going to be a photographer. A real one."

"Beau!" My face flamed. He had promised not to tell anyone.

"Sorry," Beau said. And he meant it. But still, it was as if my secret had been spilled on the floor—in front of SueAnn of all people.

SueAnn eyed me. "A photographer? Girls aren't photographers."

There it was, everyone's first reaction, the boot trampling my dream. I didn't respond.

"But there are women photographers," Beau said. "Sam told me about a famous one. Dorothy something."

"Dorothea," I corrected him in a small voice. "Dorothea Lange."

"Right," Beau said. "Sam's going to be like her and travel all over—"

"Beau!" My face felt hot and damp. He was telling SueAnn everything.

"Shucks, Sam," Beau said. "You're not doing anything wrong."

I swallowed. Beau didn't get it. He was a boy, he was white, and his family was probably the wealthiest on Linley Island. He could afford to dream. It was different for a daughter of a dirt-poor Japanese farmer. Dreaming was against the rules. Dreaming was dangerous.

"'Sides," Beau said, "you should see her photos, Sue. Sam's good. She's even better than Mr. Simmons." Beau grinned, waiting for my reaction.

I suppressed a smile. It wasn't the best compliment. Ancient and cantankerous, Mr. Simmons had taken the same portrait for decades, lining people up in front of the camera and shooting them straight on in something like a family mug shot. But he *was* our little island's official photographer. And Beau only said things he meant. A tiny seed of something warm glowed in my chest.

"Really?" SueAnn asked. "You'd travel? By yourself? That's *improper.*" There was a flat sureness to the word.

I stared at the worn toes of my boots. Most people thought like SueAnn. My brother, Charlie, was supportive. But Kiki, my social butterfly of a sister, couldn't understand why I'd dream of spending hours behind a camera, and Dad had been livid when I'd kept back a few cents from my cleaning jobs to buy film last spring. Even my mother, before she died, hadn't known my photography was more than a hobby.

"I just play at it." My chin fell to my chest. "It's not like I think I could be a real photographer." The words burned in my throat, as hot and dry as ash.

SueAnn nodded, satisfied. Beau gave me an exasperated look and opened his mouth to argue. But SueAnn pointed out the barn door. "Oh, Beau, the snow. It's coming down fast."

Beau looked out the door at the snow now whirling in frenzied flurries. He stepped forward, posting himself at one side of the door so he could look out at his shiny blue Studebaker.

"Shouldn't we drive back?" SueAnn asked. "We're already late for Hank's, and the roads in this neighborhood . . ." Unlike the paved streets that ran over most of the island, the corner everyone called "Japantown" was crisscrossed with rutted dirt roads.

"Yeah," Beau sighed. "We better go before it sticks."

SueAnn nodded smartly, then sashayed across the hay-strewn floor toward the door, dismissing me as easily as my dream.

Beau hesitated, then walked back. He leaned so close I could have counted his freckles. "Don't listen to SueAnn," he whispered. He smelled like suede and shaving cream. "Enter the contest. And stop making yourself so . . . small."

I swallowed. He made it sound so easy. But it wasn't, not for me.

"Okay, Ace?" he asked.

I half smiled at the corny nickname he'd given me when I told him I wanted to be a photographer. He'd confused photographers with reporters, but I loved the name anyway. It was a secret, something just ours.

"I better get back to SueAnn." Beau put his hands in his shearling-lined jacket pockets.

"Beau," I blurted.

I checked the door. SueAnn was gone. She couldn't get out of the barn fast enough. But was she just outside? Would she hear me if I asked Beau the questions burning in my throat?

Were they a couple now? And if they were, would that change things between him and me?

I felt a desperate need to know— but as Beau's eyes lingered on my face, I couldn't form the words. I had told Kiki more than once that Beau and I were only friends. For one thing, he was white. I was Japanese. It just wasn't allowed.

But now, faced with the possibility that he might be dating someone else, I felt a little sick.

"Sam?" I jolted at my brother's voice coming from the barn door. "Is someone here?"

"Hiya, Charlie." Beau stepped into the light. "Just me."

"And SueAnn," I added, not knowing what Charlie would think if Beau and I were alone.

"Look, I've gotta go. I'll talk to you soon?" Beau asked.

I nodded.

Beau strode out of the barn. I stared as the snow fell in his wake, crushing the entry form inside the folds of my skirt.

Charlie's gaze followed my movement. "What's that?"

For a moment I waffled. But if there was anyone I could tell, it was Charlie, who for as long as I could remember had been both my hero and my confidant.

"Beau brought me an entry form." I handed him the paper. "For a contest."

Charlie took the form in his bad hand. Damaged in a childhood accident, it remained withered even now, the only part of him not built like a tank.

I chewed my lip as Charlie read. His dark brows rose as he finished reading, and he looked up, beaming. "You have to enter."

I let out a deep breath, unable to keep from smiling. "You think so? I'm not sure I have a chance."

"Of course you do." Charlie's voice was clear, certain.

I wished I were so sure. Then a thought struck me. "But if I do enter and somehow win, I'll put the money in your college jar."

Charlie shook his head. "Nah. You don't have to do that."

For less than a second, I dreamed again of a camera. But I looked at Charlie, at his face still full of certainty for me. He'd always been the person who "got" me. I knew what he would do if I were the one waiting.

"If I win, it's yours," I promised. "That's what we all want."

"All?" A shadow flitted across the high, broad planes of Charlie's face. Our mother—we called her Okaasan—had wanted college for Charlie more than anything. He'd been accepted and was preparing to move to Seattle. But when Okaasan got sick, Dad asked Charlie to postpone for a year to help on the farm. And this fall, a year after Okaasan's death, Dad had used Charlie's fund to make the mortgage payment—it was that or lose the farm. So Charlie had to put off school again.

"Thanks, Sammy," Charlie said, his voice rough. He handed me the form and grimaced. "I've gotta turn compost."

I slipped the entry into my skirt pocket. "I should get on with my chores, too." I stepped back into the chickens' pen and picked up my rake.

Charlie trudged toward the other side of the barn. "Jeesh. This place is a dump." Metal clattered as he waded through a mess of hoes and spades, some usable but others broken or crumbling in rust. "Why doesn't Dad ever throw anything—"

Charlie broke off and cursed.

I spun around. "What is it?"

Charlie stood beyond the wire fence of the chicken pen, a sick look plastered across his face. "Rats." He pointed to the wood barrels at the back of the barn.

The rake slid through my fingers. "They got into the spring seed?"

Charlie nodded.

The wire door jangled and the chickens squawked as I climbed out of the pen. I stumbled through the mess of tools till I reached my brother.

"No. *No.*" I stared down at the barrels. Rats had chewed through their bottom rims, leaving holes like Swiss cheese. Shining seeds dribbled through onto the droppings-strewn floor.

Next year's crops depended on those seeds.

Fear and something sharper flickered over Charlie's face. "I have to tell Dad."

Dad glowered as he rushed in, only steps behind Charlie. His long, wiry eyebrows hooked up at the ends, and his eyes were sharp.

"How much?" Dad asked, his accent thicker, the way it got when he was upset.

"Maybe half," Charlie said. Dad and I followed him through the barn. "They got this barrel pretty good." Charlie tapped a hollow-sounding barrel with a pitchfork. "That other one's down maybe a quarter or a third."

Dad whirled on me. "You didn't notice?"

I folded my arms and bowed, making myself as small as possible, but my stomach burned—hadn't he been in the barn a hundred times, too? But in seconds, the anger turned to guilt. Why hadn't I noticed? I could have saved the seed—and so much money.

"And you used the *wood* barrels?" Dad glared at Charlie, pointing at a stack of banged-up metal canisters in the opposite corner of the barn. *"Baka na koto!"*

I squirmed and stepped backward. Dad's slip into Japanese was a warning sign. Unlike Okaasan, who spoke mostly Japanese, Dad usually spoke English with us, arguing that it would help us blend in better.

Veins crisscrossed Charlie's fists as he gripped the pitchfork's handle. "You only said to get it into the barn."

Dad scowled. *"This* is the reason I use metal."

Charlie grimaced.

"Without seed—" Dad smashed both fists on the barrel. I cringed, and Charlie froze. Behind me, the chickens scrambled, a jumble of feathers and squawks. I half expected rats to run out of the barrel, but instead, there was a soft, slippery rustle, and more seed flowed onto the floor.

"We cannot miss the payment," Dad said, stress weighting each word. "Not when we're so close. Nothing can get in the way."

"Nothing?" The word came out pinched, and Charlie's shoulders swelled as he dug the pitchfork's rusty tines into the dirt floor.

I stepped closer and tried to take him by the elbow, but he didn't feel my touch through his jacket. "Just like last time?"

Dad's nostrils flared. "This is as much about your future as college. The farm is in your name."

Charlie's eyes tightened to slivers. "Only because you couldn't use your own." State law didn't allow noncitizens to own land. And though Dad had been here since he was a teenager, US law didn't allow Japanese immigrants to become citizens.

Dad reddened. "The money you've saved from your job at the brickyard—" He didn't finish, but Charlie knew what he meant.

"No." Charlie jabbed the ground with the pitchfork. "I've already lost too many semesters. All my friends are halfway through degrees. I stayed when Okaasan got sick. I stayed even when you stole my college fund."

"*Stole?*" Dad's expression hardened.

Charlie hesitated. I wanted to pull him back, as if from the edge of a cliff. But his face shifted, and I knew I was too late. "You weren't the only one to save that money. Okaasan meant it to go to my tuition. I heard you, in the hospital." His eyes glinted. "You promised *her.*"

The air in the barn imploded. "*Damare!*" Dad squared his body to Charlie's. "You *will* help your family."

I held my breath. Charlie's fists looked like they might crush the pitchfork's handle. Though he and Dad were short, they both had the same sturdy, bearlike build. Either could cause real hurt.

Dad took a shuddering breath. "Just one more year," he said, his voice strained but softer. "You will go to college. We just need to get through this last payment. This land, all this work—it's for you. It's your future."

For a moment, Charlie said nothing. I squirmed, fingering the edge of the folded paper in my pocket.

"I—" Charlie hesitated, then looked straight at Dad. "I don't want it. The money I made at the brickyard—I'm going to use it for college." Charlie held Dad's eyes another second before letting the pitchfork fall to the ground. "I'm getting off this island." His voice broke as he turned and strode out of the barn.

"Charlie!" Dad took a step toward the barn door. But Charlie didn't come back.

Hunching, Dad gripped the barrel, then glanced at me and scowled. "Clean this mess up," he said, stalking past.

The barn door slammed, and Dad's crunching footsteps faded, leaving only the wind's songlike whistle and the clucking of chickens. I stepped forward and squatted, surveying the mess of rat poop and strewn seed.

I sighed and pushed my way through Dad's scattered equipment, trying not to imagine rats scurrying around my ankles as I picked my way toward the metal bins in the corner of the barn.

Outside, the wind stuttered—a haunting *wah-shah-shah*. Even within the walls of the barn, I could feel the sharp draft. "Oh, Okaasan," I whispered. "If only you were here."

The bins clanged as I dropped them next to the barrels. I hoisted the first waist-tall barrel onto my knee—I could manage now that it was half-empty—and began pouring the seed into one of the metal bins. The first seeds pinged against the metal. But as the mound grew, the seeds landed with a shushing sound that reminded me so much of when Okaasan poured dry rice into a pot. She never measured, just eyed it.

"If you were here, what would you do?" I whispered to the wind, setting the empty barrel back on the ground. As I leaned forward, the entry form fell from my pocket, fluttering and then resting on the spilled seed.

I bent down, picked up the paper, and ran its silky smoothness through my fingers. What if . . .

Fifty dollars. Fifty could make a real difference—for both Dad and Charlie. It was a long shot. I'd have to earn the money to buy film and have it developed. And I'd have to shoot a photo better than any I'd taken before. But if I could somehow do both, maybe there would be less fighting. Maybe it would even feel like we were a family again.

I would do it. I'd find a way to get film, and I would enter.

I tipped the next barrel and let a rush of seed flood the tin.

# CHAPTER 2

# AN EMBARRASSING FALL

When I finished cleaning up, the snow had stopped, but the windows of our worn, white house were dark. Before Okaasan's death, the windows had twinkled. I imagined opening the door to her tinkling welcome—*"Okaeri"*—and the smell of scalded soy sauce. I could almost hear Charlie's good-natured teasing as he, Kiki, and I snuck tastes of her cooking.

But if I went inside now, there'd be no greeting, only the ticking of Dad's clock echoing through the empty house. After fights, Charlie disappeared. More than likely, Dad was gone, too. And Kiki, preferring her friends, hadn't come home after school.

I couldn't bring myself to again sit alone in the empty house. I slipped my hand into my pocket and patted the slick paper of the entry form. If I could just find the perfect photo . . . I didn't have my camera with me, but that didn't matter. Film was so expensive that I thought long and hard before I took photographs, "snapping" mental practice photos, using my fingers to frame future shots.

What should I shoot? I knew photographers in bigger cities would be able to shoot big things—rallies, parades, maybe even riots. But important things didn't happen on our little Washington State island.

I made my way through the orchard, noting gnarled branches with lots of contrast, stubborn leaves that refused to fall, and, under a fresh dusting of snow, lush moss, fresh-as-spring lettuce, denying our mild winter. Above, the day's last clouds inched their way across a tangerine sky—could I capture that brilliance if I paid the steep price of color film?

Finally, I found myself in a clearing, where a pond marked the intersection of the Omuras' orchard, our little lot, and the Tanakas' yard behind us.

Wind rippled the black surface of the tiny cow pond. Though snow and ice laced the edges of the water, its center remained unfrozen, like a dark eye. It made me think of a photo I'd seen in *Life*. The magazine had called the photo of a brilliant green cornfield an "aerial shot," and it had been taken from an airplane. I stared at the thick cherry branch above the dark pond. Though I didn't have a plane, maybe I could get my own aerial shot.

I slipped my jacket off, folding and placing it at the base of the tree, then stopped to listen—just the wind and a few lonely birdcalls. No movement but the quivering of the fruit trees' bare arms. I hitched my skirt, pulling it between my legs and tucking the hem into my waistband, and climbed.

The tree's rough bark scraped my arms and the skin above my wool socks, but I wormed my way up the trunk, worn boot-soles and all. I straddled a thick branch and scooted out above the pond, then lowered my stomach and chest. Shoots of smaller twigs jabbed my stomach. When I jerked away, my skirt came untucked, swinging free. Clumps of snow and dried leaves fell into the dark water, disturbing its dappled reflection of the sky's last light.

*Not quite like the professionals*, I thought. I gritted my teeth and tried again, this time gripping the branch with my knees. I held my hands out, index fingers and thumbs squared to make a frame, and scrolled over the pond.

The south corner was picturesque. Thick, red-veined reeds bowed to kiss the water's surface. It was the shot I'd feel most comfortable taking—the pretty nature shot. But I knew it wasn't enough.

Not for the prize money. And not for my one chance at having a photo published.

A dark corner of the pond caught my attention. From the time I was little, I had been told to stay away from the deep, northeast section of the pond, in which previous families had sunk an old plow, rusted barbed wire, and other trash. Tangled in the wire was an old gray door, its wood swollen from several years in the water. I could still read the yellow paint that marred its face: *Get Out*. Dad had scraped away the third word—*Jap*—before he tore it off the hinges so Okaasan wouldn't see it. Then he'd bought a new door from the mill—a fancy, carved door unlike any in the neighborhood, painted a creamy robin's-egg blue—and installed it before Okaasan even knew our front door had been vandalized. My fingers dropped as I remembered her shy smile and the way her lips twisted as she whispered, "We cannot afford this, Matsuo." Later she must have heard that our neighbors' doors had been vandalized the same night. But she never let on that she knew the new door had been anything but a gift.

In the dimming light, the old door looked eerie, a reminder of months of fear. The local Farmers' Association had blamed Japanese growers for low produce prices that harvest, and some people had wanted to run us off. I held my hands out in front of me, framing the light-flecked, somehow threatening corner.

I knew at once. This could be my subject. This made me *feel*. Was that what the contest judges wanted? I had no idea. But I had to get this shot.

I edged forward on the branch, trying several angles. At one point, my foot slipped, sending another cascade of twigs into the pond. My heart raced as I realized I could have fallen. I would have to be more careful when I took the real shot—the thought of losing my camera made my stomach clench. But I clung with my knees and tried framing the shot once more. This time I centered my pretend shot on the shining green growth between the *Get Out* and the barbed wire, letting the human element take a background role. There was something about the way the live plants contrasted with the crumbling metal and the peeling paint . . .

A crackling of dry leaves interrupted my thoughts, and I froze. At first all I saw were orderly rows of bald trees. Then I saw the figure making its way through the orchard. It was too tall to be Charlie. I closed my eyes, willing whoever it was to stay far away. How could I explain myself? I couldn't say I was planning a photo—look how SueAnn had reacted.

A twig snapped a few rows away. The figure was making his way toward the pond!

I tried to scoot closer to the trunk and gather my skirt. In the fluster of movement, my boot skated off the branch. Hot, sharp pain slashed my thigh, and cold, light nothingness gaped above and beneath me.

In what felt like slow motion, my eyes locked on my neighbor, Hiro Tanaka. Charlie's friend watched, open-mouthed as I tumbled toward the dark surface of the water. Did I look as surprised as he did?

Water folded over me, and everything went black.

The thought of my camera seized me—was it ruined? No, it was safe at home. For a split second, I relaxed, then realized I needed to swim.

I paddled toward what I hoped was the surface of the water. Though Charlie had tried to teach me, I wasn't a strong swimmer, and my boots and skirt seemed to pull me back each time I kicked. My lungs ached, and for a moment, terror seared through me—what if something was caught in barbed wire? Then a firm hand closed over my wrist and tugged so hard it hurt.

Water broke over my face, and I took a ragged breath. "Are you okay?" Hiro's low voice cut through my splashing.

I coughed. "I—I'm fine." Cold buzzed in my ears, and the wind stung my skin. I fought the heaviness of my skirt and waded to the bank of the pond, collapsing on all fours at the base of the cherry tree.

"Here." I was vaguely aware of Hiro releasing my wrist as I blinked water out of my eyes. Hiro grabbed something from the ground—through the hair covering my face, I recognized my jacket, still folded. He knelt next to me and, wrapping his long arms around me, pulled first my jacket and then his own thick coat over my shoulders.

"Oh, but you'll be cold," I said, teeth chattering.

Hiro's wiry fingers were quick and deliberate as he tugged his suede bomber's hat onto my head. He picked me up and set me on my feet. "My house is closer," he said, looping his scarf around my neck. "Would you like to come dry off?"

"I just need to get home and get into some warm clothes," I said, stepping the other way. I'd have to go through the orchard to get to my house, while his was just around the hedge. But I couldn't bear to tell anyone else—even his kind father—what had happened.

"I'll walk you." He offered me his arm.

"That's okay," I started, but as I turned toward my house, I stumbled, and Hiro caught my arm—or rather, the triple-layer bundle of wet and dry clothes that encased it. And then, instead of letting go, he matched my stride.

"It's no trouble."

I swallowed, uncomfortably aware that my arm now dangled in his. No boy except Charlie had ever taken my arm, not even Beau. I imagined how mismatched the two of us looked. Kiki had said more than once that Hiro was the handsomest of the Japanese boys in her grade. And in all these clothes, I must look like a bundled-up baby. I prayed no one would see us—especially Kiki.

"What were you doing?" Something underneath Hiro's voice made me wonder if he was fighting laughter.

I frowned and wiped my forehead on my free shoulder, pressing it into the soap-smelling wool of his coat. How could I explain?

"Were you taking photographs?" he asked.

I stopped and faced him. My heart pounded. "How did you know?"

"Should I not know?" His skin, just the color of barley tea, crinkled at the corners of his dark eyes, and the muscle under his cheekbone twitched.

My face flamed. "I don't . . . usually . . . tell people." What must he think of me? Up in trees, falling into the pond, pursuing a man's profession?

Hiro cleared his throat. "I'm sorry if I'm prying. It's just my window looks out on the orchard. I've seen you out with your camera."

I could have jumped back into the pond.

Hiro smiled. "I'd love to see your work."

I broke away from his gaze and stumbled forward. But the word *work* rang in my mind. It seemed too important a word for my little efforts. But when I dared to look back at Hiro, I couldn't trace a hint of jest in his expression.

Besides the throaty cry of a bird, our steps were the only sounds in the orchard. I couldn't think of anything to say. Hiro was a senior like Kiki, two years ahead of me. And he'd always been Charlie's friend more than hers or mine. Of course, in the last couple of years he'd grown tall and handsome, and now Kiki seemed keen to get better acquainted.

We reached the split-rail fence that separated our lawn from the Omuras' orchard. I could see our door. Light streamed through one window on the lower floor, and smoke spilled out the chimney—someone had come home. I winced, realizing whoever it was would see me and want to know what had happened. Then I thought of them seeing me with my arm in Hiro's. "I can make it from here," I told him.

"I've seen you this far." He let go of my arm and hopped over the fence in one fluid motion. "Might as well see it through." He held out his other hand. I took it—it was warm even in this cold—and he pulled me over the fence.

"Thank you," I said, pulling my hand from his more roughly than I meant to. I wrapped my arms tight around myself, and he didn't try to take my arm again. But as I took the final quick, hard steps up the porch, he followed, jogging to keep up.

Just as I reached for the door, the iron handle turned. Kiki stood in front of us, her sharp eyes focused behind me.

# CHAPTER 3

# A CERTAIN KIND OF SISTER

"Hiro!" Kiki's voice was as light as water. "What a surprise!" My sister shook her head so a few ringlets cascaded over her shoulders. She had piled half her hair on top of her head, coiling and pinning it into a nest of jet-black curls. The other half hung in shiny ringlets around her soft, lovely face. It was more effort than most girls on Linley put into their appearance, and the curls looked like something you might see on a poodle's hind legs. But last year, the school had voted her "most likely to become a Hollywood starlet," which, according to her, was a real accomplishment. The only other Japanese kid to win any category was Joe Nakano, who'd gotten "most likely to own a Chinese restaurant."

"I didn't see you in science class today—were you there?" Kiki asked Hiro. I stood on the front porch, the wind cutting through both coats Hiro had bundled over me, but Kiki had eyes only for the tall figure behind me. I was used to being ignored, but I wished I could get past her and into the house.

"I was there," Hiro said.

Kiki gave him a coy look. "I should have sat by you."

Hiro's lips pulled into a small smile. Was he one of Kiki's admirers? Maybe that's why he'd wanted to walk me home.

"Er, here," I said, shrugging off Hiro's coat. I held it out to him, and he startled, as if I'd interrupted the trance Kiki had put him in.

"What happened to you?" Kiki's eyes widened as she saw me for the first time. Where Hiro's eyes crinkled at the corners and mine were plain, the size and shape of an apricot pit, Kiki's were deerlike.

Deeply set and luminous, they pulled you in, and might have given her a serious look except that they flicked up at the outer corners in flirtatious wisps. But now they swiveled, hard and appraising, from me, to the coat, to Hiro. "What were you two doing?"

"I got wet," I said, my voice more defensive than I'd intended. "Hiro helped me." Hiro took the jacket and folded it over his arm. "Thanks," I mumbled, pulling off his hat and scarf.

Kiki's face relaxed. I wasn't a threat. She stepped closer to Hiro, laying a few fingers on his arm. "Thank you so much for helping my kid sister. It was . . . gallant of you."

I rolled my eyes.

"Sure, of course," Hiro said.

I slipped past Kiki and looked back. Hiro's eyes met mine, and for a second, I felt a prickle of something like regret. Maybe there was something I should say—I could thank him again, or . . . or what? But then I saw Kiki's fingers, still resting on his arm. The two of them looked so right together. He really was handsome, and she was more beautiful than I'd ever be—a matching set.

My boots squelched as I stepped inside, closing the door behind me. I slipped off the boots and padded across the entry and into the kitchen, leaving wet toe-prints on the linoleum floor.

I hauled a giant pot to the sink and pumped water until my arm ached. Balancing the pot on one hip, I hoisted it over to the potbellied stove, where I set it atop the large, flat stovetop. Then I plopped down on the floor and waited for the water to get hot enough for a bath.

The heat warmed my face first, then my hands. As I let them fall into my lap, I blanched—the entry form! It had been in my coat pocket. What if it had gotten wet when Hiro wrapped my coat around me? I dug into my pocket, feeling queasy at its dampness.

I pulled the form out slowly, afraid of what I might see. But the paper looked exactly as it had before. A little colder, maybe, but not wet. I let out a breath.

The front door opened and shut. "Oh, Sam!" Kiki squeal-whispered, rounding the wall that separated the entry from the kitchen. "I have to thank you for falling into that pond!"

"What?" I slipped the form back into my pocket.

Kiki ran to watch Hiro's retreat from the kitchen window. "Hiro told me what happened—well, not exactly, but he said he'd walked you back from the pond." She turned from the window to me and grinned, but her eyes weren't unkind. In fact, they were warmer and somehow more gentle—like they had been before Okaasan died. "I'm sorry, but also . . ." She waltzed toward me and leaned on the kitchen table. "See, I've been trying to find a way to talk to Hiro about the Sweethearts' Ball. And tonight"—she nearly glowed in the light of the gas lamp that stood on the table—"I planted the seed."

"What does that mean?" I asked, not sure whether to be peeved or to laugh. Something inside me stirred, remembering how much closer Kiki and I had been before Okaasan died. Kiki had always been a little vain and obsessed with boys. And my "strange hobbies" had always annoyed and confused her. But even with our different interests, we'd shared chores and a room and had turned to each other when we needed to talk. We'd been companions, if not exactly friends. I missed that.

It was as if when Okaasan died, Kiki had needed something to distract her. She'd thrown herself into climbing the social ladder, insisting that she was fine, and hadn't wanted to talk even when I *needed* to. I was no longer used to her chatting with me like this . . . And I was afraid of how much I liked it.

"Give me two weeks," Kiki said. "Maybe even one, if I'm lucky, and he'll invite me to Sweethearts'. I'm sure of it."

I raised my eyebrows. "How do you figure?"

She shrugged. "Oh, all the usual. I 'just mentioned' Shelley had said something about the dance, then asked him if he'd invited anyone yet. So of course he reciprocated and asked if I had a date. And I said"—she batted her lashes with fake shyness—"'I'm waiting for an invitation from the right person.'" She came out of her act, shrugging again.

"That works?" I asked.

She grinned. "Of course."

I frowned, both impressed and a little disturbed. How could it all be so . . . methodical?

"Why are you still in those wet things?" Kiki frowned and walked—or rather, floated—to the closed-in back porch where clean laundry hung in lines. She pulled my sweater and one of her own skirts from the clothesline. "Here. Change into this."

"I'm waiting on the bathwater," I said. "And I'm covered in pond scum." But I was a little touched. For money's sake, Kiki and I had to share clothes, but she usually didn't volunteer.

Kiki set the clothes down and knelt beside me, picking bits of moss from my hair. "By the way, I saw Beau today. I was visiting Shelley, and Beau and a bunch of other kids came over to study with Hank."

*Bunch of other kids*, I thought. *But not me.*

"Anyway," Kiki went on, "Beau told me about the contest."

I hunched closer to the stove. "He told you, too?" Something wriggled in the pit of my stomach.

"He told me to convince you to do it. And you definitely should!" Kiki said. "I mean, it's fifty dollars! Maybe I should enter, too." Kiki pulled a leaf out of my hair.

"Th-thanks." I let out a breath. While it wasn't exactly a vote of confidence, at least she approved of entering. "Do you think Dad will let me use some of my cleaning money to buy film?"

Kiki gave me an incredulous look. "You're going to ask him?"

I swallowed. There had been a time when Okaasan had regularly given me nickels from my cleaning money. I'd always used them for film. But for over a year now, Dad had insisted every penny go to the farm or to Charlie. "I mean, if I'm trying to win money for the farm . . ."

Kiki shook her head. "Don't you remember what happened last time?"

I bit my lip.

Kiki pulled another leaf from my hair. "Look, just don't get caught."

I swiveled to face her. "What? Just take it?"

She shrugged. "I do." She stuck her leg out and pulled up her skirt to reveal brand-new stockings. "All the time."

"Kiki!"

She shrugged and pushed her skirt down. "If I'm going to do all that dang sewing for Mrs. Clark, I'm going to get something out of it. I still put half or so in the jar." I squinted through my wet hair and the kitchen door to the parlor, where Charlie's college jar stood on the mantel. Unless Dad took it first, my cleaning and Kiki's sewing money went into the jar with Charlie's pay from the brickyard. "Anyway," Kiki added, "why is it our job to save up for Charlie?"

I squirmed as she pulled her fingers through my hair. There was a part of me that understood why it didn't seem fair to her. After all, I wished that I could go to college, too. But Charlie was the oldest— and he'd been waiting so long. "But of course we should help him."

"Even if we give Charlie everything, who's to say Dad won't just take it again?"

"That was for the farm," I said. "He had to." But doubt clouded my voice.

"Oh, c'mon. We're going to lose the farm anyway." Kiki tugged hard at a snarl in my hair, and I resisted the urge to cry out.

"What do you mean? This is the last year. Then it's ours."

"Do you even know why Dad took Charlie's fund? Why he didn't just make a late payment or something?" Kiki scooted on the floor between me and the stove. I didn't answer, and Kiki raised her eyebrows. "When Dad bought the farm, he signed this contract. It said that if he ever came short on even one payment, even if he'd paid every year before, the entire farm would go back to the old owner. Even if it's the very last payment. And we won't be left with a dime."

I swallowed. "Why would he take such a big risk?"

"How else would he have gotten them to sell to an 'Oriental'?" The word came out pinched and harsh. Kiki pulled her knees under her. "Dad's had to ask for help every year, even before Okaasan died. All that money in Charlie's fund came from Okaasan's parents— well, except for stuff like Okaasan's sewing money and our odd jobs. But *most* of it. She saved the money they sent her every New Year's. And every year, Dad needed a chunk of it to come up with the mortgage."

I nodded. I hadn't known so much of the money was from our grandparents, but I'd known we weren't making it on our own.

"When Okaasan got sick, Ojiichan"—Kiki used the Japanese for "grandfather"—"wanted her to go to the hospital sooner. He even sent a telegram."

I winced. We all wondered if she could have been saved. But none of us regretted waiting as much as Dad.

"After she died, Ojiichan blamed Dad. He stopped sending money. That's why Dad took the rest of Charlie's fund. He used up all Okaasan had ever saved. But this year, there's nothing for him to draw on. There's no way he's making this last payment."

A heaviness settled over us. Though the stove's heat baked my cheeks, I felt cold. A part of me didn't want to believe Kiki. But it all fit together. "How do you know this?" I asked.

Kiki shrugged. "I saw the letter from Ojiichan. And everything else . . . Well, Okaasan told me things."

The pit of my stomach contracted. It was true. Kiki had always had a special relationship with Okaasan. And to Dad, Charlie was help on the farm and his hope for the future. Which left me.

I curled forward, trying to bury the familiar, lonely ache. "Does Charlie know?"

Kiki shook her head. "He knows the last part—where Dad took his fund. And he knows if they don't make the payments they'll lose it all. But he doesn't know everything about Ojiichan." She gave me a softer look. "I don't like it when they fight, either."

The fire popped. "You don't really think Mr. McClatchy would—"

Kiki gave me a disbelieving look. "Old Mr. McClatchy, Beau's grandfather, made Dad sign that form. He was the only one who would sell to the Japanese, and he made all of them sign that same contract. Think of the Nagatas and the Okawas. Or the Tanos— that was after Old McClatchy died and Beau's dad took over."

I squirmed. The Nagatas and Tanos had left the island after losing their farms. The Okawas had stayed, but they'd never recovered and now worked as laborers on a white man's farm.

Kiki narrowed her eyes. "Did you really think he'd make an exception just because you're friends with Beau?"

I blinked. Mr. McClatchy had never been friendly. And once, when I'd gone with Dad to make a payment, I'd gotten the feeling McClatchy was disappointed Dad had managed it.

Kiki leaned forward, sitting a little higher on her heels. "Sam, this friendship with Beau—are you really just friends?"

"Of course!" My cheeks flamed. There it was again, that question. I felt it when Beau and I laughed together at school, or when we met at the pharmacy for a cola. People stared as if they wondered. As if they disapproved.

But now, as I remembered SueAnn standing so close to Beau in the barn, I wondered, too. Was I really just afraid of losing Beau's friendship? Or did I wish we were more?

The fire popped again. I stood and made my way around Kiki. The stove's metal door whined as I pushed it shut.

When I turned back, Kiki's eyes were hard and knowing.

I forced a smile. "But Hiro, huh? How long have you liked him?" The words felt awkward in my mouth—like I was trying on a "regular sister" costume, and it didn't quite fit.

Kiki shrugged. "Oh, I don't know that I *like* him, necessarily. But I do need a date to Sweethearts', and he's my best option."

I frowned. "'Best option'?"

Kiki sighed. "He's handsome, of course. And he's the only Japanese boy with his own car. But he's no Johnny Sullivan." I knew she was bold, but I was still surprised at how freely she talked about a white boy. "If I was dating Johnny, I might even have a chance at Sweethearts' Queen." She shrugged. "But a lot of white boys don't date . . ." She frowned, the confidence on her face slipping. "Anyway, Hiro's the best of the Japanese boys."

I scowled. Could she hear herself? "Hiro deserves to go with someone who likes him for more than his car." The words were out before I could stop them.

Kiki's eyes hardened. "Like who? You?"

"That's not what I said." I hated that my voice shook.

Kiki scrambled to her feet. "Maybe if he asked, you could go out for once, instead of huddling in our room—pretending you're some kind of photographer!"

I reeled back, as if she'd actually hit me. I scraped for something to say, but nothing came.

A flash of something—remorse?—crossed Kiki's face, and her voice softened. "I didn't mean that." The soft tone of her voice made it worse.

*Pretending*, she'd said. Was I so pathetic? I couldn't look at her.

"It's just that you—you barely go out at all." Kiki thought I felt bad about her comments on my social life. Of course that's what *she* would focus on. "I mean," she continued, "even with Beau, you hardly see him except at school. Don't you want to make friends?"

The word *pretend* still stung, but I tried to concentrate on what she was saying. Was she right? I wasn't a social butterfly like her. But there was a group of kids I sat with at lunch. They were more Beau's friends than mine, and I hadn't been invited to the study group today . . . but maybe that was just because I lived so far from the center of town. "I have friends."

"Real friends?" Kiki's voice sounded skeptical. She knelt next to me. "Aren't you lonely?"

*Lonely.* The word clawed at every raw wound. "Of course!" I wanted to yell. But it wasn't friends that made this gaping hole I could never fill. Before SueAnn had glued herself to Beau, I'd felt fine with the state of my friendships. The hole was Kiki. It was Dad, it was Charlie. It was the family that had shattered when Okaasan died. *That's* what I was lonely for.

But as I raised my eyes and looked into my sister's face, my tongue stuck to the roof of my mouth. She wouldn't understand. If I tried to tell her what I really needed, I'd ruin the first talk we'd had in weeks. And Dad and Charlie clearly couldn't take any more pressure. I bit my tongue.

"I'll try to do better," I said slowly, letting Kiki think I'd try to make more friends. But really, I just needed to keep the friend I feared losing.

# CHAPTER 4

# SUBHUMAN

*December 5*

Even filtered through the trees, white morning light glared on the truck's windshield. I edged closer to Charlie, until I could feel his warmth on my side. Though the half-cab truck was so cold that his breath made puffs of mist, he whistled as he drove Kiki and me to school, as if last night's fight had never happened. On my other side, Kiki used the passenger-side window as a mirror, smearing crimson lipstick on her mouth. I sighed, sending a filmy haze into the air in front of me.

The truck lurched, making a horrible screeching sound, and I had to brace my hands on the dash. Kiki's lipstick jerked, painting a red streak across her front teeth.

"Jeez!" Kiki glared at Charlie.

Charlie regripped the steering wheel and grimaced. "Sorry. Pothole. This dang road . . ." When it rained or snowed, the roads in Japantown could turn into pure mud.

"Here, we're almost to the pavement," Charlie said as we neared the Mercantile. Hiro's father, Mr. Tanaka, owned the shop, with its bright red door and windows cluttered with pasted signs. It stood on the edge of Japantown, the only shop in our neighborhood.

Charlie made the turn from the unnamed dirt road onto Farmers' Freeway, a paved street that would take us toward the center of the island, where the school was located and where all the white families lived. As the truck settled back into its rhythmic creaking, Charlie grinned. "I guess it's kind of like a roller coaster. Maybe we should charge for tickets."

"You're in a good mood," I said, settling back into my seat. Next to me, Kiki cleaned her teeth with a handkerchief.

Charlie shrugged and looked back at the road. "Sure. Why not?"

"I thought you'd be . . . crabbier, I guess. After last night, I mean."

"Hmph." On my other side, Kiki leaned forward and cocked her head at Charlie. "Yes, he *does* seem happier, doesn't he?"

Charlie glanced at her and cleared his throat, shaking his head so slightly that I might have missed it. Then he shrugged. "Just feels like today's going to be a good day."

Kiki smirked. "Right. I'm sure *that's* what it is."

"What? What's going on?" I asked.

Kiki's lips parted, and for a second, she seemed close to telling me. Then she shrugged and leaned back. Facing the window again, she examined her curls, making sure every pin was in its proper place.

I sighed and turned. "Charlie?"

"It's nothing," Charlie said.

"But, Charlie—"

"Drop it, Sam." There was an edge in Charlie's voice, and I sat back, stung. Charlie had a secret? *I* was the one he shared things with, just like he was the one I confided in. Why did Kiki know? And why wouldn't he tell me?

I shifted, so Charlie and I were no longer touching. Thick silence fell in the cab. When I dared to look over, Charlie's eyes were filled with something I couldn't decipher. Was it fear? I couldn't understand how this new look fit with the cheerfulness Kiki had teased him for.

The radiator was on full blast when I walked into my civics classroom. A few kids had scattered themselves throughout the room.

Mr. Percival sat in the front, staring into a silver hand-mirror and combing his mustache with a matching comb. I hoped Beau would come soon. My lips twitched as I imagined telling him I'd decided to enter the contest.

My desk stood in the back of the room, far from the radiator and next to a cold row of paned glass windows. I didn't take off my coat as I sat down and got out my things.

In a trickle of students, I saw him. Beau's cheeks were flushed, and his parted hair shone with wax. He laughed. Something about the way he strode, with his trumpet case swinging in one hand and his suede bomber jacket hanging loose, made him the very picture of an American boy.

He caught my eyes and smiled. I grinned and slid forward in my seat. But before I stood, I heard a brassy giggle.

SueAnn's gold curls shone against the blood-orange, store-bought coat she wore. Beau tilted his head toward her, and her mouth nearly touched his ear as she whispered. The two laughed in unison this time, and something seized in my stomach. Had they come to school together? That made two times in a row. I slumped down against the hard chair-back.

Beau swung his bag and trumpet case to the floor, sliding into the desk in front of SueAnn. His low voice wove with her harsh giggle until Mr. Percival called the class to order. I tried to focus my attention.

Percival's reedy voice was uneven. "Who can define the word"—his knobby elbows strained his starched shirt as he wrote—"*nationalism*?"

I peeked over at Beau. His long, trousered legs spilled into the aisle as he bent over his notebook.

"Anyone?" Percival asked. He scanned the classroom, and his eyes narrowed as they settled on me. "Let's see." He looked down and checked his roll, even though I'd been in his class since September.

"Miss Saa—Saack-a-motto? Can you tell us how nationalism was defined in chapter twelve?"

I resisted the temptation to glance at Beau. The ideas I'd read last night sifted through my mind, as uncatchable as seawater. "Is it kind of like patriotism?"

Percival frowned. "The *difference* between nationalism and patriotism is *exactly* what last night's reading was about. Anyone else? Miss Clark?"

As SueAnn scrambled to formulate another guess, I sank into my seat and surrendered my attention to the windowpane beside me. Fog and the radiator battled on the glass, leaving tiny rivulets of condensation that dribbled into the gaping sill. Between the streamlets, I made out my filmy reflection. Flat face. Sharp cheekbones. Stick-straight hair that fell past my shoulders.

At the board, Percival had his back to us as he scribbled a phrase under the word *nationalism*. "Unity solely because of a shared background. Patriotism, on the other hand"—he moved to the other side of the board—"is born out of admiration for the nation's values." Percival finished writing the definition with a flourish.

I peeked again at Beau. His blue, impossibly bright eyes caught mine, and he winked. I swallowed, and my eyes darted around the classroom. No one had noticed the wink—except SueAnn. She glared in my direction.

"Japan is a prime example," Percival said. The word *Japan* snagged my attention. ". . . of the dangers of nationalism." I checked the clock, willing the hands to move faster.

"The Japanese believe"— Percival raised his eyebrows—"their emperor is a god."

I felt eyes around the classroom swivel toward me, quizzing me for confirmation. My face flushed. Out of the corner of my eye, I saw Henry Goto, the only other Japanese student in the classroom. His cheeks burned.

"Their *god* is their commander in chief, if you will. This—combined with the fact that they're primitive and prone to violence"—a rush of heat flared through me—"makes Japan a war-mongering nation. And the problem is compounded because of a culture of *nationalism*." He turned to the board and underlined the word.

I felt the girl beside me staring. The scratching of pencils seemed deafening. Worst of all, in the front of the classroom, Beau's head bowed over his desk as he scribbled his notes.

Percival turned back to the class. "You've all read accounts of the conflicts going on in the Orient? We've seen this problem in Manchuria."

*Manchuria.* The word was like a puncture. Anger leaked out of me, leaving an icky, dirty feeling in its place. It was the feeling that overtook me each time I heard about the Japanese atrocities in northeast China—whether in class or on the radio. For over a decade, Japanese soldiers had attacked the region, often bombing homes and shooting civilians in their brutal quest to conquer and enslave the Chinese.

Percival's reedy voice was matter-of-fact. "Murder. Torture. Rape. Over and over, the Japanese have proved subhuman."

Shame and indignation warred inside me. I thought of my parents. Dad had a temper, but he'd rubbed Okaasan's feet every night, and always gave me or Kiki the sweet heart of the watermelon. And Okaasan, my soft-spoken, self-sacrificing mother—how could anyone compare her to those soldiers?

But I had seen the photographs in the newspaper, and they haunted me. I was American, a citizen who'd never once left the United States. Yet my face, my hair, my skin, and something invisible, indefinable, made me different from the pink-skinned kids around me. When I'd seen those photographs, I'd felt shame.

"With nationalism, you have a mistaken feeling of superiority in your country, no matter how horrible its actions. That pride leads to arrogance and war. Patriotism, on the other hand"—Mr. Percival pointed to the flag hanging over the blackboard—"requires a country to live up to its principles." His voice rang. "That's the American way."

Silent pride vibrated through the classroom. My classmates sat a little straighter, as if they'd been transformed from an assortment of individuals to one cohesive group.

But I was not part of it. I was locked out.

The bell buzzed, and Mr. Percival looked up at the clock. "We'll discuss chapter thirteen on Monday," he said, his voice deflating back to its normal, bored tone.

Around me, students had come out of their trances, slamming their textbooks and shoving pencils into cases. Across the room, Henry ran out before anyone else, his books and jacket jumbled in his arms.

I closed my notebook and looked around me. I felt like a notice had been plastered across my face. And while I wasn't sure what it said, I knew I was the only one in the room wearing it.

I stooped to put my books in my bag, but a stinging wetness erupted on my cheek.

I brushed my face. A spitball fell into my palm.

The air felt hot as I looked around. Scooter Clyde grinned at me, his eyes hard. I shook my hand, and the spitball fell to the floor. Scooter stood slowly, unfolding his long body like a cat stretching after a nap. He combed his fingers through his auburn hair and strolled toward the front of the room.

I held my breath, trying to stave off tears. Blinking, I made my way to the front of the class. "Hey, Sam," Beau said.

I turned toward him. He leaned against his desk, all loose angles and smiles. Only a slightly embarrassed look toward Mr. Percival made me think he'd even noticed the lecture.

SueAnn stood next to him, tossing her hair and simpering. I could still feel the spit on my cheek.

My throat tightened and I stalked past, ignoring Beau's faltering smile.

# CHAPTER 5

# FITTING IN

Beau gave me several searching looks during lunch, but with SueAnn lurking, we didn't talk. Instead, I half listened as Hank Madsen, on my left, and SueAnn, across the table between Beau and Ruth Allred, bantered over a slice of cake.

But my attention wasn't really on them. I kept sneaking looks at Scooter. At the next table over, he joked with his friends—as if the spitball had meant nothing. Only that's not how it had felt.

"Sue, you said you'd bring gingerbread to the study session," Hank said, leaning back to make room for his long legs under the table. "But you didn't. So . . ."

SueAnn faked a pout, but she pushed a wax paper package toward him. "Fine, then. Enjoy."

Hank pounced on the package, opening it to reveal a slice of angel food cake with white frosting. A heavy ache swelled in my chest, taking over before I could stifle it. My mother had made angel food cake for every family birthday.

She hadn't known how when we were little, instead making beautiful Japanese desserts—soft, squishy *manju* and sweet *ohagi*. But when Kiki was in second grade, she'd brought home a slice of American-style cake and announced to Okaasan that everyone in her class brought cake to share on their birthdays. Okaasan didn't speak or read English, but she asked a friend to translate a recipe into Japanese, then practiced till her cake looked and tasted just like the sample Kiki had brought home. All because she wanted us to be able to share with our classmates like the other kids.

I swallowed the hard lump in my throat and looked down at my lunch. It was little things like this, little things that came up when I wasn't prepared. Loneliness for my mother seared through me.

"Scrumptious." Hank hammed up every bite. "Maybe even worth letting you parasites cheat off my work." SueAnn rolled her eyes, but on either side, Beau and Ruth laughed. Hank was undoubtedly the smartest kid in our class. I could believe he'd done most of the work.

Ruth tucked a honey-brown curl behind her ear. "Thank you for your help, Hank."

"Yeah, thanks, Hank. I really might not have finished without your help." Beau gulped down a big bite of his sandwich. "And it's so much more bearable to do it together."

I sipped from my thermos. Did they not realize I was sitting here? That they'd gotten together without me? That I'd had to do all the homework alone?

Why hadn't I been invited? I'd been sitting at this table with Beau all year. But I still wasn't one of them. And it usually didn't bother me, but with Beau growing closer to SueAnn . . .

I'd told Kiki I had friends, but now I remembered her question: *Real friends?* A squiggle of doubt lodged in my stomach.

I surreptitiously looked around the lunchroom, at the groups clustered throughout the space. Chatter echoed against the hard floors and bare walls.

The cafeteria doubled as an auditorium, and, pushed against the north wall, there stood an empty stage. Just in front of it, opposite the kitchen, a group of Japanese girls crowded around a table of their own. It wasn't *all* the Japanese girls—there were those like me and Kiki who sat with other friends. But the girls at that table had banded with other Japanese kids. I watched as Mae Goto said something, her hands moving in time with her mouth, and the whole table erupted in laughter.

Maybe if there'd been another Japanese girl in my grade, that's where I'd have sat. And maybe she could have been a real girlfriend—someone who *wanted* to spend time with me, rather than just putting up with me like the girls at this table—and Kiki. Then I wouldn't have to spend so much time worrying about whether I'd lose my best friend to SueAnn.

But even as I thought it, I wondered if it would have made a difference. The truth was I'd spent lots of time with the Japanese girls a year older than me, girls like Mae and her best friend, Mariko Tsukuda. We'd grown up in the same neighborhood, after all, and had played as children when we weren't working on farms with our parents. And I'd spent plenty of time tagging along with Kiki when she visited Alice Nakano and Edna Okawa, the girls her age.

But as we'd gotten older, our interests had diverged. Kiki had thrown herself into a different social circle. And I didn't fit, just as I didn't quite click with the girls I sat with now. My dreams were too big, and I knew the girls would disapprove of the things I wanted to do, thinking them unseemly, like SueAnn did, or boring, like Kiki did.

But Beau understood. He felt about the trumpet the way I felt about photography.

"What is this?" SueAnn's voice broke through my thoughts. On the other side of the table, SueAnn grabbed a book that partly stuck out of Ruth's bag: Steinbeck's *Grapes of Wrath*. "You're reading *this*?" SueAnn asked, holding the book up for everyone to see, her voice scandalized.

Ruth's round, soft face flushed. "Yes. I just started it."

"My mother says this book is pure trash," SueAnn said. "Ruth, the district board *banned* it."

I took a long swig from my thermos, trying to avoid attention. I'd read *Grapes of Wrath*, too. Mr. Tanaka had given it to me two weeks ago, when he protested against SueAnn's mom's campaign for it to be banned.

Still, Ruth and SueAnn were friends and had been for years. Their friendship was probably the reason I'd never gotten to know Ruth better. Why was SueAnn singling her out now?

Ruth seemed to shrink as all eyes turned to her. "Wh-why does she think it's trash?" she asked quietly.

SueAnn made a scoffing noise in her throat, but she looked a little uncertain. "Well . . . it promotes communism . . . I think."

"Promotes communism?" Ruth asked. "How?"

SueAnn looked around, as if hoping someone else had the answer. Then she sniffed, sitting taller. "I don't know. It's not like I read it, obviously."

The pink in Ruth's cheeks deepened, but she said quietly, "It doesn't seem like trash to me. I think it's . . . beautiful."

My eyes flicked to Ruth's. There was a firmness to her answer that surprised me. She was always so quiet. I hadn't expected her to stand up to SueAnn. And from the scowl on SueAnn's face, I didn't think she'd expected it, either. "I think my mother knows more about this kind of thing than you, Ruth," she said.

Ruth hunched over her lunch. Next to me, Hank squirmed, playing with a few crumbs of cake, while on the other side of the table, Beau stared across the room.

I frowned. Why didn't either of them tell SueAnn to knock it off? I opened my mouth . . . then shut it. I couldn't convince SueAnn of anything, not like Beau could have.

But he didn't speak. I put my fork down. "I've read it," I said. My voice was a little hoarse. "And it's not trash."

SueAnn's eyes narrowed. "You *read* it? The whole thing?"

I nodded. "Yes. And it was really good."

SueAnn gave me a disgusted look. "My mother says—"

"Aw, come off it, Sue," said Beau, his voice low. "Who cares? Just give Ruth her book."

SueAnn pursed her lips, but let Beau take the book from her

hand. He passed it to Ruth, who gave him a small smile, then met my eyes. "Thanks," she mouthed.

"I wouldn't read a book on Sam's recommendation," SueAnn muttered loud enough for everyone to hear.

I ignored her.

When the last bell rang, I clumped out onto the school grounds, bracing myself against the wet cold. In the parking lot, a group of Japanese girls lingered next to our family's dilapidated truck, chatting with Charlie, who leaned coolly against the tailgate. Nothing about his relaxed stance indicated that he was still worried about what had happened this morning. Kiki already sat in the cab.

"C'mon, Sam!" Kiki hissed through the open door as I walked up. "I'm trying to finish some sewing in time to go out with the gang!" She kept glancing toward the school, to where Johnny Sullivan stood, laughing on the curb with a bunch of his basketball buddies, his hair almost white in the sunlight.

I slid into the cab. Making goodbyes to his admirers, Charlie hoisted himself in after me. He started the engine, and it roared and settled into an uneven mix of grinding and clanking.

A slight smile lingered on Charlie's lips, and I followed his gaze—which of his many admirers could make my brother smile like that? And was this his secret? But I was disappointed. Charlie stared right through the cluster of giggling Japanese girls, instead looking at a group of white kids lingering by the school doors.

My stomach lurched when I saw a gleam of dark auburn hair in the middle of the group: Scooter Clyde, walking with his brother Mack and his sister, Jean. I turned away.

# CHAPTER 6

# McCLATCHY'S GENERAL

*December 6*

On Saturday, we drove into town to go shopping. Dad pulled the truck into a parking spot and killed the engine. The broad white facade of McClatchy's General, Beau's dad's store, loomed above us, its siding plastered with posters advertising Coca-Cola and Christmas toys. We didn't shop at McClatchy's often. Instead, we bought at Mr. Tanaka's store, the much smaller—and usually cheaper—Japantown Mercantile. But Dad had to order seed from McClatchy's, and the Merc didn't carry shoes.

Charlie popped open the passenger-side door and slid out. I hopped out after him. Charlie had half a foot on me, and my dismount was much less graceful. The cold pavement was hard, unyielding, as it met the worn soles of my toe-pinching shoes.

It was past time for a new pair. And now that I'd caught up to Kiki, both in height and shoe size, I wouldn't have to make do with her hand-me-downs. But that made me feel even worse—why did I have to grow now, when money was so tight?

"C'mon," Kiki said, taking my hand. As Kiki danced me toward the store entrance, Dad slammed the driver's-side door, rattling the truck like its next ride might be its last. In the gray afternoon light, my father looked older than usual, his inky black hair spangled with gray.

"Remember, Kiki." Dad's eyebrows crashed together. "We must buy *conservatively*. This extra seed . . ." He peered at Charlie, but

Charlie kept his face blank. The seed had to be bought. They'd sort out the money later.

Kiki didn't dare argue, but when Dad looked away, her mouth shifted into a pout, and she dropped my arm. "We're going to end up in clearance stock," she whispered, and she trudged toward the store—if you could call the way Kiki moved trudging. Even sulking, she was graceful, and her ebony hair shone in the winter light.

I turned to the displays behind the sparkling windows. Each table was bedecked with Christmas luxuries: walnut-handled knives, mannequins draped in silk scarves, a shiny red bike with a gold bell.

But none of them were anything compared with the camera. The shiny chrome Leica sat in a cream velvet box next to its buttery-smooth leather case. I leaned against the window, my breath billowing into a cloudy heart on the glass.

The photos I could take with such a camera! I let my eyes fall on the thick white notecard propped against the velvet: *Price Upon Request*. I'd never make that request. But maybe someday, after Dad paid off the farm, after we got Charlie to college, maybe *then* I could get a new camera. Not a Leica, of course, but a Kodak or an Argus. If the crops did well . . .

I frowned. "If the crops do well" was Dad's favorite answer for everything.

"You coming?" Kiki huffed. I tore my eyes from the Leica. Dad and Charlie had already gone inside, and Kiki stood holding the door open, one hand on her hip.

"Coming." I gave the slim camera and its delicate chrome buttons one last look, then followed my sister into the store.

The store's warm air engulfed me, and a bell tinkled as the door closed behind us. Dad and Charlie stood at a table at the far end of the store, looking through the seed catalogs. Without thinking, I turned to the checkout counter, where Beau usually worked after school and on weekends. He wasn't there, but his father was. Behind the counter, Mr. McClatchy scolded a cashier. McClatchy was a big man, at least six feet four and solid. Compared with him, the bald clerk was tiny.

"Who are *you* looking for?" Kiki asked, a smug smile tugging at her lips as she followed my gaze to the counter.

I glanced around, and my eyes fell on a display of shoes near the window. I swooped over to it and held up a pair of black lace-ups. "What do you think of these?"

It worked. Kiki flew to the display. "They're a little too blockish, aren't they? But what about these?" She pulled a pair of blush suede pumps from their stand in the front of the display. "Look at the cunning little toes. Have you ever seen anything more beautiful?"

I checked the paper tag hanging from the "blockish" boots—six dollars and fifteen cents. "Goodness!" I blurted. My voice carried over the hum of the store. I glanced over at the counter, where McClatchy still lectured the cashier. Neither had noticed my outburst. "We won't be getting those," I whispered.

Kiki glanced over. "Too much? Well, I don't really like them anyway." Kiki rubbed her finger over the pale, velvety suede. "I suppose these wouldn't do," she said wistfully.

"No, I suppose they wouldn't. Not for working on the *farm*." I let the weight of my voice fall over her.

Kiki made a face. "If only Dad would let us go to Seattle. We could visit the department stores. Can you imagine? The Bon Marché—or Frederick and Nelson!" She turned to the rack of shoes in front of us, disgust etched over her fine features. "There are so few choices here."

I didn't say anything. Kiki could be vain and ridiculous, but arguing never got me anywhere. Besides, if we could afford it, I would have loved to buy pretty shoes—not pumps, but Oxfords or penny loafers or something just for school. I opened a new box and slipped a pair of olive Mary Janes out of their paper wrappings, fingering the bright brass buttons.

"Saa-aam, look who's here." Kiki's voice curled smugly around each word. I glanced up. On the other side of the window, Beau got out of his Studebaker. He paused, gazing at our truck, then started toward the store doors.

I felt a small, not unpleasant lurch in my chest. But I kept my voice light. "We really should be looking at work boots," I said, ignoring Kiki's smirk. I laid the shoes back in their box.

The door opened, and the bell chimed. I let myself glance up as Beau strode in. "You're late," Mr. McClatchy called from the counter.

Beau's cheeks were rosy from the cold, and I noticed that he held his trumpet slightly behind him, as if shielding it from his dad. "Just a little." He fumbled with the handle of his case. "Rehearsal went a couple of minutes over."

Mr. McClatchy scowled. The trumpet was everything to Beau, and as far as anyone on Linley could tell, he had the chops to make it in music. But Mr. McClatchy said it was a waste of time.

Beau scanned the store. His eyes landed on me. He stowed his trumpet under the counter and walked toward me.

I turned back to the shoes. My face burned. I wished Kiki wouldn't tease me. It made it so much harder to act normal.

"Sam?" Beau's voice wavered.

I slipped the shoebox back into place. "Hi, Beau." Was my face as red as his?

"Hiya, Beau," Kiki said, a devilish gleam in the corners of her eyes.

I gave Kiki a scathing look and pretended to browse the shelves, drifting a few feet away. Beau followed me.

"Hey, I got the feeling you might be kinda sore with me," he said.

I hesitated. "Really?"

Beau looked up, and his blue eyes met mine. "You're not?" Beau picked at a strip of cellulose tape left on the shelf. "'Cuz in civics class yesterday . . . I dunno. And then at lunch, you seemed mad." Beau peeled the tape away from the shelf, taking a few specks of paint with it.

"I just had things on my mind." I turned to the shoes and let my fingers stream over the rows. Had he really not noticed how awkward that class was for me? Or how uncomfortable lunch had been?

Beau nodded. "Okay. Good. Anyway, did you think about that contest?"

For a moment, I felt irritated. He was so eager to think everything was fine. But explaining would only make me feel bad again. And this was the moment I'd wanted yesterday at the beginning of civics.

"Yes." I let myself grin. "I'm going to do it."

Beau swelled. "Good. Do you have a photo you want to submit?"

I shook my head. "No. I know the shot I want to take. But I need to find a way to earn some money so I can buy film."

Beau tilted his head. "I'll give you some."

I shook my head. "No. I can figure something out."

Beau gave me a look, both exasperated and amused. "Just let me get you the film." I was about to argue, when he added, "Look. If you want, we can call it your Christmas present."

I bit my lip. There was nothing I'd want more. "Really?"

He nodded. "Absolutely. Let me bring it to you—say tomorrow?"

"Tomorrow? Okay."

Beau's eyes darted to the floor. "And maybe . . . There's something I wanted to talk to you about." His voice dipped low. "Privately."

My tongue felt fat and slow. "Privately?" What could he need to tell me? The unwanted thought of SueAnn came again into my mind, and my breathing quickened. Was he going to tell me they were official?

My stomach clenched. I didn't want to know. But if I hoped to keep him as a friend, I had to let him tell me. "S-sure, okay."

"Let's meet at our spot," Beau said, his voice going back to normal. "Say ten o'clock?"

I nodded.

"Swell." Beau's blue eyes bored into mine, and my heart crashed against my ribs. I was almost sure that tomorrow he would tell me he was going with another girl. And that would mean losing him, at least a little.

I took a deep breath and pretended to check the price tag on a pair of shoes that were much too large for either Kiki or me.

"Beau!" Mr. McClatchy called from the other side of the store.

Beau sighed. "All right. I'll see you then, Ace."

Ace. My feelings bubbled like froth on the shore.

Kiki glided up beside me, again holding the pink pumps. Her eyes glittered. "What was that all about?"

I swallowed. "Nothing." *Nothing,* I repeated to myself, trying to bury my feelings. I turned to the shelves in front of me. Three rows of black lace-up work boots stood at attention, lined up from the largest to smallest. Aside from sizing, they were identical, as boring as they were useful. All I had to do was find the right size.

"Come on, Oneesan," I said, using the Japanese word for "older sister," something I only did when I was trying to sweet-talk Kiki. "You know these will be better for the farm. And"—I checked the price tag—"they're less than half the price."

Kiki groaned, but put down the pumps. "Someday I'm going to own at least four pairs of shoes. And I'll tell you this—not one of them is going to be for working on the farm."

"And yet somehow the farm will survive." Kiki and I turned.

Charlie stood behind us, grinning. Kiki stuck her tongue out, but that only made Charlie's grin spread.

I laughed. I couldn't help but adore Charlie—for my whole life, he'd been everything that Kiki wasn't for me. He'd let me follow him all over the island, treating me like a favorite brother, taking me fishing and hunting and cliff-jumping even though I was four years his junior. He'd let me in on everything. Maybe that's why I minded his secret so much now.

Charlie picked up a shoe, tossing it with his withered right hand. "Shoe hunt going badly?"

My lips twitched. "No, we're doing great."

"We're doing *okay*," Kiki huffed.

"It's about time you got new shoes," Charlie said, without a hint of regret over the money that wouldn't go to his college fund. "Make sure the soles are real rubber. If we end up going to war, they might have to last the duration."

I checked the soles and loosened the laces. Kiki grumbled under her breath as she did the same.

I slipped off my own battered shoes and pulled the boots over my feet. They were heavy, stiff with newness. I stomped around a few times, rocking back and forth, testing their fit against my heels and toes. Kiki bent down—a curl fell prettily over her frowning face—to check the leather toes of her pair.

"They're perfect," I said, pulling them off and tying the laces together.

"They'll do," Kiki sighed, gazing back at the pale pink heels.

# CHAPTER 7

# MR. McCLATCHY

Dad finished filling out his order, and the four of us made our way to the counter. The clerk stood closest to the door, next to the register, while Beau stood on the far side going over an inventory binder. Between them stood a collection of candy jars. Mr. McClatchy took out a twist of horehound candy and handed it to a girl with nutmeg curls, grinning at her mother.

Dad stuffed his battered hat beneath his arm and picked up the boots we'd chosen, tugging at their uppers, then flexing their soles. He checked the price tag and sighed, but set them next to the register with his order and a tin of axle grease.

"Will this be all?" the tiny, bald clerk asked.

"Yes, thank you." Dad reached into his faded coat for his wallet.

"Um, Arnie?" Mr. McClatchy called. He patted the little girl on the head and closed the candy jar, then sauntered toward the register.

The clerk's hand froze over the boots. "Yes, sir?"

Even leaning against the counter, McClatchy towered over both the clerk and my dad. Like Beau, he was as pale as milk, but he didn't have the warmth of freckles. The bones of his face were bull-like, and he'd lacquered his thinning light brown hair to his scalp, giving him an all-around boulder-like appearance. Only the swell of his stomach, just straining the silver buttons of his waistcoat, revealed any softness.

"You forget the new protocol?" McClatchy gestured to the woman behind us.

Arnie mumbled an apology, blushing. "Right . . . I can ring you up now, Mrs. Lowe," he said, pushing our things to the side. I froze. My body felt heavy, as if it might be anchored to the floor.

After a long moment, the woman edged around us, avoiding our eyes. She fumbled with her packages. "I need a tin of tobacco for David," she said. I flushed and peeked over at Beau. His lips pressed together.

"You understand, of course," McClatchy said. He pointed at a small white sign next to the cash register: *Management determines the order in which customers may be helped.* "Nothing personal. It's just all this business with war rumors. We've found some customers prefer not to wait in line with Orientals."

Beside me, Charlie tensed. I put my hand on his arm.

Dad nodded. "We hope the rumors will come to nothing."

Charlie's eyes flashed. "Dad, we don't have to buy here," he said, his voice too loud. "We can order from Seattle."

The little girl and her mother stared. Past them, Beau set his papers down. My face burned.

"Stop making a scene," Dad said. His eyes darted to McClatchy.

"But, Dad—"

*"Damare,"* Dad ordered, his voice low but lashing.

Charlie clenched his jaw. "Fine." He whirled around and stormed to the exit.

The door crashed closed behind him. Charlie's stride didn't break as he passed each of the picture windows, then our car, heading south, away from home.

When I turned back to Dad, his face was stony. Kiki stared at the floor, her cheeks splotched.

"I apologize for my son's behavior," Dad said, bowing his head toward McClatchy.

McClatchy's jaw twitched, and his hard eyes landed on me. I

cringed and folded my arms, trying to make myself as small as possible. Did I look as dirty as I felt?

Looking at the woman across the counter, McClatchy smoothed his expression. "Teenagers, right?" He smiled. "Don't worry, Sakamoto. I understand."

"Thank you," Mrs. Lowe murmured to the clerk, taking her change and her groceries.

Arnie picked up one pair of boots. As he tap-tapped on the register, McClatchy leaned forward. "New shoes for your girls, Sakamoto? Little expensive, aren't they?"

Dad nodded, bowing slightly. His fingers played nervously with the brim of his hat. "We're glad you stock such good ones."

I chanced a glance at Beau. He bent over the inventory sheets, his long white fingers fiddling with a stub of pencil, his ears as red as raspberries.

McClatchy picked up Dad's order form. "More seed?" His eyebrows arched. "And you're adding flowers this year?"

Dad nodded, his fingers quickening, rotating the hat like a Ferris wheel. "Last year's strawberry prices weren't as good as we'd hoped, so this year I'm going to divers-'fy." Dad stumbled over the new word.

"Diversify," McClatchy echoed. "You sure that's a good idea? With that last payment coming up?" A smile forced its way across his face.

Dad bowed lower. "You'll have it on time. I promise."

McClatchy barked one short, rough guffaw. "For your sake, I better! Not many are crazy enough to take the terms you did." He shook his head. "My father didn't think you'd make it this far, Sakamoto. But I have to hand it to you. You've done better than we could have guessed. Sure would be hard to lose everything now, so close to the end." His smile widened. "Though I guess for me it'd be good, huh?"

"That'll be eight fifty for the goods," the clerk said, his voice small. "And the seed is sixteen dollars."

Dad set his hat on the counter and pulled his cracked leather wallet from his pocket. He counted out the bills, then a stream of nickels and dimes.

"Please come again," the clerk said, handing Dad the goods without meeting his eyes.

Dad handed Kiki and me our shoes, then pocketed the receipt and the tin of grease.

As we made our way to the door, Beau called, "See you, Sam." His voice was a little too cheery, and he gave me a weak smile before glancing at his dad.

"Bye, Beau," I said, not able to keep irritation out of my voice. How could he pretend nothing had happened?

From the corner of my eye, I saw McClatchy watching, his eyes narrowed.

# CHAPTER 8

# AN UNPLEASANT RUN-IN

The door slammed behind us, and the tang of cedars and the ocean washed over me. I filled my lungs, trying to cleanse myself of the feeling I'd gotten under McClatchy's stare.

"Wait here while I go to the post office," said Dad, his voice sharp. I didn't argue. He needed a moment to calm down. Kiki and I settled on the cold curb in front of the store. I cradled my new boots in my lap.

Dad shuffled across Main Street. His battered hat and coat showed even shabbier in the broken sunlight, and the leather of his dusty shoes was cracked. These were his good shoes, too, not his work boots. He must have changed them to come into town, I realized, guilt-stung as I fingered my new rubber soles.

Dad disappeared into the post office, and I snuck a glance at Kiki. Her cheeks still flamed. I fumbled with the laces of my shoes, then took them off and replaced them with the stiff new boots. Still sitting, I stamped. The icy road didn't lick the soles of my feet anymore.

Kiki sighed, and I followed her gaze. Just past the drugstore, an emerald-green Cadillac—the Clarks' family car—pulled up to the town's only stop sign. "Oh, please no," I whispered.

Kiki's nose wrinkled. But a second later, her face was smooth, as if I'd imagined the look. The Cadillac rolled forward. I tried to see who was driving. Mr. Clark wasn't so bad—he ignored us. But Mrs. Clark, for whom Okaasan had done countless sewing jobs, had once called me "a poor little orphan."

The car purred past the drugstore and barbershop, and the smell of gasoline filled the air. As it pulled next to Dad's truck, I groaned. "Darn." Through the windshield, I saw Mrs. Clark, her thin lips pressed into a straight line. Next to her sat SueAnn.

Mrs. Clark put the car in park, and SueAnn got out, smoothing her blood-orange coat. Her steel-gray eyes locked on me, immediately hardening. Panic crept into my throat. If she and Beau had gotten together, how long could my friendship with Beau last?

I couldn't surrender him to her. I just couldn't.

SueAnn didn't stop glaring even as her mother fussed with her collar. "There, much better," Mrs. Clark mumbled, patting her daughter one last time.

I rolled my eyes. Of course SueAnn had to look her best before she might see Beau. And yet, even as I inwardly mocked her, I stared at her shiny, bouncing curls.

The two of them stepped toward the store, and I shifted my stare to the ground, hoping they would pass without stopping. But Mrs. Clark's sturdy green heels clicked to a standstill in front of me.

"Why, you poor little birds," she said. "Why are you sitting out in the cold?"

"Hello, Mrs. Clark," Kiki said, standing. "We're just waiting while our father posts a letter."

"I see," said Mrs. Clark. For a moment, there was silence. Then, "Hem hem." I followed Mrs. Clark's heels to her nylons, then her pea-green overcoat, and finally to her simpering face. She peered at me, clearly waiting.

I got to my feet. "Hello, Mrs. Clark."

Mrs. Clark beamed. "Hello, Samantha. Susie, shouldn't you greet your classmate?"

"Hello, Sam," SueAnn muttered.

I gritted my teeth. "Hello."

"Very nice," Mrs. Clark said. SueAnn gave her mother a

not-subtle look. "How is your family, dear?" Mrs. Clark asked, turning to Kiki. Her voice dripped with saccharine sweetness. "It must be almost a year now since your mother died. Is that right?"

"We're well, thank you," Kiki said. It had been over a year, but Kiki didn't correct her.

Mrs. Clark turned to me. "I do miss your mother. No one on Linley can tailor like she could. The woman I hired after her butchered a beautiful wool gabardine." She paused, as if waiting for us to comment. I bit my lip. Then her voice changed, almost to a chirp. "Now *you* show great promise," Mrs. Clark said with a squinty-eyed smile at Kiki.

Kiki dipped her head, almost curtsying. "I'm glad to hear you like my work." Her voice was a full note higher than usual. I avoided looking at her. We couldn't afford to lose Mrs. Clark's business, but I hated this groveling version of my sister.

"Yes, quite talented," Mrs. Clark said. She looked around as if trying to think of more to say.

The wind shifted and light filtered through the clouds. Didn't they have shopping they needed to do?

SueAnn smirked at my boots. "Those new?"

I gritted my teeth. "Yes." Not wanting her to think I was ashamed, I added, "I just picked them out." I held one foot out for her to see.

A wide smile broke across her face. "They look just like the boots repairmen wear."

I blushed. Next to me, Kiki gripped her boots tight.

Mrs. Clark hushed her daughter. "Susie, the Sakamotos are farming people. I'm sure they're perfect for people like you," she said, giving Kiki a radiant smile. This time, Kiki didn't return it.

I didn't trust myself to speak. My hands trembled as I tried to remember that we needed Kiki's sewing jobs—when a screeching truck pulled up.

Hiro's truck was even worse than Dad's. Next to Beau's gleaming Studebaker, the truck looked like it belonged in the junkyard, but it was his own. And today, his dad, who usually drove a big black Cadillac, sat in the passenger side.

"Hullo, Sam, Kiki," Hiro called. He grinned extra big, and I flushed, remembering the last time we'd met. He jumped out of the truck and closed its door in one swift movement, then walked around and opened the door for his father.

Next to me, Kiki straightened.

"*Arigatou*," Mr. Tanaka mumbled, struggling to keep his dark wool overcoat wrapped around him as he slid—or rather dropped—out of the car. He stood at least a head shorter than his son.

Mr. Tanaka buttoned his bright silver buttons as he walked, and the two of them stopped next to Mrs. Clark. Mr. Tanaka nodded politely, though perhaps not warmly, but Mrs. Clark didn't return the gesture. Mr. Tanaka had crossed Mrs. Clark on more than one issue, and I guessed she was one of the townspeople who thought him "uppity."

Mr. Tanaka caught my eye and beamed. "Miss Kiki. Miss Sam." His eyes wrinkled into crescents behind his silver-rimmed glasses.

I lowered my gaze, bowing deeply. Next to me, Kiki nodded. To me, it would have felt wrong not to bow, but Kiki never bowed in front of our white neighbors.

"Thank you again for the book," I said, remembering this was the first time I'd seen Mr. Tanaka since he'd given me *Grapes of Wrath*.

"Ah, Steinbeck. An author *every* student should read," he said without looking at Mrs. Clark. She sniffed. "Did you like it?"

I ignored Mrs. Clark's daggerlike gaze. "Yes. Well, kind of. It made me sad."

Mr. Tanaka nodded. "Of course." He slipped into Japanese. "Sometimes we are like square pegs in round holes . . ." Unlike

Dad, who spoke English whenever white people were present, Mr. Tanaka regularly slipped into his first language. He never worried if those he spoke with answered in English, like I was prone to do. And he cared even less if those he *wasn't* speaking with gave him uncomfortable looks. "But I should save my lectures, *ne*?"

I shook my head. I loved that Mr. Tanaka spoke to me about *real* things, without dumbing it down. But Mrs. Clark swooped in.

"Well, Susie, it seems the Sakamotos have many friends. I only hope in the future, they will learn to choose their associates more carefully." She turned to Kiki and me with her horrible syrupy smile. "I don't blame you, poor darlings. You're good girls at heart. Character-building is such a difficult thing. It must be so hard without a mother."

I stood rock-still, yet again stunned into silence. Mrs. Clark opened her mouth, about to say something more, when Hiro interrupted.

"Of course, having a mother doesn't always guarantee character," he said, with a glance at SueAnn.

I coughed, just managing to cover an escaping snort. Mrs. Clark's eyes widened. "Come on, Sue," she said in a voice free of sympathy. She marched SueAnn into the store, letting the door slam.

"I can't exactly say I *approve*, Hiro," Mr. Tanaka said, still in Japanese. But his expression was amused.

Hiro laughed. "She deserved worse." He answered his father's Japanese with English, just as my siblings and I had often answered Okaasan.

I beamed. "Thank you." I lowered my voice. "Again."

Hiro's smile reached his eyes.

"That was brilliant," Kiki said, stepping halfway in front of me. "What are you doing here anyway? Who's minding the store?"

Hiro gave his dad a furtive look. "Henry Goto's taking care of the Merc. I'm helping Dad here change the motor oil in his car. We ran out."

Kiki batted her lashes. "Well, I'm glad to run into you."

Hiro tipped his head, then made his way to the door. But his dad paused, leaned forward, and whispered, "We're not out of motor oil. He thinks I don't know he hid it. He just wants me here so he can figure out what to get me for Christmas." Mr. Tanaka put his finger to his lips, and I laughed.

Kiki sat back down on the curb, watching Hiro through the store window. "Utterly swoonworthy," she said.

"A little," I admitted. "And he defended you." My voice cracked, but Kiki smiled.

She set her boots on the curb next to her. "This whole disaster of a trip will be worth it when he asks me to Sweethearts'."

I stared at my sister, wondering how it would feel to be so sure of myself.

# CHAPTER 9

# THE CAP

*December 7*

The brickyard—deserted on Sunday—was located on the northern tip of the island, the "Cap," halfway between Beau's house and mine. Cold seeped through the thin wool of my coat, spreading across my back, as I lay on a pallet of bricks. I was sure Beau had said to meet at "our spot" at ten. But it was half past, and he still hadn't come. I stared at the sky and sighed.

Above me, a leafless tree reached, fragile, toward the sky's misty underbelly. I let my hand float up, my fingertips tracing swirls in shades of sky. *What would it feel like to graze a piece of heaven? Like cotton candy? Or maybe silk*, I thought, remembering the kimono my mother had brought from Japan. She had only worn it once a year, when she danced for Obon, the festival for the ancestors put on by the island's Japanese families.

We hadn't gone to Obon this year, but I'd gotten the kimono out, not to put it on, but to lift it, fluttering, from its box. If I rubbed the silk between my fingers, the fabric was cold and grainy. But flowing over my open palm, it had almost no feel. Just lightness and movement, like water. Or maybe—I stared upward—like sky.

"What in the Sam Hill are you doing?" Beau snickered.

I dropped my arm and pushed myself upright. My wool cap slid forward, covering my eyes. I tugged it back in place. "Waiting," I snapped, more embarrassed than annoyed.

"Shucks, don't be mad. My mom took my car to some Sunday

school thing. I had to walk." Beau picked his way through the brick rubble, flashing me a smile like a tooth-powder model. "You gonna tell me why you're flapping your arm in the air?" His grin widened, and dark warmth flooded my face.

"I was just thinking . . ." I paused. I couldn't tell him about the kimono. Or that I'd been imagining what the sky felt like.

"Always thinking," Beau said, gently ruffling the hair that peeked beneath my cap. My forehead burned where his fingertips had grazed it.

Together we walked to the cliffs on the northern edge of the brickyard. Far below, the ocean threw itself against rocky crags, and grainy salt kissed my skin. Beau hitched his long legs into a crossed position, stretched his arms, and leaned back, nearly touching me. I shifted, making a spot for him to stretch into, but he didn't notice. What would it be like to be so unworried, so unapologetic about the space you took up? I pulled my arms tight around my knees.

"Merry Christmas," Beau said, pulling something out of his jacket pocket. His fingers brushed mine as he put the box in my hand. I rolled the film in my palm—its weight felt full of possibility.

"Thank you," I whispered.

He grinned. "Thank me by winning that contest."

I swallowed and stared out at the ocean. A ferry trolled across the sound. Behind it, Seattle was just visible.

The Cap had been Beau's and my favorite spot for as long as we'd been friends. A five-minute hike down the cliffs took us to Beau's favorite fishing hole. Down the other side, we could climb to a bald eagle's nest. And when the brickyard was closed, it was the perfect place to sit, look out at the ocean, and talk. It was where I'd spilled my dream of being a photographer and where Beau had first played his trumpet for me. It was where he'd comforted me when Okaasan died. And now it would be where he would tell me—what?

My stomach flipped. SueAnn and I could never be friends. But I couldn't lose him.

A part of me wanted to run away, to avoid whatever Beau was going to say—but I closed my eyes, and the words wormed their way out of me. "So what's your big secret?" I asked, failing to keep my voice light. The waves crashed below, and above, the sky was huge and open. Between them, I felt tiny and unprotected.

Beau hesitated, then pulled a letter from his pocket. "I entered a contest of my own." Beau's words tumbled unevenly from his mouth, but he grinned.

I didn't move—this wasn't the information I'd steeled myself for—and Beau had to press the letter into my hand. I examined his face, alight but pulsing with nervousness I wasn't used to seeing.

I unfolded the letter. "Dear M-Mr. McClatchy," I read, stumbling. "We are pleased to offer you a scholarship for the band track of next summer's National Music Camp." I blinked up at Beau. His grin widened as he took in my reaction. "Of hundreds of applicants, your audition stood out. We look forward to seeing you in Michigan in a few months."

For a second, relief flooded me. He wasn't officially with SueAnn—or at least that wasn't what he wanted to tell me. And then relief gave way to joy.

"Beau!" I squealed. "This is amazing! When do you go? And how long will you be gone?"

Beau's face clouded over. "Well, that's the thing." He took the letter and refolded it. "I haven't told my dad."

"Oh." Beau was so confident . . . except around his dad. Mr. McClatchy said he was waiting for Beau to "grow out" of music. But surely an honor like this would change that. "The National Music Camp—won't he see how big this is?"

Beau shrugged. "Dunno . . . He says 'music is no kind of future for a McClatchy.'" His voice dipped low in imitation of his father's.

"They're giving you a scholarship, though."

"But not the travel expenses." The light in Beau's face faded.

Something pulled at my heart as I recognized the hopeless look in his eyes—I knew this feeling well. But on Beau, the doubt looked wrong, out of place.

"Surely he can afford to send you."

"Oh, he *could* . . ." Beau whispered, looking out at the ocean. The resentment in his face reminded me of Charlie.

I frowned. "What are you going to do?"

"I don't know yet. You're the only person I've told."

Out at sea, the ferry slid behind a rocky outcropping. The dark water stretched flat. "Wait, really—the only person?"

He nodded. "I can't tell Mother until I figure out how to tell Dad."

"But what about . . . I mean, haven't you even told . . ." I stuttered, blushing.

"What?" Beau's eyebrows arched.

"Haven't you told SueAnn?" My voice scratched over her name.

"Naw." Beau shook his head and his nose wrinkled. "She'd just be mad that I wanted to spend the summer away. Anyway, we're not official."

"You're not?" A clean breeze gusted around us, and the sky suddenly seemed brighter.

Beau gave me a strange look. "No. And I'm not sure . . ."

My heart pounded, its rhythm pulsing in my ears. "What?"

He shrugged. "I dunno. She's always . . . there."

I had to fight the smile threatening to break across my lips. "Oh?"

"Sometimes, I think I'd rather . . ." He frowned and looked me hard in the face, like he was working out a puzzle. For a split second, everything seemed to rock back and forth with the waves below.

I looked away, trembling, feeling somewhere between relieved and . . . unsteady. I'd thought I was losing Beau to SueAnn, but instead, he was thinking of calling it quits—and maybe something more.

Even though neither of us had moved, Beau felt closer. Over the echoing croak of a raven and the ocean's steady throb, our breaths intertwined. Beau's came in rough gulps, but mine trembled at the surface. The air felt heavy with all that was unsaid, while below, the waves launched themselves against the rocky cliffs, punishing them for daring to reach toward the sky.

Beau startled. "Do you hear that?" he asked.

I listened. A familiar engine clanked beneath the ocean's thundering. We looked east down McClatchy Road. My father's truck roared toward us, dust flying in its wake. I stood up, squinting, then relaxed when I realized Dad wasn't driving. "It's Charlie," I said. "But . . . he's driving too fast."

Beau and I stumbled over brick rubble, meeting the truck as it screeched to a stop in the yard.

Charlie jumped out. His face was rigid.

"Charlie?" I called.

"Get in the truck, Sam." Relief filled my brother's face, but there was a sharp edge in his voice.

"What is it, Charlie?" My eyes met Beau's—his eyes reflected my own alarm.

"What's happened?" Beau asked.

Charlie's eyes flicked to Beau, then back to me. His shoulders fell. "The Japanese—they just attacked Hawaii."

# CHAPTER 10

# PEARL HARBOR

The truck's engine rumbled as we cruised toward Beau's house. "We were listening to the radio—to the baseball game," Charlie said. "An announcer interrupted. Said Japan bombed a naval base in Hawaii. Pearl Harbor, he called it."

My brain couldn't keep up with Charlie's words. Could this be real?

"They're sure it was the Japanese?" Beau asked from my other side.

Charlie grimaced. "Yes."

"But why?" I asked. "Everyone says the Japanese want us to stay out of the war."

Charlie shook his head. "There's no way we're staying out now."

I took a sharp breath. If war was coming, so was the draft. I glanced at Charlie's right hand on the steering wheel. After Dad took his college fund, Charlie had tried to enlist. He'd been so angry when the recruiter classified him 4-F. Now I could only feel grateful.

But Beau was already sixteen. On his next birthday, he'd be old enough to serve.

I turned to stare at him, and saw the horror I felt etched on his face. He reached for my hand. Even with everything else going on, my heart thudded as his warm skin slid over mine. I felt Charlie watching, but I didn't draw my hand away.

Beau's neighborhood had always felt like a different world. Large brick houses lined the road. The lawns were edged, the picket fences mended, the driveways filled with newer, cleaner cars than those in Japantown. I'd never felt welcome here, exactly . . . But I felt even more out of place today.

When we got to the McClatchys', Charlie stopped. The engine idled as we stared up the redbrick pathway. The house's wide doors were open, and Mr. McClatchy's frame filled the entrance. I swallowed.

"Oh no," Beau whispered. My brain stuttered as he pulled his hand from mine. My fingers closed in a lonely fist.

McClatchy charged down the brick walkway. "You!" he bellowed, pointing a long finger at Charlie and me.

"Time to go," Charlie said through his teeth.

Beau pushed the squeaking truck door open and stepped out on the gravel drive. Cold air replaced his warm body at my side. "They were just giving me a ride home," Beau mumbled as he slammed the truck door. He fumbled with the gate and scooted past his dad.

But McClatchy marched up to the passenger side. "Open this window," he ordered. I snuck a glance at Charlie. He frowned. Trembling, I rolled the window down.

"From now on . . ." McClatchy growled, his voice as coarse as sandpaper. I slunk toward Charlie.

"Sir . . ." Charlie began, his hand still on the gears.

McClatchy took a deep breath. He grabbed the frame of the open window. "You're no longer welcome here. Beau's not to visit your home. And at school, you just stay away."

My brain stung as if I'd been slapped. I opened my mouth, but no words came. My eyes flicked to Beau . . . but he didn't meet my gaze.

"Sir, there's no call for this," Charlie said. He put his bony right hand on mine. I could feel his pulse—fast and hot. "We had nothing to do with this."

McClatchy's knuckles bulged on the ledge of the truck window. "You're Japanese, aren't you? Don't tell me your dad doesn't shop at that Japanese store. How much of that money goes back to your emperor?"

Charlie's hand tightened on mine. I wanted to argue, but I froze, as voiceless as a rock. "I was born right here on Linley," Charlie said, his voice stiff. "I'm as American as you."

McClatchy lunged forward. His head and an arm breached the window. I jumped back, nearly sitting on Charlie.

"My father fought in World War I! And his granddad fought in the Civil War!" McClatchy's cheeks flamed, red and splotchy. "What has your family done for this country? Take our jobs, take our land. You—" He spat on the floor of the truck. "You're nothing but a couple of Japs."

The word hit like an actual blow. Air slammed out of my lungs.

Charlie revved the engine. "Take your arm out of my truck," he said through gritted teeth.

McClatchy glared. "'Sir.'"

Charlie looked up at him. "What?"

"Say 'sir.'" Spittle flecked McClatchy's mouth.

The muscles in Charlie's face pulled. I put my hand on his arm.

"Sir." Charlie nearly spat the word, but McClatchy pulled himself out of the window, wiping his mouth on his sleeve.

Charlie shifted into gear and backed up, making a three-point turn. My hands trembled in my lap.

McClatchy stood there till we left the circle. At the bottom of the hill, I turned to see if Beau was watching. But he was gone.

# CHAPTER 11

# BACK AT HOME

Outside the truck window, the trees blurred as I blinked back tears. The word *Jap* rang in my mind. I kept thinking of the day six years ago when Beau and I had become friends. I had found Mack Clyde holding a sack full of kittens that he planned to throw off a bridge. Scooter had pushed me down when I tried to rescue them, but just then Beau had pedaled up to us on a shiny new bike. When I told him what was going on, he promised Mack and Scooter a pound of horehound candy from his dad's store if they'd let him have the bag of tiny, mewing fluffballs. Beau and I spent the end of the summer caring for the kittens and finding them each a home. And then, when the kittens were gone, we'd continued to get together.

I bowed my head, holding my temples and trying to get Mr. McClatchy's ugly word out of my mind.

Why, I wondered, couldn't Beau speak up for me the way he had for those kittens?

Charlie pulled into our driveway. The ground crunched beneath him. A dark Cadillac was already parked on the rutted dirt.

"Looks like Mr. Tanaka's here." Charlie shifted into park, but left the keys in the ignition. "Sam, McClatchy's a jerk, but he'll calm down. Just give it time."

I nodded. But as I thought of Beau, standing behind his dad, his head hanging, I wasn't so sure.

Warm air and the sound of rapid Japanese engulfed us as we entered the house. A fire blazed in the parlor, where Dad and Mr. Tanaka were joined by Mr. Omura, a wide-faced man in an elegant three-piece suit. Mr. Omura and his wife lived on the other side of the orchard. He owned the Japanese bank. He owned the orchard, too, but for years, he'd let it grow free, leaving its cherries and apples to kids and the birds.

Seeing Dad with the other men, I realized how gray his hair had gone in the last year. He was thinner, too, than the last time the three men had sat around the coffee table, as they had so many times before Okaasan's death, back when Dad still laughed.

But besides Dad, everything looked the same. The oil lamp twinkled on the table. Next to the sofa, the mahogany console radio played softly, its brass knobs winking. Only the men's solemn faces and rigid posture betrayed that this wasn't a social call. That and the low, round voice of a newscaster thrumming from the radio, just loud enough for me to catch the words *airplanes*, *civilians*, and *fatalities*.

Mr. Tanaka leaned forward on the rocking chair as he spoke in Japanese. "Surely, Omura-san, they wouldn't suspect us of treason solely because of our race!"

Sitting next to Dad on the sofa, Mr. Omura shook his head. "But Mr. Roosevelt *must* enter the war," he said, also in Japanese, his words fast and thick with fear. "Japanese Americans will be caught in the middle. And the agent asked about *us*. We are 'suspects.'" He said the last word in English.

"Suspects?" I mouthed to Charlie. His face was solemn.

"They're being cautious," Mr. Tanaka said. "They can't really think we would take Japan's side." He leaned farther forward, resting his elbows on his knees. "Take me, for example. I've lived here three times as long as I lived in Japan. My son was born here."

Mr. Omura shook his head. "But already, I've heard rumors. My friend from Seattle telephoned. He said the FBI took his neighbor. They didn't even allow him to change out of his bathrobe."

"They're arresting Japanese?" I asked, my higher voice and English words crashing like cold water over the men's conversation. All three turned.

Mr. Tanaka pushed his glasses up his nose. "We still know very little," he said, his low Japanese calmer than seemed reasonable.

I imagined how Charlie and I must look, standing in the doorway, mouths open, eyes wide. But how could there already be arrests? It had been only hours since the attack—even less since the radio announcement.

Dad cleared his throat. "Hiro and Kiki are in the kitchen. Please join them."

Charlie gave Dad a look, but Dad only rubbed his clean-shaven jaw. Charlie put his hand on my shoulder.

I wanted to stay and hear more. But the men were silent, obviously waiting for us to leave. I followed Charlie across the entryway and into the kitchen. There Hiro and Kiki sat across from each other at the table, hunched over a tin of *senbei* and the kitchen radio. Hiro was absorbed in the news, but Kiki, who was facing the door, looked up. Her shoulders lifted and fell as she took a deep breath. Relief, then irritation flitted across her face.

"The public of Honolulu has been advised to keep in their homes," the radio announcer said, his voice crisp and deep. "There has been . . ." Scratchy static sounds scrambled the announcer's words. Hiro adjusted a knob, and the radio cleared. "We cannot estimate just how much damage has been done, but it has been a very severe attack."

"It's inconceivable," Charlie said, walking up behind Hiro.

Hiro swung around and stood. He held his hand out to Charlie, and they locked hands for a brief moment. Then Hiro turned to me. "Kiki said Charlie went to get you over an hour ago. Glad you're safe," he said. I nodded, feeling a self-consciousness that surprised me.

"When did you get here?" Charlie asked. I took a seat next to Kiki.

"About half an hour ago." Hiro turned the radio lower and leaned forward. "We were at the ferry, picking up a load for the Merc. That's when we heard." He closed his eyes. "The ferry captain put the radio on the loudspeaker, and everyone—the ferry workers, the people waiting to get on, everyone—we all stopped and listened. Minutes later, these men came and told everyone they weren't going to relaunch." The corners of his mouth turned down. "Then they singled Dad and me out and told us we weren't allowed to pick up our goods."

Charlie frowned. My own mouth tightened. In my mind, I saw Mr. Tanaka and Hiro, standing all alone in a sea of unfriendly faces.

"But they let everyone else?" Kiki asked.

"We were the only Japanese."

Charlie splayed his mismatched hands on the table, his tendons set in hard ridges. Next to me, Kiki shook her head.

"When we got home," Hiro said, "we got a call from John Allred." Mr. Allred, Ruth's father, worked for the town as an assessor. "He wasn't supposed to call, but he's too decent not to. He told us an agent from the FBI called and asked him a bunch of questions." Hiro's voice got low. "Asked him to prepare a list of home addresses for all the Japanese on the island."

I let out an involuntary yelp. Charlie swore under his breath.

Hiro hesitated. "The agent also asked who might have extra influence on the Japanese community—bankers, priests, teachers." He grimaced. "Shopkeepers. Landowners."

A chill spread over the room. My mind raced. All the men sitting in our parlor would be on that list.

"What will they do with the information?" I asked. None of this made sense. What did a bombing in Hawaii have to do with anything on Linley?

Kiki's eyes narrowed. "They must just be gathering information—right?"

Hiro shrugged. "I have no idea. But Mr. Allred said he vouched for us, told them we were all good, hardworking citizens."

"All right, you're right. Of course." Dad's harried Japanese rang through the entry, and seconds later, he, Mr. Omura, and Mr. Tanaka stood in the kitchen doorway. Mr. Omura scowled, and Dad looked irritated but resigned.

Hiro snapped the radio off, and Dad cleared his throat. "Sam, build up the fire in the stove. Charlie, the fire in the parlor is already going. Go up to my room. Bring down any Japanese books. And Kiki, go to the attic. Get the letterbox and the family albums."

"Why?" I asked, trying to put his orders together.

Dad sighed. "Mr. Omura recommends ridding our house of anything that might tie us to Japan—in case we're searched by officials."

"You want us to burn our things?" My voice came out sharper than I intended—I sounded more like Kiki than myself. But the photo albums—Okaasan's albums. He *couldn't* mean to burn them.

Kiki scowled. "Why would *we* be searched? We're . . ." She stumbled over her words. "I mean, look, we're not like some of the *really* Japanese families—" She stopped, glancing over at Mr. Omura.

Everyone stared at her, and she blushed.

"I just mean we're more American." Her chin jutted forward.

"Go," Dad said.

Kiki reddened further as she tripped past Hiro. I stood to tend to the fire. Its coals already glowed hot, but Dad wanted flames.

Only Charlie didn't move. "This is—" His hands shook. "It's not fair." Charlie turned to Mr. Tanaka. "Don't they have to have evidence before they arrest us?" Charlie's voice quavered. "And wouldn't they have to prove it at a trial?"

Mr. Tanaka pinched the bridge of his nose. "That's what the Constitution says," he answered in English. "But Mr. Omura has convinced your father that there's danger."

Dad nodded. "It's better not to give them any reason . . . We can't be split up."

Charlie shook his head but stalked up to Dad's room.

My mind raced through the albums Dad had ordered Kiki to fetch. The first few pages of one album held Okaasan's only photographs of her family, of herself as a child. Another held a photo of Okaasan's home in southern Japan, taken just weeks before she boarded the ship that brought her to America. How could Dad ask us to burn these last bits of her story?

When Kiki's steps creaked on the stairs, I worked up my courage. "Dad?" My voice trembled. "Dad, the albums—we aren't going to burn *everything*, are we?"

Dad's eyes narrowed. "Samantha."

Mr. Omura gave me a gentle look. In Japanese, he explained, "You should get rid of anything that makes your family appear sympathetic to Japan."

I nodded. *"Wakarimashita,"* I said. *I understand.* I switched back to English. "But, Dad, the pictures of Okaasan . . . Couldn't we"—I swallowed, but I knew I'd regret it forever if I didn't try—"couldn't we hide those photos?"

I braced myself, sure Dad would yell at me next. But when I looked into his eyes, they glistened. "Where would you hide them?"

Kiki entered the room, carrying the letterbox on top of several leather-bound albums. Her cheeks flamed, but she held herself straight.

I thought hard. "There's a dead tree in the orchard, with a rotted hollow. If we take the photos out of the albums, they ought to fit." I remembered the orchard was Mr. Omura's. "If that's okay with you, sir," I added in Japanese.

Mr. Omura hesitated, studying my face, then Kiki's. He nodded. "It's risky. But the orchard is open to everyone."

Uncertainty crossed Dad's face as Kiki set the albums on the table. She lifted a cover, and the black-paged album fell open to a photo of Okaasan as a young woman. It was the picture she'd sent to my dad when their marriage had been arranged.

Dad stared at the photograph. Okaasan wore a flowered kimono. Her face was younger and lighter than I remembered, her expression serious, as if she knew she was taking on an entirely new life.

Dad swallowed and nodded. "Okay."

# CHAPTER 12

# HIDING MEMORIES

Mr. Tanaka and Mr. Omura excused themselves to make other visits, but Hiro stayed behind. He and Kiki shared the sofa facing the coffee table, sitting so close they might have been touching. Something rumbled inside me as I watched them go through the albums, pulling photos from pasted corners and stuffing them into a cookie tin.

I looked away. How could Kiki make even a situation like *this* work in her favor?

Dad fingered the title on the spine of a book before laying it atop the burning pyre in the fireplace. The fire blackened, swallowing one book after another. Even with the windows open, the room smelled of smoke.

I worked next to Dad, emptying our family butsudan, the ebony altar at which we honored our ancestors. Dad had ordered me to throw away its contents—the incense burners, bells, and delicate wooden platforms on which we offered Okaasan gifts like persimmons and rice balls. He allowed me to keep only a simple photo of her inside. To anyone who didn't know, the shrine would look like a basic cabinet, with no connection to Japan. It would have been impossible to disguise if it had been fancier. But for once, I was grateful that this was all we could afford, even as I regretted all that I'd just thrown away.

"What about that?" Kiki asked, distracted from her flirting as she looked above the fireplace.

I looked up at the sword, clasped in iron brackets above the mantel. The sword had been passed down from generation to generation. Our grandfather had given it to Dad when he left Japan.

Dad's shoulders curved. He stepped up, his slippers soundless on the brick hearth as he lifted the sword from its mount. He pulled the sword from its scabbard—the metal gleamed in the dancing light of the fire before he resheathed it.

"We'll have to throw it in the cow pond," he said. "It should have been Charlie's one day." No one else could see—his back was to Kiki and Hiro. But from my spot at the butsudan, I saw his face. It held the same drawn expression I'd seen the night Okaasan died.

Dad held it out to me. "Set it on the table."

I took the sword by its wooden handle. The weight surprised me, and the fire-warmed scabbard felt alive in my bare hands. Centuries of men had owned it before my father, men who'd had dreams and worries and families of their own. Some of them had lived before the United States was even a country—the realization shivered up my spine. I set the sword on the table.

This was all so wrong. We were losing our treasures—and we hadn't done anything! Shouldn't someone step in and stop this?

My hands itched for my camera. If I didn't know Dad would object, I would have taken a picture of the sword—and some of Kiki and Hiro pulling photos from their albums, of the stripped butsudan, of Dad's books burning. There was so much I would have liked to capture. Something inside screamed that this moment needed documentation.

But I looked at Dad's worn face, lit by the flames engulfing his books. Now was not the time to ask.

Hiro stood, holding the tin. "We're done removing the photographs."

"Shall I hide them?" I asked.

Dad nodded. "Go."

"I'll come with you," Hiro said. "I should be on my way anyway."

Kiki's eyes flashed to me for a split second, and I thought she'd insist on taking my place. But she turned to Hiro, her face sweet. "I'll feel much safer knowing you're with Sam." She pulled a deep peacock-blue scarf from the coffee table where we'd used it as a tablecloth. She slipped it beneath the tin Hiro held, then tied the four corners together in a topknot, making a sling. She let her fingers linger as they grazed Hiro's hands.

"Oh . . . Good idea," Hiro stuttered. I raised my eyebrows, but Kiki ignored me.

Dad didn't notice Kiki's brazen flirting as he stared into the flames. "Go now, Sam. Don't let anyone see you. And, Kiki, go through all the rooms. See if there is anything else that could link us to Japan."

My heart lurched—Okaasan's kimono. It lay in its box under my parents' bed. For a second, I wavered. Kiki might not even think to look under the bed. And what if Dad discovered what I was doing? But also . . . what if he burned it while I was gone?

"Can you wait just a second?" I asked Hiro. "I'll just . . . grab something." I ran to my parents' room and threw myself on the floor next to the bed. I stretched until my fingers found the sharp corners of the box. Kneeling, I opened the plain wood lid, then unfolded the inner paper wrappings to reveal white blossoms embroidered on a gray silk background. I tucked the silk bundle between my ribs and my coat. The fire would not have Okaasan's kimono.

The wind outside was sharp as Hiro and I trekked across the yard with the knotted package of photographs. In silence, we climbed over the fence and picked our way to the rotted hollow. All the trees were bare of leaves, but the gnarled trunk, half knocked over, still stood out. I cleared the hollow with my bare hand and set the tin inside, pushing it back as far as it would go, so if it rained, the package wouldn't be in the direct downpour.

Hiro scraped a bunch of dead leaves from the orchard floor and piled them on top of the package, camouflaging Kiki's scarf.

I stepped back. "Think anyone will notice?"

"Looks good to me," Hiro said.

In silence we stared at the tree. I calculated the things we were losing: the sword, the letters, the books . . . And maybe these photographs, memories printed in light and chemicals, now at the mercy of the elements.

I clutched the silk bundle closer to my body.

"You okay?" Hiro asked.

"Yeah. Well, no," I admitted. "But what else can we do?"

Hiro nodded. "Right. But I kind of envy you." He peeked over at me and saw the confusion on my face. "Your dad's willing to do all this to keep your family safe. My dad . . ." Hiro kicked one of the tree's wrinkled roots. "He has this . . . *faith*, I guess, that in America, these things work themselves out." He paused, and his next words were barely audible. "But what if he's wrong? I mean, he's not going to burn anything. What if the stuff he doesn't burn ends up getting us . . ." He didn't finish.

I swallowed. From this side of things, taking the kimono was reckless, irresponsible. "Your dad's probably right," I said, but I felt the words slip, high and doubting, as they left my mouth. "My dad's overly cautious. He . . ." I hesitated, but I felt I could tell Hiro. "He's afraid."

Hiro dug the toe of his shoe in the dirt. "I guess I wish a little of your father's carefulness would rub off on my dad." He glanced at the lump on my side. "Sam, do you want me to take something for you? Like I said, we're not burning things, so . . ."

I looked down at my coat. "Oh, this? No. I—I think I have an idea."

Hiro nodded. "All right." He didn't press, but I found I wanted to show him. I unbuttoned my jacket, and gray silk spilled out. I caught its folds before they floated to the ground.

Hiro's eyes lingered on the kimono, then on me. "Your mother's?"

I nodded, stroking the silk, remembering how it had fluttered as Okaasan danced. The other dancers wore reds, plums, and pinks. But Okaasan's kimono was the color of the ocean after it rains, sprinkled with only a handful of tiny white blossoms. Everyone said she was the best, more graceful than even the younger dancers. I thought she looked like a butterfly, but Dad said, "No, a butterfly's beauty is flighty and showy. Your *okaasan*, she's like the sea." I asked what he meant, and he didn't say. But I watched the way his eyes never left her, the way they followed her lithe, farm-hardened hands.

A clean, salty breeze swirled through the orchard, and the embroidered blossoms shivered on the silk. "I can't burn it," I whispered.

"Of course not." Hiro's brown eyes were warm and deep, like maple syrup in a clean bowl. I remembered that he had lost his mother, too, when we were both in elementary school. The realization thickened the air around us, and I became very aware of his eyes searching mine. I jerked my head down, so my hair fell around my face. I wasn't sure what I was feeling—not exactly afraid— vulnerable, maybe?

"I'm sorry," I said, tucking the kimono back into my coat. Even in the icy air, my cheeks felt warm. "I'm sure you have things to do. Thanks for your help."

Hiro didn't say anything as I buttoned up my coat. But I felt his gaze as I dashed away, back toward the barn.

The smell of the chickens hit me as I opened the barn door. Clark Gable rushed the gate, bobbing his head for scraps. With his gleaming black tail-feathers and golden breast, the rooster belonged at a state fair, not on our barely-making-it farm. But he had been my mother's favorite, and that kept him safe from both the frying pan and the fair.

I paused and threw a handful of scratch his way. "Mind if I keep something in here?" I stroked his silky back. Clark hooted a low, contented note.

I pulled out an old packing crate and filled it with clean straw. It wasn't ideal. If our house got searched and someone found the kimono stuffed in a crate in the back of the barn, it would be worse than if they found it in the house. It would look as if we had something to hide.

"But I can't let Dad burn it," I said, maybe to Clark, maybe to myself. Maybe even partly to Okaasan. I buried the kimono in the straw.

As I set the lid on top of the crate, Clark watched. And I must have dreamed it, but it looked as if he approved.

# CHAPTER 13

# RETURN TO SCHOOL

*December 8*

Monday's sky was bare and solid, like today was the start of something different, like nothing before had kept its place. Even the road to school seemed strange. How had I never noticed the frosted purple reeds bowing over the deep ditches on both sides?

I sat squeezed between Charlie and Kiki in the middle seat of the truck. Charlie hunched down in his bomber jacket, his gloved hands gripping the scuffed steering wheel as the truck bumped over ruts. I took a deep breath and tried not to worry about Beau and Mr. McClatchy.

Next to me, Kiki hummed "Blue Champagne" as she rustled through her bag. The schmaltzy ballad was jarring—so wrong with all that was going on. But all morning, Kiki's face had been plastered in an oddly cheerful smile. Now she pulled her gold tube of lipstick from her bag and dabbed her lips, turning them a rich, bright red.

I rubbed the toes of my new boots together, trying to scrape the already dried crust of dirt from the soles. Thinking of Beau, I wished I had taken a little more time to comb my hair.

"Can I see the paper again?" I asked Charlie.

Kiki huffed, her breath billowing like ocean fog. "Don't give it to her. It's creepy, the way she pores over that photo."

Charlie frowned but pulled the paper out from his jacket's inside pocket. "She has to understand what's going on . . . We all do."

"But she already spent half an hour this morning—" Kiki started.

"Let her be." Charlie's voice was quiet but hard, and Kiki was silent as I unfolded the paper.

*WAR! JAPS BOMB PEARL HARBOR: 1,500 KILLED.* The headline spanned the entire width of the paper. Beneath it was the grainy newsprint photograph.

I still couldn't believe it—couldn't make my brain swallow it. Even after seeing the photo before, it made something inside me stop. Real ships. Real people. Gone. Disappeared into black, clotting swirls of smoke.

The entire hull of a huge battleship was invisible—sunk or burned, I couldn't tell. What must have been the deck was gone, too. Only a few broken beams and shards of board still floated, split from the rest of the wreckage. A tower was visible, swirled in dark foaming smoke. It leaned to its side, forty-five degrees, toppling. Caught mid-motion in the photo. But not in real life.

Kiki sucked in her breath. "It's unnatural," she said. She leaned against the window. "And I don't want to see it."

Maybe she was right, but I couldn't stop myself. I kept staring at the smoke, scanning the water, hoping to see someone alive, maybe swimming or in a lifeboat. But there was no one. Only smoke and light and dark and the lines that made the photograph both terrible and stunning at the same time.

"No!" Charlie braked to a lurching stop. I looked up, and the paper fell to my lap. The Merc's paned-glass windows had been covered in scarlet paint: *JAP STORE.*

"We should help them," I said, twisting in my seat as I prepared to get out.

But Charlie shifted and began to troll past the angry words. "I need to get you to school. You'll be safe there. I'll stop by on the way back." His voice trembled. "Look, I don't want you girls walking home from school. I'll come to get you and take my break late."

"We'll be okay," I said. "We can get a ride."

"We can ask Hiro—after he gets to school," Kiki added, her eyes flashing at the idea.

Charlie thought for a moment, then said, "Okay. But promise you won't walk." We both nodded.

As we hit the paved road to town, I looked back at the Merc, the sentry at the gates of Japantown. I wished I had my camera and framed the shot in my mind: the ugly words, the lonely building.

*Click.* A shutter went off in my mind, capturing so many feelings.

Except for a flag at half-mast in front of the bank, Main Street looked as it had before the bombing. But I couldn't help thinking that it felt colder than it had on Friday. Finally, we reached the redbrick schoolhouse. Students trailed through the parking lot and stood in clumps outside the front entrance, where the flag, also at half-mast, snapped angrily, caught in swirling gusts of wind.

Charlie slowed as we neared the school, and the truck's brakes squealed, loud as foghorns. I hunched down as everyone turned and stared.

So many eyes. So many expressions. Some curious, uncertain. Others hard, angry. A group of Japanese girls my age huddled next to the building, eyes darting. Frightened.

Kiki made a strange swallowing noise. I followed her gaze to a line of boys standing between our truck and the front door. Scooter Clyde and his blond, bull-like brother Mack stood in the center of the group. They had turned to face us directly, arms folded over their chests. My breath caught.

"Go inside straightaway," Charlie said. His mouth tightened as he looked at the line of boys.

Kiki shook her head. "No. We have every right to be out on the grounds . . . and anywhere else."

"Then at least wait till they go inside." But before I finished,

Kiki swung the truck door open. She squared her shoulders, took a deep breath, and stepped out of the car without a word.

I sat frozen, torn between running to catch up and pleading for her to get back in the truck. Charlie propped the driver's-side door open and planted one leg outside.

"Kiki!" Alice Nakano hurried from behind our truck. She waved her hand above her head.

Kiki glanced backward at Alice, her eyes as hard as the boys', then whipped around. Alice faltered, and Kiki strode toward the school without another look. The line of angry boys broke as she walked straight through them.

"Hiya, ladies!" She waved at a group of white girls. The girls, including Kiki's best friend, Shelley, fidgeted and eyed each other, but opened the circle to make room.

Charlie shook his head. "Well!" I wasn't sure if he was impressed or disgusted. I was both.

Alice followed slowly in Kiki's wake, crossing the line of boys with her arms tightly folded. She passed Kiki without looking up and made her way toward the group of Japanese girls huddled against the school wall.

As I edged toward the open door and pulled my book bag over my shoulder, I saw a flicker of strawberry blond. Beau stood on the far side of the mass of students. Next to him, SueAnn saw me staring. She glared, then cupped her hand around Beau's ear and whispered.

Beau's eyes flashed toward me. Shoulders slumped, he turned and walked toward the door. SueAnn followed him.

"Oh, Sam," Charlie said. I couldn't look at my brother, couldn't stand to see the sympathy in his eyes.

The school bell rang, and the other students finally looked away. They converged, like cattle, at the door, just like they did every day. Like nothing was different. Like today was just another school day.

Only it wasn't.

The wind snatched dust from the schoolyard and tossed it in spirals. Through the open door, a gust tugged at my hair, pulling it out from under my scarf and batting it around my face. The flag whipped hard, its red and white stripes proud and fierce.

My eyes stung, and I bit my lip. Then I slammed the truck door and strode toward the school.

When I reached my first class, I tried to remember the way Kiki had broken through the line of boys. It felt awkward with my book bag, but I pushed my shoulders back and raised my head. The room hummed, a combination of the radiator and whispered conversations. Mr. Percival wasn't there yet, but Beau, sitting in the front of the room, was already bent over his desk. I took a deep breath, then—before I could chicken out—marched up to his chair, four desks in front of mine.

"Beau?" I whispered.

Beau didn't raise his head.

As the silence lengthened, I knew I should walk away, saving face before anyone noticed. But I couldn't move my feet. I still expected my best friend to support me . . . like I would've supported him.

"Beau, please," I whispered.

Beau glanced up, his eyes meeting mine for a split second. "I can't, Sam."

"Why?" My voice cracked. Beau stared at his desk. My cheeks felt hot. "Why are you doing this?" My whisper was harsher than I'd expected, like the question came from some deep part of myself I hadn't known existed.

When he still didn't answer, I swallowed and quickly straightened. I checked to see if anyone was listening. No one, not even SueAnn, had heard. She'd swiveled around in her seat to listen as

Scooter trumpeted the things he'd heard about the bombing to a group of students.

"They say over a thousand men were killed on those ships." Scooter's voice was slow and nasal.

"So many?" asked SueAnn.

"Yup." Scooter had slicked his rust-colored curls against his head, making his freckled face look even wider. His long body was too big for his desk, and he'd propped his legs on the iron rail of the chair next to his, blocking the aisle. "Most of 'em drowned."

The horrible picture from the newspaper swam in my mind. I still couldn't believe it had happened. And that it was the Japanese . . . A feeling heavier than gravity pulled on me.

"It's just so terrible," Ruth whispered. Her round face shone almost white against her brown curls.

I made my way down the aisle, hesitating when I came to Scooter's long legs.

"Excuse me," I whispered.

Scooter ignored me. He smoothed the front of his oily hair with his fingers. "My dad said the Japs are targeting islands. Linley could be next."

"Linley?" Ruth asked, fading even lighter.

Scooter's jaw spread into a smirk. He *liked* scaring Ruth. And that—combined with Beau and everything else—made me mad.

"*Why* would they do that?" My voice was louder than I'd intended. Scooter stared. "I mean . . ." The classroom had gone silent, and every person in the room stared at me. "Pearl Harbor is a naval base. What good would it do to hit us?"

Scooter's mouth curled. "You sure know a lot about how the Japanese think." He sat up, planting both feet on the ground.

My hands trembled. I forced myself to leave them at my sides. What had I been thinking, speaking up to someone like Scooter?

"Tell us, *Slanty*"—Scooter stood up, and the top of my head didn't even meet his shoulders—"who *is* next?"

I glanced behind me. Beau was still hunched over his desk—the only person not staring. My stomach balled up in a tight knot.

I turned back to Scooter. "I don't know . . . I'm not . . ."

Scooter stepped forward, closing the gap between the two of us. "Not *what*?"

But before I answered, Mr. Percival walked into the classroom. "All right, class. Composition books out."

I stood, not sure what Scooter would do if I tried to pass him.

"All of you," Mr. Percival said in his reedy voice. "Sit," he said, his voice more annoyed than concerned. "That means you, too, Mr. Clyde."

Scooter glared at Mr. Percival, but he sank back into his seat.

I could still feel people staring at me, and my legs felt weak, but I scrambled to my desk. I slung my book bag onto the back of my chair, then sat down. Every part of me was on fire.

*Slanty?* The word burned. And Beau hadn't said a thing.

# CHAPTER 14

# AN ASSEMBLY

Just before civics ended, Principal Carroll called the student body to assemble in the lunchroom. President Roosevelt was going to address the nation by radio broadcast. SueAnn flounced up to Beau as we lined up at the door, giggling like we were going to a pep rally. I trailed behind.

The halls smelled of cleaning supplies and body odor. The clatter of shoes mixed with echoing chatter. As we got closer to the cafeteria, administrators and secretaries stood on both sides of the hall, herding us. I felt their stares, like I was the only person they really needed to corral. I told myself not to let my imagination run wild, not to lose my composure right here in the hallway. But still, a prickle danced on the back of my neck.

"Quickly, quietly," the school librarian directed, shushing us with a finger over her mouth.

At the cafeteria entrance, the crowd slowed. Through the open cafeteria doors, I saw all the lunch tables stacked against the walls. The stage had been set up in the front of the room, and dark wood benches had been lined up in two sections, with a wide aisle between. The front rows were already filled with students, though most were standing instead of sitting.

As my class made its way toward the benches, Mr. Pratt, the boys' gym teacher, jerked my arm roughly. "Back of the room," he said, already scanning the crowd and moving to stop another Japanese student.

"What?" I asked. He was gone. But as soon as I got past the

crowded doors, I saw. All the Japanese students had been herded to the back of the cafeteria, where they sat in two long rows. Three yards of empty space separated them from the rest of the students.

Miss Lambson, my English teacher, patted my shoulder as she stepped past me. For a moment I thought she might explain, or even tell me this was a mistake, but she only called for her own class to sit in an assigned area. I stood, frozen, as SueAnn patted the open bench on her right. Beau slunk down next to her.

A violent heat spread through me. I'd spent all morning staring at the back of Beau's head. Now I was being herded to the back of the auditorium like an animal—and he didn't even care. Blinking, I marched to the back of the room. I couldn't dodge the stares from both sides of the aisle.

Kiki sat alone, back straight and proud, like she'd chosen the best seat in the room. Only the splotches blazing across her cheeks gave her away. I slid into the seat next to her. "You okay?" I asked. She gave me a withering look.

Alice and Mae made their way down the aisle. They slid into the row behind us. "That Kiki, with all her airs," Alice whispered loudly. "But here she is, still sitting in the cheap seats."

I glared, but Kiki didn't look back.

Principal Carroll's rolling voice filled the room. "Please take your seats if you have not already done so." He stood in the center of the stage, his greased hair melted against his forehead.

"Students." He cleared his throat into a megaphone as the last stragglers sat. "You may remember today's broadcast for as long as you live." He paused to let the weight of his words soak in. "I urge you, listen closely. You will tell your children about this."

He gestured to two boys, and they pulled a radio phonograph in front of the stage. The principal set the cone-shaped horn in a stand so it pointed out at the student body, then tuned the radio dial.

There was a piercing crackle. The student body shifted in their seats as static filled the room. I glanced at Beau. He craned his neck to watch the principal, totally oblivious to me.

I sat back as the round voice of a radio announcer flooded the room. There was a break, and then the voice of the president echoed through the cafeteria.

"Yesterday"—the president's voice was slow and measured but penetrating—"December 7, 1941—a date which will live in *infamy*—" The word made me tremble. "The United States of America was suddenly and deliberately attacked by naval and air forces of the Empire of Japan." He paused. "The United States was at peace with that nation."

Several of the Japanese kids looked down. Even Kiki squirmed in her seat.

"The attack was deliberately planned many days or even weeks ago. During the intervening time the Japanese government has deliberately sought to deceive the United States by false statements and expressions of hope for continued peace."

"Dirty sneaks!" a student near the front yelled.

"Cowards!" another yelled. A senior in the front section turned around and gave us a dirty look.

I swallowed hard. The bombing seemed so underhanded—not at all like the samurai stories my father loved to tell. Even though I was born in the United States—and had never even been to Japan— I felt dirty.

"I regret to tell you that very many American lives have been lost," the president continued. "Always will our whole nation remember the character of the onslaught against us. No matter how long it may take us to overcome this premeditated invasion, the American people in their righteous might"—his voice trembled—"will win through to absolute victory."

In front of me, students clapped, magnifying the applause on the radio.

"We will gain the inevitable triumph—so help us God." The president paused for more clapping, louder and longer. Then he said, his voice strong and deliberate, "I ask that the Congress declare that since the unprovoked and dastardly attack by Japan on Sunday, December 7, 1941, a state of war has existed between the United States and the Japanese Empire."

From the radio, there came whooping, cheering, and a long round of applause. In front of me, the student body yelled and whistled. A few even threw their coats above their heads.

I didn't understand. How was this something to celebrate? This was war—killing and dying and hate. The terrible newspaper photograph flashed in my mind. How could anyone cheer?

# CHAPTER 15

# FALLOUT

The rest of the day was haltingly, achingly slow. From second period on, I was sent to the back of the room in each of my classrooms. At lunch, I started toward my usual table. Ruth slid to make room, but SueAnn glared at her. And Beau still wouldn't look at me. So I swallowed and walked on.

I didn't see Kiki, and, thinking of how she had treated Alice, I doubted she'd welcome me anyway. So I gingerly made my way to the Japanese girls' table. They'd moved from their usual spot in the front of the cafeteria to a seldom-used table on the side of the room, and they ate in near silence.

"Can I sit here?" I asked.

Alice gave me dagger eyes. "Is your sister coming, too?"

I shrugged, and Alice rolled her eyes, but Edna nodded. "Of course," she said, and Mae scooted close to Mariko, leaving me room on the edge of the bench.

I sat and got out my lunch, letting my eyes slide to my old table. Ruth kept glancing at me as she and SueAnn chatted on one side of the table. On the other side, Hank seemed to be telling a story. His hands flapped wildly, and Beau doubled over laughing.

I gritted my teeth. How could Beau be so thoughtless? It was like six years of sitting together every lunch were just erased, and something inside me felt like it was tearing.

❧

When my last class ended, I hurried to Kiki's locker, hoping she'd wrangled a ride with Hiro. But when I found her, Kiki's eyes were red and swollen.

"Are you okay?"

Some of Kiki's curls had come unpinned, framing her face in frazzled wisps. "What do you think?" she asked, her voice sharp enough that people looked. She jerked her locker open.

"Charlie said to get a ride . . ."

"I know what Charlie said," Kiki snapped. "But Hiro wasn't in any of my classes. He never came."

I grimaced, thinking of the horrible words painted across the Merc. "Should I call the brickyard and ask Charlie to come?"

"Do what you want," Kiki said, stuffing a thick textbook into her bag. "I'm not going home. I'm going into town with some of the gang."

"Wait, what about me?"

"Car's full." Kiki banged her locker closed. "And anyway, I'm not going to ask the only friends I have left to bring along my kid sister."

"But—"

I stared at Kiki's straight back. Her book bag struck her hip as she marched away. Students streamed past, and my stupor melted, turning first to anger, then disgust. I ran through my options. Should I call Charlie? He'd be furious that Kiki had left me. Even as angry as I was, I didn't want them to fight. But he'd be even madder if he found out I'd walked home alone.

*Bam.* Something hard slammed my shoulder. My bag fell to the ground. I crumpled to my knees.

"That's right. Bow, Slanty." I looked up at Scooter's broad face. His jaw spread into a grin that made his cheeks look like the handlebars of a two-speed.

He leaned forward and scooped up his textbook, then strolled past, whistling "Yankee Doodle" as he merged with the other students. His brother Mack followed him. Mack's stare was like ice.

I knelt in the middle of the hall. My left shoulder throbbed, but everything else was numb. I didn't understand. Why did Scooter throw the book? Why did they hate me? I hadn't *done* anything.

"Are you okay?" a soft voice asked.

Ignoring the pang in my shoulder, I nodded.

"I can't believe he did that," the girl said, picking up my bag and handing it to me.

I looked up at the girl's kind, full face and hazel eyes: Ruth Allred. She gave me a half smile, then stood up, waiting for me to stand, too. I pulled my book bag onto my good shoulder, then tested my left arm. "Anything hurt?" Ruth asked.

I straightened and shook my head, even though my shoulder throbbed. "No. Thank you."

Ruth nodded, then slipped into the stream of students, exiting as quietly as she'd entered.

I walked out into the whistling wind. The sky swirled, dark and moody. Remembering my promise to Charlie, I looked around the parking lot, searching for someone I lived near—and knew well enough—to ask for a ride.

But no one from Japantown was waiting on the curb. No Japanese kids loitered in the parking lot at all.

My shoulder still throbbed, and I felt antsy at the lack of people who looked like me. I was about to go back inside and call Charlie when a dark sedan stopped in front of me. Hiro reached across to prop the passenger door open. "Sam!" he called.

I hadn't recognized Mr. Tanaka's car, but my fear drained into the pavement beneath me.

"Can I give you a lift?" Hiro asked.

"Yes, please," I said, not even bothering to hide my relief. The car was full of notepads and loose papers. Hiro shoved a pile onto the floor.

"My father's idea of an office."

I hardly noticed the mess. "Kiki said you weren't in class."

"I was at the Merc with my dad. But Charlie called. He wanted to make sure you guys had a ride."

Charlie had called. My insides softened at the realization, and I leaned back, making myself as comfortable as I dared, careful not to disturb the papers, though there seemed to be no organization to the piles. "I'm sorry about what happened to your store."

An unreadable look crossed Hiro's face. "Thanks," he said, his voice gruff. "Is Kiki still inside?"

I looked down. "She—she got a ride."

Hiro's eyes narrowed. "She left you here by yourself?"

I shrugged. "There wasn't room for me in her friend's car." The excuse echoed weakly in the space between us.

Hiro's eyebrows plunged, but he shifted into gear. We sailed out of the parking lot without so much as a clink. The smoothness reminded me of Beau's car, and I turned to look at the parking lot. But there was no sign of the Studebaker.

"Did you listen to the broadcast?" Hiro asked. "About war being declared?"

"They played it at school."

Hiro shook his head. "Dad's been getting calls all day." I believed it. The Merc was the hub of our neighborhood. Japantown was too small to have a mayor, but Mr. Tanaka was about as close as it got.

"What kind of calls?"

Hiro's eyes swiveled from the road to me, and the look on his face was evaluating. "You should know," he said, and something in his face made me brace myself. "You remember that we'd heard men might be arrested?" Hiro sighed. "The *Seattle Star* reported that over seven hundred Japanese have been arrested already."

I gasped. "Seven hundred? In one day? How?"

"There were arrests back in November in Los Angeles. Dad thinks the government has been keeping watch, and maybe planning this, for some time."

"I—I don't want to believe that." My voice shook.

"I've scared you." Hiro slowed the car. "I shouldn't have told you."

"No. I'd rather know than not." The air swam around me. "Has anyone here been taken?"

"From Linley?" Hiro shook his head. "Not so far. But Dad got calls from a couple people who had property vandalized like ours. And, well, that was the other reason Charlie called—there's talk that the brickyard might fire Japanese workers."

"What?" I jolted, and winced at the surge of pain in my arm. "But why? Don't they need workers? I mean, the draft might be coming." I stopped short. Hiro would be draftable on his birthday.

"I know. Seems like a bad move to me, too. And Mr. Bush says he's got plenty of orders to fill. But there's been pressure." He stopped, something catching in his throat. He looked at me, again with that evaluating expression. "There's . . . people demanding it."

"Already?" It was so premature. We hadn't even been at war for a day. They already wanted to fire people like my brother, just because his parents had been born across the ocean?

Hiro shrugged. "It'd be a real blow. No one's looking for farmhands right now. I don't know what families will do if Mr. Bush caves to the pressure."

I shook my head. None of this made sense.

In Mr. Tanaka's warm car, we glided to the end of Farmers'

Freeway. When we got to Japantown, Hiro slowed, pulling off onto packed earth freckled with deep potholes. The car lurched up and down.

Then Hiro jerked to a stop. "What—"

Together we stared at the two vehicles parked in front of the Merc's door. One was Dad's old truck. The other was a big black car with one word painted in gold on its side: *Sheriff.*

# CHAPTER 16

# ACCUSATIONS

"Open this door!" The snarling voice carried across the parking lot.

Hiro cut the engine and bounded out of the Cadillac, leaving the keys swinging in the ignition. I rushed after him, my bag pounding against my thigh. I stumbled when I saw who was speaking.

"We know someone's in there!" Mr. McClatchy yelled, his breath billowing like smoke. He stood with two other men on the Merc's plank porch, hammering the bright red door with his fist.

"Elroy, this isn't a great idea," said Mr. Allred. The slope-shouldered man tried to place himself between McClatchy and the door, but McClatchy ignored him, turning instead to glare at Hiro and me.

Hiro skidded to a stop, breathing fast. Though McClatchy was tall, Sheriff Palmer was even taller, broad with rounded features and a doughy complexion. Next to them, bespectacled Mr. Allred looked even shorter than usual.

The door rattled and opened a crack. "Gentlemen, we are closed." Mr. Tanaka's voice was strained but level. "Please come back tomorrow." He looked so small compared with the men on the other side of the door.

"Heard you had a bit of a day," Sheriff Palmer said, jerking one thumb at the window. The words I'd seen on the drive to school had been scraped from the Merc's windows, but angry drips of red marred the wood sill. "Thought I ought to make a call." The big man stood at the door, but as he spoke, McClatchy shoved the door open, forcing Mr. Tanaka to step backward.

"You have no right—" Hiro said.

The sheriff followed McClatchy into the store. McClatchy narrowed his eyes as my father emerged from a dark aisle. Hiro strode to his own father's side, and I scampered to Dad.

Sheriff Palmer gestured again at the window. "Looks like you've got things sorted out."

"Mm, yes," Mr. Tanaka said. "Perhaps you could have been more helpful if you'd come sooner."

Outside the door, Mr. Allred hesitated on the porch. He spread his hands, palms up. "They came to my house with some property assessment questions," he explained. "When they said they were coming here, I insisted on accompanying them—as a witness."

"I understand," Mr. Tanaka said, tucking his shirt where it had come undone. "What can I help you with, Elroy?"

McClatchy's jaw tensed when Mr. Tanaka used his name. "Well—" McClatchy's eyes swept over the aisles. "I guess you could call me a concerned citizen. See, it seems to me that you do a lot of *international* business."

Mr. Tanaka remained unfazed. "Yes?"

"And most of that business is with Japan?"

"Where is he going with this?" I whispered. Dad shook his head and stepped backward.

Mr. Tanaka cleared his throat. "There have been trade restrictions lately . . . But over all my years of business? Yes, definitely."

McClatchy glanced sharply at Sheriff Palmer. "There, he admits it."

"Admits what?" Mr. Tanaka asked.

Sheriff Palmer gave Mr. Tanaka an uncomfortable look. "What Elroy here means to ask is"—he gave an almost peevish backward look at Mr. Allred—"how do we know you aren't . . . sending things—and maybe information—back the other way?"

Hiro growled.

Mr. Tanaka gazed up at McClatchy. "You mean to ask, how do you know I'm not a *spy*?"

Mr. McClatchy's mouth twitched, and Sheriff Palmer flushed.

Mr. Tanaka sighed. "Gentlemen, do you have any evidence to support these allegations?" Mr. Tanaka paused as he looked from McClatchy to Palmer. "Anything that would rationalize running across the island, barging onto private property, and making accusations that could be considered slander?" As the sheriff fidgeted, Mr. Tanaka answered his own question. "You don't . . . because I am *not* what you suggest."

I snuck a glance at Hiro. His eyes were riveted on his father.

"You know . . ." Mr. Tanaka hesitated, then made a decision, his eyes glinting. "Sheriff, John—" He nodded at Mr. Allred. "I should state for the record that McClatchy has voiced his displeasure about the competition my store offers his establishment on multiple occasions. He offered to buy me out last year—for pennies on the dollar. In other words"—his steely eyes fixed on McClatchy—"accusations this man makes could be motivated by issues other than concern for his country."

McClatchy flushed a deep, dark red. "Are you saying that I—I . . ."

"I am only making a statement of fact that I think ought to be known. To witnesses."

McClatchy glared at Mr. Tanaka, then at the sheriff. "You gonna let him talk to me that way?"

The sheriff shifted from one foot to the other. "Ah, we don't need that kind of talk, Tanaka."

Mr. Tanaka nodded. "I've said all I needed."

"How dare you?" McClatchy sputtered. "I— I— Your kind has no right!"

"My kind, Elroy?" Mr. Tanaka smiled bitterly.

McClatchy's eyes narrowed. "That's Mr. McClatchy to you."

Mr. Tanaka ignored McClatchy, turning to the sheriff. "I have the right to refuse entry to my private property. You ignored that right when you forced your way in. So unless you have a warrant—which, I believe, you do not—I ask that you both leave."

I held my breath—could Mr. Tanaka get away with talking like this? Sheriff Palmer chewed the side of his cheek. He glanced at Mr. Allred before scratching his head under his hat. "He's right, Elroy."

"But—" McClatchy started, his face still red.

"Look." Sheriff Palmer turned, as if he were speaking only to McClatchy, but his voice carried through the store. "Let's just go. Those federal agents will look into it."

Fear raced up my spine. "Federal agents?" I breathed. Dad shifted, and Mr. Tanaka's eyes flashed to Hiro.

The flush faded from McClatchy's face as he took in our reactions. "Yeah. Federal agents." He sneered. "I guess we'll just have to wait."

McClatchy swaggered to the still-open door, following the sheriff outside.

"I'll vouch for you," Mr. Allred promised in a low voice.

Mr. Tanaka held himself tall, but his face seemed to droop. "Thank you, John."

Mr. Allred followed McClatchy and Palmer out to the waiting patrol car, and Mr. Tanaka locked the Merc door. For a moment he was lost in his own thoughts. Then he gave us a warm smile. "Well, that was interesting."

Hiro shook his head. "Did you have to talk to him like that?"

Mr. Tanaka stared at his son, the smile fading from his face. "I will not let them make me afraid."

"It's like you want to be arrested." Hiro glared.

"These arrests won't stick," said Mr. Tanaka. "The American public will speak out."

"The American public?" Hiro seemed to burst with everything

he was thinking. "The American public just painted 'Jap Store' across your window. The American public just forced its way into our store!" He broke off, shaking but silent.

Dad scowled.

Mr. Tanaka's voice remained mild. "Still, I trust that if we go to court, the Constitution will prevail."

"You say it as if you're already planning on prison," Hiro scoffed.

A sad smile spread across Mr. Tanaka's face. "Well, I would of course *prefer* not to be arrested."

Hiro shook his head. "It's not funny." His eyes met mine. In them, I saw the fear and confusion I felt.

"If the feds are coming to make arrests on Linley, we must prepare." Mr. Tanaka turned to Dad and spoke in Japanese. "Sakamoto-san, if it comes to it . . . will you watch over my son?"

Dad grimaced. *"Iu made mo nai."* It goes without saying. Mr. Tanaka sighed, then nodded once, more relaxed now that he'd made plans for his own arrest. But in the window's reflection, Hiro's face looked older than I'd ever seen it.

*I AM AN AMERICAN.* Mr. Tanaka used a calligraphy brush to ink the letters onto a scroll of parchment. Two cans of vegetables sat on either end to weight the sign while it dried. "It'll go in my window when it dries," he said in Japanese. He stood at his counter, lit only by the grayish light streaming through the window behind him. There was something so straight about the way he stood as he examined his handiwork, something determined in the way his lips met.

I wished again that I had my camera. His resolve, his honor, and his hope all seemed worth recording. I sighed. Had it been only days since I'd imagined nothing political ever happened on Linley?

"You doing okay?" Hiro asked.

I nodded and looked up at him. "What about you?" I tried to read his shadowed face.

"Sometimes I wish he'd just behave."

"Sam," Dad called. I pulled my eyes away from Hiro. "Where is your sister?" Dad asked. There was a tiredness in his voice that made me wary of angering him. In all that had happened, I hadn't had a chance to get a good look at him. Now I saw that his clothes were flecked with chips of dried red paint and his hair was sweaty.

I hesitated, trying to think how to answer without lying or getting Kiki in trouble. "She had plans with friends," I said. "They'll give her a ride home."

He scowled. "Always with her friends." I bit my lip. But he only said, "Charlie is here." He jutted his chin at the westward window, at our truck just turning into the parking lot. Charlie sprinted from the truck, and Mr. Tanaka let him in.

The moment I saw Charlie's face, I knew something was wrong. "We did all we could," he said, mostly to Mr. Tanaka, his palms up. "But at the end of the shift, they let us go."

*Let us go.* The words rang in my mind, their gentleness in such contrast to their meaning.

"We will fight this," Mr. Tanaka said. "There has to be something we can do, even if we have to take it to the courts."

Charlie nodded, but his motion was mechanical.

The look on Dad's face was even worse than Charlie's. This could mean the farm.

"Sam," Charlie said, turning to face me. "There's something else I think you need to know."

He stepped toward me and took my hand. The gesture made my heart race. What was he about to say?

Charlie swallowed. "McClatchy is behind the firings at the brickyard."

"What?" My brain stuttered. How could Mr. McClatchy have anything to do with Charlie's job?

"He came by early this morning. He and Mr. Bush argued,

but McClatchy's a key investor who could replace Mr. Bush if he wanted. So Mr. Bush let us go. And there's more." I already felt as if my hands and feet had turned to stone. Could I take more? "As I was gathering my last pay, Mr. Bush said McClatchy specifically wanted *me* gone."

"Why you especially?" My words were high and strangled.

Charlie's eyes darted to Dad. "Mr. Bush said McClatchy told him, 'I'll die before I let those Japs own Granddad's land.'"

Dad's face was gray.

I shook my head. "That's . . ." Crazy? Horrible?

Charlie's shoulders fell.

"We'll find you another job, Charlie." I squeezed the hand that held mine. "We can still get your tuition."

Charlie pulled away. "Who'd hire me now? And anyway, what will a college education matter? All anyone will see is a Jap."

"It's only been a day. Give it a few months . . ." But even as I said it, I realized there was something to what Charlie was saying. Things were changing. And if Charlie's dreams were disappearing—what about mine? Becoming a photographer already seemed impossible. How much harder would it be if everyone saw only a Jap?

# CHAPTER 17

# POSTCARDS AND PROMISES

My head reeled. How could the world feel so different today than it had yesterday?

I needed a moment to take it all in. While Mr. Tanaka questioned Charlie further, I slipped down one of the store's dark aisles. The store smelled of ginger and sawdust. Its shelves were filled with mismatched goods, both Japanese and American. Cracker Jacks were stocked next to bean-jam sweets. Mason jars sat next to rice paddles.

But my favorite was the ladies' section on the east side of the store. The small column of shelves was filled with bolts of traditional *katazome* fabrics, a display of porcelain dolls, and beautiful Japanese ceramics. I knelt down at the shelf where Mr. Tanaka kept delicate-faced dolls. I sighed. She was still here—the heart-shaped face, the rosebud lips just hinting at a smile, the sun-gold kimono with pink cherry blossoms, each edged with a thin embroidered line of sparkling silver thread. Despite everything that had changed in the last few hours, this at least remained the same.

Kiki and I had coveted this doll when we were young. She had never sold—no one around here could afford her. But because she'd always been here, and I'd visited her so many times, she seemed a *little bit* mine. I stroked her silk kimono with one finger. The silk was as soft as newly fallen snow except where my finger brushed over the raised silver embroidery.

A knot tied itself in my stomach—the kimono in the barn. Agents were coming, and McClatchy was out for blood. Was I putting my family at risk? For what—a dress?

Yet it was a piece of my mother. I shook away the doubt and thumbed through a stack of postcards displayed on the shelf above the dolls. Each depicted a nature or village scene. Most were traditional Japanese watercolors, but a few were woodblock prints. As I looked through them, the cards blended together—none standing out, all fairly bland. The majority were black-and-white reproductions, but the more expensive color replicas were filled with pastel colors. They all seemed the same.

"You like those?"

I whipped around. Hiro stood behind me, his frame blocking my light.

I glanced at the cards. "They're . . . pretty."

He gave me a searching look. "You don't sound very impressed."

I felt a smile flicker across my lips. He was so direct—so much like his dad. I was surprised to realize I didn't mind him coming up to me, even if I had wanted to be alone. "I just prefer photographs."

Hiro folded his arms and waited.

"I mean . . ." I had to think. "Well, when I look at photographs, everything's *real*. People have wrinkles, their clothes have smudges and tears. It's true life, captured. In these paintings, everything's too . . . pretty."

He nodded slowly. "I never thought of it that way." He stared at me, his eyes solemn and unlaughing. "Is that what you're trying to do—capture real life?"

A surge of self-consciousness caught in my chest—I felt exposed. And I didn't like the feeling.

"You're embarrassed again," Hiro said. "I don't understand. Why?"

Why? Because girls weren't supposed to have these kinds of dreams! I didn't have the right to want this. But I didn't say any of that. I shrugged.

"So what exactly were you doing the other day—in the tree?"

I scrutinized his face. He didn't seem to be teasing. "I was trying to get an aerial shot. Just something I saw in a magazine."

"Like from an airplane?" he asked, catching on quick. I nodded. "That's pretty neat."

A trickle of pleasure ran through me. "I was lucky. I was practicing and didn't have my camera on me. When I take the real shot, I'll have to be more careful."

Hiro looked at me thoughtfully. "My dad takes photos."

"Yeah. He's given me some tips," I said. Back when Okaasan had let me keep some of my odd job money, Mr. Tanaka had noticed that I bought film. I'd been too shy to tell him how interested I really was, but he'd lent me a book once.

"Did he tell you he just bought a new camera?" Hiro asked.

I shook my head.

"Would—" Hiro hesitated. "Would you like to take it out sometime?"

I felt unbalanced. I had never let anyone watch me work. "Together?"

"Only if you'd like," Hiro said. I must have given him a funny look, because his face flashed through several emotions. "I just thought you might appreciate it. It's a good camera," he added. "A Leica."

My breath caught in my throat, and my heart raced. "A *Leica*?" I asked. "Like the one in the window at McClatchy's?"

Hiro smiled. "Actually, a better model."

I found it hard not to talk fast. "Are you sure your dad wouldn't mind? I mean, if I could take my shot with a camera like that!"

Hiro's mouth twitched as if he was working not to laugh. "Well, obviously you'd need to avoid falling in the pond this time. But as long as we're careful, I'm sure he'll let us. I think Dad needs me tonight, and I work every afternoon this week. But how about Saturday? Say, before supper?" Hiro asked.

I nodded, hitching my bag over my shoulder. "That'd be fine."
*Any* time would be fine.

I was nearly floating as Hiro and I walked back up to Mr.
Tanaka's counter. Dad and Charlie seemed surprised by my grin,
and I felt ashamed to have forgotten, for a moment, everything that
had happened.

"We should go," Dad said. "Unless there's something more we
can do, Tanaka-san?"

"We can take it from here." Mr. Tanaka stepped back, examin-
ing the banner he'd attached to the inside of the window. The light
shone through, showing the print on the other side.

The big brass bell jingled as I followed Dad and Charlie out the
door and down the porch stairs. Even though it was almost six,
the evening sky seemed brighter than it had less than an hour before.

I looked back at the sign, its thick black letters so solid and sure.
My fingers itched for my camera.

*I AM AN AMERICAN.* Mr. Tanaka knew who he was.
McClatchy and Sheriff Palmer couldn't make him doubt himself.
Even the fact that his country refused him citizenship didn't dis-
suade him. Would I ever feel so certain?

"Sam!" Hiro loped down the stairs, his hair falling into his eyes.
He held something in his hand. "Here." He handed me a postcard.
"On the house."

I took the card, holding it by its edges. It was one of the expensive color prints—a woodblock of a single mountain peak.

"It might be too pretty," Hiro said, "but it's my favorite, for what
that's worth."

"You shouldn't give it to me, not if it's your favorite."

Hiro waved. "Keep it," he said, turning and jogging back to the
store.

As the door closed, the bell rang again. I walked to Dad's truck, studying the postcard in my hand. Its colors were more saturated than most of the prints had been. The whole scene was painted in blues and blacks, except for a swash of brilliant orange across the mountain, like a sunset. Only days earlier, I'd imagined capturing Linley's sunset with my camera—had this artist felt the same? If so, he'd succeeded. Keeping the rest of the print dark let the orange burst from the page.

I could see why Hiro liked the print. I tucked it into my bag, sliding it between the pages of my notebook so it wouldn't bend.

"What was that?" Charlie asked. I felt Dad's eyes evaluating me.

I hesitated, then smiled. "I think I've made a friend."

After dinner that night, Dad fell asleep in the dark parlor, on the sofa that faced the butsudan. The nearly empty cabinet was open. A half-drunk bottle of sake sat on the side table next to Dad.

I sighed. When Okaasan was alive, the bottle had been a tiny ceramic cup.

I tiptoed over to where the butsudan sat on an armoire and gazed at the framed photo inside. Okaasan's face was restful, filled with that deep acceptance that made her peaceful to be around. Though the incense was gone, I clasped my hands and bowed. "I miss you," I whispered. I covered Dad with one of Okaasan's crocheted blankets and trudged upstairs.

"Close the door!" Kiki hissed as I entered the room we shared. Bundled in a coat and scarf, she stood next to the open window. Cold air swirled through the room.

"Sneaking out again?" I pressed the door closed. "Aren't you worried Dad's going to find out one of these days?"

Kiki rolled her eyes. "He's done for the night—I could probably go out the front door without waking him."

"Where're you going?"

"Probably the Point," Kiki said. She leaned out the window.

"At night?"

Kiki gave me an annoyed look. "There'll be tons of us. We'll be fine."

"Who?" I asked.

"Shelley, Fred, Johnny—just a bunch of us."

"No other Japanese kids?" I asked.

Kiki glared and didn't answer.

Outside, someone whistled. Kiki combed her hand through her hair, then stuck one leg out the window. She paused, one leg in and one leg out. For a moment I thought she might invite me to come along.

"If Dad wakes up, cover for me, will you?" Without waiting for an answer, Kiki shimmied out the window. She climbed down the ivy-choked lattice and ran to the car waiting next to the orchard.

As the car pulled away, I tugged the window closed. *Cover for her* . . . I scowled. How was it that I spent so many nights alone? If I was honest, I was jealous of Kiki. Besides Beau, most of my friendships were shallow. I didn't fit in with the girls at school, who knew their place better than I did. I didn't usually mind—I'd rather spend my time learning photography than going to parties anyway. But I *was* tired of being alone in a silent house. Kiki was always gone. And Dad . . . Even when he was here, he was still . . . not here. And Charlie, too, was absent lately, gone night after night, never telling me where he'd been. It was so different from how it used to be. It had to have something to do with his secret.

I threw myself onto the bed. My foot hit something hard. My book bag lay at the foot of the mattress. I pushed the bag off, and as it fell, a sliver of orange caught my eye—the postcard from Hiro.

I leaned over and pulled it out. In the flickering lamplight, the orange and dark blue were deeper, and I noticed tiny details in the texture of the mountain. To make the print, the artist had to cut each of those details out of the wood before he painted it and then pressed it, like a stamp, to make the print on paper. It was remark-able now that I thought about it.

I stood and walked to the vanity. Wedging the postcard between the mirror and its frame, I pondered how the best part of my day had been that conversation at the Merc.

# CHAPTER 18

# IT'S HAPPENING

*December 13*

The week passed slowly. Charlie unsuccessfully looked for work. So did other brickyard workers, especially after a freeze was put on all accounts at the Japanese bank. School settled into a silent but uneasy routine. I sat in the rear of each class. I ate lunch at a table of Japanese girls who huddled together for something like safety. I stared at Beau but didn't speak to him. And I spent class breaks avoiding Scooter, who still hissed "Slanty" each time he crossed my path.

Underneath it all was the constant worry about what might happen if agents came. From the way Charlie and Dad checked the front window each time an engine neared, I knew Sheriff Palmer's threat was on their minds.

Saturday's promise of the Leica was the one bright spot in my week. When the day came, Hiro and I met in a section of Mr. Omura's orchard, a sloppy area kitty-corner from my own backyard.

"Shall we go straight to the pond?" Hiro asked. "Or practice first?"

"Let me try it with my feet on solid ground," I said.

"Then let's head this way." The cased Leica hung from Hiro's shoulder on a long leather strap that reached to his waist. He strode in front of me, kicking his way through the ankle-deep grass. I followed in the trail he made. When we got to a rocky outcropping, Hiro paused. "The ground's uneven here," he said, holding out his hand. His long, tapered fingers stretched toward me, and I took them.

It was different than with Beau—like I'd only just become aware of my hand. I thought of Kiki, and guilt flushed through me. As soon as I was down, I let go. My hand tingled as cold air licked my skin.

Hiro jumped down and walked—almost glided—past me. His steps were slow and deliberate, and I got the feeling he was being careful not to push me too fast, given the difference in our strides. We were quiet as we made our way to the center of the orchard, silent except for the crunching of our steps on fallen leaves.

We came to a bit of a clearing, a place where the trees weren't quite as close. The sun dropped, sending pink light shimmering across the misty orchard. Hiro stopped to stare at the blushing light in front of us. "Nice, huh?"

"More than nice." It was like something out of a fairy tale. I sighed, knowing it could only last minutes. Was everything good fleeting?

"Ready for the camera?" he asked.

"Absolutely." My face broke into an idiotic grin.

Hiro unhooked the leather case and pulled the Leica out. I took it as carefully as I might a baby bird. I was used to the boxiness of my old Brownie, but the Leica was small, more the size of a pocketbook than a camera, only around the weight and thickness of a tin of sardines. My hands trembled as I thought of how much it must cost.

"Are you going to look through it?" Hiro asked, leaning against the tree. His eyes gleamed. "Or just hold it?"

"Right." I bit my lip and brought the camera in front of me. Instead of holding it against your stomach and looking down into the viewer, the Leica was made to be held right up to your face. I raised it to my eye, blinking when my eyelashes brushed the little window viewer. Everything appeared so clear and crisp compared with the Brownie's mirror.

I didn't dare move my feet, for fear of tripping, but I turned my head. As I focused on what I was pointing at, the images shifted. I started noticing things—a shard of bark pulling off a tree trunk, a shriveled black leaf clinging to a branch. The box disappeared and the images flattened. I tilted the camera. Branches splayed out in patterns across a gray sky—that mute, deep vastness that hung above us, watching.

I lowered my shot, looking again at the untrimmed yet still somehow orderly rows of the orchard framed in the little black-rimmed viewer. I felt a rush of affection that surprised me. How was it possible for me to love this combination of trees and dirt and fog almost as I might a person? Yet that was what I felt for my island as I stared at it, transformed in the viewer. It was like looking at an old friend in a whole new way.

"You like it?" Hiro asked.

I lowered the Leica. "It's wonderful."

Hiro stared, as if reading me like a book. Even though he was several feet away, he felt too close.

I put my hand in my pocket, wrapping my fingers around Beau's canister of film. Its smooth weight reminded me of that last happy moment I'd had with Beau at the Cap. Again, I felt . . . guilty.

I cleared my throat. "Let me just get a good look at how to put the film in," I said. "Then we can go to the pond—I'd like to try to get that aerial shot. But I'll have film left. Maybe as a thank-you I can take your portrait?" I let my eyes dart up to his face.

"Not sure I'm portrait material," he said, cocking his head apologetically.

"Well, I mean, it's a Leica. That'll make up for anything, right?" I bit my lip. Was I flirting? And—ugh—did I sound like Kiki?

But Hiro grinned, revealing a set of dimples I hadn't noticed. The phrase "movie-star good looks" flashed through my mind.

I hurriedly bent over the Leica, fumbling with the latch to the film compartment. "I was also thinking about—" I hesitated, unsure how Hiro would take my next idea. "That sign your dad put up at the Merc—I keep thinking how brave it is. And how it . . . makes me feel sad but proud at the same time."

I glanced up, hoping that nothing I said had rubbed Hiro the wrong way. He frowned, his face turned toward his house. "I know what you mean," he said slowly. "I don't like that Dad's putting his neck out there. But it is brave."

"Would you mind if I took a photo of it?" My words clipped over each other.

Hiro's features softened. "You don't have to ask."

"I know . . . But—do you mind?"

"Course not."

I let out the tiniest of sighs and smiled up at him. "I keep a journal of photographs," I admitted, not sure why I was telling him so much. But I found I wanted him to understand. "I clip photos from magazines and the newspapers. They're sometimes just really good photographs—artistic, interesting, or with techniques I want to try. But my favorites are the ones that"—I tried to find the words—"tell stories, I guess. And make me feel. And sometimes even document something before it disappears," I added, thinking of the photo of Pearl Harbor.

I looked up at Hiro, worried I'd said too much. His expression was the most piercing yet.

"Sorry, I got carried away," I mumbled, finally opening the compartment with a click.

"My dad's sign makes you feel that way?"

I nodded, feeling exposed but also relieved that he understood. I opened Beau's canister and pulled out the roll of film.

"Then after you get your photo of the pond, let's go down to the Merc," Hiro said with a decided nod.

I smiled. "That would be perfect. And maybe we can get a portrait in, too."

Hiro's eyes crinkled. But as I settled the film inside the camera, a long, low cry echoed through the orchard.

"What was that?" I asked. Hiro turned.

Another wail rang across the orchard. We looked at each other. "That's Mrs. Omura!" Hiro said. Something dark and cold buried itself in the pit of my stomach.

I clicked the camera closed. Hiro was already running. Nestling the camera next to my body, I followed, my short, skirt-hobbled strides not nearly fast enough for Hiro's long, loping gait. He bobbed up and down as he ran over the furrows, getting farther and farther ahead of me.

Loud barking joined the wailing. When a low branch suddenly reached for me, I ducked.

Hiro slid to a stop near the south edge of the orchard. He crouched low in the bushes next to the waist-high picket fence separating the orchard from the Omuras' front yard. As I caught up, he turned sharply and gestured for me to get down.

My ears were filled with a rhythmic throbbing, and my breath was jagged. I huddled beside Hiro, still cradling the Leica. Frost seeped through my skirt, turning wet as it touched my skin.

The barking continued, and another cry, this time rougher and more strangled, sliced the air. I peered through a break in the bushes. Tiny Mrs. Omura swayed on her front porch. A mustached Caucasian man in a black suit and snap-brim hat stood in front of her, holding out his arms. Two fluffy white Akitas barked from behind the screen door.

"No." Hiro's face drained. "It's actually happening."

Where the road met the front walk, a taller, sallow-skinned

man guided Mr. Omura. My neighbor's wrists were chained by handcuffs.

The world constricted.

"Where? Wh-wh-where you take?" Mrs. Omura asked.

The men didn't answer.

Hands shaking, I held up the Leica. I didn't have time to think—but something in me *needed* to get this shot. I raised the camera to my eye.

*Click*. Mrs. Omura, blocked by the agent as she reached for her husband.

*Click*. Mr. Omura, handcuffed, being pushed by the agent toward the car.

*Click*. Mr. Omura, head bowed, shame etched into his face, as the agent forced him into the back of a long black car.

The tall man slammed the car door, shutting Mr. Omura inside, and the man on the porch finally lowered his arms.

Mrs. Omura's sobs stuttered and went silent. Soundless tears flowed down her face as the mustached man trudged to the waiting car. As the engine turned, Mrs. Omura clutched her sides, holding herself together.

Mr. Omura didn't look back. He sat, head bowed, as the car peeled away. We watched it roll toward the main road, its metal flashing. When it turned out of sight, Mrs. Omura crumpled to the front porch, her child-sized body shaking.

Hiro and I looked at each other. As one, we stood. We picked our way over the fence and through the bushes, together glancing at the road. The car was gone, its motor barely audible in the distance, but the road still felt full of threat.

The dogs pawed at the screen door, their nails clicking furiously. Mrs. Omura—sweet, elegant Mrs. Omura, always so shy and proper—just lay there, her forehead against the decking, whispering in Japanese that I couldn't understand.

"Omura-san?" I stepped onto the wooden porch.

Mrs. Omura raised her head. Her face was twisted. I patted her back, not sure what else I could do. But after a few moments, her eyes focused on me. Tears still streaming down her face, she sat up and pulled her legs under her, kneeling, ladylike. *"Gomen nasai,"* she said, her voice breaking as she bowed low, her head against the wooden slats once again. *"Moushiwake arimasen."*

"No, please don't," I said in Japanese, horrified that she was apologizing. She tried to stand up, and I crouched to help her.

"Are you all right, Omura-san?" Hiro asked, also in Japanese. She nodded, but swayed and grasped my offered hand tightly. Hiro looked at me, and in his eyes, there was a deep, dark sadness. It was a look I knew and understood, the look of losing someone—for Hiro and me, our mothers. For Mrs. Omura, her husband.

"I'll go get Dad," Hiro said.

I nodded. He jogged down the stairs, then ran, fast and almost wild, toward his house.

"Mr. Tanaka can help," I said, still in Japanese, hoping my words were true.

Mrs. Omura nodded, but swayed again.

"Please, let's sit while we wait," I said. Mrs. Omura nodded, and we sat on the porch steps, both facing the road where her husband had disappeared. Her hand still clutched mine. Behind us, the dogs whined but no longer barked. Every so often, a stifled sob broke her silence like a punctuation mark. I patted her hand, feeling powerless to do more.

It seemed longer, but it must have been less than ten minutes. Hiro came back with Mr. Tanaka, both huffing and sweating. Mr. Tanaka ran up the porch first, and Mrs. Omura fell into his arms. His hat fell from his head as, like a bursting dam, she let her suppressed cries explode over him, her body jerking as if she were actually breaking. Mr. Tanaka stroked her head. "We will find him. We will find him."

The way Mr. Tanaka held Mrs. Omura frightened me. It was like one might hold a crying child, with none of the hesitant formality that held our community together. The invisible structures had tumbled. There was nothing left but this.

"Omura-san," Mr. Tanaka whispered.

Mrs. Omura stopped crying. She looked up from Mr. Tanaka's tear-soaked shoulder. Swollen rings rimmed her eyes. *"Gomen nasai,"* she apologized.

Mr. Tanaka swallowed and straightened, swapping his scared, confused face for that of the knowledgeable, calm shopkeeper. "We will straighten this out," Mr. Tanaka said in Japanese. "I will go home and make some calls. This is a mistake. Of course it's just a mistake," he repeated, his brow furrowing.

Mrs. Omura sniffed and bowed. *"Arigatou gozaimasu."*

Mr. Tanaka motioned toward the door, and Mrs. Omura tottered to her waiting dogs, taking Hiro's arm when he offered it to her.

"They *must* release him," Mr. Tanaka said under his breath as he bent to pick up his hat. "It's unconstitutional."

Mr. Tanaka called Mrs. Yamaguchi on the Omuras' phone. Mrs. Yamaguchi was a widow who'd run her own farm since her husband's death several years earlier. "There's no one like her. She'll know how to help," Mr. Tanaka assured us.

Mrs. Yamaguchi arrived in a sun-faded pickup minutes later, carrying a battered valise and a basket laden with food. "This is so wrong," she said in Japanese, pushing her way through the door. *"So* unjust. But we will get through this." She set the valise on the floor and the basket on the table. I had only ever seen Mrs. Yamaguchi in town or on the road—inside the tidy entry, she somehow filled the room. She was an inch shorter than me, but wide, loud, and unconventionally beautiful—her clear eyes and deep brown, sun-spotted skin radiated warmth.

She wrapped one of Mrs. Omura's aprons around her waist. "I'll prepare my special tea. She'll be asleep before you get home." She pushed me and the Tanakas toward the door with hands as strong as my father's, then turned to Mrs. Omura, nearly picking her up in a giant hug.

As the door closed behind us, Mr. Tanaka said, "Miss Sam, you must go home. If agents are making arrests . . ."

My heart lurched. What if they'd come to our home, too? I hadn't heard cars go that way, but what if while I'd been busy in the orchard, or inside with Mrs. Omura . . . A cold kind of dread froze my rib cage, making it hard to breathe.

"I'll walk you," Hiro started, but I shook my head.

"Stay with your dad." I handed him the Leica. "Thank you," I said automatically, and I ran, leaving the Tanakas behind.

# CHAPTER 19

# SACRIFICES

The frosted dirt road felt cold and unyielding, the air too still. A raven cawed, then all was silent except for the wind and my hurried, scuffling steps. It felt like it took longer than it ever had to reach the house, but as I walked up the drive, Charlie opened the door.

"Sam." The dark stillness in his face validated my fears.

"Dad?" I whispered.

He nodded. "An hour ago. They took him."

The whirring of my heart seemed to stop cold. "Omura, too," I said, and Charlie closed his eyes. My legs quivered beneath me. Nothing felt real. "Why?" I asked.

Charlie shook his head. "They only said they needed him for questioning. But the things we've heard from Seattle . . ."

He didn't have to say more. "Where's Kiki?" I asked.

"On the phone. She's trying to reach Mr. Tanaka."

"We left the Omuras' at the same time. They're closer. He should be home."

"Not anymore," Kiki said, coming up behind Charlie. "I spoke to Hiro. The agents just got to their house." My lungs froze mid-breath. "They're taking Mr. Tanaka, too."

Charlie made more phone calls and learned that almost every man with Japanese citizenship had been hauled away.

As he hung up the phone, I stood next to the stove, listening to the ticking of the clock from the parlor. Dad's absence seemed to fill the room, and I fought a feeling of panic.

Kiki sat at the table, her face in her hands. "Who could we call?" she asked.

Charlie didn't answer, and I felt my throat constrict.

Where had they taken Dad? When would they release him? I thought of the article Hiro had told me about: seven hundred arrests in one day. My breath came in shallow, fast waves, like froth lapping on the shore. The year since Okaasan died had been so painful. How could I bear losing someone else?

"Sam?" Charlie walked across the room and stood next to me. "It's going to be okay," he said. I nodded, but my thoughts still swirled. "We'll figure it out," he added.

I nodded again, still feeling as if the world was constricting around me.

"I promise, Sam." As Charlie put his hands on my shoulders, the deep note in his voice broke through my thoughts. He stood so close I could feel the heat radiating from his body. "We'll get Dad back." His eyes locked onto mine. There was a sureness in his gaze that I latched on to. I forced myself to take one deep breath. Then another.

I remembered how Charlie had always let me follow him, never making me feel like a tagalong. I remembered how he'd stepped up when Okaasan died, quietly doing her tasks so that Kiki and I could continue going to school. And I remembered how—like now—he always seemed to know what I needed better than anyone.

He'd been absent lately, but he was still the best brother I could have hoped for. And I trusted him. If he said we'd figure it out, I knew we would.

The three of us turned off the lights, pulled the drapes closed, and settled in the kitchen. Lit only by the dark glow of the stove, we fell silent. None of us thought to go to bed upstairs or even to sit on the sofa in the parlor.

At first, Charlie paced, and Kiki stood at the window. But

eventually we all fell asleep, Charlie slumped across the table, Kiki and me huddled by the stove, heads resting against each other.

The sound of an engine woke me. My neck ached—how long had we slept? The fire had died, and in the cold, every part of me had stiffened.

"It's coming closer." Kiki's eyes were wide. I listened. The engine was coming right up to the house. Kiki and I held our breath as Charlie peeked out the kitchen curtains and into the pitch-black night.

"I think it's him." Charlie dropped the curtain and rushed to the door.

"Thank goodness!" Kiki and I extricated ourselves from the blanket we shared. We got to the door in time to see a dark sedan pull away, its headlights gleaming.

"You are okay?" Dad asked as he crossed the threshold. "They did not hurt you?"

Charlie shook his head. Dad released a deep breath.

"Good. Good." Dad stumbled across the entry and fell into a chair at the kitchen table without even taking off his shoes.

Charlie picked up the blanket Kiki and I had left on the floor and threw it around Dad. I added wood to the stove, then struck a match. I stared into the black burn that consumed the kindling, sniffing back tears. My chest heaved silently, as if fear had frozen me, and now that it was melting, I might fall apart.

"Everyone sit down," Dad said.

Charlie caught my eye. He touched my shoulder lightly, then walked to the table and lowered himself into the chair across from Dad. Kiki slid in beside Charlie. I swallowed hard and stumbled into the seat next to Dad.

Dad wiped the flat of his hand over his face. "They collected all of us, every *issei* man on this island."

"Only *issei*?" Charlie asked. Because Japanese hadn't been

allowed to immigrate to the United States for a generation, the *issei*—first-generation immigrants—were mostly elderly and had been in the US for decades.

"Except for Mr. Kinoshita's son, Keizo," Dad said. "Probably because he studied in Tokyo. They questioned us for hours, then let some of us go. But not Omura-san. And not the Kinoshitas, Mr. Kinoshita or Keizo. And not Reverend Saito. They are being taken to the mainland." His hand trembled, and he flattened it against the table. "To a prison."

The news settled over us like a frost.

"For how long?" Charlie asked.

"And why them?" The idea that any of them might be a threat was ridiculous.

Dad shook his head. "I don't know. What we've heard from Seattle is that they are taking *issei* men from all over."

"Not women?" Kiki asked.

"Not that I know of."

"Who brought you home, Dad?" There was a gentling in Charlie's voice—the same softness he'd used at Okaasan's bedside.

"John Allred. He says the agents questioned him about us. They did interviews with several members of the city council. He vouched for me. And for Tanaka-san, who he knows even better. He says he'll continue to speak for us, but . . ." Dad turned to Charlie. "If I am taken . . ."

"You can't be!" In a flash, I realized this was how Hiro had felt when his dad made the same request.

Dad silenced me with a hard look, and I felt ashamed for my outburst. "There's no time to pretend. Better to prepare. If I am taken, Charlie, you must keep the family together till I get back."

Charlie sank in his seat. "Okay."

"I don't know what will happen with Omura being gone. It could be that the Japanese bank will remain closed. Even if it opens,

there's no guarantee they'll unfreeze our account. If . . ." Dad hesitated, and Charlie's face dropped as he realized what Dad was going
to demand. "We may have to use more of your savings. When the
bank opens, we may be able to pay that back." Charlie's eyes narrowed, but he didn't look up from the table.

"I've been thinking about what happened at the Merc. Tonight
shows us how much is at stake. We *cannot* behave like Mr. Tanaka.
It's too risky." His eyes paused on me, then Kiki, finally landing on
Charlie. "This is no time for pride—we must show we can cooperate. We must prove our loyalty. We must do anything to keep our
family together, even if it means bending."

Charlie's jaw worked in time with the ticking clock. Kiki and I
shifted in our chairs.

Dad skidded his chair away from the table, still staring out
the window, past the bare branches of Okaasan's persimmon tree
and into the Omuras' orchard. "Charlie, I need to go through the
contracts with you so you will know . . . In case . . ." Charlie stared
sullenly at the table, then, frowning, slid back and stood. He followed Dad out of the kitchen and up the stairs.

*Why Mr. Omura?* The question ricocheted in my brain. I couldn't
shake the image of Mrs. Omura, crumpled to the ground, and my
thoughts went to the barn, where I'd hidden the kimono. What if the
agents had found it? Would Dad have been sent away with Mr. Omura?

Behind Kiki, the fire crackled greedily, licking at the open grate,
ready to be fed. Kiki stared out the window—her pained expression
made her look thinner than she really was.

"Are you scared?" I whispered.

Kiki's eyes slid to me. "I—" For a moment she looked confused.
Then she straightened. "No. They let Dad go. We've done nothing
wrong."

"But they *took* Mr. Omura."

Kiki shrugged. "Maybe he really is a spy."

My stomach wrenched. "You cannot mean that."

Kiki's face reddened, but she slid away from the table and stood in one fluid, infuriating motion. "It's the FBI. I'm sure they know more than we do." Without looking back, she swept out of the room, leaving me standing all alone.

I turned back to the stove and stared into the angry flames. Less than an hour ago, Kiki and I had huddled, heads together, in front of that stove. Now I felt as distant and different from her as ever.

I couldn't sleep. Whenever I closed my eyes, I saw Mrs. Omura, her face twisted, her forehead crushed against the wood porch. If I opened my eyes, staring into the deep, purple midnight that clung to the corners of the room, I saw men in black suits coming for my family.

When soft gray light peeked through the window, I slipped out of the house. Aches coursed through me as I made my way to the barn. "I can't do it," I whispered into a gentle gust of wind. But I kept walking—because Okaasan would have done anything for her family. She *had* done everything for us. And she had always faced what was real.

*This* was real. This surreal, unfair, awful week was real.

The chickens startled, but Clark didn't crow as I entered the barn. I pulled the crate out and pushed the straw away, exposing soft gray silk. A hint of Okaasan's rose-scented soap mixed with the smell of straw. I took a long breath, then lifted the fluttering silk from its box. The sleeves of the kimono fell from their folds, revealing the smattering of tiny flowers near the cuffs. I swallowed hard, remembering the feminine, precise wrist motions that had made the blushing petals tremble like real cherry blossoms.

I hesitated and, in a breathless rush, did the thing I'd wanted to do since I was a little girl. I slipped my arms into the kimono, first one sleeve, then the other. The silk was cool and barely rustled as it fell over my shoulders. Like water, it tumbled in a sheath to my ankles. Though Okaasan had been taller than me when she died, it fit perfectly.

I let the kimono slither from my shoulders, catching it before it hit the barn floor. I must have grown . . . Like everything else, I had kept going . . . without her.

This was too much to ask. The fragile seams I'd repaired in the last year were re-ripping. I wrapped my arms around myself and gritted my teeth, letting the pain course through me, punishing me for what I was about to do.

I took three deep breaths. Dad was trying to keep us safe. Okaasan would have wanted that, too—she had never put anything over the family's welfare. I folded the kimono and carried it inside.

I stoked the fire in the potbellied stove. Letting the silk flow over my hands one last time, I laid the bundle in the stove. Heat waves blurred the blossoms, and the edges flickered. As flames lapped up the fabric, I closed the stove door.

*Creak.* I whipped around. From the stairs, still wearing her nightgown, Kiki stared at me, her face hard and her eyes bright.

I turned back to the stove. "Forgive me," I whispered, staring through the grate into the brilliant orange heat.

# CHAPTER 20

# THE SEARCH

*December 14*

The sun had risen, but the kitchen still smelled of burnt silk when a brisk knock sounded on our door. I dropped my scrubber and a dish in the sink. In the parlor, where she was sewing, Kiki stood. She reached over to the humming console radio and snapped it off.

Dad, still in his pajamas, and Charlie, dressed but with his hair uncombed, were down the stairs in seconds. Dad gestured, and Kiki and I found our spots behind him. There was one more brisk knock, and Charlie opened the door. The dark frames of two men made silhouettes in the bright morning light. My whole body went numb as I recognized the men I'd seen at the Omuras'.

"Mr. S-Sakamoto?" one said, reading from a clipboard. He was tall and sallow-faced, and he opened his jacket just enough to show the badge pinned on the inside. "My name is Frank Judd. My partner Boggs and I are federal agents. You met some of our colleagues last night?"

Dad nodded. "I was released."

"Yes, well, we've been ordered to search every Japanese house for contraband." The agent pushed into the entry. He would have run into Charlie if Charlie hadn't stepped aside.

"Contraband?" Dad repeated.

"Do you have a warrant?" Charlie asked.

The man pulled a light-blue document out of his inside pocket and absently slapped it in Charlie's outstretched palm. He sauntered forward, his shoes tapping loudly. Agent Boggs, a mustached man with squinty eyes and a cigar between his teeth, followed.

"Is there anything you're looking for specifically?" asked Dad. "We'd be happy to help."

Neither agent answered, and neither removed their hats. Instead, they wordlessly strode to the kitchen. I had to back up when Boggs walked past. His cigar dropped ash on the freshly swept linoleum.

Judd, smelling strongly of aftershave, made his way to the counter and opened the drawers next to the sink, while Boggs flipped through a pile of mail on the kitchen table. When he stopped and smelled the air, I froze. Would the smell of the burnt silk make them suspicious?

But Boggs only took another draft from his cigar. The smoke he blew was cloying—sweeter and thicker than the smell of Okaasan's kimono.

"If there's anything we can help you find . . ." Dad began again.

"Look, we've just got to search the house," Judd said. "Then we can talk. I'll take the other room," he said to his partner. Dousing us in his cologne, he wandered back across the entry and into the parlor. Dad followed.

Kiki folded her arms tightly across her ribs. "Why are they searching *us*? Shouldn't they be looking for real spies?" I drew my lips together. Charlie came over and put his thin right hand on my shoulder.

"Radio," Boggs called, staring dully at the radio on the kitchen table.

"One in here, too," Judd called. Through the entry, I saw him slip a yellow tag onto Dad's console. "Radios are contraband," he explained to Dad. "They'll have to come with us."

Kiki took a sharp breath, but Dad nodded. Judd lugged the

console to the entryway, and a few moments later, Boggs set the tagged kitchen radio on top of it.

"What do they think we're going to do?" Charlie asked, loud enough for the agents to hear. "Tune in to some broadcast from the emperor? They're *one-way* radios."

"Charlie." I slid my arm around his waist. "Please."

Boggs returned to the kitchen. He gave the stove a long look, and I again worried about the smell of burnt silk. But Boggs took another puff from his cigar and made his way out to the entry. "Kitchen's clear."

"Let's check upstairs," Judd answered. "You stay here," he added, looking at Dad.

The four of us waited in the kitchen, standing awkwardly at attention.

"When will we get the radios back?" Kiki asked.

Dad shrugged, and when his shoulders fell, his face fell with them. "I know as little as you."

Kiki huffed. "How are we supposed to live without a radio?" I gave her a look, and her eyes narrowed. "Not just for my music, though I don't see what's so wrong with that. But what about the news, for hearing about things like blackouts and bomb drills?"

"We will have to make do," Dad said.

But next to him, Charlie shook his head. "She's right. This is wrong. We shouldn't let this happen."

"Behave, Charlie," Dad said. "*Shikata ga nai.*" *Nothing to be done.* He whispered the words, but I was shocked that he would use Japanese while the agents were in the house.

When the agents returned to the kitchen, Judd held Dad's rifle, and Agent Boggs was holding the old Brownie. It had been in my drawer, next to my only pair of pantyhose, and a sticky, hot feeling surged through my chest. Had they gone through everything? What else had they touched?

"We'll have to take the gun and the camera," said Agent Judd, pulling a paper tag and a pencil out of his pocket.

I burst forward. "No!" The camera was battered and leaked light, but I needed it.

"Hush, Samantha!" Dad ordered. Judd gave me a cold look as Boggs set the camera on the radios.

"Sir, the camera is my little sister's," Charlie said, stepping forward. "It's so old. What harm could it be?"

"I'm sorry, but it's on the list." Judd attached a paper tag to the rifle. "Can't have the enemy getting photographs of our geography."

Charlie strangled a snort. "We're not taking photos for the enemy with a beat-up old Brownie."

Agent Judd shrugged. "You'll get it back eventually."

"When?" The edge in Charlie's voice was growing.

Judd ignored him.

"Soon? After the war?"

"Look, kid. I don't know. I just write your name on this tag and take it in."

"The war could go on for years." Charlie nearly shouted. "How do we know you'll ever give it back?"

"Let it be, Charlie!" Dad said.

Judd raised his eyebrows. "That's not my concern."

Charlie's nostrils flared. "Then what is your concern?"

"Step aside, boy," Judd hissed. He stood like a guard, holding the rifle with both hands, as Boggs gathered up a load of our things. Together, the two agents took our belongings to the car.

I ran up to my dad. "Can't we do something?" Dad didn't know how I'd planned to enter the contest and help with the mortgage. But couldn't he hear in my voice how important this was?

"Cut it out," Dad hissed. "Both of you. This is something we just have to accept."

"How can you say that?" Charlie asked.

"But, Dad, please!" I said.

Dad's eyes widened. "We've already lost one family member. Do you really need there to be more?"

I felt like I'd been slapped. The weight of everything hit me—the threat from McClatchy, the arrest of Mr. Omura. Now the kimono and the camera. There were too many losses. And while losing the camera was losing a dream, when I looked at my Dad's face, tight and filled with shadows, my heart was filled with an even deeper fear. I couldn't lose my family.

I turned to Charlie. "He's right. There's nothing we can do."

Charlie glared at Dad. His shoulders rose and fell with each huffing breath. My hands were shaking.

While Judd finished searching the house, Boggs asked me to show him the barn. Relief trickled through me. I'd made the right decision about the kimono. He would find nothing.

Coatless, Kiki and I walked the agent out to the barn. Its worn wood shone silver in the bright sunlight. As Boggs opened the barn door, I sighed. This, at least, would be safe.

Boggs peeked inside, then wrinkled his nose at the smell of the chickens. He shut the door.

Something curdled in my chest. That was it? He wasn't even going to search?

He took a long drag on his cigar, then threw it on the ground, snuffing it with his heel. He leaned one way, then the other, stretching, and then headed back to the house.

He hadn't even gone inside the barn.

I had lost a piece of Okaasan for nothing.

# CHAPTER 21

# THE FIGHT

"What were you thinking?" Dad's voice echoed off the kitchen's rose-papered walls. "Right now we can't give them any reason to think we're disloyal. You could have been taken, Charlie."

"The whole thing is bogus," Charlie mumbled. "What could Sam do with that old camera? And the radios?"

Stuck in the corner of the room, Kiki and I held our breath.

"It's not about what we would do," Dad says. "It's about what it looks like."

"Who cares what it looks like?"

"*Dameyo!* We have to show we're American." Dad's voice lashed like a whip. "That's the only thing keeping us from getting sent off with the Kinoshitas and Omura."

"*Dameyo*, Dad?" Charlie's voice was cold. "If you're so big on showing how American we are, why don't you use English?"

Dad's eyes bulged. "*Bakatare!* We wouldn't know where they'd taken you. We wouldn't have any clue what was happening to you. Like Keizo Kinoshita. His mom doesn't know if he's even still in the country."

Charlie's whole body hardened. "And you still say we should all obey? Even when people are being taken?"

Dad's voice fell, each word heavy. "We cannot risk splitting the family."

The dark vein in Charlie's forehead throbbed. "This isn't a family," he muttered. "It hasn't been since Okaasan died."

Silence fell on the room. For a moment, I thought Dad might hit Charlie. Then his shoulders fell.

The clock in the parlor chimed ten times.

Dad took a deep breath. "This is a trying time for the whole nation. Cooperating is the only thing we can do to help. It's our duty." He rubbed the back of his neck. "And we owe each other loyalty. It's my job to keep you all safe."

Charlie's jaw worked back and forth. "Mr. Tanaka says it's our duty to use our voices. To make this a country we *can* be loyal to."

Dad shook his head. "Mr. Tanaka . . . He is asking for trouble."

Charlie cut him off. "I don't want to hear it. Not again."

Dad hesitated, then swallowed. He nodded.

Kiki and I shared a look. Had Dad just backed down?

Then Dad looked at me, and there was a depth of sorrow in his face. "I'm sorry about your camera," he said. The words sounded rough, as if they cost him great effort.

I nodded. I didn't want to fight. And the camera was gone.

"Aren't you surprised?" Kiki asked after Dad and Charlie went out. We both were on our hands and knees, scrubbing scuff marks from the kitchen floor. "Dad basically gave in to Charlie. He even said sorry to you."

I nodded, but didn't speak. Charlie had put something into words. I could still hear the slicing harshness of his voice. *This isn't a family—it hasn't been since Okaasan died.* It was something I'd felt, but hearing it out loud made it so much worse. More real. It felt as if the split had solidified, and we would be broken forever.

I had hoped that if I won the photo contest, the prize money would somehow hold our family together. It seemed laughably stupid now. I wasn't Charlie, heir to the farm, or Kiki, the confident girl everyone knew was going somewhere. I was just Sam—the youngest, the spare, one more mouth to feed in a family that was barely making it. How could I have thought that *I* could make a difference?

# CHAPTER 22

# BEAU'S NEWS

*December 15*

I hadn't recovered from the weekend, but Monday came anyway. By the time the school day ended, I'd gotten enough dirty looks and cutting remarks to last the rest of the year. I hurried out of class, hoping to catch my ride with Hiro before the Clydes saw me. But as I ran-walked through the mostly clear hallway toward Hiro's locker, I ran straight into a tall, suede-covered back. I looked up into a shock of strawberry blond that made my heart thud.

"Beau!"

Beau blanched. His face went slack. He turned and began to stride away.

My head felt fuzzy, and my heart pounded. "Wait!"

Beau paused. Trickles of students filed around us, their carefree conversations echoing off the walls.

"Sam, I can't—"

"Please?" I hated the pathetic note under my voice. But I'd been staring at the back of Beau's head for a week now. And everything else was falling apart. I needed my friend. "Please, Beau. I don't understand. And I need to."

Beau squirmed, turning his head and looking at the other students. Then his eyes met mine—in them I saw the misery I felt. "Meet me out by the dumpster," he whispered. "I'll come in a few minutes." He merged into a stream of students.

ॐ

I told Hiro and Kiki to go ahead without me. Hiro's eyes were questioning—he knew Dad had told me not to walk home. But he didn't ask questions. And Kiki was thrilled to be alone with him. "If he asks me to Sweethearts', I'll tell you first!" she promised before sashaying after him.

I waited behind the school. The smell of the dumpster seeped into my clothes.

Maybe Beau wouldn't show up. But I couldn't bring myself to leave—not if there was a chance I might get an explanation. Even if he told me he hated me, at least I'd hear it from his own lips.

After a good fifteen minutes, my tailbone hurt from sitting on the concrete. I stood and walked past the dumpster to the edge of the school, where I could see the nearly empty parking lot. I relaxed when Scooter Clyde was nowhere to be seen. But I wondered if Dad or Charlie would worry that I wasn't back yet.

Then I saw Beau coming toward me. His head was bowed and his round shoulders hunched. My heart thumped.

Seeming to sense me, Beau looked up. His eyes hardened as he closed the distance. "What do you want?" Beau looked toward the parking lot, his fingers twitching. If I didn't say something quick, he'd turn around and walk away.

"I—I need to know why," I said. Beau stared out at the school grounds. "I can't believe it's just because of what your dad said." My voice got higher and faster, and I felt ashamed, but I couldn't seem to stop myself. "Is it because you're afraid of what people will think if you're friends with . . . a Jap?" The word, in my own voice, fractured the air.

Beau spun around and grabbed my arm. I cried out, more out of surprise than anything, but his grip was unyielding. He pulled me close to the dumpster. The air reeked.

"Don't use that word," he said. I held my breath—he hadn't let go of me, and I didn't want him to.

"I don't understand."

Beau sighed, his eyes on the dumpster. "You were there. You saw my dad."

"But he's never liked me!"

Beau's jaw flexed. "I don't want to get you in trouble."

"I don't want to get you in trouble, either," I said. "And I know things have changed. But even if we can't go to the Cap or to each other's houses, can't we at least stay friends when we're at school?"

"No, Sam," Beau said. "My dad—this isn't just about me and you anymore." He scrunched his forehead. "Sam, he's out to get . . ."

"Get what?" Relief slipped into my voice. Beau was finally telling me something real.

Beau let my arm fall, and my heart fell with it. "Look, don't tell anyone, but a few days ago, these men came to our house—they were from the mainland. They came with the sheriff and a list of names." He gave me a weak smile. "Never thought I'd meet an FBI agent."

Something inside me chilled.

"The sheriff told them Dad was a city leader, so they asked Dad if he knew anything about anyone on the list . . ." He squeezed his eyes closed. "Dad told the agent there were two men who got lots of mail from Japan and that one ran a store and the other had a bank."

I fell against the dumpster, sliding down into a crouch. "Mr. Tanaka. Mr. Omura."

Beau nodded. "I was there when the sheriff came last night to tell Dad about the arrests. Dad said he wished they'd taken the store owner." Beau sounded sick.

I shook my head. *This* was how the agents decided who to arrest?

Beau crouched beside me. "At breakfast the next morning, Dad told me again that he didn't want me talking with you." I looked down—I didn't want to hear this. "Your dad was born in Japan, right?"

"What does that matter?" I gave him a dirty look.

Beau shook his head. "I don't mean . . . It's just . . . Sam, my dad said he could get any Japanese man locked up. And he said if I spend time with you . . ."

I felt slow, like I was trying to walk in the ocean. "How can he do this?"

Beau grimaced. "He's used to getting what he wants."

I stared, not sure if it was Beau or the smell that turned my stomach. "Mr. Omura, threatening Mr. Tanaka and my dad. He's horrible!"

"He's my *father*, Sam. And . . . he's not the only one. It's complicated."

I huddled next to the dumpster. The cold sank deeper into my bones and heart.

"Look, I've got to go," Beau said, standing. "I'm already late."

"Wait!"

"I just wanted to warn you." Beau started to walk away.

"Beau!"

Beau turned around. "I can't be friends with you anymore, Sam." The words were cold and distant.

"Beau . . ." My voice echoed against brick and metal. My heart felt like ice.

Hands in his pockets, Beau walked away.

I made it as far as town before a beat-up black truck came rattling toward me.

Hiro slowed and rolled his window down. "Would you like a ride?"

I blinked, still stunned from my encounter with Beau. "Aren't you headed the opposite way?" Hiro was driving toward the school, not home.

"Actually," Hiro said, and he seemed nervous, "I was kind of wondering if I might find you." He regripped his steering wheel. "After I dropped off your sister, I had some errands in town . . . But I'm done now, and I just wondered if you'd made it home, seeing

how I usually give you a ride, and I hadn't seen you as I drove out."
His eyes flashed up to mine as he rambled.

"Oh. Um, thanks." I didn't know what to make of his jittery
explanation, but I was touched that he'd thought of me. "A ride
would be great."

Hiro turned the truck around, and we headed back toward
home. As we got to Japantown, Hiro sighed. Cars filled the Merc's
parking lot. "Dad's still at it."

"At what?"

"He's holding a meeting. Trying to start a protest. Y'know, of
the firings at the brickyard."

"A protest? People are going to protest?" My heart seized. What
would Mr. McClatchy do if he found out?

"Not all of them," Hiro said. "Most are there to tell him not to
make waves."

I looked back as we passed the parking lot. There had to be at
least ten cars. And given what Beau had told me . . .

A fresh surge of hurt went through me at the thought of Beau,
and I hesitated. Beau had asked me not to tell anyone. But I hadn't
promised. And the Tanakas—how could I let them go unwarned?

"Hiro, has your dad ever considered shutting down the Merc—
just till this all blows over?"

Hiro frowned. "I've asked him. Especially after Old Man
McClatchy came that one time. But you've seen how he is."

"It's just, I was talking to Beau." Hiro stiffened, and my cheeks
warmed. "He told me something about Mr. Omura." I plowed on,
trying to get it all out. "Those agents visited McClatchy, asking
about different families on the island. He told them that Mr. Omura
got lots of mail from Japan."

"He said that? To agents?"

I nodded, and Hiro let out a sharp breath. Even with the truck
radiator cranked to high, I could see his breath's hazy outline. "Did

he mention my father?" Hiro's voice was dull, as if he already knew the answer.

"Yes. Beau said he told them your dad got lots of mail, too. And"—I didn't want to say it, but they had to know—"after Mr. Omura was arrested, McClatchy said he wished it had been your dad."

Hiro swerved to the side of the road and slammed the brakes. The engine shuddered and died. Hiro didn't face me, but his profile was as hard as stone. His stillness unnerved me.

"I didn't mean to scare you."

"Scare me?" He swiveled to face me. "I'm not afraid. I thought Dad was being daft with this protest, that he ought to get rid of his Japanese stuff, learn to toe the line. But hearing this . . ." He shook his head. "Maybe Dad's right. This world needs a big change."

My chest tightened. This reaction was the opposite of what I'd hoped. Did Hiro not understand how much danger his dad was in? "Hiro, Beau's dad said he could get anyone Japanese arrested. If your dad keeps antagonizing him—"

"*Beau's dad* is just going to have to get used to it." The scathing note in Hiro's voice sliced the air.

I sat back hard and bit my lip. Silence as thick as quilting filled the truck's cab.

Hiro cleared his throat. "I—I didn't mean that. Sorry." He rubbed the bridge of his nose. "It's just a lot to take in . . ." He turned the key in the ignition, restarting the engine.

Hot tears prickled behind my eyes. I felt like an idiot. How could I be near tears because of one frustrated sentence? But as I leaned into the cold, hard window, exhaustion sank deep into my bones.

# CHAPTER 23

# KINDNESS

*December 16*

Hiro phoned the next morning to let us know he was sick. Charlie took us to school and said he'd pick me up—Kiki again had plans with friends. As I sat through my morning classes, I fiddled with the empty film canister that had been in my pocket since that day in the orchard. I didn't like how I'd left things with Hiro. Had I been wrong to warn him? Did he think I was judging him? Or that I questioned his father's patriotism?

By the time I got to lunch, I had decided to apologize. I was mulling over whether to take Hiro rice porridge after school or wait a couple of days till he got better when my thoughts were interrupted.

"Can I sit here?" The gentle voice came from behind me.

I turned to a pair of hazel eyes and a bush of caramel curls: Ruth Allred.

I swallowed a slimy mouthful of green beans. "You want to sit . . . here?" All around us, the cafeteria echoed with the sounds of students chatting and laughing.

Ruth nodded. I glanced around. My table was empty. A couple of Japanese girls I usually ate lunch with had gotten the same bug as Hiro, and the others were still getting their food.

But white kids didn't sit at this table. Even though it had been less than two weeks since Pearl Harbor, it was essentially a rule. A few Japanese kids—like Kiki—had been lucky enough to retain their spots in white cliques. But *no* white kid wanted to sit with a Japanese group.

Still, Ruth slid her tray next to me. She sat, unfolded a handkerchief, and placed it on her lap. I chewed silently. Around the room, gazes stumbled on Ruth. At the old table, Beau and Hank stared, and SueAnn's expression was unmistakably hostile.

Ruth smiled shyly. "Um, what did you think of Mr. Percival's lecture this morning?"

I shrugged. Mr. Percival had spent the better part of the hour talking about the shortages the war would bring to the country. "S'okay, I guess." At least it was better than when he talked about the Japanese.

Ruth grinned sheepishly, her full cheeks dimpling. "Sorry. I know there are better things to talk about than *civics*. It's just that's the only class we have together. But we can talk about something else . . ."

I nodded, but inside I was thinking, *Like what?* Why was she sitting here?

"So . . . what do you like to do?" Ruth asked. Her fingers twisted in her lap, but her nervousness didn't seem to be about the student body around us. Her eyes were focused on my face—as if she was worried what *I* thought of *her*.

"Um, I don't have a lot of spare time," I said. "When it's warmer, I work on my dad's farm a lot."

"Oh, really?" Ruth asked, and her eyes lit up. "That's neat."

It wasn't the reaction I'd expected. I raised my eyebrows. "Working on a farm is neat?"

"No, really!" she insisted, blushing. "My dad's not a farmer, but he has an incredible garden. I help him weed and mulch and fertilize—it's my favorite thing." Her eyes dropped with her voice, and her face flushed peach. "I guess that's not normal, is it?" Her eyes drifted back, now filled with a look I knew well—the fear of judgment.

My face relaxed into a smile. "Probably not. But I can see loving it—gardening, I mean, not fertilizing."

Ruth grinned, and she speared a bean. "Anyway, I can't imagine how . . . fulfilling it would be to have a whole farm and see it all come to life."

I suppressed a laugh. "The way you say it is more romantic than it really is."

"Yeah. I guess it must be different as a hobby than when everything depends on it." Her eyes held no shadows of pity or judgment.

"That's for sure," I said.

A wad of something sailed in an arc through the air above our table, landing on the floor next to our feet.

"Wha—?" Ruth bent to pick it up.

I looked around. Scooter and his group of pals snickered as they pointed our way. My stomach squeezed. Ruth picked up the balled-up newsprint and unfolded it.

*JAP LOVER!* The words were scribbled over the top of an article about battles in the Pacific. Ruth crushed the paper back into a ball and let it fall to the ground.

"Why are you sitting here?" The question bubbled out of me before I could stop it.

"You want me to go?" Ruth asked, her voice faltering.

"That's not what I mean . . . But don't you worry?" Scooter's group tried to muffle their laughter as a teacher scolded them for throwing things. "I mean, sitting with me is sitting with . . . the enemy."

I looked back at the old table. SueAnn had turned so her back was to us, but Hank kept sneaking glances our way, and Beau stared, a strange, maybe sad look in his eyes.

Ruth shook her head emphatically. "You're not the enemy.

Scooter's a caveman. I mean, we've all known you forever, and all of a sudden we're supposed to think you're a spy or something? I refuse to believe that." Her voice was stronger than I'd ever heard it, though her face was as fair as ever.

"But sitting with me . . . It'll make you a target."

Ruth tilted her head. "Am I making things worse for you?"

I shook my head. "I don't think so. They hate me regardless," I said, glancing over at Scooter.

Ruth exhaled a tiny, satisfied sigh. "Then . . . I can handle it," she said, shrugging. "I mean you were always with Beau. But"—her cheeks went pink—"I always kind of wished we could be friends."

Her words hung in the air. The truth was that I had felt the same thing. And somehow I dared to say it. "Me too."

We went back to eating, both hiding shy smiles.

# CHAPTER 24

# CRUELTY

I kept catching myself grinning during my afternoon classes. It felt so good not to be avoided by someone. I felt better than I had in weeks as I pushed my way out to the parking lot, not minding the jostling or the cold.

It had snowed during the day, and the wind was bitter. Kids raced to their cars. I found a spot on the curb where I could wait for Charlie as cars filtered out of the lot.

I watched Kiki and her friends get into a dark Ford. A gleam of blue caught my eye. Beau's snow-frosted Studebaker sailed smoothly out of the lot. Car after car pulled away.

I scanned the drive, hoping I might see Charlie and the truck. But instead, my eyes landed on a rust-red head. Across the driveway and a couple of rows in, Scooter Clyde hoisted himself onto the railed side of his father's pickup. Three of Scooter's gangly friends stood in a semicircle on the gravel below him, as did his older brother Mack. I'd forgotten to avoid him.

Just a few students still scurried to the gate or waiting cars. Where was Charlie? Why weren't the Clydes hurrying away like the rest of the students? I pulled my coat tighter and scanned the parking lot again. Was there someone from Japantown I could ask for a ride? Or maybe if I could find Ruth . . .

But the lot was almost empty.

Then, in a moment that felt both rushed and slow, Mack turned, and his flinty eyes caught mine. He hit Scooter's leg with the back

of his hand, gesturing at me with his chin. The way they eyed me
made the wind feel colder.

I couldn't wait for Charlie. I tightened my grasp on my book bag
and walked toward the schoolyard gate. I'd have to pass the Clydes,
but there'd be a road between us.

If only they'd just ignore me. I focused my stare on the gate that
split the parking lot from the main road, wishing the boys weren't
closer to it than I was.

"Hey, Slanty!" Scooter yelled.

My stomach clenched.

"Hey!" The wind swirled Scooter's words with other sounds—
the faint *ding* of a chain hitting the flagpole, the loud rustling of the
trees. I pretended not to hear and walked faster, steps unsure as I
hit patches of ice.

Scooter jumped down from the truck. "Slanty!" He hustled
toward me, not running, but fast enough that my breath caught
in my throat. Legs rubbery, I walked faster. But some voice inside
warned me not to run.

I drew parallel with the boys, with the driveway and two parking spots between us. We were at almost even distances to the gate.

But the boys dashed ahead. Scooter stood between me and the
gate, his three friends tailing him like a scraggly pack.

I looked around the parking lot. A farm truck, carrying two
skinny boys in overalls, slowed as it approached us. The boys eyed
us, their faces serious, then puttered past. My insides sank, but I
tried not to show it.

When the truck was through the gate, Scooter's mouth spread
into an ugly smile.

"What do you want?" My voice sounded small.

Scooter laughed, then looked around at his gang. "Well, I'd say first
up, you owe us an apology. We've been calling you for a while now."

"I don't respond to that name," I snapped.

Scooter's eyebrows arched. I was as stunned as he was, but that same little voice told me this was my best chance.

"Now if you'll excuse me." I pushed past Scooter and his friends. One after another, they stepped aside, each time surprising me. I kept my eyes on the gate, starting to believe they might leave me alone.

Then I saw Mack. He sauntered up several feet behind the other boys, to one side of the gate. Blond and naturally thicker, Mack looked more like a man than a high school student. "C'mon now, don't be like that," he said. His soft drawl wasn't jeering or nasal like Scooter's. It was silky . . . but sharp-edged.

I paused, taken aback, then kept walking. But as I passed him, Mack stepped forward. He grabbed my arm and jerked it, forcing me to face him. My shoulder wrenched, and I gasped.

Mack's face was set in a stormy, closed-mouth scowl. I glanced around. None of the boys were laughing or talking now. Their faces were somewhere between scared and excited. A chill of real fear radiated through me.

"I just want to negotiate"—Mack's voice warped—"some diplomatic relations."

An icy numbness now spread through me. My bag had slipped off my right shoulder when Mack grabbed me. I grasped the shoulder strap with my right hand, preparing to swing if I had to.

"Leave me alone."

"Mm," he said, stepping closer and forcing his face into my eyeline. "We could do that. If you'll deliver a message to your brother."

I met Mack's light eyes. "Charlie?"

"Charlie," Mack said through his teeth. "You tell *Charlie* to watch himself."

I looked around, bewildered, but Scooter was nodding, his face as hard as Mack's. What had Charlie gotten himself into? Was this his secret?

"Mack! Teacher!" one of the boys whispered from behind me.

Mack let go of my arm and stepped back. A dark sedan pulled out of the faculty lot and onto the driveway. It slowed, then stopped, and a male teacher rolled down his window. "You all okay?"

"We're good, Mr. Michaels," Scooter said.

"You tell your brother," Mack whispered. Then he turned and strolled past me, to where the other boys posed in a semicircle.

"You sure?" the teacher asked, looking from the boys to me.

I stood, frozen. It would be smart to speak up, but I felt Mack's glare, and I couldn't make the words come.

"We don't want any loitering," the teacher said.

"Yeah, sure," someone said. When Mr. Michaels didn't drive away, the boys drifted back toward Scooter's truck.

Mr. Michaels watched till they crossed the driveway, then rolled his window closed.

Most of the boys kept walking toward the truck, but Mack and Scooter stood on the edge of the drive. The sedan disappeared through the gate. I looked forward—the gate was only a few feet away.

I took a deep breath, then strode toward it. The back of my neck tingled. I tried to keep my stride even, but I wanted to run. Only three more feet. Two feet . . . Would they leave me alone once I reached the main road?

*Thwack!*

Something hit the side of my head, and I slipped, slamming to the ground on my hands and one knee. A snowball skidded in front of me, broken open to reveal a rock the size of a tobacco tin inside.

My brain felt slow. It took a moment to look back. Mack smirked, his broad shoulders rolling as he brushed ice and gravel from his hands.

My palms smarted. The side of my head rang with pain. My knee burned. I touched my head, then examined my fingers. A smear of blood marred their tips. My palms were skinned and full of asphalt.

"Careful, Slanty!" Mack's humorless laugh echoed around me. "Wouldn't want anything bad to happen to you."

I stood up slowly. My left knee was torn and bleeding, but I kept walking, risking another backward glimpse. Scooter had turned around. He strolled back to the parking lot, flanked by laughing friends. But Mack still glared.

I turned back to the road and stepped forward, trying to hold my head high. But as the gravel turned to paved road, I couldn't help myself. I ran.

When I got close to Japantown, I stumbled to a stop. My heart thudded in my ears, and my breath came in ragged gasps. I sat down on the edge of a ditch, taking care not to bend my stiff knee. Now that I wasn't running, I had time to truly feel my injuries. My head felt fuzzy and tender. My hands were scraped, and my shredded knee burned. I imagined how I must have looked to the boys—silent, afraid, then scampering away. On top of everything else, shame flared through me.

The sun glared down, its light sterile and white. The trees threw weird, squatty shadows on the orchard floor, and even though I'd spent years playing in the forests, the sounds—the rustling leaves, the cry of a killdeer, the throaty squawks of a cormorant—seemed unfamiliar and threatening. I peeled my skirt away from my skin. Fresh pain seared up my leg. The wound wasn't deep, but it was already swollen and stuck with bits of gravel.

Some distance away, an engine thrummed. The low sound crescendoed. For a moment I tried to reason with myself—it couldn't be Mack or Scooter. They'd embarrassed and scared me—hadn't they already won?

But then I remembered Mack's cruel eyes. A sickening fear flushed through me as the engine came closer.

I stood up fast, and the orchard spun around me. Pain burst through my leg as I hobbled away from the road again, awkwardly crawling over a split-rail fence. But still the engine closed on me. I dropped my book bag and kept running, trying to ignore each jolt of pain.

The engine cut off and the door slammed. "Sam!" The sound of my father's deep, round voice broke through my panic.

I turned around. My father jumped out of our truck, and for a moment, I was a little girl. Dad was here. Everything was going to be okay.

"You're hurt?" Dad asked, pulling himself over the fence and running toward me. His face was pale.

"I'm fine." I bit my lip. Seeing my father run toward me was almost too much.

"Where is your sister?" Dad asked.

I stumbled, stiff-legged, toward my father. "She's fine. She's with her friends." I winced as I wobbled on my bad leg. "How did you know to find me?"

"Charlie sent me to pick you up. When you weren't there, I came to look for you. But then I saw you running . . ." My dad put his hands on my shoulders and looked me over. "What happened, Sam-chan?" He hadn't called me that pet name in years.

I swallowed hard and blinked. "I . . ."

Dad's eyes bored into mine, as dark and shiny as watermelon seeds. I couldn't lie to him.

"Someone chased me," I said. "But I can't tell you who."

"Why not?"

I took a long, slow breath that tasted like blood after so much running. *Because he couldn't do anything about it*, I thought, thinking of what had happened with the Brownie. Or at least he wouldn't . . . And that felt just as bad.

"What good would it do?" I whispered.

Conflicting feelings flickered across Dad's face. I thought he might yell at me. Then he sighed. "You are right."

I nodded, partly relieved but partly disappointed.

Dad helped find my bag and took me to the truck. I propped my leg on the dashboard.

"We need to pick up Charlie. He's at the Tanakas'." Dad spun the steering wheel to avoid a pothole.

The truck swerved, and I clenched my teeth against the shooting pain in my knee. "Why is Charlie at the Tanakas'?"

"Mr. Tanaka asked him to come over." The Dad from my childhood disappeared, leaving the brooding Dad I'd grown used to. "He wants him to join his boycott."

# CHAPTER 25

# AT THE TANAKAS'

"He what?" I remembered what Beau had said behind the dumpster. Mr. McClatchy could get any Japanese person arrested—and he had it out for our family. "Dad, Charlie can't join the boycott."

Dad nodded. "That's why we're going to get him."

McClatchy's threat hovered as we wove through Japantown, turning on the road east of ours. The Tanakas were the only family on their small drive. Their home was larger than most in Japantown—made of dark brick and trimmed with carved wood—but somehow slightly shabby. Dead weeds filled the flower beds, and paint peeled on the windowsills.

Dad parked behind the Cadillac. "I think it's a bad idea for me to go inside. I don't want to argue with Mr. Tanaka. Maybe it's best if you get Charlie."

"Me?" I looked down at my scraped hands and the blood that soaked through my skirt. But I was relieved Dad didn't want to argue.

I hobbled from the truck to the Tanakas' front door, crossed my hurt knee behind the good one, and knocked.

After several long seconds, Mr. Tanaka opened the door, first a crack, then wider. "Miss Sam." He startled at my appearance. "Are you okay?" he asked in Japanese.

"I'm fine," I said in a voice that didn't invite questions. To show I didn't mean any disrespect, I bowed awkwardly, trying not to put extra weight on my leg. Behind me, the truck door slammed shut. Dad stood by the side of the car with his arms crossed.

"We're here to pick up my brother."

Mr. Tanaka looked out at Dad and gave an understanding nod. "This must be hard for him." Mr. Tanaka gestured for me to come in, then went back to the parlor. Despite the larger proportions and finer finishes, the layout of the house was exactly like ours—parlor to the left, kitchen to the right, and an entry with stairs in the center. The doors to both the kitchen and the parlor were open. Charlie stood in the parlor, facing the fire, arms crossed.

I arranged my hair so it covered the scrape on my face, again hiding my knee behind the other leg. Charlie would see me soon enough, but maybe I could avoid an explosion in front of the Tanakas.

"I've said what I need to say," Mr. Tanaka said, now in English. His voice was steeled with belief but polite. "The choice is yours, Charlie."

From my spot next to the kitchen, I couldn't see Charlie's expression, but heard the slump in his voice. "I believe in what you're doing . . . but there are people I need to protect. I need to think about the consequences, both with my dad and with . . . others."

"Take your time. Think about it." Still speaking low, Mr. Tanaka and Charlie walked past me and out the door. I started to follow, but paused. A photo of Hiro's mother stood among a collection of framed photographs on a spinet piano in the parlor—she looked so much like her son. I stepped forward, trying to see a little more clearly.

"Looking for someone?"

I jumped, and a fresh surge of pain went through my knee.

"I was only kidding," Hiro said. His expression turned from teasing to horrified. "What happened to you?"

I took a steadying breath. "I . . . fell on my way home. Skinned my knee."

His eyes searched me, landing on my cheekbone. "Someone did this to you. Who?"

I shook my head.

"Leave it be."

Hiro's head snapped up. "Wait—on your way home?" His face grayed. "Because you didn't have a ride."

"It's not your fault. Charlie was supposed to pick me up—not that it's his fault, either."

"I should have come." Hiro's face crumpled, and for the first time I noticed the blanket around his shoulders.

"You're sick."

Hiro shook his head. "I still should've . . ." He gave my knee a baleful look. "Here, let me clean that up."

"Oh, but my dad and Charlie are waiting."

"It'll only take a minute," he said, ducking into the kitchen.

Hiro came back with towels and a medical kit. He had me take off my shoes—I felt horribly rude when I realized I was still wearing the mud-plastered boots—while he filled a pail at the sink.

"Right here," he gestured, helping me lower myself to the floor.

"You really don't have to do this."

Hiro stared at my knee. "*Kuso,*" he swore under his breath as he slid two towels beneath my leg.

The gash seemed larger under his stare, and I fumbled with the edge of my skirt, pulling it to cover everything but the actual wound.

"We've got to clean it first." Hiro poured the contents of the pail over my knee in three surges, washing both blood and debris onto the towel below. "This will sting," Hiro said, pulling out a dark glass bottle of Mercurochrome. My knee burned as he doused the scrape, and I bit back a gasp.

"Sorry," he said, teeth gritted. He held a gauze bandage inches above my knee. "Do you mind?"

It was only then that I realized how careful he'd been not to touch my exposed leg. My face felt warm, but I nodded.

Hiro's touch was light as he placed the cool bandage on top of the scrape. His hand froze for a moment. His eyes were hidden by long dark lashes, but his cheeks reddened as he carefully pulled my skirt up an inch. "To secure the bandage," he said in a hoarse, low whisper. He pulled a strip of clean cloth from his kit and wrapped it around my leg. His fingers were careful, just brushing my skin as he tucked the two ends under.

Our eyes met, and I swallowed. All I could hear was my own breath.

"That should get you home," he said. "Shall I do your palms?" He held out his hand.

My knee still tingled, and every fiber in my body stretched toward him. It was a feeling more intense than I knew what to do with. I willed myself to shake my head. "They're just scraped. I'll take care of it at home." I stood and took a deep breath, one laced with the sharp tang of the Mercurochrome. Hiro nodded, not quite looking me in the eye, somehow looking as shaky as I felt.

"I should go," I said. But I didn't want to leave. And I still hadn't apologized. My stomach tightened as I tried to work out the wording. "By the way . . . I wanted to say I'm sorry if I said things yesterday that made it seem like . . . like I didn't trust you or your dad."

Hiro took a step back. "Don't apologize. I'm glad you told me."

I gave him a skeptical look.

"No, really. I still wish Dad would stop riling people up. But hearing what McClatchy said . . . Well, it helps me understand." Hiro frowned as he tried to explain. "I mean, before, I thought if Dad toed the line, we'd avoid all this ugliness. I thought we could be safe, at least. But after you told me what McClatchy said, I realized that the prejudice isn't about *us*. It's about *them*."

"Meaning"—I digested his words—"we're already not safe?"

Hiro frowned. "Yeah. I think that's why Dad feels so strongly."

My stomach sank. Maybe Mr. Tanaka was right. Mr. Omura was gone. Our things had been taken. Even before Pearl Harbor, the McClatchy family had made Japanese families sign ridiculous contracts that made it almost impossible to keep their farms. Still, I'd meant to warn the Tanakas, not egg them on.

"'The nail that sticks out gets hammered,'" I whispered, remembering the Japanese proverb.

Hiro nodded. "I'm still worried that Dad's sticking his neck out too much. But at least I understand why."

"Won't you at least warn him?"

Hiro smiled. "I already have."

I sighed, not feeling quite as relieved as I'd hoped.

After a second of awkward silence, I picked up my boots and walked stiffly out to the entry. Across from the kitchen, the parlor fire still roared, its flickering gleam darting along the dusty walnut paneling, the faded velvet sofas . . . and the collection of framed snapshots on top of the dusty spinet.

Something like the feeling of light jumped in my chest. "Hiro, those photos I was looking at earlier—who took them?"

"Those are Dad's," Hiro said. "You can go get a better look."

I stepped into the parlor. At the spinet, I bent down, staring into each photograph. There was the photo of Hiro's mother. But there were also landscapes—a deeply contrasted photo of the Cap, a carpet of strawberry fields, and a shot of a beach I didn't recognize.

I put a trembling hand into my coat pocket and wrapped my fingers around the empty canister. Maybe my dream of entering the photo contest wasn't over. I hardly dared to hope.

"Hiro, when the agents came, what happened to the Leica?" *Oh please, let this be one of the things Mr. Tanaka rebelled over.*

Hiro's lips twitched, and his eyes sparkled. "They would have had to find it to take it."

My heart leapt. "You hid it?"

He shook his head. "No. But we left it in the orchard on our way back from the Omuras'—Dad had a feeling it might be better."

"And they didn't ask you to gather all your contraband?"

Hiro grinned. "Oh, they did. But Dad wasn't too worried about being helpful."

I beamed at him. "Oh, Hiro, can I use it? They took my Brownie, and there's this contest I've just got to enter. That's why I'm trying to take that aerial photo I told you about."

"Of course you can use it," Hiro said.

I wriggled the empty canister out of my pocket and held it up. "The film's still in it, right?"

"Yes." He hesitated. "But what about developing the film?"

I hadn't thought of that. If I sent film for development, would I get my family in trouble? Or lose Mr. Tanaka's Leica? I slid the canister back into my pocket. Without a way to develop the film, I'd already lost the contest, and with it, my one chance at saving the farm and maybe even my family.

A crazy, wonderful thought sprang into my mind. "I—I might know someone who could help," I whispered. Yesterday, I would have thought my dreams were doomed. But today's lunch made me reckless enough to hope. "Do you know Ruth Allred?" I asked.

"Mr. Allred's daughter—she's in your grade, right?"

I nodded. "I have to ask, but I think she might help me."

Hiro raised his eyebrows. "Great. And I have to retrieve the Leica. But we could do that now if you like? Then you could take your photo tonight."

I smiled. It was tempting. But . . . "Dad and Charlie are waiting," I said. "And you're sick."

Hiro gave me half a smile. He hesitated, then said, "Little better now."

Something about the way he said it made me blush. "I really should go."

He nodded. "Take care of yourself, okay?"

Remembering all he'd said about Mr. McClatchy, I meant it when I said, "You too."

Outside the house, Dad, Charlie, and Mr. Tanaka stood in a cluster next to the truck. Their voices were low. Thankfully, they seemed to be talking about something besides the boycott.

But as Hiro and I hobbled up to the truck, Charlie's eyes widened. "What happened?" he asked.

The dirt crunched loudly beneath my feet as I walked up to them. I glanced at Dad. He frowned.

"I fell when I was walking home from school," I said, faking an embarrassed smile.

Mr. Tanaka's lips tugged into a tight line, and behind me, I heard Hiro's sigh. I closed my fists, vainly trying to hide the scrapes on my hands.

Charlie's expression shifted from shocked to angry. "You fell onto your knee"—he gestured at the bandage Hiro had given me—"and the side of your head?" His eyes stopped on the spot where the snow-covered rock had hit me.

I didn't know what to say.

"*Who* did this to her?" Charlie asked, this time glaring at Dad and then Hiro.

Dad shook his head.

"She didn't tell me, either." Hiro frowned.

A little part of me thought about telling Charlie what the Clydes had said. I wanted to ask why they'd singled him out. I wanted to find out if this was his secret. And I wanted to warn him. But I saw the hard lines in his face, and I knew if I told him who'd hurt me, I wouldn't be able to stop him from going after them.

"No one," I insisted. "Charlie, I just fell." I could hear the false note in my voice. I pressed my lips together and hurried to look away from my brother, afraid of what he'd read in my expression. My eyes met Hiro's. It was less than half a second, but in that short time, I saw Charlie's anger mirrored. I flinched.

"Why are you protecting the person who did this?" Charlie asked. "Was it Beau?"

"No! Of course not."

"Then why won't you tell me? Who else do you care about enough to protect?"

My face burned. Why did he have to use the word *care* right now? I willed myself not to look at Hiro and stood straighter, ignoring the pain it sent through my knee. "Who do I want to protect?" I asked. "Who do you think?"

Charlie looked at me sharply, questioningly.

I felt so tired. I wanted to let Charlie take care of me, and a part of me even wanted him to fight for me. "Charlie, if you get hotheaded and charge into a fight, with everything going on right now, *who* is going to get in trouble?" I bit my lip, fighting a rush of emotion.

Charlie's face was so tight I could see the muscles in his jaw. "I'm not going to do something stupid." But his voice was softer, as if he knew as well as I did that was exactly what he might do.

"I fell," I said stubbornly, and I hobbled to the car, knowing that behind me, Charlie and the Tanakas were looking at each other awkwardly. I ignored them.

I sank into the worn seat and scooted to make room for Charlie.

Though I needed to warn him to watch out for the Clydes, it would have to wait.

Charlie slouched next to me on the bench. He still looked angry, but under the anger, I saw worry. My insides softened.

It felt wrong to keep a secret from Charlie. We'd always confided in each other. As Dad started the truck, I wondered, when had that changed?

# CHAPTER 26

# TWO FRIENDS

*December 17*

I wanted to ask Ruth for her help right away, but she was late to civics the next morning. At lunch, the other Japanese girls, as enamored with Ruth as I was, chatted with her the whole time. I wasn't able to ask her about developing the film until the five-minute bell rang.

"Ruth?" My pulse pounded in my ears. So much rode on what I was about to ask.

"Yes?" Ruth bundled her utensils into her lunch pail.

"May I ask you a favor?" My voice trembled, and Ruth stopped what she was doing. "I take photos," I confessed, not quite meeting her steady hazel gaze. "I have for years, actually, and . . . I'm pretty serious about it."

I glanced up and into Ruth's face. There was no shock or laughter in her expression, only waiting.

"Anyway, there's a contest I want to enter—a photo contest. See, there's a cash prize, and I'm trying to win some money for my family . . ."

Ruth nodded. "What can I do?"

I hesitated, feeling the weight of the favor I was about to ask. "Our cameras were taken away after the bombing." I felt a twinge of shame. "By FBI agents. I'm not supposed to have a camera, so I'm borrowing one from . . . someone. But he's not supposed to have a camera, either. And I'm not sure how to get my film developed."

"Of course—" Ruth said.

"Wait. I have to explain." I took a deep breath. "There are photos on this roll of film that people won't like . . . and there are people who are looking for ways to get us in trouble. It could get *you* into trouble." Guilt washed over me. I was asking Ruth to put herself in danger, and all because she'd been kind.

Ruth's expression was thoughtful as she finished stowing her things. The lunchroom was nearly empty, and we were probably going to be late for class. "My dad told me about the people who are trying to get you in trouble." Her lips pressed together for a moment, and her eyes sparkled. She pulled her book bag on her shoulder. "I want to help. And I know it will be okay with my parents."

Her answer was the one I'd wanted. But I didn't feel the relief I'd hoped for. Instead, I felt confused. "Why?" I blurted, just as I had the first time she'd sat at the Japanese girls' table. "Why are you different from the others? Why would you do this for someone like me?"

"Someone like you?" Ruth shook her head. "Sam, don't say it like that."

"But everyone else—even Beau . . ." I swallowed. "They hate me." The word *hate* came out as a whisper.

Ruth looked uncomfortable. "I don't think *everyone* hates you."

I smiled bitterly. I knew Ruth was trying to make me feel better, but it was such small comfort. "Right. Maybe not quite *everyone*."

Ruth frowned. "I'm sorry. I didn't mean—"

I shook my head. "No, I know you didn't. And you're right. Maybe for some of them it's not hate, exactly. But they are afraid. Some of me. Some of what everyone else will think if they associate with me." I looked into Ruth's flushed face. "Why are you different?"

Ruth thought for a moment, then sighed. "I shouldn't be different." Her answer sent a chill through me. "I mean, I grew up with these kids. We've gone to school together all these years. Had the same teachers. Roamed the same forests and beaches. I would say it's because of my dad. But Dad grew up here. And his father, too." She shrugged. "Maybe he read a few more books. Or maybe sometimes I've felt a little like I didn't belong myself. I don't know."

Her hazel eyes were bright. "But, Sam, you shouldn't have to ask why I'm willing to be your friend. They're the ones who should be asking why they aren't."

I blinked, trying to process her words. I'd gotten so used to the idea that something was wrong with me. In my head, I could see what Ruth meant. But some part of me still struggled to believe it.

Ruth put her arm in mine. The familiarity of her touch surprised me—but felt natural. "Sam, I'll help you however I can. Really. Now, let's hurry to class—maybe we can make it before the bell."

"She said she'd develop it?" Hiro's face mirrored my elation. Out the window of his truck, pine trees flipped by. "Then you just have to take the shot. Let's go get the camera."

"Right now?" I laughed. "Just go take a prizewinning shot? It's that easy?"

Hiro grinned. "For you, sure." He gave me a look that made my stomach squeeze.

I blushed and turned so he couldn't see my face.

There was something different about the way Hiro was talking to me today. He'd taken Kiki—who for once didn't have arrangements with friends—home after school, then had come back and picked me up after I finished a biology lab.

Like that day when I'd stayed to talk to Beau, Hiro had come back just for me. A part of me knew he felt some sort of duty to make sure I didn't run into trouble again. But another part felt like he . . . wanted to give me a ride. Was I imagining it?

I thought of the way Kiki talked about boys liking her, and I shook the idea from my mind. I didn't want to start assuming things like she did.

"There's a lot that has to come together," I said.

"Like what?" he asked.

"Well, the lighting's the trickiest part to time. You have to shoot when the light is right, or it doesn't matter what else you do."

"Is this light not okay?" Hiro asked.

I looked up at the sun. The shadows it threw were hard and cold. "It depends what you're photographing, I guess, and how you want the final shot to feel."

My eyes darted to his face. He gave me a look that said, "Go on."

"Some light is soft. Some is harsh. It can make your shot feel upbeat. Or moody. Or warm or stark or even eerie. It depends what you want. People think you just point the camera and press a button. But really so much has to go right. Everything has to shuffle into place just so." I gazed out the window at the harshly lit forest. "You have to find the right subject at exactly the right time, with the right light, from the right angle. And that's all before you even touch the camera settings. The aperture, shutter speed, even the film—they can all completely change the feel of the photo." I held up my fingers, as if marking a shot. "Then—click! You have less than a second to capture it. But when you do, it's magic."

I let my fingers fall to my lap and peeked up at Hiro. His lips twitched. "I got carried away, didn't I?"

Hiro's eyes crinkled. "You definitely know what you're doing."

I bit my lip. I wasn't trying to show off. "It's just . . . It's what I love about photography."

He nodded. "Is this light wrong, then?"

"For the photo I'm thinking of."

"Guess I'll take you home, then." His mouth twisted, and the look he gave me—disappointment, maybe?—made my stomach squeeze again.

Hiro pulled onto Main Street. "What's that?" I asked, point-ing at a trio of figures gathered in front of McClatchy's General. But before Hiro answered, I recognized Mr. Tanaka's suit. The dark figures were holding signs. "They're really doing it?" I whispered.

Hiro swallowed hard. "Dad's absolutely determined."

"But why at McClatchy's store? I mean, I know he's behind the firings, but it's so . . . dangerous." Fear chilled me.

"It wouldn't make sense to protest at the brickyard—no one would see them."

As we neared the store, Hiro's jaw clenched. I could see the fig-ures clearly. Mr. Tanaka, Frank Kinoshita, and Mr. Yoshida stood stony-faced in front of the wooden deck. Frank, whose father and brother had been taken with Mr. Omura, wore a sandwich board that read *Rights for All Americans*. Next to him, Mr. Yoshida, a quiet man I wouldn't have expected to protest, held a sign that read *Support Linley Workers: Boycott McClatchy's General*. Mr. Tanaka stood in front of both of them, holding a stack of flyers.

My heart hammered at the thought of what could happen to the three men. "Are you going to join them?"

Hiro shook his head. "I'm supposed to mind the store after I drop you off." He hesitated, and I wondered what he would have done if he hadn't had to watch the store. Almost as if he knew what I was thinking, Hiro whispered, "What I said before . . . I under-stand why Dad does this now. But he went all over Japantown, to the people who actually got fired. Only Frank and Mr. Yoshida were willing to stand with him. How does he expect to convince anyone else? What if he's sticking his neck out for nothing?"

I pursed my lips, feeling like I ought to say something but unsure what would be right. On the one hand, I admired Mr. Tanaka's bull-headed bravery. But I was also relieved that Charlie wasn't with him.

I swiveled and looked up at the big, white-faced building. I hadn't been inside since the day McClatchy made us wait for service.

The building looked unfriendly. Signs in the still fully stocked windows indicated a 10 percent sale on Christmas items. "Looks like McClatchy hasn't sold his Christmas merchandise yet."

"No one's in the Christmas mood. Everyone was shocked by Pearl Harbor, and now the war . . . Business has been bad for us, too." Hiro's jaw flexed.

As we drove past the store and the boycotters, a pang shot through me. I lifted my fingers to again frame a shot.

"Hiro, can we grab the Leica?" I needed to capture the scene, not for the contest, but for myself. Because the sight of the three lonely, likely-to-fail figures made me feel something I couldn't name.

Hiro drove to his house, where we grabbed the Leica, then doubled back to Main Street. I would have liked to take the photo with my lens nearly touching the ground—a "worm's-eye view" I'd learned from a photography book. But we had to stay in the car, parked on the side of the road, so no one would see the camera.

Still, I got a pretty good shot. I captured the whole storefront, so the photo showed the smallness of the three dark figures in comparison to the looming white building. The harsh lighting worked, too—the cold shadows made their boycott seem even more endangered and futile.

I swallowed as I lowered the Leica. I hated something about the scene, but I *needed* this photo—both its sadness and its bravery. As we drove away, I knew that if I hadn't gotten the photo, the scene would have haunted me. Maybe it still would.

As we drove into Japantown for the second time, my stomach squeezed. I didn't want to be dropped off. And we had more film. The lighting was wrong for the photo I'd been planning, but maybe we could take some other shots?

I almost asked . . . but I knew Hiro was supposed to watch the Merc. "Thank you so much," I said, holding the encased Leica out to him.

"Keep it for now, just in case you need it," he said, his hands on the steering wheel as the road beneath him turned rough.

"Are you sure?" I asked, stroking the buttery case. I was awed at the idea of having free access to a Leica, but afraid of its worth—and of what could happen if I were caught with it.

"I'm sure." Hiro turned onto our lane. As we drove past the Omuras' orchard, he gestured at our driveway ahead. "You have a visitor."

I sat up straight and squinted. An emerald Cadillac idled in our driveway. "What's she doing here?"

Hiro pulled up to the drive. Kiki stood next to the Clarks' passenger-side door, a smile plastered on her face as SueAnn passed a large package through the window.

I slid out from the cab, coming around the truck just as the Cadillac backed up. It rolled so close that I could have counted the freckles on SueAnn's smirking face. I jumped back, away from the tires. "If I were a boy . . ." I said, teeth clenched.

The Cadillac roared away, and I turned back to Hiro. A smile tugged at the corner of his mouth.

"What?" I asked.

"Nothing." Hiro raised his hands, palms up.

Kiki sashayed forward, still holding the box with both arms. "Hiro! Back already?" Her eyes gleamed.

"What was SueAnn doing here?" I asked, stepping between her and Hiro. I had to force my jaw to relax.

"Nothing much." Kiki tightened her grasp on the box.

"A dress box?" I asked, even though the look on Kiki's face was clearly a warning.

"It's none of your business," she said.

I shook my head. "You got paid in clothes again, didn't you?"

Kiki stiffened. I had guessed right.

"We're all trying to save the farm and you're groveling to SueAnn, of all people, for dresses . . ."

Kiki's eyes narrowed. "You're just jealous of her and Beau."

My hands trembled against my wool skirt. I could feel Hiro's eyes on me. "You don't know what you're talking about," I said through my teeth.

I couldn't look at Hiro. I turned away and left him to Kiki.

When Kiki stomped inside a few minutes later, I thought she would yell at me. But instead, she dropped into a chair next to the stove. "What is wrong with him? I thought he'd have asked me by now."

A stitch caught in my chest. I didn't want to hear Kiki talk about winning over Hiro. In my spot on the floor, I buried myself in a newspaper article. There'd been a riot in Seattle.

"If he doesn't ask soon, he'll miss his chance." Her voice rose. "I won't wait forever."

I tried to focus. The article said a mob of more than a thousand had gone around Seattle breaking the windows of businesses that hadn't complied with the city's first blackout. How did people turn so wild? There was an accompanying article about blackouts in Linley. For the foreseeable future, we were to have our lights out by eleven.

"Of course, maybe it's for the best," Kiki mused. "If I forget about Hiro, I can focus on . . ." She halted mid-sentence.

I finally put the paper down and looked at my sister.

At my attention, the corners of Kiki's mouth tightened into a thin smile. "Let's just say, 'a bigger fish.'"

I straightened the paper with a flick. I would not beg for more information.

# CHAPTER 27

# A WARNING

*December 19*

School was scheduled to let out the Friday before Christmas, and the break couldn't come soon enough. On Wednesday someone stuffed all the Japanese kids' lockers with pamphlets titled "How to Tell a Jap from a Chinaman." On Thursday, I found a piglike cartoon of a Japanese girl scribbled on a bathroom stall. And there was always Scooter. He'd bought a small brown card that read "Jap-hunting license." The card carried a crude illustration of a yellow-faced, slant-eyed head mounted to a plaque like a trophy stag's. Scooter kept it in his wallet, flashing it at me when we passed in the halls. Each time, my heart jumped into my throat, and the rest of me—including my mouth—went numb.

I'd even started dreading the rides to and from school with Hiro. Despite her comment about a "bigger fish," Kiki had doubled her efforts to get Hiro to ask her to the dance. She no longer left school with her friends, and she used each ride to flirt without subtlety.

When I finished my last exam on Friday, I trudged out to meet Hiro and Kiki at his truck. But when I got to the parking lot, I saw something I hadn't expected.

"Charlie?" My brother leaned against the truck's front bumper. At first, I grinned. But then, across the parking lot, I saw Scooter and Mack sitting on the rail of their truck bed, glaring our way. In the three days since they'd cornered me, I hadn't passed on their warning.

My smile slid off my face. "What are you doing here?"

"I'm here to pick you up—for Christmas break," Charlie said, but he looked past me, toward the school.

"Let's get in the truck," I said, pulling on his sleeve.

"Why?" He stared at the entrance, unaware of the angry looks from the Clydes.

"Just . . ."

A grin broke across Charlie's face, and I turned to see who he was smiling at. But I didn't see any of his admirers from our neighborhood in the direction he was looking. Only . . .

My face and neck went cold. Jean Clyde—Scooter and Mack's sister—grinned back at Charlie.

This was his secret.

"Get in the truck, Charlie." The way I said it startled him.

"Sam?"

"Get in the truck." I chanced a glance at the Clydes' truck. Scooter and Mack had jumped down. "Kiki can get a ride with Hiro." She'd prefer it anyway. "We've got to go!"

Charlie gave me a questioning look, but he obeyed. We both slid into the truck, shutting our doors in unison. Charlie had to turn the ignition twice before it started. He backed out, and we puttered off school property.

"What happened back there?" he asked.

I twisted to look through the back window. No one followed us. But Jean Clyde stared after our retreating car, her thin face framed by a full head of dark curls.

"Charlie, are you"—my voice wavered—"seeing Jean Clyde?" I felt a little ill. How could Charlie have kept something like this secret from me?

Charlie was silent. His handsome eyes flicked up, and for a moment he inspected the rearview mirror.

I twisted again. The road behind us was open. Jean had disappeared in the distance.

Charlie sighed. "I was going to tell you. But . . ."

"But what?" My words jammed against each other, hard and awkward. Was this why Charlie was always gone? Why I was always home alone?

"I didn't know if it was safe."

I winced. He didn't know if I was *safe*? "You thought I would tell people?" My words sailed through the air like fastballs. "But you told Kiki?"

He stumbled. "No. I never told her. She just figured it out. And I didn't think you'd tell anyone. But . . . I didn't know how you'd take it." There was a vulnerability in his last sentence. Even hurt and indignant, I could hear that this had been a burden on him.

"You could have told me. I would never have . . ." Tears welled behind my eyes. I stared out the passenger window at a sign hanging in the post office. Charlie had kept something huge a secret. From me. Even sitting right next to each other, I somehow felt as if I'd lost him.

Charlie sighed. "What was that at the school?"

I took a deep breath. "*They* were looking at us. The Clydes."

Charlie made a sound in the back of his throat. "Jean's brothers?"

"Yes."

"I don't think they know . . ."

"They know, Charlie!" It all spilled out. "They told me to tell you—the day I got hurt—"

"They did *that*?" Charlie said, his voice strangling the last word. "Your face, your knee—they're the ones?"

I ignored him. "They said to tell you to 'watch yourself.' Charlie, they know!"

Charlie pulled air through his teeth. "We were so careful."

We were silent for a minute. Feelings swirled inside me—betrayal, regret, anger . . . loneliness. We puttered through Main Street, then turned onto Farmers' Freeway.

"Charlie . . . How serious is this?"

Charlie stared at the road ahead. When he finally looked at me, his eyes said it all. This was something real.

And then I understood. This was why waiting to go to school was such a big deal. This was why he hadn't joined the boycott. This was why he'd been willing to put up a barrier between himself and our whole family. Jean was more than just a girl to him. He wasn't just my Charlie anymore.

# CHAPTER 28

# A VICTORY

*December 22*

The Christmas party was put on by the Japanese Christian Church, but all of Japantown came. Pews had been shoved to the sides of the room to create one large, open space. In the corner, someone had set up a Christmas tree, its branches loaded with origami and seashell ornaments. A table brimming with a pot-luck buffet stood in the middle of the room.

Children in their starched and ironed best ran wild around the buffet, spilling rice balls and snatching *konpeito*. Their parents stood in small groups, eating and talking. Some of the groups were cheerful, swapping gossip like any other year. Other clusters huddled, their whispers rippling with fear. Kiki stood in the middle of a flock of boys, beaming in a garnet party dress.

"Merry Christmas, Sam." Hiro walked up to where I stood alone by the punch bowl. Charlie followed close on his heels.

"Merry Christmas." I combed my bangs with my fingers.

Charlie beamed. "Hiro, tell Sam what you just told me," he said, helping himself to a glass of punch.

Hiro grinned. "Dad thinks McClatchy is going to let Mr. Bush rehire his Japanese workers."

I looked from one boy to the other. Their faces both shone. "Really? McClatchy?"

Hiro nodded. "I didn't think Dad could do it, but it's true."

"How?" I asked.

*"Shitsurei."* From behind me, Mrs. Yamaguchi approached, carrying a pitcher to refill a punch bowl, and Hiro stepped away from the buffet. As Charlie and I followed, Hiro told us the story.

Mr. Tanaka and the two other men stood in front of the store all Friday. On Saturday, six more men joined them. Hecklers—that some people speculated McClatchy had hired—threw water and then ice balls at the group, but the men stood their ground.

"Shoppers started to stay away," Hiro said. "And not just Japanese shoppers, either. Some of the white brickyard workers realized that if McClatchy could threaten the foreman, their *own* jobs would be in danger if they ever crossed him. There was even one man who came to shop and then *turned around to go home* after talking to Dad."

"Amazing," Charlie said.

"The guy said, 'I worked alongside a couple of you folks. Hard workers. Earned my respect.'"

I shook my head, my grin spreading.

"The store was closed on Sunday, but today, McClatchy finally came out. Only three days left till Christmas, and he still has all this stock. Dad said he came out with his hands in his pockets, head down like he was going to walk right past," said Hiro. "But he stopped. He said, 'If you'll move aside until Christmas, I'll speak with Bush about hiring 'em back.'"

"He actually budged!" Charlie crowed. "Man, I wish I had been part of it!"

"Just like that?" My grin slipped. It seemed too easy.

"Well, we're not done yet," Mr. Tanaka said in Japanese as he and Dad came up behind us, each holding plates full of pink rice and sashimi. A small crowd of men followed, listening. "There's still a possibility that McClatchy could renege. But if things work out, come January, you'll be back at work."

Charlie lifted his punch glass in the air. *"Yatta!"* Success!

"With your wages, we'd have a chance at the mortgage," Dad said in Japanese. His grin was as goofy as Charlie's.

As the men toasted each other, cheering when someone pulled out a flask of something stronger than punch, I stumbled to an empty chair. I wanted so much to believe Mr. Tanaka had won, that Charlie would get his job back and the farm would be saved. But as I thought of my conversation with Beau, something dark squirmed in the pit of my stomach.

# CHAPTER 29

# CHRISTMAS DAY

*December 25*

Snow fell all Christmas day, but it didn't dampen Dad's spirits. He sang his Japanese folk songs, making up for off-pitch notes with extra volume, sending Kiki and me into fits. Charlie had been in high spirits since the Christmas party. Now he stretched himself over the parlor sofa as if, for once, there was nowhere he'd rather be.

After breakfast, Dad surprised all of us with small *furoshiki*-wrapped bundles. We exchanged surprised glances—and shy smiles. Kiki cooed over her little bottle of scented spray, and Charlie beamed as he fanned through the pages of his collegiate dictionary.

"Yours was the hardest," Dad said to me, looking uncertain.

I peeled away the corners of my bundle's wrapping. In the center were four clean, square planks of pine, a set of what looked like miniature chisels, and a small bottle of ink. I looked up at Dad, puzzled.

"I saw you had a woodblock print on your mirror," Dad said, twisting a bit of discarded wrapping and watching my expression. "I thought maybe you could try printing yourself, at least until you get your camera back."

I fingered the smooth wood, inhaling its sharp-sweet scent. I hadn't expected Dad to notice the print. Or to realize how much I had missed my camera. I thought of the Leica, wrapped and hidden in the chest of drawers I shared with Kiki, and felt a pang of guilt.

"Thank you, Touchan," I whispered, slipping in the name we'd called him as young children. Dad flushed pink.

After a lunch of pickled radish, fluffy white rice, and fresh fish, Dad fell asleep in the parlor. Charlie and Kiki both were busy in their rooms, giving me a moment to myself. And—maybe because of the woodblocks Dad had given me—I found myself thinking of Hiro, wondering what his Christmases with only his father must be like. Did either of them think to make a special dinner?

When Okaasan was alive, she always made *manju*—sweet red-bean-filled rice cakes—for the neighbors at Christmastime. This year, I'd made *manju* for the first time. They were misshapen and flat, but the taste was right. And maybe the Tanakas weren't the type to mind misshapen *manju*.

I put the steamed cakes onto one of Okaasan's prettiest plates, then wrapped it in a clean dishcloth. I listened. Dad snored in the parlor. No sounds came from the rooms upstairs. For a moment I hesitated. Should I invite Kiki to come with me?

I bundled myself in my coat and tiptoed through the little add-on. I made barely a sound as I closed the side door. Once outside, I looked up at the window Kiki and I shared.

I slowly turned back toward the Tanakas. Some part of me didn't want her to come.

I knocked on the Tanakas' ornate wood door, my stomach fluttering.

The door swung open. Mr. Tanaka's deeply dimpled grin shone in the electric light of the entry. "Miss Sam!"

"Merry Christmas." I held out the plate and bowed.

"What is this?" He lifted the dishcloth corner. "Ah, *oishisou*!"

"I'm sorry they're smashed."

"They look delicious. Please, come in." He waved me through the open door. "Hiro, we have a visitor."

Mr. Tanaka's flannel slippers slapped as he led me into the house. I slipped my shoes off in the entry.

"Sam." Hiro loped down the central steps, one hand skiing down the carved banister. "What are you doing here?"

"She brought us *manju*," Mr. Tanaka said, popping one—whole—into his mouth. *"Oishii,"* he mumbled around the too-big bite.

I smiled.

"Come. Sit down." Mr. Tanaka led me into the parlor, pushing aside a stack of books to put the plate on the coffee table. He and Hiro settled in armchairs on one side of the table, leaving me the entire burgundy velvet sofa on the other side. While Hiro and I spoke English, Mr. Tanaka seemed to flow in and out of Japanese and English as if they were twin currents.

"So tell us," Mr. Tanaka said. "Has your brother heard from the brickyard yet?"

"Not yet."

"It is taking McClatchy so long." Mr. Tanaka sighed.

Hiro's lips twisted. "What if he only said he'd hire people back to get you out of the way for his Christmas sales?"

It was the exact question I'd had since the day of the Christmas party. But I didn't want to be here while they discussed it.

Mr. Tanaka folded his arms. "Of course I have wondered myself. If so, we'll just have to protest again."

Hiro shook his head. "It's not safe."

Mr. Tanaka stared into the electric light above us, as if praying for enlightenment. Then he looked at me and smiled. "Enough of this boring talk, *neh*? Tell us, how was your Christmas?" Hiro still looked unsure, but he leaned back in his armchair.

"It was nice. Relaxed."

"Oh, that's good to hear. Any presents you're particularly pleased with?" Mr. Tanaka asked.

I let a smile soften my face. "Actually . . ." I turned to Hiro. "Dad bought me a set of chisels and things to try my hand at woodblock printing. He saw that print you gave me. I have it hanging in my room . . ." I trailed off, feeling as if I'd said too much.

"You do?" A hint of a smile crept across Hiro's face.

"Dad thought maybe I was interested in printing. Especially since the camera was confiscated."

"I was sorry to hear about that," Mr. Tanaka said.

"Thanks. At least it's an old one. Not like your Leica." I looked shyly at Mr. Tanaka. "Thank you for lending it to me."

"I'm glad you're using it. Makes me happy that I didn't tell those agents about it." He winked.

Sitting back in his seat so his dad couldn't see him, Hiro shook his head as if babysitting an especially naughty child.

"I'll bring it back soon," I promised.

"Nonsense, use it for as long as you like. Hiro tells me you're quite the photographer."

I blushed. "It's just a hobby."

"Really?" Mr. Tanaka's tone required the truth.

"I mean, I'd like to be a photographer. Maybe. If things settle down."

"How long have you been taking photos?"

I hesitated. "Five years."

"Since you were only eleven?" Hiro asked.

"I guess." I looked from Hiro to Mr. Tanaka. Neither seemed shocked or amused at anything I'd said so far.

"So young to know what you want," Mr. Tanaka said. "How did you get interested?"

I leaned forward. It didn't make sense, but—just as with Ruth—I felt lighter as I spoke. "It started when I saw this photograph in a newspaper, of this mother and her children during the Depression. They were laborers—pea-pickers. And it . . ." I shrugged, unable to express exactly how it had made me feel.

Mr. Tanaka stood up without speaking and went to an oak file cabinet in the corner of the room. Hiro and I shared a confused glance as he thumbed through several folders, finally pulling out a brown file.

He opened it, shifting through the pile of cut-out newspaper articles as he settled back in his chair. He held up a yellowed clipping. "This photo?" he asked.

"That's it!" I said.

"A famous one." In his hand, Mr. Tanaka held the Dorothea Lange photo I'd described. I'd seen it before I started my journal, and I hadn't clipped it out, but the woman's chiseled face and haunted, somehow knowing eyes were as I remembered.

"It's a form of protest, that photo," Mr. Tanaka said simply. "A voice."

*A form of protest. A voice.* A puzzle piece clicked into place inside me, and I understood Mr. Tanaka and his boycott. He *had* to protest like I had to take photos. Both were ways to speak out—if only I could muster the courage.

I hadn't meant to stay, but as the sun set, shedding brilliant color through the parlor windows, the three of us continued talking. Hiro told us about his Japanese American friends who'd joined the army the year before. After Pearl Harbor, one had been discharged outright, while another had been reassigned to do janitorial work at a camp in Arkansas. "Waste of good boys," Mr. Tanaka said.

Then Mr. Tanaka told me that Mrs. Omura wasn't doing well. "Mrs. Yamaguchi told me that all Mrs. Omura says, over and over, is *shikata ga nai.*"

*Shikata ga nai. Nothing to be done.* Dad had said that exact same phrase when my camera was confiscated. "Do you think it's true?" I asked. "That there's really nothing to be done?"

Mr. Tanaka frowned. "I guess that's not the way I see the world, or I wouldn't have held that protest. But a lot of folks around here do. And I see something valuable—even virtuous—in their"—he searched for the right word—"cooperation?"

I didn't understand, and Mr. Tanaka noticed.

"In your dad's case, he sees accepting these . . . insults as a way to keep you all safe. I know others who choose not to protest to be patriotic—they say it's a way to make things easier for a government that's already strained." He shrugged. "It's noble, really. And in a way, accepting their circumstances allows them to move forward, to make the best of their lot rather than fighting for a different one."

I bit my lip. It made sense—the way he was saying it—in my head. I could see the honor in it. But my heart was beating fast. Some part of me *couldn't* accept it. No one should have to make that big a sacrifice.

Mr. Tanaka smiled, as if knowing exactly what I was feeling. "I obviously have some trouble with that idea. And they probably see my protests as un-American. But I choose to believe that we also have a duty to hold this country accountable. Maybe that's how to make this country what it ought to be, even if it makes *me* a pain in the—"

"Dad!" Hiro burst out.

I blushed, and the phone rang. Laughing, Mr. Tanaka stood and went to the hall to answer.

"Tanaka residence. Taniyuki speaking."

There was a silence. Too long a silence. The fire crackled, unheeding and harsh. Hiro stood and walked to the doorway.

"I see." Mr. Tanaka's voice was stripped of emotion. "Thank you for the notice." He gave Hiro a long look. Then, back into the phone, he added, "I know you did everything you could, John . . . Thank you. I feel the same about you."

Mr. Tanaka hung the phone on its hook. He swiveled to face us. "That was Mr. Allred," he said. "Agents are coming to arrest me."

# CHAPTER 30

# ANOTHER ARREST

I felt dazed and helpless. Mr. Tanaka rushed upstairs to change. Hiro scrambled to pack a suitcase.

"Shall I call my dad?" I asked as Hiro rushed past with a pair of gloves.

"It's better he not get involved," Mr. Tanaka said, coming back down the stairs in a charcoal suit. "There's nothing he can do."

Hiro handed his dad a hat. His eyes were wide, his hair mussed. "I can't believe we're here."

Mr. Tanaka placed one hand on Hiro's shoulder. "No matter what, keep going."

Hiro leaned into his father's hold. His hair fell forward, partially covering his eyes. "What if I can't?"

From my spot in the parlor, I felt as if I were witnessing something private, even sacred. I looked down at the dark wood floor.

"You can," Mr. Tanaka said. "You will. We will find a way to bring these cases before the courts. It will all work out." His voice was measured, but it quivered as he added, "I didn't mean to leave you."

All three of us heard the engines. Through the parlor window, I saw two dark sedans pull up to the Tanakas' gate.

Mr. Tanaka lifted his hand to touch Hiro's cheek. "I will do this. For all of us." He dropped his hand and squared his shoulders, then nodded at the door. Though Hiro's lips quivered, he darted forward and opened it, and the three of us stepped out onto the porch.

The air outside felt like a cold wall. A door slammed and Agent

Judd walked up to the gate. Agent Boggs got out of the passenger side and stood next to his partner.

"They're the FBI agents who searched our house," I whispered to Hiro.

"Mr. Tanaka?" Judd called.

"Yes, that's me," Mr. Tanaka said, adjusting his grip on the suitcase's handle. I stared at the second car. No one had gotten out, and the way the light played on the windows made it impossible to see who was inside.

"It looks like you know why we're here," Judd said.

Mr. Tanaka nodded.

"You won't give us any trouble?"

Mr. Tanaka gave him a long, hard look. The agent cleared his throat and strolled to the back door of the car. He propped it open.

"Dad—" Hiro said.

Mr. Tanaka stared into Hiro's eyes. *"Gaman shite,"* he whispered. *Endure.*

Mr. Tanaka bowed his head, and for one second, I thought he might falter. But he straightened and strode to the gate. Boggs held out his hand for the overnight case, and Mr. Tanaka handed it to him.

Judd pulled something silver out of his pocket. Hiro swore. When Mr. Tanaka held out his hands, I understood. The agent locked the handcuffs around Mr. Tanaka's outstretched wrists. Something clicked closed around my heart.

Mr. Tanaka walked to the propped-open car door and climbed inside. Without a backward glance, the agents got into the car and pulled out with a rumble.

As the second car followed, I took a sharp breath. Next to me Hiro swore again. McClatchy was sitting in the passenger seat. The two cars disappeared in the twilight.

"Oh, Hiro."

Hiro's face was wan as he stared down the dark, fir-lined road.

"You should go home, Sam. If they came for Dad, it's possible they're going to other homes, too."

The world went blank for a moment. I collected myself. "Okay. Come with me. You shouldn't be alone."

Hiro shook his head. "This is where I belong."

"But maybe there's something my dad can do?"

Hiro sighed. "My father's been trying to help Omura for weeks. They've blocked him at every turn." For a moment, neither of us spoke.

"Sam." Hiro lifted his head, and his eyes—those warm, usually laughing eyes—were like flint. "It will take time, but I will find a way."

I nodded. "I know."

I ran through the orchard and up the porch, not stopping to shut the front door. I burst into the parlor. Dad lay on the sofa. His coarse hair stuck to the side of his head, and his face was peaceful for once. My arms and legs went soft. At least for now, he was okay.

I knelt on the pine floor. "Dad, I have to tell you something."

Dad's eyes fluttered as if he were still in another world. "Miku?"

My mother's name sent a pang of loneliness through me. "No, Dad, it's me."

Dad blinked.

"It's important."

Dad sat up. "Yes, right. What is it?"

"Dad . . . Mr. Tanaka was arrested."

Dad and Charlie drove to town, ordering me and Kiki to stay home and keep the phone available. At first, Kiki and I couldn't stop talking about what had happened. How could Mr. Tanaka be gone? Why had Mr. McClatchy been there? And what could Dad and Charlie do? We still didn't even know where Mr. Omura was.

But as it got later and later, Kiki and I spoke less and less. Rain pattered on the roof, then began falling in earnest. Its tapping drone filled the house.

It was black outside when Dad and Charlie finally stumbled in the front door, both soaking and covered in mud.

"What happened?" I flew down the stairs. "Where's the car?" We hadn't heard an engine.

Charlie wiped his hair from his dripping forehead. "We got stuck in the mud. We'll have to go back when it dries out."

"What about Mr. Tanaka?" I took Charlie's coat as Kiki brought rags from the kitchen.

"There was nothing we could do," Dad said, pulling off his boots. His face was ashen.

"Are you okay?" I grabbed several of Kiki's rags and wrapped them over Dad's shoulders.

"Dad was incredible!" Charlie's eyes were bright, even feverish.

I looked from Charlie to Dad. Their expressions couldn't have been more different.

"I was a fool," Dad said.

Dad refused to say more about it, and he trudged upstairs for dry clothes. But while Kiki and I warmed water on the stove for Dad's and Charlie's baths, Charlie told us what had happened.

"We went to Sheriff Palmer's, and McClatchy was there. Probably celebrating or something." He made a face. A dark heat snaked through my stomach. "Anyway," Charlie said, "at first Dad talked all careful—you know how he is. 'Sir, might there have been a mistake?' That kind of thing. Then McClatchy said Mr. Tanaka had 'forgotten his place'—those were his exact words. And I don't know why, but that set Dad off. It was like he was a whole different person."

I didn't know whether to be terrified or proud. "What did he say?"

Charlie laughed. "It was everything we've always known but no one's ever said, like that McClatchy wanted to get rid of Tanaka's store because it was competition, that he takes advantage of people, that he's a bully. But you should have seen him! I mean . . ." Charlie's eyes glowed. "McClatchy and Palmer were shocked."

"Won't Dad get in trouble?" Kiki asked. I chewed my lip. Mr. McClatchy had gotten the last person to cross him arrested.

Charlie's smile faded. "I don't know. McClatchy spoke out against Mr. Tanaka. But I think Mr. Tanaka was already on some kind of list." His brow scrunched into folds. "McClatchy did say there was no way he'd show any leniency to 'such an ingrate'— that the farm would be his by fall."

I wrapped my arms over my stomach. "He was never going to show leniency."

Charlie sighed. "That's true."

I stared at the door of the potbellied stove. It was slightly ajar, and angry orange flames licked the air. Something in my stomach flickered with them. McClatchy had done so much damage. He'd ruined things with Beau, gotten Charlie fired, and had some part in Mr. Omura's and Mr. Tanaka's arrests. I thought of Mrs. Omura, crumpled on her porch, and of Hiro's ashen face. "I don't know how, Charlie, but we've got to make sure Dad doesn't default."

Charlie nodded. "We'll do our best."

I shook my head. "No, not just our best. We *have* to save the farm. I will not let McClatchy win."

# CHAPTER 31

# AN AFTERNOON OFF

*January 5, 1942*

Determined to help Dad pay off the mortgage, I spent the rest of Christmas break going around town, asking if anyone needed any cleaning or sewing done. I was able to get some work, mostly alterations on outfits that had been Christmas gifts, and Mrs. Allred paid me to scrub down her whole house even though Ruth insisted on helping me and could have done it herself.

When the high school opened in January, Alice Nakano had moved. Her dad, who had lost his job at the brickyard, had decided to relocate to Kansas, where he had family and hoped to find work.

Hiro was also missing from school. When Charlie drove us past the Merc parking lot, I'd seen his car, its windows broken and the word *Jap* painted across its side.

"When did that happen?" I asked. But neither Charlie nor Kiki knew.

At lunch I sat on the corner of the Japanese girls' lunch table. Ruth was meeting with the school counselor and Edna was sick, so with Alice gone, it was just Mariko, Mae, and me.

"I miss Alice," Mariko said, cutting a bite-sized piece off her sausage.

"Think we'll all have to move?" Mae asked. "My dad still hasn't found work."

"We won't be able to move," I said. "Not with the travel freeze." Days after Alice left, the attorney general had banned travel by all "suspected enemy aliens"—which meant us. I choked down a bite of canned spinach.

"Sheesh," Mae said. She scrunched the barely there freckles on her nose. "They don't want us here, but they won't let us leave."

"My mom said that if things keep going this way . . ." Mariko started. But I didn't hear. Across the lunchroom, Beau and SueAnn took their seats, sitting together, like always. But unlike other times, they weren't with friends—they sat by themselves. A sliver of envy squiggled through me as Beau set SueAnn's tray in front of her.

Then I heard Hiro's name. "Did you see his car?" Mariko asked.

"Poor guy," Mae said. "It's enough that his dad got taken."

"That makes five from Linley," Mariko said. "How many more will they take?" Her thick hair fell over her shoulders as she leaned forward. "Do you think any of them are actually spies?"

I froze, mid-bite.

"What? Are you serious?" Mae's forehead wrinkled.

"I mean, Mr. Tanaka got packages all the time," Mariko whispered. "It'd be easy."

My stomach heaved. I waited for Mae to put Mariko in her place. But Mae just shrugged. "Yeah, but . . ."

"It would be so easy for him to slip a message into an order."

"Can you hear yourself?" I burst out. "Of course he gets packages. He's a shopkeeper!" Both girls stopped eating and stared. "You know him," I said. "You know Hiro."

Mariko's face flamed. "It was just a question."

I shook my head. "Aren't things bad enough without this kind of . . ." A lump formed in my throat.

"She didn't mean anything." Mae looked down at her plate.

For one moment, the three of us sat in awkward silence. Then I stood. "I've got to finish an assignment," I mumbled, and I rushed out of the cafeteria, leaving my tray on the table.

I had never in my life ditched school, but I could barely breathe.

How could I keep going to class, pretending everything was normal, when even Japanese kids were looking at our friends as possible spies? When people like McClatchy were running things? When Mr. Tanaka had been taken and Dad could be arrested at any minute?

I walked straight through the hall, toward the front entrance. The door felt heavy, and I wondered who might be watching. But I had to get out. It felt as if my lungs might burst.

The wind hit my face, and the doors slammed behind me. I gulped at the cold, sweet air.

I made my way through the parking lot without pausing. I'd imagined skipping school before and always thought I'd feel nervous and excited. But I was neither. I felt angry . . . and alive.

The road was empty, the light gray and cold. When I got to the Japantown intersection I paused. The Merc stood in front of me, its curtains drawn and a *CLOSED* sign hanging under Mr. Tanaka's *I AM AN AMERICAN*. But Hiro's truck stood in the parking lot. Teethlike shards of broken glass stuck in the frames of its windows. Ugly, hand-painted letters marred its side.

It felt like I'd been headed here all along.

I tramped up to the door and knocked. The curtain twitched and the handle clicked. Hiro opened the door. Shadows ringed his eyes and his hair was tousled, but he smiled.

"Sam. What are you doing? Isn't it"—he checked the clock above the register—"still school time?"

"I couldn't take it today."

"You ditched?" He raised his eyebrows. "Guess I can't judge."

"I—" My anger burned away any shyness. "Your truck. I'm sorry."

"Yeah." I waited, expecting anger. The tired look he gave me was much worse. "Anyway"—Hiro pulled the door wide—"you want to come in and get a drink from the fridge? No charge."

I looked through the door. The store was dark, illuminated only by the curtain-filtered light of the windows, but still comfortable and familiar.

"Um, sure. Thanks."

Hiro walked to a fridge at the back of the store and plucked a bottle from its shelves. "Here you go," he said, handing me the cola.

We sat side by side on two stools at the checkout desk. I drank greedily. Even though it was cold out, I'd sweated as I walked, and the smooth cola slid down my throat. I pressed the chilled bottle to my forehead and let the school day melt away.

"What are you working on?" I asked. The usually spotless counter was covered in crinkled papers and folders, with paper clips strewn throughout.

Hiro frowned. "These here are invoices," he said, pointing to one stack. "These are the inventory charts—they aren't so bad. I've been doing those for years. But these bills"—he pointed to a third stack—"I'm having trouble figuring out which ones have already been paid . . ."

"Yikes," I said. The checkout desk was so small that each time I shifted on the slick seat, my knee bumped Hiro's, making my stomach do little flips. I crossed my ankles and pulled my elbows close to my body.

Hiro nodded at the other side of the counter. "Then this is Dad's stuff on the brickyard—not that I think anything's going to happen there." His lips curled. "And this file—" He flattened open a folder of lined yellow paper. "It's the list of people Dad was calling and writing on Mr. Omura's behalf. He obviously didn't succeed, but I don't know where else to start." He sighed. "I've got to figure out where they've taken Dad and find a way to get him out. But I also can't let the store fail." The muscles in his jaw pulled tight. "I'm not gonna let McClatchy run us off."

Just looking at the papers made me feel flustered and helpless.

But I swallowed. "Okay," I said, in a passable version of Okaasan's "time-to-work" voice. "What do you want me to start with?"

Hiro eyed me. "Are you sure? It's—"

"I'm sure," I said, surprised at how my words slightly satiated the burning in my chest.

Hiro gave me an appraising look. "All right. Then here we go." Hiro pulled a list from the Omura file. "These are the representatives and senators for this area. Dad was writing letters to each of them weekly."

I nodded. "So we will, too."

Hiro set me up with stationery and a pen. As he phoned suppliers about invoices, I wrote letter after letter, begging congressmen and councilmen for information about Mr. Tanaka's whereabouts. My hand cramped, my back ached, and still I wrote.

When Hiro said we should stop, my hand was a claw. Yet my anger had burned away, leaving me feeling full and relaxed, the way I sometimes felt with a camera in my hands.

"Looks like we're in for a storm," Hiro said as we stepped out of the dark Merc. The wind swirled, pulling at my hair. I squinted upward. The cloud-crammed sky was gray. But each cloud was rimmed in dazzling light, and all around us, the trees, bushes, even the dirt, appeared crisp—the shadows deep and the highlights warm and glowing. In my mind, I saw the shot of the pond I'd planned for the contest.

"Hiro"—I spun toward him—"the lighting is perfect."

"Let's go," he said, already locking the door.

We jumped into the ice-cold truck. With the windows broken, the engine's cranking was even louder.

"Will you come with me?" I asked. "Not just to my house but to get the shot?"

Hiro grinned. "Of course."

"Thanks." I looked away to hide my matching smile.

We drove for a few minutes in silence—but a comfortable silence.

"You know," I finally said, "the contest I'm entering has a cash prize. I know it's a long shot, but if I won . . ." A lump rose in my throat. I wanted it so much. "Mr. McClatchy is so sure we're going to default and he'll get the whole thing back. I can't let that happen."

Hiro nodded. "That's how I feel about the store. That's why I won't be coming back to school."

"You won't graduate?" I couldn't imagine it. Hiro had always been the one Japanese boy we knew would go to college.

"I'll continue my correspondence courses. As long as I pass them, I should have the credits I need. But I have to run the store during the day. Or McClatchy wins."

His eyes met mine, blazing. And in the look we shared, there was a promise: We would not let that happen.

# CHAPTER 32

# THE PHOTOGRAPH

As Hiro drove to the house, I watched the sky, feeling as if I were racing the sun. The wind whipped at my hair and face through the jagged windows. But all I could think of was the light.

I ran first up to my room, where I grabbed the camera, then back out to where Hiro stood waiting next to the fence. A cold drop of rain fell on the tip of my nose. Hiro blinked as a drop hit him, too. "We should run," he said.

"I'm afraid of breaking it." I held up the Leica.

"I'll take it," Hiro said, and together we jogged to the pond.

At the pond's edge, Hiro took the camera out of its case and—with a gentleness that made me shiver—hung its strap around my neck. "Good luck, Miss Sakamoto." With his hair swept out of his face, his eyes were even clearer. They locked on mine, and for a second I forgot the light.

Hiro knelt down and linked his hands together. "Step on."

I let him boost me, feeling self-conscious. But with a few more scrambling steps, I was able to throw my leg over the branch I'd chosen. I scooted out over the pond as the rain began falling in earnest.

"Is your photo ruined?" Hiro called from below.

I sighed. The reflection I'd imagined was gone—the rain had robbed the pond of its glassiness. I held the camera up to my eye, without much expectation.

But what I saw through the viewfinder wasn't what I'd expected.

Instead of ruining the shot, the rain gave it texture. In the unusual light, each drop sent out rings of shine and shadow. The texture became the subject of the photo, and the door, with its painted *Get Out*, seemed small and insignificant. As it should be.

"It's even better than I hoped."

Hiro beamed. Rain streamed over his smooth brown face, and something caught in my chest.

I gulped and set up the shot.

The light was so perfect that even as I struggled with a whirl-pool of feelings, I took several more photographs on the way home. I took one of the orchard, its regimented rows of trunks growing into chaotic arms, another of the peeling barn, its dark square-ness in contrast to the winter-muted growth around it. I took one of Okaasan's persimmon tree, of the few bright orange bulbs still clinging to its uppermost branches. And with Hiro's permission, I took a picture of his truck, its knife-edged shards of window glitter-ing in the changing light.

Hiro didn't hover as I worked, but he stayed nearby, sometimes watching, silently trying to see what I saw in the subjects, other times strolling a few rows away from me, quietly engaged in his own thoughts.

When he was looking in the other direction, toward the Omuras', I pointed my camera, hurriedly fumbling with the lens till he came into focus. With his hands in his pockets and a knee slightly bent, there was an ease to Hiro's posture. The texture of his sweater contrasted with his smooth skin, and he looked slightly upward, so the light hit his face, illuminating the openness in his expression. When his eyes landed on me, I took the shot.

I blushed, and Hiro's eyes lingered on me for a moment, but he didn't say anything.

"Thanks for coming with me," I told Hiro when we got to the fence.

"Thanks for inviting me." Hiro folded his arms. "I liked seeing you work. I can tell you're really good."

A cool draft ruffled my already wind-mussed hair. I couldn't meet Hiro's eyes. For me something had shifted, and the thought of him walking me to the door now scared me—it could mean more somehow.

But he didn't offer. "I'll see you tomorrow?" I could tell he was looking into my face, but I couldn't look up to read his expression.

I scrambled over the fence, not sure if I was relieved or disappointed.

"Where have you been?" Dad demanded. I had only just stepped inside. Dad stood in the kitchen doorway, glowering as I shrugged off my book bag, hiding the Leica in my coat.

I hung my wet things on a peg. "I helped Hiro write some letters," I said, fussing with my tangled hair. I didn't add that I'd been there since lunch.

"You should have called," Dad said, stomping out of the room. His angry footsteps echoed through the entry, and his door slammed shut.

The clock in the parlor read quarter to six. Time had gotten away from me. "Sorry."

At the stove, Kiki stirred a thick curry.

"Smells good," I said.

"Mm."

"You okay?" I asked.

Kiki shrugged and kept stirring.

"Sorry I was late—thanks for covering supper." It wasn't actually my turn to cook—and there were plenty of leftovers in the icebox.

Kiki stared into the bubbling curry. "You were with Hiro?" Her voice was too casual.

I nodded.

"Just Hiro?" Her hand froze, mid-stir.

I hesitated. Could Kiki sense my jumbled feelings? "He . . . the store was closed."

Kiki set the spoon on its rest. She picked up two of Okaasan's thick hot pads.

"I just helped him write letters to congressmen." I couldn't tell her about our photo-taking adventure. It felt . . . private.

Kiki dropped the pot onto the wood cooling board. "You don't have to explain anything to me, Sam," she said, in a quiet, measured voice. "I'm not interested in Hiro. Not anymore."

"No?" I swallowed. The word had come out disbelieving—and maybe a little hopeful?

Kiki gave me a hard look. "You know what it was that got me over him?" She leaned toward me. "I realized that dating a Japanese boy, right now, was social suicide."

I stared. With everything that had happened, how could she still worry about this stuff? "Are you saying you want to date a white boy? Johnny?"

"Date him? I don't know. But I *can* focus my energies on relationships that will help me instead of . . . taking other people's castoffs." She arched an eyebrow at me.

"That's not what I'm doing." I blushed. "I'm not doing anything."

"Right. Just like Charlie's not doing anything." Her sharp laugh sounded like barking. My jaw tensed—she didn't know that I knew about Jean. And I wasn't going to tell her.

*Taking other people's castoffs.* Did she really think that? I wasn't trying to do anything except help.

And then Hiro's face, blazing with determination, came to my mind. He was so . . . good. So brave.

My whole body felt hot as I realized how it must look to Kiki. Of course she'd think I liked him. Who wouldn't like a boy like him? She probably thought I didn't have a chance.

*And she was right*, I thought, remembering how he'd stopped at the fence . . . Still, my stomach fluttered as I thought of the moment we'd shared in the rain.

# CHAPTER 33

# THE FARM

*January 12*

Over the next week, Hiro and I wrote at least fifty letters. During classes and lunch, after school and before bed, I wrote the city council, congressmen, and local newspapers. But no one offered to help.

When I wasn't writing letters, I scrounged up sewing and cleaning jobs. I took our chickens' eggs to the Merc, where Hiro sold them free of commission. I convinced Dad to let me go through his mess of broken tools and sold metal parts for scrap. But still, the jars on the fireplace seemed unfillable.

The Japanese bank hadn't reopened, and aside from a few odd jobs, Charlie was still unemployed. Finally, Dad went to town wearing a pressed suit to meet with a man—Mr. Jenkins—who sometimes gave loans the bank wouldn't consider.

"Think Dad'll get the loan?" I asked Charlie as we waited for Dad to return. The two of us squatted on the porch, repairing the berry nets Dad would put over the strawberry plants to protect them from birds and other critters.

"Don't know. Dad's a risk," Charlie said, using his penknife to saw through a particularly bad tangle. "From the lender's side, it's a bad bet."

I tied a strand of twine to close a tear. My fingers felt twitchy. I kept glancing at the road. I had always hoped Dad could save the farm, of course. But now, with everything that had happened, I felt as twisted as the nets I was working on. Dad had to win—or McClatchy would.

"Are Jenkins's rates as bad as people say?"

"He usually charges two to three times as much as the banks—which'd add another five years to the mortgage, maybe more. But with the shape we're in, I'd bet that if Jenkins gives Dad a loan, it'll be even higher."

The day was sunny but frigid, and we had only finished half the nets when our fingers got too stiff to keep going. We were inside for a break, warming ourselves with barley tea, when Dad got back. The floorboards murmured under his slow steps, and before he shut the door, cold flooded the kitchen.

Dad hung his hat on a peg and turned to us. The side-to-side shaking of his head was almost imperceptible. He trudged up the stairs.

"Well, that's that," Charlie whispered, setting his mug on the table. He wiped his face with the flat of his palm, the way Dad did.

"We don't have a chance? Really?" My voice was too high. We'd almost failed so many times—it was hard to believe that this time it was real.

"I don't see how . . ." Charlie said. The space behind my eyes felt heavy and full. I blinked. Charlie slid his chair back and stood. "Look, I've got to get out of here. If he asks, I'll be back by nine." Charlie went to the door and began working the knot on his shoelaces.

"Charlie?" I wanted to ask him not to go. Couldn't he stay away from Jean for a while, just until it was safe?

"Yeah, Sam?" Charlie said, shoving a foot inside his boot.

I hesitated, remembering the way Charlie had looked when I asked about Jean, like she was everything to him. "I— Please be careful."

Charlie smiled. "Yeah, sure," he said, already putting on his other shoe.

Through the kitchen window, I watched Charlie stroll out to the truck. I put my hands around my mug of tea. The last of its warmth was fading.

Dad came down in his work clothes half an hour later. He didn't ask where Charlie and Kiki were, or even speak to me. I let him have a five-minute head start. Then I followed him.

The farm was about a quarter mile northeast of the house. The uneven dirt path that led there was dusted with frost and tracked with Dad's footprints, subtle as fabric that had been rubbed the wrong way. I followed the tracks to the perimeter of the property. The farm's borders were marked by other farms on three sides, with an uncleared wilderness on the west. From a hilly spot in the wild glen, you could survey the entire plot.

It was there that Dad sat on a fallen tree, looking out on the even mounds of mulch-covered strawberry plants, the bare ground where we'd plant new seed come spring, and—farthest from us— the section where he'd hoped to try flowers this year.

He saw me before I crossed the southern ditch. His face was full of ache, but somehow—samurai eyebrows and all—soft. He patted a spot next to him on the log. I hurried over, out of breath, and sat beside him.

"Look at that sky," Dad said, peering up at the lavender-gray expanse. "The sky was that color the day your mother died. Before then, I didn't know it could be that color. I always thought it was supposed to be blue. Maybe gray or black. But that day"—he spread his hands, gesturing above us—"purple."

I nodded. I remembered that day's curious storm.

Dad swallowed, then gazed out over the farm. "Did she know what her life would be when she agreed to come here?" His voice was low. He didn't mean for me to answer. "I had been working in Hawaii, sending money home to my parents. Then I decided to come to Washington. My parents were worried that I was getting older, so they asked the matchmaker to find someone for me." I froze, and the hairs on the back of my neck stood up. I had never heard this story from Dad. He always let Okaasan tell it.

Dad shook his head. "They sent me a picture, but I didn't think it was possible she could be that beautiful. When she got off that boat, I thought there had been some mistake. She was even more beautiful. I didn't think she could possibly be meant for me."

He bent over and dug his fingers into the dirt. "She could have married anyone in her own village—probably in the whole *machi*. I couldn't understand why she'd come all the way over to work this land with me." He paused. Regret cut into the lines of his face.

"But she remembered you," I prompted.

A ghost of a smile painted itself on Dad's face. "I guess so."

Okaasan had told me her side. Back in their village in Japan, she had seen Dad stop a man from beating a beggar, and some piece of her heart knew she would marry him. Years later, when she heard the matchmaker was looking for a wife for Matsuo Sakamoto, she asked her parents to speak for her. They had opposed their only daughter leaving Japan, going to an unknown country to marry the third son of a farmer so poor he'd had to send his son to work in the sugarcane plantations. But Okaasan had known her heart, and her parents had such affection for her that they let her make her own choice, something nearly unheard of at that time.

The story had been filled with romance when Okaasan told it, glowing so she looked ten years younger. But now, as Dad told it, his eyes drifting to the scarred land in front of us, I saw the sacrifice she'd made. How often had Dad wondered if she regretted her choice?

Dad let dirt sift through his fingers, falling in granular trails to the ground by his toes. "How can it all be for nothing?"

"Is there anything we can do? Maybe if—" I broke off. What

possible solution was there? He'd been scraping together the funds for years. What idea could I offer that he hadn't thought of?

The last of the dirt fell from Dad's palm, then he brushed his hands against each other. "We can only go forward, making as much as we can of the harvest, and then hope that by some miracle . . ." A wild, desperate war waged on his face, playing across his furrowed brow. "Charlie doesn't understand. But before he was born, they made laws—no Japanese man could become a citizen. No noncitizen could buy land. I was stuck." I'd heard this before. But I didn't interrupt.

"I'd been here for so long—I wasn't Japanese anymore. Hadn't finished my Japanese education. Had taken on manners and likes and dislikes from America. But I couldn't be American either—they wouldn't allow it.

"Then when Charlie was born, I was able to buy the land in *his* name. It wasn't a good deal. Maybe I was a fool to take it. But I thought that if I owned a little piece of this country, my son would never have to feel like *he* didn't have a home."

A gust of wind swirled around us, filled with the smell of earth. My heart hurt for Dad. If only he and Charlie could understand each other. Why did it have to be so hard?

Dad stamped both feet on the land beneath him and stood. "We've got to find a way. We've just got to find a way."

Dampness soaked the back of my legs. I watched my father pace the rows I'd seen him walk so many times, willing the land to produce. Only this time, even if it did produce, it wouldn't be enough.

I bowed down and spread my own fingers into the loamy mixture of frost and soil. This dirt held my parents' sweat and dreams. I swallowed the lump in my throat.

Then I got up and, quietly, so as not to disturb Dad, walked back to the house, praying to the lavender sky for a miracle.

At home, I ran up to my room, to the dresser where I'd stored

Mr. Tanaka's camera. I pulled the Leica's case over my shoulder. I still had a few shots on the roll of film that Beau had given me. The same roll . . . It seemed impossible. So much had happened. Sometimes I still wondered if it could all be a dream.

I pulled my coat over the camera, then snuck outside, doubling back to the farm. My heart thumped as I considered how Dad would react if he saw me. But I had to get this shot.

I was out of breath and jittery as I made my way up the road. When I got close to the farm, I scrambled into the brush on the side of the road. I pushed my way through the wet grasses and sharp ferns, coming back out only when I was on the other side of the farm. I rested my camera in the V of a particularly thick tree.

Dad still walked the rows, pacing with a desperation that fractured my heart. In contrast to the even lines of dark dirt, he was all curves, his head bowed, shoulders slumped, his back folded forward, almost as if he wished he could crumple in on himself.

No man who had worked as hard as he had should feel this way—the thought seared through me like a flame. I wanted to scream, to hit, to shake. But instead, I raised the camera and pointed it at my father.

# CHAPTER 34

# A BAD NIGHT

*January 17*

Over the next few days, Dad didn't speak about our conversation on the farm. But nightly, I found him staring into the fire, his face shifting from depressed to frantic.

Kiki threw herself into her social life. And Charlie was gone more often than Kiki, never telling us where he'd gone, but I guessed he was meeting Jean. Even when the army designated Linley, like other parts of the West Coast, a "restricted area," Charlie refused to be worried. He rolled his eyes when we were told Japanese people had to obey a five-mile travel restriction. And at least twice in the first week, they broke the new eight o'clock curfew all Japanese were supposed to follow. Dad stormed at the two of them, telling them they were risking more than they knew. But they didn't care.

They were both gone again, and I'd holed myself up in my bedroom, sitting cross-legged on the bed with the pieces of a dress Mrs. Allred had hired me to take in, needle poised in the air.

Dad blustered into my room. "Where are your brother and sister?" From the knees down, Dad's pants were soaked with mud.

"I don't know," I stammered, holding my needle in the air.

"Why don't you ever know?" His eyes were hard—mean. "Your brother never showed up. I can't do the ditches myself!"

The pit of my stomach clenched. It wasn't fair for him to take this out on me. I was doing all I could—sewing, cleaning houses.

Every moment I wasn't at school or helping Hiro, I spent making money for the farm. I was working on a job right now, this very second. Heat rushed up my neck.

The door opened downstairs, and laughter rolled up through the floor—Kiki and Charlie had walked in together. Dad's eyes narrowed as he whipped through the bedroom door.

I shoved Mrs. Allred's dress to the side and ran after Dad.

The laughing dropped off as I reached the top of the stairs.

"Do you know where I've been all afternoon?" Dad stood mid-staircase, dripping mud.

Charlie's hand paused over the coat he was hanging on its peg, and Kiki's eyes went wide. I chased Dad down the stairs, not sure how to make things better, but too terrified of what he might say—or do—not to follow.

Something flickered across Charlie's face, and he closed his eyes. "The ditches. I'm sorry."

"Sorry?" Dad said. "You run around all over town, never offering to help. Then the one day I ask you to do something—"

"I said I'm sorry. I forgot!"

Dad shook his head. "You think it's no big deal. You said yourself—you don't want the farm."

Kiki's eyes met mine. Her expression held all the helplessness I felt. Charlie lifted his chin.

"You don't even think about all that your mother and I did to earn that land for you," Dad spat. "You stay out past curfew, ignore the travel restrictions. You put our family, your sisters, in danger. When will you think of your duty?"

Charlie's face went red. "I—"

"You don't deserve the farm—or the Sakamoto name."

For a moment, Charlie's face blanked, as if he'd been slapped. Then anger flooded it. "Fine." He grabbed his coat back up. "If that's how you feel."

Charlie's shoulder struck Kiki's as he stalked to the door, and a bundle I hadn't noticed fell from under her coat. Two dresses, one a dark green party dress, the other a floaty deep blue gown, slipped to the floor.

Dad yelled after him, "You see, your sisters, they both take in sewing to save the farm. And you're leaving?" His face had gone red, and his voice echoed off the walls.

Charlie looked down at the two dresses. "There you go again. You're so wrapped up in that farm—" He shook his head, and a smirk snaked across his face. "You haven't known what's going on with any of us in years." Okaasan's light-blue door slammed behind Charlie.

Kiki and I stared at each other. Dad trembled on the stairs.

"Should I go after him?" I whispered.

"Stay where you are," Dad ordered.

Kiki knelt down and pulled the dresses into a bundle. Dad turned and walked up two steps. He stopped.

"What did your brother mean?" Dad asked, his back to us. Kiki's hands froze. "Your sewing—it *is* to help with the farm?" Kiki swallowed. Dad turned around. "Kiki?"

Kiki's voice trembled. "I needed a dress for the Sweethearts' Dance."

Dad's eyebrows shot toward his hairline. "You bought those dresses?"

Kiki shook her head quickly. "No, no. The blue one is SueAnn's—the Clark girl's. Mrs. Clark hired me to alter it."

"And the other?"

Kiki flushed. "They gave me it as payment for a couple of the jobs I've done."

Dad's eyes widened, and he stomped down the stairs. "You took a dress? Instead of cash?"

Kiki didn't respond.

Dad's neck was roped in veins. "We're losing the farm, and you're worried about frills?" Dad spat out a stream of harsh Japanese. His hands struck the air with each syllable.

Kiki interrupted. "It's not my fault! Or Charlie's. You should never have signed that deal."

"You know nothing about how it was." Dad's chest heaved.

Kiki narrowed her eyes. "Charlie's right. If it weren't for the dang payment, Okaasan could have gone to the hospital . . ."

"Kiki, no!" I said.

". . . earlier. She might have *lived*."

Dad rushed forward. His hand flew into the air. Kiki turned her head to the side, and I squeezed my eyes shut. But the slap never sounded. And when I opened my eyes, Dad's hand was pressed to his chest. Kiki looked up at him, her eyes flashing. My breath stuck in my throat.

Dad's face crumpled. "I wouldn't have . . ."

Kiki's face didn't soften.

"I didn't mean to." Dad's face drained. He turned and started back up the steps, his hand still clutched to his chest.

Kiki waited until his door clicked shut. "He'll drive us all away."

My breathing came fast and hard. "You were too cruel."

Kiki gave me a sharp look. "Like he doesn't know."

I remembered his expression that day on the farm. "That's why it's cruel."

Kiki stood up, hugging the dresses in her arms. "Well, I guess it's my choice what I say. And what I do with the money *I* earn. This *is* America, isn't it?"

Kiki took the two dresses to the parlor, where she set them next to Okaasan's sewing machine, then came back. Her face hardened into a false smile as she passed me. "By the way, in case you didn't know"—her smile puckered, and she raised her eyebrows—"I heard SueAnn's going to Sweethearts' with Beau."

I'd known this was coming, but my stomach still fell. Kiki flounced up the stairs, slamming the bedroom door.

I stumbled to the stairs and collapsed on the bottom step. I had so many thoughts and feelings swirling through my brain and body that I didn't know where to start. I imagined Mrs. Omura, telling herself *"Shikata ga nai." Nothing to be done.* That's how I felt.

# CHAPTER 35

# AN INCIDENT

*January 18*

When the first few rays of light hit the smoky sky the next morning, I took out the Leica. There were a few frames left on my roll of film, and I didn't want to waste them, but I also wanted Ruth to have the film developed as soon as possible. She'd have to send it by mail, and it could be several weeks before I got my photos back.

Kiki still lay asleep in her bed. Her jaw hung open. One curler had come undone, a springy coil hanging in front of her mouth. It wobbled with each breath she took, and I felt a smidge of satisfaction that she couldn't look perfect all the time.

I slipped outside, wearing only my nightgown, the sweater I'd layered over it, and my work boots. Dad didn't get up this early in the winter, but still, I hurried. I needed to take my photos and hide the camera before he woke.

I tromped over to the barn, my bare feet sliding in my boots, and hurried inside. The chickens startled as I entered its warmth, swiveling their heads and standing. Several let out trilling coos, and Clark Gable took slow, confident steps toward me. I opened their feed pail and scooped out a handful. I sprinkled it on the ground.

Clark clucked to his hens, a high, soft sound, then stood waiting, eyes flashing, head erect, as the hens gathered around him and gobbled up the feed.

"Always such a gentleman," I said, leaning over the pen to stroke his arching black tail-feathers. "You mind if I take your portrait?"

The light in the barn wasn't great. But this wasn't a photo for a competition. This was just for me. I loved this little rooster, and Okaasan had loved him even more, and I wanted a snapshot.

I took the camera out, pointed it, and waited. Clark didn't cooperate at first, turning his back to me. But then he turned his head. As the shutter clicked, I knew I'd gotten exactly the shot I wanted.

A shattering crack split the air outside. I whirled around, tightening my grip on the Leica. Had a car backfired? This early in the morning?

Without thinking, I rushed out of the barn. From near the house, on the other side of the barn, I heard male voices. An engine squealed.

I sprinted toward the house, coming around the barn as my father flung open the front door. A black pickup peeled past the Omuras'.

"*Nanda kore*," Dad swore, running down the driveway. Kiki stumbled through the doorway behind him.

Through the trees I saw the pickup take the turn fast, screeching as it disappeared in the direction of town.

I stumbled back to the driveway, where Dad stood staring at our truck. They'd shot the windshield and—across the hood of the car—painted the word *Jap* in slanted, cramped strokes. The back two tires were slashed. Dad sank to his knees. "*Kuso.*"

The front yard blurred.

Kiki ran past, her curlers jumping. "What the hell?" she yelled at the silent road beyond. Dad didn't reprimand her.

"What will we do?" I whispered. We couldn't afford two new tires. And without the truck, how could we keep up the farm?

Dad said nothing at first. Then, staring at me, his eyebrows plummeted into a sharp V. "What is that?"

It felt as if our yard had drained of air. I remembered without looking that I was clutching the Leica. I couldn't even make a sound.

Dad's face turned to steel. "You are disobeying me, too? After all that has happened?" His voice, though soft, cut through me like a sword. I couldn't meet his eyes. His bony knees pulled at the threadbare pajamas he was wearing, dirt and wetness soiling them.

Dad shook his head. "You too . . . Does no one care for our family's safety?"

Shame flooded me. All Dad wanted to do was protect and provide for our family. And now he thought I was against him. "I'm sorry," I said. "I'll take it back."

Dad pushed himself up. Still shaking his head, he shuffled inside, his bare feet leaving the slightest of impressions in the icy gravel.

I felt broken as I stumbled through the orchard to the Tanakas' house. Mud pulled at my boots, and beneath my nightshirt, my legs were covered in goose bumps. I should be embarrassed to visit looking this way. And this was Hiro—I had all sorts of feelings to sort through. But this morning, I couldn't summon the will to care.

I had risked our family's safety. I had wanted to save the farm, maybe save our family itself—those were good things. Even punishing McClatchy seemed like a worthy cause.

But a little part of me knew I'd also wanted to prove my own worth, to carve out a space for myself. Now that felt presumptuous.

How had I thought I could be the hero? What about my little life had made me so conceited?

I tapped Hiro's door. It took him several minutes to open it, and when he did, his hair was shoved into a vertical cliff above his head.

"Sam!" He tried to rub the sleep from his eyes. "What's going on?"

I couldn't make words come. I handed him the camera.

He looked at it. "Why?"

"My dad."

"He found it?"

I nodded. "Sort of."

"And he's making you give it back?"

I shook my head. "No. But . . ." I wanted to tell him about the hurt I'd seen in Dad's face, about how he had said, "You too?" It felt like the weight of my guilt could crush me. Telling Hiro would be a release.

But I was also ashamed of how I'd dared to think I could make a difference. And of giving up that dream.

"I can't do this anymore." My voice broke as I shoved the camera into his hands. "It's too hard."

"But you're so good. What about the contest and the prize money?" Hiro started, but I shook my head, already backing down the porch. I wanted to let him convince me. I wanted the Leica in my hands. I wanted the pictures I could only see through its black frame. I wanted the voice I felt when I took a shot that said something.

But I thought of the betrayal I'd seen in my father's face, of the way he'd shuffled, broken, back to the house. I had to give this up. And if I didn't give it up now, I'd never be able to.

"Sam—" Hiro called, but I was already running to the orchard, the grass bowing beneath my steps.

# CHAPTER 36

# THE BASKETBALL GAME

*January 30*

Charlie came back a day later, when he heard about the truck. But though Charlie finished clearing the ditches, he and Dad were more distant than ever. Dad didn't reprimand him for leaving, didn't even scold when Charlie continued disappearing each night. But he didn't say anything else to him, either.

The next Friday, there was a basketball game with a team ferried over from a school in Tacoma. Hiro invited all of us—Charlie, Kiki, and me—to come with him. As we drove through town, I let Charlie and Hiro carry the conversation. I hadn't felt the same around Hiro since I'd given back the Leica. I felt uncomfortably aware of how much he knew. It seemed strange and somehow wrong that only he knew how I'd hoped to save the farm—and how I'd given up.

Once we got to the gymnasium, Kiki had eyes only for the game—or maybe for Johnny Sullivan, who played on the team. The way she carried on, she could have been one of the cheerleaders, and more than once, Johnny looked up from the game to grin at her.

On one side of the gym, the school's sparse marching band sat in three rows near the court. They squealed a rhythmic jumble of notes that sounded familiar, but was off-tune enough that I couldn't name the song. I leaned forward, realizing that the clear, bright sound of Beau's trumpet was missing. I scanned the band, but he wasn't there.

I found him sitting high up in the bleachers with SueAnn and Hank. His eyes were glued to the band, ignoring both the game and SueAnn, an aching look etched on his face. Had he given up the trumpet? Had his dad won that battle, too?

I turned my attention back to the group I'd come with. Charlie had gone somber, seeming to forget me and Hiro as he stared at the crowd—always, I noticed, keeping Jean Clyde in his field of view. With his reverie and Kiki's preoccupation, Hiro and I—sitting to the right of the others—were left to our own conversation.

"So . . . any response to our letters?" I asked over the cheers of the crowd and squeaking shoes of the players. I asked more out of habit than hope.

"Actually," Hiro said, pulling an envelope from his pocket, "I got a letter."

"What?" The game disappeared along with Kiki and Charlie. "From who?"

"My dad."

I gaped. "Why didn't you tell me this as soon as you picked us up?"

Hiro slapped the letter into my hand. "It's not as good as it sounds. Go ahead, see for yourself."

I opened the letter, and my insides dropped. Except for *Dear Hiro*, every line of the letter was blacked out. "What—"

Hiro pointed to an official-looking stamp at the top of the page. It read, *Censored: War Department*.

I turned the letter over in my hands. "Did the envelope say where he is?"

Hiro shook his head. "Nothing." He showed me. The Merc's address was scrawled in the center of the envelope, and there was another *Censored* stamp. But that was it. "He could be anywhere."

I sighed and handed the letter back to Hiro. He took it and slid it into the envelope.

"Thanks for all the help." His eyes met mine. "I don't know how I would keep going without it."

I swallowed. "Of course. You're my . . . friend." My cheeks burned, and I tore my eyes from his, only to find Kiki staring at us.

Our team lost, but except for the sulking players, no one seemed to notice. Everyone was too busy getting ready for the bonfire the student officers were hosting at the Point. "We better get home," Hiro said. The curfew was still in effect, and besides that, the beach was outside our five-mile limit.

Kiki sighed. "Why don't we go to the bonfire?"

"Kiki!" I shook my head. "People have been arrested!"

Kiki shrugged. "They're really going to arrest me for going to a bonfire?"

I narrowed my eyes. Even without the curfew, the Point could be dangerous after dark. But that didn't mean anything to Kiki.

As we made our way down the bleachers, Kiki ran into friends. The rest of us let her take her time, slowly trickling toward the door.

When we were smack-dab in the center of the crowd, my eyes landed on the Clydes and their gang. They glared at us from across the gym, and I was almost sure I saw Scooter point.

My neck and arms tingled. "C'mon, Kiki." I grabbed her arm.

"Ouch! Wait, I'm—Sam, you're hurting me."

"Sorry," I said, but I yanked her arm again. Charlie and Hiro hurried after us. Once we were past the crowd, I let her go, but I still hurried.

"What was that?" Kiki asked.

"Don't want to miss curfew," I muttered.

Hiro gave me a funny look—we still had nearly an hour—but he kept pace as we made our way through the halls, past the front office, and out to the parking lot.

Charlie kept up, too. He hadn't said a word since the end of the game, and as we all piled into the broken-windowed truck, he stared at the school. Jean and a group of girls huddled together near the entrance. Behind them, Mack and Scooter Clyde stared back.

# CHAPTER 37

# BREAKING CURFEW

When Hiro dropped us off at home, Kiki claimed she was too tired to eat and slunk upstairs while I fixed dinner. Since the fight, Charlie had avoided meals with Dad, and he slipped off without even coming inside. Dad and I ate dinner alone.

After we ate and I cleared the dishes, I went up to my room. From the moment I swung the door open, I knew something was wrong. The dark room felt hollow, bigger than it really was. My stomach tightened, and I turned to the window. It gaped open, flooding the room with brisk air. I crossed the room and looked out—the sky was drained to its last dregs of light and color, littering the yard with long shadows. It was unusually quiet, abandoned by the familiar symphony of chittering and chuffing. Under the quiet, the wind whistled low and long.

I wrestled the window closed, then let my eyes rest on the bed. Kiki's pillows were tucked into the shape of a body under the quilt. Did she really think she could trick me?

A second later, I realized that she'd never meant to fool me. The pillows were for Dad. She *knew* I would never tell. And she expected me to cover for her.

I threw one of her pillows on the floor. I was tired of protecting her, of waiting at home while she got away with everything. How could she be so cavalier? If she were caught after curfew, it could mean a huge amount of trouble, not just for herself, but for Dad.

For a split second I wanted to march to Dad's room and tell him where Kiki had gone—she could only be at the beach. But I remembered the fight they'd had over the dress.

Still, people had been jailed for breaking curfew or passing the five-mile travel ban. Kiki was flaunting both. I went back to the window and stared down at the truck stuck in the driveway on flat tires. I'd have to ask for help.

Dad was in his room, so I put on my coat and slipped out the side door. "Charlie?" I shouted from the porch. There was no answer, and I didn't run into Charlie on my way through the yard. Was he breaking curfew, too?

I sighed and made my way through the dark orchard to the Tanakas' house. Hiro's hair was mussed when he came to the door. "Sam?" There was a look on his face I couldn't quite place—almost as if he were hopeful. He hurried to let me inside.

"Sorry. Were you sleeping?" It seemed too early—something that probably should have tipped me off to Kiki's ruse.

"No, no." He closed the door. "Just working on one of my correspondence courses." He gestured to the lamplit table in the parlor, covered in books and papers. He combed his hair away from his forehead with his fingers. "What's going on?"

Behind me, the walnut door screened away everything outside. In the buzzing electric light, I felt safe. But Kiki—and maybe Charlie—were out there. "I think Kiki went to the beach. I know it's past curfew . . . but would you mind giving me a ride? I want to bring her home before anything . . ." I stopped. What if I got Hiro in the exact trouble I was trying to avoid for Kiki?

The hollows under Hiro's cheekbones went taut as he frowned. "Let me get my keys."

As we got close to the Point, on the bank above South Beach, Hiro puttered into a pullout and parked next to a sleek sedan. He silenced his engine and its churning was replaced by teasing, singing, and laughter—safe sounds. Just beyond the thicket that ringed the pullout, a bonfire glowed on the beach, circled by animated silhouettes—boys and girls swaying, jostling, running.

Through the broken windows of Hiro's truck, I breathed in the clammy air, a mixture of salt water and bonfire. The smell brought back memories of swimming in the freezing water with Charlie and Kiki till my lungs ached, of the whole family roasting freshly caught fish over driftwood fires.

My father always said the Point was dangerous after dark. But surrounded by sounds of teenagers at play, I wondered if maybe it wasn't all that bad. Had I worried for nothing? I certainly didn't want to fight with Kiki. And yet . . .

*Abunai*. Okaasan's word for danger rose to the surface of my mind like a bubble. Kiki's desire to pretend everything was fine made her blind, so determined that if she was in trouble, she might not see it. And if anything happened, I would never forgive myself.

The bank was steep, but there was enough light to pick our way down its crags to the rocky beach. "Hey, Hiro!" one boy greeted as we passed him. "How've you been? Haven't seen you in a while." His voice trailed off, and I knew he'd suddenly remembered that neither Hiro nor I was allowed to be out.

"I've been real good, thanks," Hiro said, his voice mellow and impossibly sure.

We passed SueAnn and a bunch of girls from my grade, but they ignored us as they admired a group of football players throwing a ball near the water's edge. I swallowed hard when I saw Scooter and Mack and a gang of four other boys, huddled in their own circle away from the bonfire. The Clydes were too quiet as they handed a brown paper bag around, talking in low voices, not joking or laughing like the other kids. When he saw us, Mack glared and elbowed Scooter. I put my head down and focused on Hiro's back.

Hiro led me to the edge of the bonfire. All around, kids were laughing and talking, roasting hot dogs and singing. I glimpsed Beau's gingery hair—his back was to me—and flushed. But I didn't have time to worry about him right now. Where was Kiki?

I scanned the group. It was mostly seniors, with a few juniors and sophomores mixed into the bunch. The fire gleamed on their skin, making their faces more angular and exotic. But they were all white.

Then, about twenty feet from the fire, I saw her. In the glinting firelight, Kiki's loose ebony hair looked like liquid. It mixed with Johnny Sullivan's shellacked blond, covering his shoulders, as the two of them whispered, their heads nearly touching.

Hiro followed my gaze as I waffled between shock and embarrassment. How had Kiki finally "gotten" Johnny?

There was nothing I wanted to do less than walk up to her like this. She'd hate me forever.

I took a deep breath, then turned to Hiro. "I'll go get her." Hiro shouldn't have to face her—she wasn't his sister. Besides, if he had feelings for her, this was already awkward enough. I steeled myself and walked up to the conjoined pair.

"Kiki?" Heat rushed into my cheeks.

Kiki and Johnny both bolted out of their private world. Johnny straightened. Kiki stared at me, her eyes as sharp as daggers.

"Hey, Hiro," Johnny said, holding out his left hand because his right held Kiki's. I turned to see Hiro. I hadn't even realized that he'd followed me, and I felt a surge of both surprise and gratitude. Hiro stepped forward and took Johnny's hand. Their hands dropped. Kiki was glaring up at me in a way they couldn't miss.

After a few silent seconds, Johnny cleared his throat. "You hungry?" Johnny asked Hiro. His pale skin shone in the firelight, and his chin looked weaker than ever. "I think some of the girls brought pie—and maybe some cookies."

"Uh." I could feel Hiro looking to me for approval. But I kept my eyes trained on Kiki's livid face. "Yeah, that'd be good." Johnny squirmed away from Kiki, and he and Hiro retreated toward the bonfire.

As soon as they were out of earshot, Kiki stood. "What are you doing here? I've never been so embarrassed!"

I had so much I wanted to say: how embarrassment was the least of our concerns, how Dad would be outraged if he knew she'd gone to the Point, how it was dangerous, how she could be fined for being outside our five miles and there was no money to pay it. But all I said was, "It's past curfew."

"Who cares?" Kiki crossed her arms over her chest. "It's just a stupid rule!"

"There have been arrests and even beatings."

"None of those things happened on Linley!"

I took a deep breath and reminded myself that I had to get Kiki home safely. "Kiki, just come home. Please."

Kiki didn't say anything for a moment. She stared at the girls Johnny and Hiro were talking with. The wind had picked up, and several people were getting their things together. "You didn't have to make a scene, Sam." Kiki's face was intractable, but her voice wavered. "And you didn't have to bring him!"

I was making a scene? I wasn't the one who'd gone out when everyone knew I could be arrested. I wasn't the one cuddling with a white boy in public. If anyone was making a scene, she was. But saying any of those things would only make her madder. "I couldn't find Charlie. And even if I had, we still would need a ride."

Kiki reeled back to face me. "Charlie's here, Sam. Or he was. He walked off about an hour ago." She gestured toward the cliffs behind her.

"Charlie's here?" I asked. "With Jean?" I paused and looked in the direction she'd pointed.

"You figured it out, huh?" Kiki jeered.

I stared past Kiki to the cliffs and, in the distance, Single Tree Lookout. In the twilight, the cliffs were mottled shards of blue and black and silver. "I can't believe he'd do something so fool-hardy." But Charlie had always liked the hike to the other side of the Point. If he'd come to the beach tonight, Single Tree was where he'd have gone.

My insides chilled. This was dangerous. The Point, the Clydes, the beatings that had happened in other parts of Washington. And then something snapped and I was just . . . mad.

How could Charlie be so irresponsible? I expected Kiki to do thoughtless things. But Charlie was my big brother, the person who'd stepped up when Okaasan died, the person who tried to save my camera and made sure Kiki and I got rides home from school. Our protector. How could *he* be so reckless? Not just for himself, but for Kiki, too? He'd seen her here, breaking curfew and risking arrest—and he'd done nothing? Was I the only one who cared what happened to us?

The shouts and laughter around me swirled. So many nights Charlie and Kiki had both gone out, and I'd been left at home. Why was I the one left out? I'd always thought Charlie and I were close, but now I felt alone, even more alone than before.

"What's the matter?" Kiki's eyes and face glowed, made wilder in the reflected firelight. "Aren't you going to spy on him, too?"

I felt something hard rumble up my spine. It would feel so good to slap her.

"Why are you so interested in our lives anyway?" Kiki's face shifted into sharp lines. "Is it because you can't get a date yourself?"

Cold hate coated the inside of my ribs, leaving an icy hollow in my stomach. "Fine," I said, and I was pleased to hear a steely note in my voice. "Do as you please. Get arrested, for all I care."

I spun around and stalked back toward the bonfire, keeping my shoulders and back straight. The sand pulled at my boots with each step, but I strode past the bonfire without slowing. Out of the corner of my eye, I saw Hiro and Johnny. For a split second I thought about stopping. Hiro deserved that courtesy. It would be polite, too, to say goodbye to Johnny, as awkward as it might be. But I imagined Kiki's eyes on the back of my neck, and I kept going. I didn't even mind the open-mouthed stare Beau gave me as I stormed past.

There was no one on the trail up the bank. The wind had turned slicingly cold, and the Clydes had left in the few minutes since I'd gotten there. I was glad not to face them.

Scrambling up the bank was harder than going down had been, and I had to claw at the grassy growth on top of the bank to pull myself up. The rhythmic crashing of the waves muffled the remaining laughter behind me. But as I struggled to find a foothold in the rocky bank, Hiro said my name. "Sam." He didn't yell it or call it—it might have been any word in the middle of a sentence. But I heard it, even over the waves.

I finished climbing to the top of the bank, then stopped and dusted the sand and grass from my palms.

Hiro nimbly picked out the most stable stones for footholds. "Kiki's not coming?" he asked when he reached the top.

I shook my head, not trusting myself to speak. He waited as I fought back tears. Then I turned so I was facing him. In the dim light, Hiro's skin looked darker—warmer, somehow. "I'm sorry for making you break curfew." Guilt and embarrassment lumped in my throat. "I've wasted your time."

Hiro shook his head. "I wouldn't say that." He paused, then asked, "Can I give you a ride home?"

The bubble I'd felt earlier pinged at my conscience—*abunai*.

I sighed. "You're going to think I'm crazy, but I'm going to stay. You don't have to wait, though. I'll find a way home." I made a face. "I just . . . need to know that Kiki is going to get home okay." I glanced at the cliffs and frowned. "Charlie too, I guess," I added, staring past the cars that lined the pullout and into the forest beyond.

"Charlie's here?"

"Yeah. He's probably out at Single Tree. With Jean Clyde." My voice curdled. "I guess we're just about the most foolhardy family on Linley." I tried to smile, but I didn't quite manage it.

"At Single Tree." Hiro looked at the blackness beyond the bonfire. "Would you feel better if I went and got him?"

My eyes flashed up to his before I could hide my hope. Who knew how far Charlie and Jean had wandered? It was already dark. And Hiro was as much at risk as any of us. "I can't ask that of you," I finally said.

"Oh, Sam." Hiro gave me a long, hard look—a look that felt too strong, as if it really ought to be watered down. My pulse beat hard in my ears, and I couldn't look away. "It would be my privilege."

# CHAPTER 38

# AN ATTACK

Hiro walked me to his truck, opened the door, and—like some storybook prince—offered me his hand. I took it. Even though this wasn't the first time, I felt fumbly and awkward, like an actress who didn't know her lines. But as he helped me into the truck, Hiro's careful, light touch made me think my awkwardness might be okay.

He pulled off his coat and shook his head when I protested—I was already wearing my own jacket—saying only, "Keep warm," as he laid it over my legs. Giving me one last too-honest look, he closed the door and disappeared over the lip of the bank.

Draped in his jacket, I buzzed with questions. The last few weeks tumbled in flashes through my mind: the electric pulse when he put the Leica around my neck, the embarrassed excuse he'd given when he came back to school to pick me up, his hopeful expression when he opened the door tonight. I'd been so confused about my own feelings. But suddenly it was his feelings that filled my mind.

How could he have noticed me when Kiki was always making eyes? And yet . . .

I bowed my head to smell Hiro's jacket. It smelled of pine crates and gasoline and something musty I couldn't quite identify. I liked the smell. Something near a giggle rose in my chest.

*It would be my privilege.* I listened to the feelings rippling through my core. This was different than with Beau. Pure. Quieter. Aside from the welcome flutterings, it felt almost peaceful.

A kerfuffle on the bank interrupted my thoughts. The silhou-ettes of four—no, six people pulled themselves up the bank. In the growing dark, their faces were shadows, but I could see that they were tall—boys. I inspected the group, but Hiro's and Charlie's sil-houettes weren't among them.

A twang of unease entered my mind. Why were they so quiet? They didn't laugh or jostle. And they didn't get into their cars. Their stillness unsettled me.

One of the boys pointed to a spot a few feet from the bank's edge, behind a mass of winter-bare elderberry bushes. The group shuffled to where the leader had pointed. A chill slid through me as I recognized the leader's wide, flat jaw, the straight nose. Mack Clyde. I scanned the rest of the silhouettes and found Scooter's lanky, knobby frame.

I slid down, till my back lay against the seat of the truck and I could just barely see over the frame of the broken window, hoping no one would notice the top of my head. What were they up to?

I heard the sounds of kids trickling up the bank. I peeked over the dash. Fat swirls of white smoke rose from the beach. The bon-fire was over. Wind whipped at the girls' skirts as they picked their way back to their cars. My back began to ache, and I thought of Hiro wandering out there with nothing but his woven shirt.

The trickle slowed and then stopped, and I hadn't seen Kiki. Was she still at the beach? Or had she come and gone with one of the groups, and I'd missed her?

Minutes passed. Lightning flashed over the ocean, and thun-der rumbled the car. The Clydes and their gang stirred. Smoke still rose beyond the bushes, now in a gauzy white stream. Then Johnny Sullivan's pale face and blanched hair peeked over the bank. He stopped, leaned, and pulled Kiki over the hump.

In what seemed like something out of a silent movie, one of Mack's boys ran up and socked Johnny in the stomach. The boy didn't say a word, before or after. Johnny curled over and fell to his knees.

"Johnny!" Kiki's yell split the silence. She crouched beside him.

The rest of the gang stepped out of the shadows in one synchronized unit. They paused as Mack sauntered forward. "Why—" Johnny grunted, holding his stomach.

Mack raised one booted foot and stomped hard on Johnny's back. Johnny went down with a *thwack*.

Kiki screamed and lurched to cover Johnny with her torso. In the truck, I almost screamed, too, but I remembered the truck's broken windows and plastered my hand over my mouth.

"Take that, Jap lover," said Mack. His words slurred together. He was drunk.

My mind felt slow, like it was running through quicksand and couldn't catch up. This couldn't be happening. Not right in front of me. Not to a boy that Kiki liked.

Johnny tried to pull himself up. Kiki steadied him as he stood.

"Only thing worse than a Jap is a traitor," Mack said to Johnny. "So you've got a choice. You can leave now, and *we'll* make sure your *girlfriend* gets home. Or we can deal with both of you together."

Kiki edged behind Johnny, still holding his arm.

"You want me to leave her with you?" Johnny's voice warped. He held an arm in front of Kiki. "I—I can't do that."

Mack darted forward and swung at Johnny's jaw.

"Johnny!" Kiki screamed, stepping backward.

Johnny ducked and put his hand up to block the punch. Mack's fist glanced off his scalp. For a moment, Johnny looked dazed. Then, blinking, he rushed at Mack, using his height to come from above and crush Mack to the ground. He threw blow after blow—wild, fast punches—as Mack grunted, trying to wriggle away.

It was only seconds before Mack's gang converged, pulling

Johnny from all different angles. They dragged him off Mack, who groaned as he rolled over on his knees.

Johnny jerked his arm away and lunged at Mack. But one of the taller boys yanked Johnny's hair, pulling his head back till Johnny stood, chin jutting out, his neck gleaming white and exposed. In a split second, two others rushed in and took his arms, clamping down till Johnny stopped jerking.

I had to do something. I fumbled under Hiro's seat, hoping he might have left a key in the car. I checked in the jockey box—empty—then under his mat. I felt nothing but the floor.

I turned back to the fight. Should I honk or run out or scream?

But there were so many boys. With Johnny restrained, Kiki and I didn't stand a chance.

Mack scrabbled up. He wiped his lip and nose, then spat. "You got it in you to be some kind of hero?"

*Swhapp!* In one swift hurtle, Mack landed a punch. Johnny's head snapped back.

"No!" Kiki's shout and the sound of the punch mingled, echoing into the vast night. My stomach turned.

"Let him go," Mack said, his words trailing into each other.

The boys holding Johnny hesitated, then released him. Johnny staggered, struggling to keep himself upright.

"Go get it. In the back of the truck," Mack said to Scooter. Scooter slunk down, his skinny neck nearly disappearing as he pressed his fists into his pockets. "I said, *go get it.*" Mack shoved Scooter, the strike audible against Scooter's bony chest. "Now."

Scooter squinted again, then rubbed his chest as he skulked to their truck farther down the pullout.

"I'm going to give you one more chance," Mack said, turning back to Johnny. "And before you decide whether you're going to do the smart thing"—he shook his head and let his voice slide into a drawl—"or the dumb thing, I want you to ask yourself, 'Is she worth it?'"

Scooter sidled back up to the group, holding something small and bright in one hand. The gang of boys scrambled back.

"Jeez, Mack!" one of the boys cried. "What're you playing at?"

"Aw, why'd ya gotta go bringing that dang knife?"

Everything froze and spun at the same time. A knife. I forgot to breathe. I stared at my sister—behind Johnny, she was motionless.

We didn't have a chance against the boys, but I had to do something. I leaned over and pushed Hiro's horn. Nothing happened. I tried again, but the blaring honk I'd hoped for didn't sound. For a moment I considered screaming. But Kiki had already screamed. If anyone was near, they would have heard her. Screaming would only alert the boys to the fact that I was there.

I vainly wished for the rifle, or even Dad's sword. Angry tears welled behind my eyeballs. They'd left us with no way to defend ourselves. We were sitting ducks.

Scooter handed his brother the shining knife without a word, his face set in a sullen frown. Johnny trembled. Behind him, horror filled Kiki's expression.

Mack caressed the knife. "It's a beaut, huh?" He gave Johnny a cold smile.

I stared at the crest of the bank, willing Hiro and Charlie to show up. For a second, I imagined something moved . . . but the bank stayed still.

I reached for the handle on the truck door. I couldn't stop Mack. But anything would be better than sitting here and watching.

*Matte!* From somewhere in the back of my mind, the Japanese command stopped me. *Wait for the right moment*, said the same voice.

I clutched the handle, torn. What if the right moment was too late?

"This knife is my pop's." Mack flipped the gleaming knife between his fingers. "Now, Pop, he told that trash sister of mine not to get involved with their kind." He pointed the knife at Kiki. "But Jean's as stupid as you. So now, while my big brother Donny's on his way to fight and I've got my own name in the draft, she's sneaking around with one of them!"

Mack stalked toward Johnny, holding the knife in front of him. Johnny and Kiki stumbled backward to the edge of the bank, holding hands. "Jean won't listen." Mack's voice got darker and rougher. "So instead, we've got to send a message to that 'boyfriend' of hers. That's where you come in," he said to Kiki.

Mack took a fast step toward Johnny, bringing the knife to Johnny's chin. "So . . . you gonna leave or not?"

Johnny stood still for a moment, then his head quarter-swiveled toward Kiki. She whimpered.

"What—" Johnny's voice was hoarse. "What are you going to do to her?" The question felt like a silent scream searing through my body.

"Does it matter?" Mack pressed the knife to Johnny's neck.

Johnny's eyes closed. "Please don't!" He hesitated. "I'll go."

Behind him, Kiki's face shattered.

Mack smiled and let his knife hand fall to his waist. "Smart move. Now git!"

Johnny's head inclined toward Kiki, but he didn't look at her as he pulled his hand from hers. After a few long seconds, he stumbled toward the long road where his parents' car was parked. He passed my car, and up close, I saw the swollen lump beneath his eye.

"All of you but Scoot," Mack ordered his gang. "You follow Sullivan. Make sure he doesn't come back this way. And if he stops to talk to anyone—" He flashed his knife in the air.

The boys looked at each other, then turned and walked to their car. As they passed me, I held my breath. But they didn't look into my window, even when one came so close I could see the mixture of worry and relief on his face.

As their engine turned over, I pressed myself against the door. Kiki looked like a child standing against the dark night sky. But she squared her shoulders, and, trembling, lifted her eyes to meet Mack's and Scooter's gazes.

"Oh, Kiki." I prayed a panicked, desperate prayer that someone would come. It was our only chance.

Again, I saw a flash of movement on the bank. But I blinked and found only the swaying of reeds. It might have been an animal—or maybe my desperate imagination.

I couldn't stay in the truck anymore. I couldn't leave my sister to face the Clydes alone. Though every part of me trembled, I had to do something.

I opened the door slowly. When it was only three inches open, the door squeaked. I froze. But no one noticed, so I continued. I didn't know what I'd do once I got out—go for help, obviously, but was it better to go down and try to find Hiro and Charlie? They might be all the way out at the cliffs still. Or should I head for town? It would take longer, but I was more certain I'd find someone.

From over by Kiki, Mack cackled, a rough, drunken laugh that made me shiver. "Did you see him run?"

Scooter didn't answer, didn't laugh.

"You not enjoying yourself?" Mack snapped. "Gosh-dangit, Scoot. I don't know what's wrong with you."

Scooter mumbled something.

"Well, this here's that Japanese Romeo's sister. So you best get used to it."

Hiro's coat slid from my lap to the car floor. My door was almost a foot open now—I only needed a few inches more. And it would open right onto the scene.

Mack stepped up to Kiki. "Have you seen one of these before?" Mack put his hand in his pocket and pulled out something I couldn't see. He held it up to Kiki. "This here's a license—for hunting folks like you." He laughed.

My neck and cheeks flushed—that stupid license. I pushed the door a little more.

Mack slipped the card back into his pocket. "Course, it's open season now." He went back to turning the knife in his hands.

Kiki stared past him. She'd pulled herself together, and as scared as I was, I was proud.

"Jean always was an idiot. If my father knew, he'd kill her." Mack spat on Kiki's shoes. "But your brother should have known better. Should've known that if he messed with our sister"—Mack stepped closer to Kiki. Too close—"we'd mess with his."

Kiki twitched, breaking her perfect posture.

Slowly, almost painfully, I opened my door another inch. When I looked up, it took a moment for me to realize something had happened. Kiki bolted in the other direction, her black hair streaming behind her as she made a break for the thicket of firs and berry bushes beyond the pullout. Scooter and Mack looked at each other for a moment, then, as if on a film reel that had gotten unstuck, took off after her.

"You think you can run from me?" Mack yelled thickly. "Head her off at the shed, Scoot!"

"Kiki!" I said aloud, forgetting to be careful. I froze, realizing that I'd given up my position. But neither Scooter nor Mack turned around.

"Sam!" The rough whisper made me pause. I turned in the direction it came from, to the bank. "Sam," the voice said again, and I recognized Beau's husky voice.

"Beau?"

Beau pulled himself up the bank, slowly, looking in the direction that Kiki and the Clydes had run.

"Oh, Beau," I said, feeling a rush of affection and gratitude. "Oh, I knew someone would come! We've got to go after them. It's the Clydes, Beau. Mack has a knife. He's going after Kiki." I waited for

Beau to understand, for something to register on his face. "We've got to go after them."

"But—" Beau stood there, ineffectual, goon-like.

"Beau," I said, making my voice more deliberate. "We have to go now. They could catch Kiki at any minute."

"We can't stop them," Beau said. His voice was rough with fear.

"We have to try. You should have seen what they did to Johnny."

Beau dug his toe into the dirt. He wasn't going to come. My eyes hadn't been playing tricks on me at all.

"You saw everything." It was a statement, not a question, and Beau didn't respond. I felt sick—how could he be so cowardly?

I couldn't stop the Clydes by myself. Beau was Kiki's only chance. "Beau, *please*. It's just the two of them now. Their friends are gone. And they'd never dare pull a knife on you . . ."

Beau stood there, looking like he might cry but unwilling to move.

A scream broke the silence. It was Kiki's, but it didn't sound like her. This scream was long and spiraled with pain and fear.

I looked at Beau one last time. He'd made his decision. With a nauseated huff, I said, "Then at least go and get us some help. Please!"

And without waiting for an answer, I ran straight into the thicket, in the direction of Kiki's scream.

# CHAPTER 39

# THE DARKEST NIGHT

I ran through the thicket and into the forest, listening for any sound over my own snapping steps. No birds cried. Little moonlight streamed through the dense firs, which reached up like endless pillars, disappearing in blackness. Thorns snagged my dress. My arms stung from lashing branches. I ran until I was near the spot where Kiki had screamed. I stopped and listened hard. Here, in the dense island growth, the ocean was almost inaudible—faint static. The only other sound was the wind in the trees.

"Kiki!" I whispered. No answer. "Kiki, it's me!"

Then, carried on the wind, I heard a snatch of Mack's voice. I turned toward it. The shadowy outline of some kind of structure—maybe a shed—stood in a clearing about eighty feet from where I stood. I hurried toward it, trying to keep my steps soft. The fir needles bent silently, as if they were on my side. But each time I stepped on a twig, the slight *thwick* made my insides jump.

I was twenty feet from the structure when something tumbled inside it.

"Leave me alone." Kiki's voice trembled.

Hot, electric anger pulsed through me, warring with fear. I bent down and felt around the ground till I found two fist-sized rocks. With a rock in each hand, I crept closer to the hut. Its door, barely tacked to its frame, was open. From inside, the smell of alcohol was overpowering.

"People say this one's a looker." Mack's drawl made my skin

crawl. "What do you think, Scoot?" A crash mixed with the scuffling of feet.

"Stop right there," Kiki said. The fear in her voice gave me goose pimples.

"Aw, Mack," Scooter whined. "I don't know about this."

I steeled myself, taking a deep breath. Blocking every thought, I threw myself through the broken-down doorway. My heart hammered as I took in the scene: the stench of fermentation, the shack filled with barrels, vats, and messes of tubes. Scooter stood a foot to my left, his long limbs blocking Kiki's path. She stood on the opposite side of some overturned barrels, her eyes wide and latched on Mack, who paced the other side of the mess, still brandishing the knife.

"Kiki! There you are!" I mustered lightness into my voice. In my shaking fists, the rocks felt like pebbles.

Scooter whirled to face me. "What the—" He almost tipped over. He was drunk, too. Maybe that would help.

"Sam!" Kiki's eyes darted to me, then back at Mack. Something crossed her face, a look even more frightened than before. Mack scowled.

I cleared my throat, gripping the rocks tighter. "Come on, Kiki." I thought wildly as Mack took a step toward me. "There's a whole bunch of people looking for you. A—a group of men. From town."

Mack stopped and—slowly, so slowly—cocked his head. Kiki looked from him to me, breathing hard, her hair tangled. She braced herself against a vat in front of her, as if on the verge of falling.

"C'mon, Kiks." I took a step toward Kiki, giving Mack what must have been a trembling smile. "Thanks for finding her. I'll tell everyone they can go home."

Mack squinted. "How'd you find us?"

I cleared my throat, racking my brain for an idea. "S-Someone said that Kiki came this way." I gestured to Kiki. "C'mon, we better go tell them you're safe."

Kiki eyed Mack's knife. Finally, she took a step toward me.

Mack, Scooter, and I stood, stiller than seemed possible, as, swaying, Kiki picked her way through the mess.

I reached out. With the rocks in my fists, I couldn't hold her hand, but I put my arm in hers.

"Was it Sullivan that sent y'all out to find her?" Mack asked.

Together, Kiki and I began backing toward the door, holding each other close. "I'm not sure—maybe?" I said, almost tripping over the uneven floor.

"Aw, Mack. I told ya we shouldn't . . ." Scooter started, but Mack shook his head a little, as if trying to clear it.

"This search party came all the way from town?" Mack asked. I swallowed and nodded with a sinking feeling that my lies were unraveling faster than I could weave them. "That fast?" Mack's eyes narrowed to slits.

I nodded. We were in the doorway now.

A slow smile slid across Mack's ashy face. "You're lying." Scooter looked from his brother to me.

I shook my head, adjusting my grip on the rocks. "No," I said, but I pulled Kiki closer toward me.

"Scoot, she's lyin'. It's just the two of them," Mack said.

For a second, there was stillness. Then I spun toward the doorway. "Run!" I shouted, pulling Kiki with my linked elbow.

"Get them!" Mack yelled.

In a jumble of movement, Kiki and I tumbled out the door. Her arm fell from mine as we ran. "Come on, Kiki!" I shouted, running toward the beach—and the highway.

Kiki's ragged breath came from right behind me. "You shouldn't have come! You've got to get out of here!"

"*We've* got to get out!" My lungs burned, but I surged forward.

"Run, Sam!" she said, but I could hear that she was falling behind.

"Faster, Kiki!"

"Sa-am!" Her scream stabbed the air. I skidded to a stop and turned to see her being grabbed by Mack. Her soft arms reached for me. Then Scooter's bony body crashed into mine, tackling me to the ground.

Coming to, I heard Kiki's shouts and felt Scooter's sharp weight against my chest. Still holding the rocks, I shoved and punched till Scooter rolled off me, covering his face with his hands. I scrambled to my feet, ignoring a searing pain on the back of my head. Mack had already yanked Kiki's arms behind her, pulling her to her knees.

"Let her go!" I threw myself on Mack's back. But Mack was thicker and more determined than his brother. My weight meant nothing to him. I hit his back with the rocks, over and over. "Let go of her! Let go!"

Mack grunted. Holding Kiki's wrists in one hand, he shoved me with the other. I fell to the ground, landing hard on my tailbone. One of the rocks flew from my grasp. "Get a grip on her, Scoot!" Mack roared.

In the dirt next to me, Scooter rubbed his jaw—I must have caught it with one of my punches—then stood. I ran back to Mack, raising my arms to bring the rock down on his head. But before I could, Scooter's long fingers clamped on my wrist. Thin and bony, yet strong, he twisted my arm behind me, pulling up so I had to move as he directed or the pain was unbearable. I cried out as my last rock fell from my hand, hitting the forest floor with a pitiful clunk.

Mack shoved Kiki onto the ground. "Jean says we're all the same . . . underneath." There was a sick curl in the way his voice caressed the last word. "Whaddaya think, Scoot?"

Scooter let my arms down an inch. "I don't like this, Mack."

"Chicken," Mack spat. Everything in me buzzed. I had to do something—anything.

"Maybe Jean's right. *Maybe*"—Mack leaned over Kiki—"I should check."

In a flash, Kiki's palm shot up. *Thwack!* Mack's face spun ninety degrees. Kiki's eyes were bright and wide as she lowered her hand.

Mack touched his jaw. "You uppity little . . ." His fist streaked down. There was a sickening clunk, and Kiki fell, her head rolling.

"Nooo!" The sound that roared out of me was too loud to be mine. I pulled against Scooter's grip till the shoulder seam of my dress ripped. My muscles felt as though they'd be next.

Kiki didn't move.

"You brought this on yourself," Mack growled. He turned to Scooter. "You take that one and teach her a lesson."

Scooter didn't move, but Mack turned around and pulled his knife out. "Remember, this is for Jean." He grimaced, and moonlight glinted off his teeth.

Scooter trembled, then stepped backward. "Kiki!" I pulled against Scooter's grip. My shoulders ached, and my boots slipped.

Kiki's head rolled toward me. Her eyes fluttered. "Don't hurt her!"

Scooter dragged me backward. My arms burned as I kicked and pulled. The heels of my boots skidded and bumped over rock and grass. "No! Please, Scooter," I cried. Branches lashed against my legs.

"Don't hurt her!" Kiki's raking sob rent the air. Through the thrashing brush, I saw her crawl and try to stand as Mack closed in on her. Then the moon disappeared behind a cloud, and all was dark.

# CHAPTER 40

# SCOOTER'S CHOICE

kicked and yelled till Scooter put a viselike hand over my mouth. I bit him, and he hooked his other arm around my neck, forcing me to stumble along with him.

From the dark I heard an animal's quick-silenced death cry. I couldn't breathe. The darkness swirled around me. Scooter's arm tightened. I couldn't keep up.

And then . . . he let go.

I froze. I tensed to run, but something stopped me: the stillness. Scooter didn't come at me. He didn't say anything. He just stood. And so I did, too, every fiber of my body alert and waiting. I could hear the crash of waves, and in the distance, the sound of an engine. Scooter had dragged me back toward the edge of the woods—*away* from the lonely thickets and out toward the highway.

I stared up at him. His bony shoulders rose and fell as he tried to catch his breath. His bright red hair was plastered to his sweaty forehead, and his handlebar grin was nowhere in sight.

"Git." His voice was hoarse. "Go on, git!"

The dread in my chest thawed on the edges. "You're letting me go?"

He glanced at me, the movement so quick I almost missed it. But in it, I saw excruciating wretchedness. "Go on." His big mouth turned down. "You'd best hurry."

I stood one second more, gazing at my tormentor. With all the bravado stripped away, there was something fractured in his face.

But my thoughts had to be for Kiki. I turned and ran, leaving the broken boy by himself.

The moonlight revealed a break in the dark trees—the highway. I ran until I reached it, falling several times, but ignoring the pain. The towering trees cleared, allowing moonlight to spill over me. My feet met hard, smooth pavement. "Help! Is anyone there? Help!"

"Sam?" Charlie's warm, deep voice came, like a miracle, from down the highway, from the shadowy shoulder of the road. I couldn't make out his figure, but I heard the quick *thwaps* of his soles against the pavement. There were other footsteps, too, and a clicking. Hiro and Jean emerged from the shadows with Charlie. Jean's eyes, round and dark, filled her blanched face. Hiro outpaced Charlie, reaching me first, and Jean came last, low pumps clicking against the pavement.

"Are you okay?" Hiro tried to take my hand, but I winced.

"Where's Kiki?" Charlie asked, his face wild.

I pointed behind me, toward the dark forest. "Mack," I panted. "He's got her near a shed out there."

"Probably that old moonshiner's cabin," Charlie said to Hiro, who nodded.

"Scooter's out there, too. But he let me go." I glanced at Jean, whose face was crisscrossed with horror. "And Mack has a knife."

"We heard." Hiro's mouth was set in a tight frown. How had they heard?

"Stay here," Charlie ordered. Jean let out a sound so soft it could have been the wind, and Charlie paused. "It will be fine," he whispered, taking her hand. Even in this crisis, I was surprised to see his hand around a white girl's. "Please, stay with my sister?"

Jean nodded, shaking. With one last look, Charlie and Hiro plunged into the woods.

As I watched their outlines merge into shadow, Jean put her hand—the hand that had held my brother's—around mine. My palm stung, and something white-hot welled up in my gut. This was *her* fault. *Theirs*.

Then I remembered what Mack had said. She had argued for Charlie. She had *chosen* him—even with brothers and a dad threatening her. Her loyalty was what I'd wished for from Beau.

I stilled myself and let my hand sit in hers. Hers was smaller than I'd imagined. And cold.

We waited by the side of the road, straining our eyes and ears each time we saw a flicker or heard a snap. Sometimes I thought I heard a muffled voice. Once I was sure I heard a crash. It might have only been ten minutes, maybe fifteen. But it felt uncountable.

Then three figures emerged from the trees. Charlie and Hiro walked on either side of Kiki. Her right arm was draped over Charlie's shoulder. Her left hung at her side.

"Kiki!" I cried. Jean and I started forward, but Charlie held his hand out. The trio picked their way up to the road. As they got closer, the moon lit Kiki's face. I gasped. Her right cheek was swollen. She had a cut under her left eye.

As they mounted the shoulder of the road, Kiki tripped. Charlie caught her, and she cried out, bending in half and cradling her left arm. Her shoulder looked misshapen, as if under the fabric it was twisted and lower than it should have been—broken or dislocated, I couldn't tell. Charlie and Hiro waited as she breathed through the pain. The washed light revealed smaller bruises and scratches all over her face and arms, and her dress was torn.

My stomach heaved. What had Mack done?

But there was a tension, a fragility in the way Hiro and Charlie said nothing, only waited. This was not the time to ask her. Instead, I whispered to my brother, "Is she okay?"

Charlie looked up at me, his sweat-drenched face serious. "She will be."

"I'll get the truck," Hiro said, breathing heavily. He wiped a trickle of blood from his nose. He turned to face Jean. "Your brother—he'll be okay, too."

I felt hot and ill. An ugly part of me wanted him destroyed.

Jean snatched a shamed look my way. "Thank you," she whispered.

Hiro jogged down the street, disappearing into the blackness.

# CHAPTER 41

# MRS. YAMAGUCHI

Kiki winced, cradling her bad arm, as Hiro jostled over a particularly bad rut. "Sorry," Hiro said, grimacing and gripping the steering wheel.

There wasn't really room for all of us in the cab. But no one suggested that anyone sit in the truck bed. Not after tonight. Only Kiki, who stifled cries each time the truck bumped, reclined fully against the back of the seat. The rest of us perched awkwardly. I was crushed next to Hiro, pressed into his arm to avoid bumping Kiki, who sat on my right, her left shoulder still hanging, twisted and wrong-looking. Charlie took the spot on Kiki's other side, still holding her good arm, and Jean balanced herself between him and the door, crossing her ankles and looking somehow ladylike even as her dark hair blew in the wind.

"Where to?" Hiro asked.

With a roughness in his voice, Charlie asked, "Kiki, could you wait till tomorrow for your arm?"

"What?" I stared at him. "She can't wait!"

But Kiki whispered, "The curfew."

"S-Surely in an emergency . . ."

"If we take her to the clinic, it could mean trouble." The anguish in Charlie's voice was like a wounded animal. "Probably not for her. But they'll want to know why we're all out."

Realization rushed through me. Of course. Tonight wasn't over yet. Not really. Not for Hiro and Charlie, who could be arrested for what they'd done to Mack. Or worse. Next to me, Kiki whimpered.

"We'll take you if you need it," Charlie said. The torn quality I'd heard in his voice was all over his face. "I—I'm so sorry, Kiki."

For a moment, there was silence in the car. Then Hiro cleared his throat. "What about Mrs. Yamaguchi? If the arm's not broken, she might be able to . . ."

"Mrs. Yamaguchi?" A hopeful note entered Charlie's voice. "Does it feel broken?"

"I don't know," Kiki said.

Charlie hesitated. "Would you mind if we asked Mrs. Yamaguchi to look at it first?"

I frowned at the idea of skipping the clinic and driving all the way back to Japantown. Mrs. Yamaguchi usually only helped with little things—colds and sprains, headaches. She wasn't a real doctor.

"Your arm might be dislocated," Charlie said. "She could fix that, I think. And if we can avoid questions . . ."

"Okay," Kiki whispered, squeezing her eyes shut.

We drove in near silence. Far above the road, stars shivered in the sky, not quite sparkling, muted by the weather. In slivers of the moon's wan light, I saw the dark stains on Hiro's knuckles as he gripped the steering wheel tight. I shuddered.

Besides the big question—the unspeakable question of what had happened to Kiki—one other question had been bothering me.

I turned to Hiro. "How did you know where to find us?"

Hiro's face clouded. "We ran into Beau."

Ah. I felt a stab of anger.

"I was almost to Single Tree when I found Charlie and Jean. They were on their way back. In the dark, it was slow going on the rocks." Hiro's voice twisted, as if asking me to understand. "If I had known . . ." He fell silent.

I wished I could make him feel better. But the words seemed wrong. How could I say, "It's okay" or "That's all right"? My mouth couldn't form the words. It wasn't Hiro's fault. But everything was not fine.

We went over a rut, and Kiki stiffened next to me. Her face contorted, and she failed to stifle a low groan. Then she sat back, still holding her arm at her side.

I waited till Kiki's breathing became regular. Then I turned back to Hiro. "Beau told you where I'd gone?"

Something I couldn't label descended over Hiro's face. Was it anger? Disgust? "Beau told us what happened," Hiro said, his voice flat.

"He was in a real state," Charlie added. "He told us about Johnny. He nearly cried when he told us about the knife." Heat seared through me. Beau had *nearly* cried"? What was I supposed to feel? Sorry for *him*?

"He was watching?" Kiki asked. "While they were beating Johnny—he *watched*?" For the first time since she'd emerged from the forest, her face registered something other than pain. Her eyes narrowed, sharpened by resentment.

Hiro slowed the car as he veered from the highway toward the unpaved road. "Beau told us they'd chased Kiki, and that you'd gone after them." He peeked over at me as he said that, and there was something indiscernible in his expression. "So we went after you."

The rest of the drive was rough. Hiro did his best, but Kiki's groans punctuated each dip and bump. Finally, we pulled in front of Mrs. Yamaguchi's bright yellow house.

After a long pause, Charlie turned to Hiro. "Could you take Jean home?"

Hiro nodded and looked forward. It took me a moment to realize, and then only after I'd craned my head to see past Kiki, that Hiro was giving Charlie and Jean privacy. But I was not as considerate.

I stared as my brother gave Jean a long, unbroken look. "Is there *any* chance Mack or Scooter would . . ." he whispered, his voice gentler than I'd ever heard it.

Jean shook her head. "I'll stay out of their way." Her eyes lingered on Charlie's face, unashamed, un-shy, almost bold with trust.

"What about your father?" There was an urgency below the surface of Charlie's voice.

Jean's lips twitched. "They won't tell him. Especially not if they have to explain that they got licked by Japanese boys." A hint of apology colored her voice. "It's you I'm worried for. Mack'll never let you get away with this."

Charlie shook his head. "Never mind all that. I've put you in danger." His eyes closed for the briefest moment. "All of you."

I swallowed. He was right. An aching anger swelled through me. He and Jean had played with fire. And Kiki and I had paid for it. But . . . hadn't I wanted to date Beau? Hadn't Kiki tried for Johnny? We'd all gotten caught in the hope that this world was fair. We'd all dared to think ourselves American.

"It's *their* fault," Jean said. "Not yours." My anger flickered.

I thought of the camera, of the guilt I'd felt for keeping it. I'd blamed Kiki for breaking curfew. I'd been angry that Charlie dared to date Jean. And yet . . . shouldn't Charlie date whomever he liked? Shouldn't Kiki be able to stay out till the same time as her friends? Shouldn't I be allowed to take pictures?

What Jean said made sense. We weren't the problem.

*We* weren't the problem.

My brother stared at Jean. I'd never seen this look on Charlie's face before, but it seemed natural, even fated. Charlie was more than a son and brother now. I felt at once both a snaking kind of loneliness and a calm resignation. This was as it should be.

"You're sure they won't . . . ?" Charlie asked.

Jean nodded. "I promise." Her words were heavy, as if weighted with meanings I couldn't even fathom.

At first Mrs. Yamaguchi opened the door only a crack. But when the light fell on Kiki, she flung the door wide, revealing a checkered apron over a giant sky-blue nightgown. She swept us all in through the door, gesturing us into the living room and ordering her five wide-eyed children to bed.

"You too, Kenji-kun," she ordered sternly, and a three-year-old boy with a shiny bowl cut ran after his brothers and sisters.

Almost hidden behind the wider woman, tiny Mrs. Omura wrung her hands. Both women took in Kiki's swollen cheek and cut face, then landed on the misshapen arm.

"How long?" Mrs. Yamaguchi asked in Japanese. She scrubbed her large hands on the front of her checkered apron, then gestured for Kiki to sit on a worn couch.

Kiki winced as Mrs. Yamaguchi ran her square fingers over the injured shoulder.

"Do you mean when she hurt it?" Charlie asked, also in Japanese. "Maybe three quarters of an hour?"

*"Ah, sou?"* Mrs. Yamaguchi shook her head. "Sooner is better for 'dis-u-location.'" She said the last word in English.

"Dislocation? It's not broken, then?" I knelt on the floor in front of Kiki, while Charlie took the seat at her side.

"Hm." Mrs. Yamaguchi slid her fingers down to Kiki's forearm. "Does this hurt?" she asked, her fingers pausing. Kiki winced and nodded. "How did it happen?"

Kiki looked at Charlie. "I—I fell," she said. Charlie nodded, and I frowned.

Mrs. Yamaguchi raised her eyebrows, but went back to feeling Kiki's arm. "The forearm is probably—" She closed her eyes for a moment and felt more carefully. Kiki cried out. "Ah! 'Fu-racture,'" Mrs. Yamaguchi said, again using English for the word. "But the shoulder is 'dis-u-located,' I think. Is there more pain the longer you wait?"

Kiki nodded. "It didn't hurt so much at the beginning. But now . . ." Kiki fought back tears.

"Should I call the doctor?" Mrs. Omura stood at the entry table, her finger poised over the telephone.

"Wait!" Charlie turned to Mrs. Yamaguchi. "Can you fix it?" he asked, still in Japanese.

Mrs. Yamaguchi scanned each of our faces. Her gaze felt sharp and knowing. "Is everything okay at your house? Your father . . ."

Charlie paused, then, understanding her question, answered. "It's nothing like that. But . . . we were out past curfew. And . . . there are reasons we'd rather not involve anyone else."

With one more look at Kiki, Mrs. Yamaguchi shook her head at Mrs. Omura, who put the phone down. Mrs. Yamaguchi turned to Kiki. "For the shoulder, the longer you wait, the longer it will take to heal. Shall I fix it?" She held her hands out, so that they hovered over Kiki's shoulder.

"Ye-ess," Kiki said.

"And what about the fracture?" I asked.

"It's not a full break." Mrs. Yamaguchi looked Kiki in the eye. "It might be better to call a doctor. But I can put on a splint."

Kiki gazed up at Charlie, her face covered in a sheen of sweat. She looked at the phone, then back at Mrs. Yamaguchi. "Please, do what you can." I put my hand on Kiki's knee, patting because it was all I could do.

Mrs. Yamaguchi spoke in Japanese to Mrs. Omura, who still stood by the phone, wringing her hands. Mrs. Omura hurried to the coat closet to get out a large tin first-aid box. Mrs. Yamaguchi rummaged around and found a long bandage and a wooden splint. She wrapped the wooden splint to Kiki's forearm.

She looked hard at Kiki's shoulder, then put her hand on Kiki's bicep. Kiki groaned, but Mrs. Yamaguchi's face was impassive. She placed her other palm under Kiki's arm. Then—faster than seemed possible—Mrs. Yamaguchi lifted the bicep and pulled. Kiki screamed, but Mrs. Yamaguchi pushed against Kiki's armpit with the other hand. Kiki's screams crescendoed. I held my knuckles to my teeth.

The screaming stopped. Kiki panted as Mrs. Yamaguchi bandaged her, first using a long swath of fabric to make a sling, then wrapping the arm tightly to Kiki's upper body.

Kiki closed her eyes, and for the first time since she'd come out of the forest, her face relaxed. *"Arigatou gozaimasu,* Yamaguchi-san," she said.

It was the first time I'd heard her use Japanese since Pearl Harbor.

# CHAPTER 42

# SHIKATA GA NAI

Mrs. Yamaguchi pressed both Kiki and me to stay the night, while Charlie went home to tell Dad where we were. As Mrs. Omura went upstairs to prepare a room, she gave Kiki a sad, long look. Wringing her hands, she said something I couldn't quite catch, but I heard the Japanese word for "pity" and then the phrase *"shikata ga nai."*

Mrs. Yamaguchi's lips pressed tightly. *"Shikata ga nai, shikata ga nai,"* she said when Mrs. Omura was out of earshot. Her nostrils flared. "You know this saying?" She got up and walked into the kitchen. Kiki had closed her eyes, so I followed Mrs. Yamaguchi.

"I know it," I answered, remembering that Dad had said it when the agents came, and what Mr. Tanaka had said about it the night of his arrest. I answered in Japanese, and something about using the language I'd used with my mother while in a kitchen sent a pang of loneliness for Okaasan searing through me.

Mrs. Yamaguchi shook her head. *"Nothing to be done.* She says this ten times a day." She plunged her hands into the sink full of dishes and started scrubbing. "The one thing I know—" She dunked the pan she'd just washed into a tub of rinse water, then set it on the drainboard. "There is always something to be done."

I didn't know what to say. Trying to be useful, I grabbed a white dishcloth from the table and began drying the pan.

"She wrings her hands all day. But how will that help?" Mrs. Yamaguchi scrubbed the next dish so hard, I worried it might break.

"My husband's gone, too. I have to run a farm and home by myself. If I only wring my hands, my kids won't eat."

She stopped scrubbing and peered at me. "Some people think 'nothing to be done' means quit. Just accept it. But really, the most important part of *shikata ga nai* comes next. Dot-dot-dot. You know 'dot-dot-dot'?"

"Like an ellipsis?"

"Yes." She nodded. "'Ee-rip-shee.' Nothing to be done, *so*—dot-dot-dot—you make it the best you can." She dunked the dish into the rinse water. "The most important part of the saying is the part that comes after the words. 'Make the best of it.' *Gaman shite*. You understand?" She put the dish on the drainboard.

"I . . . I think so."

Mrs. Yamaguchi shook her head. "Mrs. Omura doesn't."

As we finished the dishes, those phrases, *shikata ga nai* and *gaman*, rolled over and over in my brain. Mr. Tanaka had said that even though he chose to protest, he understood, even admired, those who had chosen to accept their circumstances. He said that accepting allows you to move on. And before he got into the agents' car, his last instruction to Hiro had been *"gaman."* At the time, I'd thought he simply meant, "endure." But had he'd used that specific word for its subtler meaning—"make the best of it"?

When we'd finished the dishes, Mrs. Yamaguchi shuttled Kiki and me up to a pink room. She brought us two short-but-too-wide nightgowns, fresh towels, and—with a swift "good night"—left us. Even though her manners were nothing like Okaasan's quiet ways, there was something comforting about Mrs. Yamaguchi's domineering mothering. It was a feeling I hadn't had in a long time.

"She's a force of nature," Kiki said after Mrs. Yamaguchi closed the door. I remembered Mr. Tanaka's words: "There's no one like her."

Kiki took the twin bed, facing the wall away from me, lying on her side to protect her bandaged arm. I lay in the trundle next to her. Above her, wind whistled through tiny cracks in the frame of a small window. The thick pink quilt was heavy and comforting on my limbs, but above the child-sized covers, cold air chilled my shoulders and face.

Out of Mrs. Yamaguchi's presence, my mind raced. I thought of Hiro yet again crossing the island after curfew. Had he gotten home safely? And how much trouble were Charlie and Hiro in? Would Mack really not say anything? Jean had seemed confident, but would Mack's pride really keep him silent?

My thoughts swirled and snaked, finally landing on Jean. How could someone so gentle be Mack's sister? I thought of what she'd said—that Mack would stay silent because he was scared of their father. How bad must Mr. Clyde be, if even Mack was afraid?

My insides squirmed at a memory—just last year, Jean had come to school with a bruise on her face. She'd said she'd fallen . . . just like Kiki.

My heart tugged as I thought of the adoring way Jean looked at Charlie, of the quiet way she'd spoken to me. She'd treated each of us like *people*, like it really didn't matter whether we were white or Japanese. I wouldn't recoil from her again.

Beside me, Kiki's breath was shallow and sometimes hitched. "Kiki?"

Kiki didn't answer, but her breathing paused.

"Do you think Jean will be all right?"

Kiki sniffed. "I hope so. She said she'd be okay."

It wasn't the answer I'd wanted. It left my insides feeling twisty. And beneath the twisting, the question that had haunted me through the evening still trembled. I waited, trying to think of the right way to ask. But there was no right way.

"Kiki?" My voice quavered.

"Yes?" There was none of her usual irritation in her voice. It was tired, patient even. It made it even harder for me to ask. But I had to know.

"What happened? Did Mack . . ."

The room was still. Behind Kiki, only a glimmer of moonlight dappled the window's icy blackness. Then beside me, I heard a sound that made my heart sink: Kiki's stifled sob.

The world had shattered. I threw my covers off, ignoring the frigid air. I didn't dare touch Kiki's arm, but I lay beside her, on top of the quilt, cradling her back, the way Okaasan used to cradle me when I was sick.

"Oneesan," I whispered. "Oh, Neesan, Neesan."

We cried together then, smothering our sobs in the mattress.

It might have been hours later—I had no sense of time—when Kiki's breathing slowed and steadied. Above me, rain tapped on the Yamaguchis' roof. I slipped from the bed to the trundle, where I got under the pink quilt once again, my stomach still knotted.

I wrapped my arms around my middle and squeezed, trying to understand, to find some sort of structure that would hold me together. But instead, a new thought crept through me. If we kept this secret, how many others did the same?

My mind tumbled with the terror of that thought until, exhausted, I thought no more.

In. Out. In. Out. I measured my breaths with Kiki's. Just before sleep took me, I looked once more at the little window. Lightning split the sky wide open, streaking the windowpane with tears.

# CHAPTER 43

# AFTERMATH

*January 31*

By the next morning, the rain had turned to snow. Outside, rocks and bushes hid under soft white caps. It was rare for so much snow to stick. Within a day—less if it rained—the sparkling mounds would disappear.

If only other things were as easy to erase.

Charlie picked us up in the morning, and Hiro showed up at our house in the afternoon, while Kiki was napping. Hiro carried a small white package tucked under his arm. He and I stood on the porch together, leaning against the wood rail.

"How's Kiki doing?" Hiro stood to my right, close enough that I could smell his soap but far enough that we didn't touch accidentally.

I looked out at the driveway. All around the useless truck, the snow was already melting. "She'll recover."

"And you?" he asked.

I kicked at icy slush, revealing the board beneath it. "I'm fine." The word *fine* hung lamely in the air.

I felt his gaze on me. *It would be my privilege.* Years had gone by since that moment at his car. The world had shifted.

It was ironic. I finally knew that he liked me. But I couldn't do anything about it. Kiki might have seen Hiro as a backup, but still . . . if I went forward with him now, it would feel disloyal, like stealing. And I couldn't do that to my sister. Not after last night.

"I have something for you." Hiro perched the white paper package on the wood rail. It was exactly the shape of a stack of photographs.

"I said I was done," I whispered.

"I know," Hiro said. "But I didn't believe you. Or at least I didn't want to."

My heart leapt traitorously, but I frowned.

"I asked Ruth to help. She took them to Mr. Simmons so we wouldn't have to wait for the post. He said he was pleased to help."

I let my eyes flick up to Hiro. "Really?" He nodded, and a lump rose in my throat. Mr. Simmons had always seemed grumpy. His portraits were posed and stiff. But if he'd seen what was on that film—the boycott, the truck, the arrest—and he'd developed it anyway . . . maybe I'd misjudged him. Especially after last night, my heart swelled at the thought that he had been willing to help.

I picked up the package. Ruth's neat handwriting lined its surface. "These are incredible, Sam!" I swallowed and reached for the paper wrapping. One fold at a time, a stack emerged. On top was the photo of the pond, its surface a textured combination of mirror and shadow, the marred door a shadowy afterthought in the corner. It had turned out better than I'd imagined.

Hiro pulled an object from his pocket. "Mr. Simmons also sent . . . this." He set a roll of film on the rail.

My heart thudded, and blood rushed to my head. I wanted the roll's smooth weight—those fifteen squares of possibility—in my palm. I craved the rightness of its click as I loaded it in a camera. I needed to harness a piece of this messy world, forcing some kind of sense onto it with the four corners of a viewfinder's black frame.

But . . . it would mean breaking the rules. And breaking the rules had already cost us too much.

The thought of Kiki crystallized my decision. "Hiro, I can't do this." I swallowed. "I'm so sorry, but could you please leave?"

"Sam?" It was as if my name scratched his throat. "I didn't mean to . . ."

He didn't understand. Maybe I didn't, either. But Dad saw my photography as a betrayal, and Kiki saw Hiro as something we'd competed over. As a family we'd been through too much. Something had to give—and I chose my family.

"Please, Hiro," I whispered. I held out the roll of film to him. "It's just not a good time—for this or . . . for us."

There was a long silence. Then—voice level—Hiro said, "Okay. I'll go." He took the film from my outstretched hand. A moment later, his footsteps retreated, first the hard steps on the stair boards, then the sound of slush on the drive.

When his truck's engine roared to life, I looked down. In my hands, the photo of the pond stared up at me, its blacks and whites and grays physical, the slick paper touchable. I had wanted this shot so much. And Hiro had made it real—even when I had given up.

I flipped to the next photo and my breath caught. Shades of gray revealed the smooth contours of Hiro's unsmiling face. His eyes were intense—as if he were capturing me, not the other way around. How had I not noticed when I'd taken the photo?

He had liked me. I hadn't seen it, but there it was, a moment snatched and printed and . . . undeniable.

And I'd just ruined everything. I stared down at the drive, at my family's footprints trudging toward the house, at Hiro's steps in the opposite direction, crisscrossing the unshoveled walk and weed-filled lawn, muddying the melting snow.

I looked up. The truck was two houses away, and through the truck window, I could just make out the back of Hiro's head.

I closed the envelope without looking at the other photos. This one alone was nearly enough to break my resolve.

# CHAPTER 44

# BACK TO SCHOOL

*February 2–13*

When I stepped into Mr. Percival's class on Monday morning, both Scooter and Beau were already in their seats. Beau's face flamed as I walked past. I couldn't focus on him, though. My heart pounded as my gaze pulled toward Scooter. I remembered how he'd dragged me. His grip had been unshakable. He'd let me go, but still . . . my hands trembled as I made my way to the aisle.

Scooter's mouth turned down, and he glanced around the room. My insides quaked. Which boys had been there that night? I felt as if I might throw up. Scooter laid his head on his desk, and I scurried past.

Throughout the class, my eyes drifted back to Scooter over and over, but he didn't raise his head. When the bell rang, he rushed out before Mr. Percival even finished giving our homework. But Beau sat, shamefaced, and as I walked past him, he stood.

"Sam," Beau called, catching up to me in the hall.

I paused but didn't look at him.

"Are—are you okay?"

I pursed my lips. My mind filled with the image of Beau's ashen face in the bushes. He had told Charlie and Hiro where we'd gone. I could at least thank him for that.

And hadn't I been praying for him to talk to me? Now he was. I forced myself to look into Beau's clear blue eyes. I opened my mouth . . .

But I remembered the way Kiki's arm had dangled from her shoulder. I swallowed and walked away.

I stashed the packet of photos in my sweater drawer, unable to throw them away even though I feared Dad finding them. Hiro spent his days trying to save the Merc, so Charlie drove me to and from school. Every morning, Kiki found a reason to stay home—one day her arm hurt. Another, she said she had a big sewing job to finish. And another, she offered to help Dad on the farm, even with her fractured forearm.

By the beginning of the next week, Kiki asked me to take her written withdrawal to the school. It saddened Dad—it had been so important to Okaasan that we all graduate—but he didn't force the issue. Charlie had made Dad promise never to ask what had happened, and the haunted look in Dad's eyes showed he was afraid to know.

At school, Mack was missing. Jean told Charlie that he'd gotten a full-time job at the brickyard. It was a relief not to run into him—though knowing he was still on the island made me nervous.

Once the bruises faded, Johnny seemed the same as always—surrounded by his teammates, loud and full of laughter. But I noticed him watching me, and one day, he made his way across the hall to my locker.

"Is she okay?" he whispered.

I slid my workbook onto the locker shelf, biting my tongue. Johnny couldn't have held off the whole gang, and Mack had a knife. Yet I couldn't help but despise him for leaving Kiki, and for waiting so long to ask if she was okay.

But Kiki wouldn't want Johnny to know how hard things had been. "She's fine," I said. "She's just helping my dad."

Johnny's flat chin bobbed up and down, and he managed a weak grin. "Good. That's a relief."

I watched him walk away, wondering if he really believed me or just wanted to. Either way, Kiki's secret remained intact.

At home, everyone toed the line. I came home right after school, and Charlie helped Dad with the farm. No one even thought of going out after curfew. There was a heaviness throughout the house. We waited, wondering if Mack Clyde would resurface. But nothing happened.

The weekend of the Sweethearts' Dance came. At the end of school on Friday, a pair of teachers brought in a big banner. They unrolled the hand-lettered sign as everyone watched. *Sweethearts' Royalty: Beau + SueAnn.*

Applause thundered through the hall. SueAnn beamed as she sidled up to Beau. A simpering grin crossed Beau's face. I turned away, waiting for the trickle of jealousy that had been my constant companion the last two months. But it didn't come.

Beau wasn't who I'd thought he was. I missed—ached—for the friend I'd lost. But the Beau in front of me wasn't that person. Maybe he never had been.

I walked away from the crowd, feeling both lonelier and lighter.

# CHAPTER 45

# A GREEN DRESS

*February 13*

"*Okaeri*," Kiki said as I walked into our bedroom. She sat on the bed, legs stretched out, ankles crossed. Her face was bare, and she'd tucked her uncurled hair under a checkered headkerchief. "How was your day?"

I slung my bag to the floor. "Okay." It still surprised me when she started conversations—I'd been ignored by her for so long. But I liked it.

"Anything interesting happen?" She looked up from the deep green fabric she was stitching. She wore the splint on her left arm, but it didn't seem to slow her down.

I squinted. "They announced Sweethearts' royalty." It seemed like the kind of thing Kiki might want to know.

"Who won?"

"Beau."

Kiki's stitching fell to her lap. "With . . . ?"

I shrugged. "SueAnn, of course."

She watched my expression. "You okay?"

I nodded. "I really am." I gestured at her sewing. "At least everyone will see the dress you altered. Aren't you cutting it a little close?"

"That was the blue one," she said. "I finished it days ago. It was pretty spectacular. And Mrs. Clark gave me a lot for altering it."

"Good. I mean, the money. I kind of wish the dress wasn't

'spectacular.'" But I grinned to show that I didn't really mind. I pointed at Kiki's sewing. "Then this . . . Are you going tonight?"

I immediately wished I hadn't asked. Kiki's face darkened. "No. Not me." She shook her head, then got up on her knees and held the emerald fabric up. "This is for you."

If I hadn't recognized the fabric, I'd never have known that it was the same dress Kiki had gotten from SueAnn. Kiki had transformed it.

"There was so much fabric in that skirt—it would have drowned you," Kiki said. "I cut it up and used the extra to make it longer."

"It's . . ." I couldn't find the right word. What had once been a short, full-skirted party dress was now a slinky gown. Kiki had added a narrow, cinched-in belt, and even a hint of a train. She'd moved the girlish placket of buttons and added a draped cowl at the bottom of a daringly deep V-back. "You did this?" I breathed, fingering the tiny hand-stitches in the hem. They were as perfect as Okaasan's.

Kiki grinned. "You like it?"

"I can't believe it's the same dress. It's so . . . sophisticated."

Kiki slid off the bed and held the dress up to me. "You'll knock 'em dead."

"Oh, but I'm not planning—"

But Kiki was already pushing the dress into my arms. "Try it on."

I stroked the shining fabric. I'd never worn anything like it. I smiled and made my way behind the dressing screen.

"What do you think?" she asked when I emerged a minute later.

I stared at myself in the mirror. I didn't recognize myself from the shoulders down. Kiki had fitted the fabric perfectly, so it just skimmed my sides, cinching in at exactly the right place. The fabric winked in the light. It was as if my head was atop some movie star's body.

Kiki sighed with satisfaction as she buttoned the gown down my back. "You look amazing." She paused. "But also like *you*."

I shivered at the unfamiliar coldness of the low back. "It doesn't *feel* like me."

"Let's do something with your hair." Kiki ignored her splint as she pulled my hair out of its braid. "Let's see . . ." She pushed me to my knees. "I need a better angle."

I almost protested. I wasn't going to the dance. I had no need for a dress. But there was a smile in Kiki's voice. She was back—not scared, not hiding. Even the pushiness felt like the real her.

"If only we'd curled it last night. But I have an idea." Kiki got out a box of hairpins, then combed the front half of my hair till it made a smooth plane. She rolled the hair around her fingers, pinning it on top of my head.

I looked sideways at the mirror. A cylinder of hair sat on my forehead. "I look like a sea creature."

"Don't be silly," Kiki mumbled, one side of her mouth clamped down to hold two hairpins. "It will look good." She back-combed the hair behind the roll, then created two nests on both sides of my head.

I reached up. It didn't *feel* like it looked good.

"Stop." Kiki grabbed my head and held it tight, so I couldn't check the mirror. "Just trust me." She pulled the hair on both sides of my face back into a ponytail, covering the tangles she'd just created, then coiled my long black hair into a bun on the nape of my neck. "There," she said, pinning it into place. "Actually, this is better on you than curls."

She twirled me to the mirror. I stared. The smooth bun was . . . elegant. "Is it too old for me?"

"No, it's sophisticated. You always look too young." She came at me with a tube of lipstick.

I stepped back and shielded my face with one hand. "No."

"You can always rub it off. Just try it."

I cringed.

"Just *let* me." She stepped forward and pulled the lipstick across my mouth in little dabs. I let my hand fall to my side as I took in the strange, velvety feeling of the makeup. It smelled less edible than I'd expected.

Kiki stood back. "Not bad." She pointed to the mirror.

She was right. I looked . . . pretty. For a moment I imagined what it would feel like to walk into the dance. I blushed as my thoughts leapt to Hiro. If only he could see me.

I glanced awkwardly at Kiki. "I'm sorry. You went to all this work. But I'm not going."

"What? Why not?"

"Well, I don't have a date."

Kiki cocked her head to the side. "What about Hiro?"

I shook my head, flushing.

"Was he too chicken to ask you?" Kiki frowned.

"What do you mean?"

Kiki squinted. "Seriously? I have eyes, Sam."

I swallowed. "There's nothing going on."

Kiki's eyes narrowed.

"I—I couldn't do that to . . ."

Kiki shook her head. "Oh, Sam. Look, I know I was a blockhead, but . . ." Kiki's lips twisted. "It was always you. Looking back, I think he chose you the day you fell into that pond." I opened my mouth— how could she possibly know that?—but Kiki held up a hand.

"So if you like him, don't lose him on my account." She grinned. "Besides, he *is* the only Japanese boy with his own car." She mocked herself in a singsong voice.

The corners of my mouth twitched. Then I sighed. "Pretty sure I've already lost him."

"Even if he saw you in this dress?" Kiki asked. I nodded, and

Kiki frowned. "Well, go to the dance anyway. You can't waste this. You look like a million bucks."

"Everyone would stare," I said, again feeling the cold air on my back.

My sister gave me a smile that was 100 percent old Kiki. "So let them stare." She stepped forward and draped a silvery wrap around my shoulders. "Look, there's a group of Japantown kids meeting at Edna's. Who knows? Maybe Hiro's going with them."

"I'm not invited," I said. "I can't just show up." But Kiki pushed me toward the bedroom door.

"It's fine—it's a whole bunch of kids." She frowned and touched the shining sleeve. "Sam, you have to go. With curfew, it's only a couple of hours. And look at all the trouble I went to!"

I looked down at the perfectly fitted dress. Guilt knotted my stomach. How could I reject her offering? I swallowed and let her guide me out of our room. At the top of the stairs I turned to her and opened my mouth. "Thank you, Kiki. This is . . ." I couldn't think of a big enough word.

She gave me a wicked look. "You tell Beau to eat his heart out, okay?"

The corners of my mouth tugged. There was so much light in Kiki's face—and a touch of her old pride.

# CHAPTER 46

# IN THE ORCHARD

Damp cold licked my skin above the dress's V-back, even under Kiki's wrap. Kiki watched through the parlor windows, so I made a good show of walking to the road, then turning south, as if heading to Edna Okawa's street. But when I got to the spot where wild berry bushes grew as tall as a man, I ducked under the fence and into the Omuras' orchard. I couldn't go to the dance. I wasn't just dateless. I was nearly friendless.

For Kiki to believe I'd gone, I'd have to stay out till just before curfew. I needed to feed the chickens anyway, so I headed for the barn. I pulled up my hem so that it wouldn't drag in the crabgrass and dirt, and I smirked. Kiki had frowned when I put my boots on, but there was nothing to be done about it—Okaasan's only pair of heels was now too small for either of us. The dress, though . . . well, it was perfect. I still couldn't get over the fact that Kiki had made *me* a dress. Even if I was the only person who ever saw it, it meant the world.

As I neared the barn, I heard the chickens squabbling. The barn door hung ajar, shuddering with the wind. "Charlie?" There was no answer. I hurried into the barn.

Soft light filtered through the cracks in the barn walls. Glittering swirls of dust fell softly to the nubby floor. Clark Gable paced the length of the wire fencing that kept the chickens on their side. "Why's the door open?" I asked, shutting it behind me and checking the latch. It clicked smoothly. "Did Charlie leave it?" I checked the ground inside the chickens' pen. The water was still a quarter full, but the ground was bare of feed.

"Well, if it was Charlie, he didn't feed you." I leaned forward, using one hand to keep my dress off the floor and the other to open the tin container of feed.

The top of my head grazed the wire enclosure. A burst of feathers and talons lunged at my eye. I whipped back.

Clark stared at me, his eyes onyx. Again he spread his wings and flung himself at the fencing. His talons flashed as he crashed into the wire only feet from me.

My heart and head pounded. I'd dropped my dress. Dust dirtied its hem. "What's gotten into you?"

Clark stared at me, his neck feathers ruffled.

I stepped toward the food. "Look, I'm just going to dish you some—"

But Clark flew at me again. The wire jangled as his talons sliced the air next to my hand.

I jumped back and took a deep breath. In one swift movement, before Clark could react, I shoveled a bunch of feed into the waiting coffee can and poured it on the ground near Clark. He didn't charge me this time. Instead, he glared, his eyes hard and sparkling, his tail-feathers gleaming.

I frowned and dropped the can back in the feed. "Oh, Clark. Don't do this." All around him, the hens scratched and pecked, but Clark eyed me, his gaze reptilian. We'd had roosters go mean before. It happened sometimes as they aged. The really bad ones attacked every time anyone tried to get near their hens, even just to feed them. If that was the case with Clark—if it got bad enough— he'd have to be put down.

Clark swiveled and stared into the dark far corner of the barn. I sighed. Maybe he wasn't going mean. Maybe he was spooked. There might have been a rat. Or maybe it was the open door and the wind.

"Please don't turn on us, boy," I said, fitting the lid on the tin. "For your own sake." I gazed at the handsome rooster, thinking of how Okaasan had loved him. I wasn't ready to lose another part of her.

I slipped out of the barn, shutting the door as the familiar ache washed over me. I tipped my face up to the sky. "Oh, Mamii." I used the name I'd called my mother when I was young. "I wish you were here."

The evening light shone soft. I closed my eyes again and tried to picture Okaasan. The image blurred. Was her hair really as smooth as I remembered? Had her only freckle been under her right or left eye? A cold thought slid through me. Was I losing my memory of her? The thought terrified me in a way Mack and Scooter couldn't.

I picked my way through the orchard in the dying light, searching till I found the gnarled, knocked-over trunk. I brushed at the leaves, surprised at how dry they'd stayed, till my fingers rubbed fabric. I lifted out the dirtied peacock-blue scarf and unknotted the corners to find the tin inside.

I pried the lid open. The picture on top was the family portrait we'd taken just months before Okaasan went to the hospital. She sat in the middle of the photograph, wearing her kimono. Dad sat next to her in his best suit. Charlie, Kiki, and I stood around the two of them. The photo was blurry—we'd laughed as the photo was taken. I couldn't remember why we'd laughed, but I did remember that Mr. Simmons, irritated, had made us pose for a second take.

There was an ease to the scene. No brimming tension. No consuming grief. We were a family. We were happy.

How could things have changed so quickly? And what else would change? With everything going on in the country, in the war, with the farm—where would I be in two more years?

And I found myself thinking of Hiro. Kiki's exasperated voice rang in my brain. *If you like him, don't lose him on my account.* And something clicked. This life was too fleeting, too changeable, to waste. I'd made a terrible mistake.

There was a crackling of leaves behind me, and I turned. As if I'd summoned him, there stood Hiro.

"Sam." Hiro's expression was solemn. He seemed not at all surprised to run into me in the orchard in the middle of winter. He didn't even mention my dress.

I laid the photo in the tin. "Hi."

Hiro rocked on his heels. I crumpled the fabric of my dress.

"You didn't go to the dance?" I asked.

Hiro shook his head. His gaze swept over me. "Did you?"

I shook my head. "No, Kiki—"

But Hiro interrupted me. "Sam, I saw you out my window, and I just had to ask . . ." I glanced toward his house. I could barely see his window. But Hiro plowed on, his jaw tight. "Look, if what you said before was for keeps . . ." Something dark flickered across his face. "If it was, just tell me. But I thought that . . ."

There was a hooded quality to Hiro's eyes, as if he was afraid of what I might say. But around the edges there was a softness—hope?

My heart slammed in my chest. In a flash of random thought, I remembered the time I'd begged Charlie to take me cliff-jumping. I'd perched on the edge of the rock, looking down at the dark, froth-laced water beneath me. This was just as terrifying. And yet . . .

"It's not for keeps," I whispered. "I think I feel . . . the opposite."

Hiro said nothing, and I couldn't bring myself to look up at him.

Then two leather boots stepped into my vision. "Sam." A smile softened his voice. My breath filled my ears, embarrassingly loud and uneven. When I dared to look up, his eyes searched my face, reading me as if I were a book. I kept my face angled toward his, but lowered my eyes, focusing on the Adam's apple under his smooth brown skin.

Too many thoughts and feelings clamored inside me. I wanted to run or at least say something to rend the thick tension between us. But as Hiro lifted his hand, I dared to stand still. Shivers of something sweet danced up and down my spine.

Hiro hesitated, then reached up. His fingers lingered on my temple just long enough for me to feel their warmth . . . and the question in them.

I took a deep breath, steadying myself, and let my gaze rise upward, first to his chin, then—shying away from his mouth—to his cheekbones, finally meeting his eyes. Something between us disappeared, and his face seemed clearer. Sharper somehow.

For a long moment, his eyes held mine. We were so close I could see specks of light in their warm, deep brown.

Hiro's hand dropped, and his fingers caught mine. They trembled, as if he might be as scared as me. My breath caught in my throat. And then, in one slow, careful movement, he brought my lips to his.

# CHAPTER 47

# HOPE AND TERROR

The kiss was brief, yet it left my lips burning. It was as if layers of doubt and disbelief had fallen around me, like silk to the floor. As Hiro walked me toward my house, I felt like I was floating.

We were coming out of the trees when we heard the chickens' calls. I stopped. "They were upset earlier," I said. "Our rooster attacked me. It's not like him." Hiro nodded and changed directions. We headed toward the barn, our hands still clasped.

As we drew nearer, the barn door trembled in the wind. A chill stole over me. "I know I shut that."

Hiro held up his hand. There was a sound under the chickens' squawking. Voices.

Hiro and I scrambled back into the orchard. The trees were too far apart to offer much protection, but we crouched beside one. I held my breath.

The voices were harsh and deep, though they seemed to be trying to whisper. And there was something else—something absent in the sounds. But what?

The door slammed against the side of the barn, and two masked figures rushed out. I leaned forward, trying to see more clearly. They wore caps and bandannas. All I could see were slits from their eyebrows to their cheekbones. One was tall, the other shorter but with broad shoulders. He dragged a baseball bat in one hand.

The one with the bat looked up at the house. "I'll bet he's in there." My spine crawled as I recognized the drawl.

"Mack," I mouthed to Hiro. He nodded.

Mack hoisted his bat to his shoulder and started for the house. "Stop!" said the taller one. "McClatchy said not to lay a hand on them."

*McClatchy?* I startled, accidentally snapping a twig under my knee.

Mack raised the bat. "What does that geezer care? The boy's got it coming to him." He swung the bat down, like an executioner's axe. My blood froze in my veins.

"I'm telling you, McClatchy will string you up," said the tall one. "Remember, 'scare only.'"

*Scare only.* Then they'd come on McClatchy's orders?

"But that Jap scum—"

"Shut up!" said the tall one. For one long, drawn-out minute, the boys glared at each other. Then Mack's bat fell to his side.

The tall one nodded. "Let's go."

Squatting beside me, Hiro rocked on the balls of his feet, on the verge of trying to follow. I put my hand on his arm and shook my head.

The thugs edged their way around the yard, heading toward the road instead of the house. Hiro sighed. "There wasn't much I could do," he said. "But if they'd headed for the house, I would have—"

I shook my head. "I know."

Hiro turned to the barn. "Why were they—"

I swallowed. "We better go see."

We trudged over the patchy ground, Hiro in front of me. My chest tightened as we neared the barn. The door creaked as it swung slowly, almost imperceptibly.

And then I saw him. A scream clawed my throat.

He swung from the doorframe. A twine noose stretched to an ugly knot around his broken neck. The scarlet crown lolled on his golden breast, and his onyx eyes were blank.

Clark's cry was the sound that was missing.

"Wha— Why—" I couldn't breathe. Clark's tail-feathers were snapped. His claws reached, taut and useless, toward the ground. One leg was broken. And they'd stuck a sign on the other foot, using one of his talons like a pushpin: *YOU'RE NEXT.*

I gasped, folding over on myself, as Hiro took me by the shoulders and turned me away.

"How could they?" I fell into Hiro, but even in his arms, I felt cold. Clark was more than a pet. I'd lost another piece of Okaasan. "We can't let Kiki see," I rasped. "If she finds out someone got this close—she's still so—"

"Shh. We won't let her." Hiro led me around the barn, back to the fence. "Sit here," he said quietly. "I'll bring him down."

He put his jacket around my shoulders. But still, I shuddered.

It was dark, and well after curfew, when Hiro and I arrived back at the house.

"Hullo!" Charlie called, trudging up the drive just as we reached it. He grinned, and behind him, my father's face was alight. It struck me as strange—I didn't think I'd seen the two of them so happy for years. Maybe ever. And yet here they were, looking as if Christmas had come early, while I felt only numb horror.

"We have good news," Charlie said as he and Dad met us at the top of the drive. His eyes flicked between the two of us, pausing on my dress.

"Tell them, Charlie," said Dad. His eyes glittered.

"Right. We've done it," Charlie said. "We figured it out. It was there the whole time. We just had to see it."

"Figured what out?" Hiro asked. After he'd buried Clark, he had wiped his hands and face, but his clothes were powdered with dirt, and his hair shone with sweat.

"The farm," Charlie said. "It's unbelievable, but . . . we can make it."

It was as if someone was trying to rouse me from a nightmare. "We can make what?"

"Slow down," Hiro said. "What's happened?"

"The farm—we can save it!" Charlie said.

"How?" I stared from Charlie to Dad.

Dad put a hand on Charlie's back. "Charlie thought of it."

Charlie beamed. "The orchard."

"The Omuras' orchard?" I asked.

"It's so simple," Charlie said. "We asked Mrs. Omura if we could farm it for her. We'll split the profits. Fifty-fifty, if we can manage it, but if not, she'll allow us to take whatever portion we need to pay off the debt, then make it up to her the next year." Charlie put his hand on Dad's shoulder. "We can *make* it, Sam."

"It will still be difficult," Dad said. "The payment is due in the middle of the harvest, so the late crops will not help. But it is . . . possible." He leaned on his heels and stared out over the orchard, a dreamy smile on his face.

I stared at Charlie's hand resting on Dad's shoulder. But as I followed my father's eyes over the orchard and toward the shadowy silhouette of the barn, my heart sank. "Dad."

Dad turned to me, and as I took in his expression, something inside me broke. I was going to ruin his first good night in months. "Yes?"

I took a deep breath. "Something happened tonight. Two people broke into our barn. Hiro and I saw them as they came out. They—" A lump rose in my throat. "They killed Clark."

Charlie's hand fell from Dad's shoulder. "They— Why?"

I shook my head. Hiro spoke in a low voice. "They hung him from the barn door."

I shivered. It was so cruel. So . . . ugly.

"This was on his foot," Hiro said. He pulled the folded note from his pocket and handed it to Charlie. Charlie and Dad read the note together. "I buried him," Hiro said. "He's behind the barn."

Charlie crushed the note in his palm.

"Thank you, Hiro." Dad's voice was strained. I blinked away tears. Dad's face was drained of the light that had filled it.

"Why the rooster?" Charlie asked. "I don't understand."

"To send us a message," Dad said.

"They also mentioned—" Hiro glanced at me.

"McClatchy," I said. "They were talking when they came out. Said McClatchy told them to scare but not hurt us."

"He sent them to kill Clark?" Charlie's voice warped. "It makes no sense."

"Could you see who they were?" Dad asked.

"They wore masks, but they were male, and young. The older one might have been in his twenties." Hiro turned to Charlie. "The other one—he drawled."

Charlie's expression broke. His lips pulled away from his teeth.

Anger flared through me. For the first time in so long, Charlie and Dad had been happy, like the old days. But the moment was gone. Stolen.

Dad's eyes flicked from Charlie to Hiro and back. Seeming to understand that he shouldn't know, he put his hands in his pockets and stared again at the orchard. "If McClatchy sent them, then the best thing we can do is follow our new plan. The land is what he wants. We won't give it to him."

Tears still weighed heavy behind my eyes, but I nodded. Dad was right.

The door creaked open, and Kiki's silhouette appeared in the kerosene's yellow light. "What are you all doing out there?" She tiptoed onto the porch, her feet bare, her arms tight over her thin dress.

Charlie whipped around, hiding his face. He sniffed twice, then turned back. "Just telling Sam some great news," he said, combing his hair back into place. His voice held no hint of the anger we'd just witnessed. "Dad and I worked out a deal with Mrs. Omura. We're going to take over the orchard. We may be able to pay that mortgage after all."

"Wha—really?" Kiki picked her way down the stairs.

Dad, Hiro, and I followed Charlie to the porch, forming a half circle around my sister.

"I can't believe it." Kiki peered at Dad. "We have a chance?"

Dad nodded, forcing himself to smile. "Yes. We do."

We all fixed happy expressions on our faces as Kiki stared around the circle. When she got to me and Hiro, her grin widened. "I can't believe it," she said again. "Who would've thought things could turn around so fast?"

I swallowed, thinking of the time we'd gone to the beach and Okaasan had spotted a whirlpool. Lately it felt as if we were always turning, as if everything was fast.

# CHAPTER 48

# HIRO'S NEWS

*February 19*

The next Thursday, I woke up to the telephone's screech. What time was it? Pale light streamed through the cracks in the curtains. I lay back, churning with feelings that hadn't gone away since Saturday—anger and fear over Clark, hope and disbelief about Charlie's new plan, and . . .

My stomach flipped as I thought of Hiro. I flopped onto my stomach and pressed my face into a pillow. Hiro and I hadn't talked or been alone since that night. But every morning I woke up feeling like my stomach was doing somersaults.

"Sa-aaam." Kiki's voice came from downstairs. "The phone is for yooo-u."

Her voice was cheerful, and I scowled.

"Sa-aam. It's Hiiirrrooo."

I blinked, then flung the covers off and tripped down the stairs in my pajamas.

Kiki stood next to the phone with an intolerably smug look on her face. "That sure got you to come quick."

"Shush," I mouthed, snatching the phone from her. "Hello?" I said, turning toward the wall. My voice came out croaky.

"Hi." Hiro's low, velvety voice made my knees feel funny—like I'd gotten up too fast. "How are you doing?"

"I—I'm okay."

Kiki snorted. "She's gaga for you!" she said in a whisper I hoped Hiro couldn't hear.

"I was worried about you after Saturday."

I turned to see where Kiki was. She leaned against the kitchen table in her bathrobe, arms crossed on her chest. Blushing, I waved her away, but she ignored me, smiling broadly. I turned back to the wall. "I'm okay. We all are," I said into the phone.

"I'm glad," Hiro said. He paused, then asked, "Did you hear that a pipe burst at the school?"

I shook my head, then remembered to speak. "No."

"They've had to cancel classes," Hiro said. "And I wondered"— his voice wavered—"would you like to do something with me today?"

"Yes," I said too quickly.

"Maybe we could go to the pictures? Or get a soda?"

"Yes."

"Yes to which one?"

"Either." I sounded too eager, but I couldn't stop myself.

"All right." I could hear the smile in Hiro's voice. "There's a double feature matinee, and Henry Goto said he could watch the store for me. How about it?"

"Yes."

"It starts at noon. Should I come at about eleven thirty?"

"Yes." Why couldn't I think of anything to say but "yes"?

"All right. It's a date."

*A date.* I slid the phone onto its cradle. I had a date with Hiro. So many things had happened in the last week. But for now, they all seemed a little less pressing.

I turned around. Still leaning on the table, Kiki grinned. "'Yes, yes, yes, yes.'"

*"Damatte,"* I growled, but I couldn't completely wipe off the goofy look plastered across my face.

"I knew you were sweet on him." She shook her head. "But

watching that—you're cooked!" She stared at me with a quizzical expression. For a second I thought I might have seen pain behind her eyes. But she smirked and fluttered her eyelashes. "Can I dress you up?"

I narrowed my eyes and stalked back toward the stairs. "Fine."

Kiki danced ahead of me. "I'll go pick out a dress!"

Kiki was still pulling at my hair when Hiro knocked. "It's not time yet, is it?" I asked.

"Drat. He's thirty minutes early." She frowned at my half-finished hair.

"Well, just pull it back, then," I said, reaching back to wrangle it myself.

"Stop!" She slapped my hand without losing her grasp on my hair. "It's so close to being cute."

Steps sounded outside the bedroom.

"Oh my goodness," I said. "I forgot to tell Dad."

My hair fell from Kiki's hands.

I should have told Dad Hiro was coming. I should have asked permission. But I had done neither, and now Dad was on his way to open the door.

"What should I do?" I asked, leaning out of Kiki's reach. I took a ribbon—it almost matched the outfit Kiki had picked—and tied my hair back in less than three seconds.

"Maybe Dad'll surprise you," Kiki said. "Maybe it won't be a big deal."

I gave her a look.

"I said 'maybe.'" She grinned.

But when Kiki and I got to the top of the stairs, Dad and Hiro stood in the entry, their heads close together.

"What's going on?" I asked.

"I got a letter," Hiro called. "From my dad!"

"Your dad?" I scrambled down the steps.

Hiro handed me the envelope. On the left-hand corner of the envelope, scrawled in black ink, was the name *T. Tanaka*. Under the name was another line: *C/O Department of Justice*. The address had been blacked out, and a purple-ink stamp marked the envelope *CENSORED*.

"I had Henry go to the post office for me. He brought this back with the newspaper and bills." Hiro's eyes were too bright, and a scramble of emotions raged on his face.

"What does your dad say?" I asked.

"Read for yourself." Hiro shifted so I could read it with my dad. Kiki huddled next to me. "There's a lot more than last time."

The page was marred with thick black marks, but Mr. Tanaka's untidy scrawl still made my heart jump.

> *Dear Hiro,*
>
> *I don't know if you have received my previous letters, so I will again begin by telling you I am safe.*

I turned to Hiro. "Safe." Hiro nodded, blinking fast.

> *I have been at ███ for nearly ███. I know you must be wondering what it is like here. You are smart, so I will not pretend ██ is comfortable. There are about █ men here. Most are business owners and community leaders. I have not seen anyone from Linley, but I have met men from all over ████. The food is not what we are used to. Often the produce is already rotting when we get it. But that is nothing to how cold it is. Even in our*

*bunks, under the thin blankets they give us, we cannot
get warm, sometimes for days at a time.*

*Worse, I believe, is the uncertainty. We have not been
told how long we will be at* ▮▮▮▮ *, and if or when we
will be allowed to take our cases to trial. Very few have
been allowed letters from home, so we do not know how
our families are. That worry, I think, is the worst of all.*

*Sometimes when things are very bad, I wish I
hadn't "stuck my neck out" as you called it. But other
times I still believe. Surely these bullies are no match
for the Constitution. Surely good people will speak
up. Am I only dreaming?*

*I often wonder how you are holding up with both
school and the store. My guess is that you are trying
to keep the store going, and I know how much that
is to ask of you. If push comes to shove, put your
education first. It seems unlikely that I'll be home
by* ▮▮▮▮ *. Sell the cars if you can and the
Mercantile if you have to.*

*I do not know if you will receive this letter. But I
am thinking of you.*

*Always,*
*Dad*

Anger and hope welled inside me. The conditions he described,
the black marks—it was all so wrong. But he was safe.

"He hasn't gotten *any* of our letters." Hiro's voice trembled. "But
if I got this, maybe they're letting letters through now. I've got to
send him something right away. Do you mind postponing?"

"Of course," I said. "We can go to the movies another time."

"The movies?" Dad looked up from the letter he still held in his hand. "You were going to the movies? Together?"

I blushed, but Hiro seemed not to notice Dad's question. "Will you come with me? To the post office?"

"Can I go, Dad?" My breath pinched in my throat.

Dad's eyes flicked from me to Hiro. Kiki took the letter from Dad and handed it to Hiro. "Of course she can. Right, Dad?"

Dad blinked. "I, ah . . . I suppose."

"Thanks," I mouthed to Kiki. I pulled my coat from the coat-rack, then stopped. "Let me get one thing," I said to Hiro. I rushed upstairs to my drawer, rustled under my sweaters, and found the white package Hiro had given me, along with the folded entry form. I had never been able to throw them away. And with my anger renewed, I had to do something. I stuffed both into my coat pocket and clambered back down the stairs.

I twirled to the door, sparing one backward glance at Dad. He stared after us, as if wondering what had just happened.

# CHAPTER 49

# A CONFRONTATION

"What can I do for you?" Mr. Walton asked as we walked into the sunlit post office.

"I need to write a letter," Hiro said. Taking Hiro's money over the clean oak counter, Mr. Walton handed Hiro two pages of stationery and an envelope.

"Just lemme know when you're ready," Mr. Walton said, waddling back to his sorting.

Hiro scribbled then stopped, scribbled then stopped. As I waited, I fingered the worn edges of the contest entry form in my pocket. I couldn't bring myself to pull it out. Dad was ready to fight for the farm, but that didn't mean he would approve breaking contraband rules. And even if I did . . . A whisper of fear that had nothing to do with Dad trickled through me.

What if I failed? What if, after all we'd done, I wasn't good enough?

I smoothed the pocket, feeling something sink inside me.

Hiro scanned his letter. "At least he'll know I'm okay." He blotted the page, folded it in thirds, and stuck it in the envelope. "Where should I send it?" he asked, pulling his father's letter from his pocket.

I squinted at the blacked-out address. "Can you see through it?"

Hiro shook his head. "Already tried."

"At least this time there's a 'care of.'"

Hiro nodded and printed, *MR. TANIYUKI TANAKA, C/O DEPARTMENT OF JUSTICE.* "Think that'll be enough?"

"Maybe you could put 'Washington, DC'? I'm sure they've got an office there."

"Let's ask Mr. Walton what he thinks."

We stepped up to the counter. "You two ready?" Mr. Walton asked.

"We have a question," Hiro said. "I got a letter from my father, and it said 'care of Department of Justice.' Where do you think that would be?"

"Well, let me think . . ." Mr. Walton scratched his thatch-colored hair.

The door behind us rattled, and I turned. Through the glass, I recognized the tall silhouette.

The door swung open. Mr. McClatchy's gaze rested on Hiro and me. His eyes narrowed, and I thought he would say something. But instead he sneered and turned to Mr. Walton. "Herb, you get a package for me?" He strolled up to the counter, positioning himself between us and the cash register.

Hiro slipped his envelope from the counter.

"Think I did see something," said Mr. Walton cheerfully. He backed up and scanned the wall-length sorter behind him.

McClatchy leered as he leaned against the counter. Without a word, Hiro stepped forward, blocking me from McClatchy's view.

"Yep. Here it is." Mr. Walton slid a flat box out of one of the slots. He handed it across the counter to McClatchy.

"Thanks." McClatchy took the box and strolled out the door. The bell rang again as the door slammed behind him.

"Now what was it you two wanted?" Mr. Walton asked. "Oh, right. Where to send that letter—"

I didn't know I would do it until I did. "I'll be one minute," I said to Hiro, and I rushed out, ignoring his startled look.

"Mr. McClatchy!" I called. I ran till he was only feet away. "Excuse me, Mr. McClatchy!"

The big man turned around in the middle of the street. Deep lines crisscrossed his forehead. Spittle clung to the corners of his lips. "What do you want?"

"Sir." I swallowed, hating that I had to call him "sir," but knowing he wouldn't answer if I didn't. "Sir, yesterday our rooster was killed."

McClatchy's face didn't move.

"Do you know anything about that?" I felt a little light-headed, as if I were watching someone else—someone bigger and braver than me.

McClatchy's eyes narrowed. "'Scuse me?"

"Do you know anything about it?" The sharpness in my voice both surprised and pleased me.

McClatchy's face went splotchy. "I don't like your tone, girl."

I flushed. There was something ugly in the way he said "girl." Anger flared in the pit of my stomach.

McClatchy turned back toward his store. I followed, daring to walk in the middle of the street. "Sir, they said something as they were running away."

"I'm sure they did," he grunted.

"They said *your* name, sir."

McClatchy's stride stuttered.

With a burst of angry courage, I called, "Did you send them?"

McClatchy stopped dead and turned to face me. "*Send* them?" His lips curled. "I didn't have to *send* them. I've been reining them in for weeks. All I did"—he stepped toward me, and, looking around, lowered his voice—"was let the leash out a bit."

It was my turn to stumble. "You're holding them back? Why would you do that?"

"Oh, not for you and that dad of yours. I just don't want anything hanging over *my* land when I get it back."

I squinted at the sun behind his head.

"Don't understand?" He smirked. "Someone kills your dad or your brother, and I might have to deal with a will. Some judge could give the new owner time to get affairs in order. Even if they just hurt them, there'd be legal questions. Might slow down the property return." He shook his head. "I want my grandfather's land free and clear."

"You can't *know* you'll get it." My voice broke. "We still have months."

McClatchy grinned. "You think you've got months?" He put his hand in his pocket and pulled out a nickel. He held it up. "Go get yourself today's paper." He threw the nickel at my feet.

I stood, watching as he sauntered back toward his store. The wind tore at my hair and numbed my face.

I knelt and picked up the nickel. We were five cents closer to the mortgage.

# CHAPTER 50

# LONG SHOTS

"Sam." Hiro came up behind me. "Are you okay?"

I pulled my gaze away from McClatchy's General and nodded. We headed back toward the truck. When we were both inside I asked, "How much did you hear?"

"I heard him tell you to read the paper." Hiro reached down to the floor of his car, where a pile of mail lay spread under the gearshift. He sifted through it and pulled out a newspaper. "Let's find out what he meant," he said, unrolling the newsprint. My stomach fell as I read the front page. *Presidential Order: Japanese on West Coast to Be Incarcerated?*

Even the wind outside went still. "Incarcerated," I whispered.

"Should I read it out loud?" Hiro asked, his voice not quite steady. I nodded. "'A new executive order, issued by the White House, enables the secretary of war to establish military areas from which any persons or group of persons may be excluded.'"

The words tumbled over me like waves. I couldn't make sense of them. But my heart seized.

"'Concerned citizens hope that this order signifies more aggressive steps will be taken to secure the West Coast. Patriots have called for the speedy internment of Japanese Americans. Many believe immediate action is necessitated by recent events, including flickering lights spotted in areas populated by Japanese.'" He shook his head.

"Flickering lights?" I asked. It was ludicrous that such little things could have turned into a real, black-and-white printed news story—and that the president might act on the rumors.

"Anyone trying to live behind blackout curtains is going to have flickering lights," Hiro said.

"People can't be buying this," I whispered. But the executive order . . .

"It goes on." Hiro bowed over the paper again. "'It is conceivable that Japanese farmers will plant this year's crops in arrow-shaped patches to tell the Japanese where to find military targets.'" Hiro slammed the paper on the seat between us. "What rubbish!"

I picked it up, scanning over the same tired accusations we'd read for months—Japanese are different. Biologically inferior. Sworn to the emperor. Treacherous by nature.

Finally, the article came back to the new order. I read it aloud. "'The president has given the secretary of war the right to enforce compliance'"—my voice caught—"'including the use of federal troops.'" I covered my mouth with my hand. "'He further authorizes the same to find shelter for those excluded from military zones.'"

"What does *that* mean?" Hiro asked. "Shelter?"

"I think it means they can put us in prison," I whispered, horrified. I read on. "'A top level source in Washington, DC, explains, "The most likely scenario is that those of Japanese descent will be banned from the West Coast and relocated further inland where they are less dangerous to national security." While some Americans may cry foul, most reasonable patriots agree: civil rights may be trampled, and some innocent may be imprisoned with the guilty, but this is a small price to stop treachery. The complete evacuation of the Japanese from the Pacific Coast just makes sense.'" The words hit like an actual punch. I felt like retching, but I choked out the article's final words. "'Why delay?'" I let the paper fall to the floor.

The post office swam as I held back tears. "Could they? Would they lock us up?" My voice broke.

Hiro shook his head. "I can't imagine. There have to be tens of thousands of us in Washington alone. Where would they put us?" But his voice wavered.

It was all too much—Mr. McClatchy grinning as he told me he'd "let out the leash." Thugs killing Clark. All that had happened to Kiki. "Why—why would they want this?"

Hiro shook his head. "Dad says fear makes people small."

Fear. But there were so few of us, and so many of them. How could *they* be afraid? The cold feeling of sheer helplessness raided my body, making it difficult to even breathe.

It didn't make sense. And yet it was the way things were. And there was nothing I could do. Nothing. *Shikata ga nai.*

"Sam . . ." Hiro's voice seemed soft and far away. "Sam, you can't let them win."

McClatchy's sneer filled my brain, but I held on to the timbre of Hiro's voice. He was right.

Something hot and steadying flared through me, fast and hungry, like a fire consuming dry stubble. And I remembered Mrs. Yamaguchi saying that the most important part of *shikata ga nai* was the unsaid ending. The dot-dot-dot. "Nothing to be done, *so . . .*" Endure. Make the best of it. *Gaman.*

The cold feeling disappeared, and I felt strong, as if the marrow in my bones had turned to steel. "You mailed your letter?"

Hiro nodded. "Sent it to DC. Hope Dad'll get it."

"He will. He's got to." I felt in my pocket. The packet of photos and the entry form were still there. "Could we . . . Would you go back in with me? I need to mail something, too."

Mr. Walton leaned back in his chair, reading a magazine as Hiro and I huddled at the counter. I pulled the packet of photos from my pocket and set them on the smooth oak surface.

Hiro read the form. "You're going to enter?"

I took a shaky breath and opened the wrapping.

There was the photo—the pond, the door, the rain. I sighed. The light and texture were perfect.

But as I slid the photo out, the paper wrapping collapsed. The whole bundle fell, photos scattering on the counter and spilling to the floor.

I knelt to pick them up. Mr. Omura in handcuffs. Hiro's truck, vandalized. Mr. Tanaka protesting, vulnerable and brave.

Mr. Walton hadn't budged, hadn't even looked up. But as I stared at the photos, they seemed as dangerous as fire.

They said so much about the last three months: the desperation, the terror. The . . . guilt.

My vision constricted. They'd taken our cameras like they'd taken our guns, leaving us unable to protect ourselves in yet another way. These photos documented and proved what had happened to us. They'd tried to strip us of that.

I stared at the photos. The pond shot was beautiful. It told a story. But fire still raged in my belly. It didn't say enough. Not anymore.

I squatted next to the photo of Mr. Tanaka's boycott. Of all the photos, this one shook me. Its harsh, highly contrasted light illuminated three small figures fighting a store so big it had always been sure to win.

Yet Mr. Tanaka's expression was determined, so certain he could make a difference.

And now he was in a prison. Had he been wrong?

Something in my core twisted. I could not accept that thought. I wouldn't. He was good. He was brave. He was . . . what I wanted to be. And this was my shot.

If incarceration was coming, the prize money wouldn't matter. But the contest was still my chance at having a photo published—of revealing these moments to the world. Maybe people would see how we'd struggled. Maybe they'd see Mr. Tanaka's bravery.

And even if they didn't . . . Well, sending it was something I still needed to do—for me.

With the breathless feeling of falling, I picked up the photo and slid it into the envelope with the entry form.

"It's a long shot," I said, gathering the other photos.

Hiro knelt to help me. "Maybe long shots are the ones worth taking."

I nodded, rewrapping the photos, and stood. "Maybe."

I walked to the counter and slipped my entry into the outgoing mail slot.

# CHAPTER 51

# SIGNS

*March 25*

The signs appeared five weeks later. The school had reopened, and I'd volunteered to make a trip to the post office after classes, just in case there was word from the contest. But as I turned onto Main Street, I stumbled to a stop. Crisp posters had been pasted on each of Main Street's eight telephone poles.

My feet seemed to sink into the sidewalk, and the air around me closed in, as if the sky itself might swallow me up. We'd heard about signs appearing in towns all along the coast. Each time, the Japanese in the area had only days or weeks to prepare before they were rounded up and "removed."

A car puttered past, and farther down Main Street, someone yelled. I startled, then steadied myself.

I had to check. Maybe the signs were just signs.

I took a few steps toward the nearest pole, in front of the pharmacy. *INSTRUCTIONS TO ALL PERSONS OF JAPANESE ANCESTRY.*

Everything went still. I scanned the document till I got to the word *evacuate*. I blinked and reread, willing the words to make sense. *All Japanese persons, both alien and non-alien, will be evacuated from this area by 12:00 o'clock noon Tuesday.*

*This* Tuesday. Six days.

It was here. We'd hoped it wouldn't come. We'd hoped it would be ruled unconstitutional, that they'd run out of funding, that they'd realize we weren't a threat. But there was no more hoping.

There were more instructions after that—something about registering, something about what to pack. But I couldn't understand it, couldn't even see the words.

I turned back the way I'd come and ran. I sprinted through the brickyard, stumbling to the Cap. The waves below hurled themselves against the sharp rock that rose in purple-green shards toward the sun. For how many thousands of years had this battle raged? Yet neither the waves nor the cliffs gave in.

I sat cross-legged, soaking in the cacophony of clashing currents and shrieking gulls. Far out, dark clouds rolled, and a vein of lightning struck the dark water.

Dirt ground into my palms, but I welcomed the pain. It was Linley soil and meant that I was still on the island I loved.

But only for six more days. A lump rose in my throat. How I loved this island, even if it didn't love me back.

# CHAPTER 52

# GANBATTE

I was too chicken to go home, too much of a coward to tell my family about the signs. I stayed at the cliffs until evening. When I finally walked into the dark house, I could feel it. They knew.

Dad sat in a stupor in the parlor, while in the kitchen, the only lighted room in the house, Charlie spoke into the phone.

"It says we must register tomorrow. Yes, we're allowed only what we can carry. Probably two suitcases for adults . . ." He rubbed his forehead with the flat of his hand. "Only what we can carry." There was a long pause, and Charlie's eyes met mine. "I'm so sorry, Mrs. Yamaguchi. It does seem hard . . ." He sighed. "I'll come by tomorrow to help. Yes, good night."

He hung the phone on its hook, his head dropping. "Mrs. Yamaguchi thought she must have misunderstood the English. She couldn't believe they'd only give us six days to pack and put our affairs in order. And she has all those kids—" Charlie's face drained, leaving him looking so much older and more like Dad than I'd ever realized.

I swallowed. How must he feel? Charlie'd been taking care of us since Okaasan died. Now he was making arrangements for our— my stomach rolled as the word came to me—arrest.

"I need to get some suitcases," Charlie said as I followed him to the entry. "The Allreds offered to sell us some secondhand." He pulled his coat from the rack and slung it over his shoulder. He glanced into the dark parlor, where Dad slumped in the shadows.

"Hiro's lending me his truck. I'll try to be back by curfew." He walked out the door, letting it slam in his wake.

I folded my arms over my chest, then turned to my father. His face was so blank that it frightened me. "Would you like me to light the kerosene?" I asked.

He didn't respond.

"Or shall I light a fire?" The parlor was freezing.

Dad looked up, as if noticing me for the first time. "If you like." There was a strangled formality in the way the words followed each other.

Still, lighting the fire gave me something to do, so I pulled two logs from the woodbox and placed them in the grate. My match flared fast, then dwindled as I lit a stick of kindling. Flames lapped up the bone-dry wood.

Outside, the wind howled, and in the parlor, the accompanying draft was laced with a cloying, woody smell. I instinctively turned to the butsudan. Dad had lit a stick of incense. But we'd thrown the incense away . . . When had Dad replaced it?

The butsudan was open, and Dad stared at Okaasan's photo, his expression only animated by the reflection of flames on the stony planes of his face. "Is there anything I can get you?" I asked. Dad closed his eyes.

I tiptoed out of the room, then sat on the bottom step of the stairs, out of sight. This strange quietness in my father frightened me. I'd seen him desperate, but this was different. I was scared of what he might do.

For several minutes, I listened to the crackling fire and the echoing tick of the clock. Then, as if out of nothing, I heard Dad's low voice. "Oh, Miku." The whisper trailed like a sound in the wind, but my mother's name made me sit forward. *"Taihen moushi-wake gozaimasen."* A wail mutilated the end of the apology. "I tried so hard," Dad said, the words strangled. "I wanted so much to live up to what you deserved. To give your children what someone else could have." His voice broke. "Oh, Miku, can you forgive me?"

I didn't know how to process what I was hearing. It was too much. I was torn, wanting to comfort my father, but also to hide that I'd heard. And at the same time, I wanted to hear more. The mystery of my father was within reach.

"We'll lose the farm." Dad's sob rent the house. "Charlie will have to start from scratch."

I stood. Dad was praying to Okaasan. I owed them both their privacy.

I tiptoed up the steps and into the bedroom I shared with Kiki. As I entered, she pulled her quilt over herself.

"Are you okay?" I whispered. She didn't answer. I sat on the edge of the bed. "Kiki?"

Her voice was muffled by the quilt. "It's just . . . a bad day."

I fiddled awkwardly with the blanket. This wasn't aloof, pre-attack Kiki, but it wasn't the Kiki who'd been getting better the last few weeks, either. It was someone between, and—like the Dad downstairs—it scared me.

"Can I get you anything?"

She sniffed. "I just need some space."

"I— Okay. I'll step outside. But if you need anything . . ." My voice was as flat and helpless as Charlie's had been on the phone.

I shut the door behind me and stood on the landing, listening to the cries of one broken family member and the silence of another. The air felt heavy with grief.

I couldn't breathe. I stumbled down the hallway to my father's room and closed myself in, holding my hands over my ears when the door still didn't block out Dad's sobs.

The smell of the room flooded my nostrils. The smell of Okaasan.

My hands slipped from my ears. Except for the unmade bed and a few clothes on the floor, everything looked exactly as it had when she was alive. The blossom-covered curtains were still bound in the ornamental knots only she knew how to tie. Her mahogany brush still lay on the dresser next to the scarf she'd worn at night. Even her slightly stained gloves still draped the back of the chair in the corner. Like the butsudan downstairs, Dad had made this room a shrine.

I made my way to the curtains and fingered a silky knot. The memory—no, the *feeling*—of my mother coursed through my body. The ache of missing her tore at my already fragile seams, yet at the same time filled me.

Outside the window, the wind rustled the trees. The storm I'd seen over the ocean was nearly here, and the sky was dark. Except—except for a patch of light around the descending sun. The clouds broke there, like whites around yolk, their lacy edges on fire.

The warmth of that vision made me feel stronger. I looked out at the orchard, its trees just starting to bud, and the thick, dark forest. Beyond the forest, I made out slices of the cliffs plunging toward the hidden ocean beyond.

This was my *home*. Wherever they sent me, whether the rest of Linley wanted me or not, I claimed it. I loved it. What anyone else thought couldn't change that. This was mine.

Like tumbling waves, another thought broke over me. Whether my family was broken or whole, I claimed them, too. I loved them. Nothing could change that, either. Whatever was coming our way, *they* were mine.

As the realization washed through me, a single phrase filled my mind: *Ganbatte ne. Do your utmost.* Okaasan's favorite encouragement rang through my head as if she were in the room, saying it aloud.

And I knew what I had to do.

# CHAPTER 53

# THE SALE

*March 26–29*

The next morning, before anyone else was up, I went through the house, cataloging what we might be able to sell—furniture, the icebox, even the stove. Writing down Okaasan's precious sewing machine was the most painful of all. But I swallowed and scribbled it down with the rest of our belongings, reminding myself that we couldn't take it. Only what we could carry, the sign said.

And if we could sell enough . . . Something hitched inside my lungs. Was this how Dad felt when he dared to hope? The farm wasn't my dream. It wasn't Charlie's. And, despite what Dad thought, it wasn't Okaasan's. But it meant everything to Dad. And if by some miracle we could pay the mortgage . . . *Ganbatte.* It was what Okaasan would have wanted. It was worth it all.

When Charlie came down, I told him my plan. He frowned but said, "Mr. Garry is interested in purchasing farm equipment. We won't get nearly what we should, but better than nothing."

"The truck might be worth something, too."

He grimaced. "It's in rough shape."

"So we won't get much, but at least—"

He nodded. "Yeah, write that down, too."

Through the rest of the morning, Charlie and I ransacked our belongings. When Dad came down, eyes swollen, Charlie told him our plan. Dad's eyes widened. "See what you can get for the seed we haven't planted. And the chickens."

Once Charlie and I had thought up everything we could, Kiki copied the list on twenty different sheets.

"I'll take these around while I'm in town." Charlie's face crumpled. He was registering our family for deportation.

The next days were filled with packing and selling. Dad and Charlie brokered a deal with Mr. Garry for the farm equipment, getting a quarter of what it was worth. But other families had gotten even worse deals, so Dad took it. The furniture had gone cheap, and the truck, too, to a squirmy-eyed man who'd come from Tacoma just to buy out Japanese families. We hadn't wanted to sell for so little, but the man said, "Better to sell than have it stolen once you're gone."

Some families treated us reasonably, though. A family called the Bennetts gave Charlie a fair price for the unused seed, and the Allreds insisted on paying full price for the chickens.

I felt ill when Charlie told me Mrs. Clark had asked for Okaasan's machine. She barely knew how to sew. When I thought of my mother, sewing by candlelight after working a whole day in the field, the thought of bargaining with Mrs. Clark made my face hot. But no one else made an offer.

*Ganbatte*, I thought, and I wrapped the machine in an old quilt.

Since Hiro was busy putting his own affairs in order, I trekked the mile from my house to the Clarks' with the sewing machine in a Radio Flyer wagon I borrowed from the Yamaguchi kids. A cool rain fell on my bare arms and head, but even so, I sweated. By the time I got off the Japantown roads, my arms screamed at the weight of the cast-iron machine. The roads outside of Japantown were smoother, but I had to pull the load uphill, and when I got to the Clarks', my hair and dress were soaked, slicked to my skin.

I knocked. Mrs. Clark's sickly smile was nowhere in sight when she opened the door. She looked both ways, as if checking to see if anyone might be watching, then tried to hustle me inside. But it took some time to hoist the machine from the rusty wagon and lug it up her steps.

When I got the machine, still wrapped in a quilt, onto the entry floor, Mrs. Clark shut the door. She gestured past the entry, to the parlor where two figures sat next to a crooning Victrola. "I believe you all know each other."

My heart thudded. Beau sat next to SueAnn, a crossword on the table in front of them. Beau squirmed.

Face blazing, I turned to face Mrs. Clark. "If we can do this quickly, I've got a lot of packing waiting for me."

"Right." Mrs. Clark pointed to the table in front of Beau and SueAnn. "If you'll set it up on that table, I'll look it over. Susie, can you clear your things?"

*Look it over.* She might not buy it, even after I hauled it across the island. I willed my mouth shut, unfolded the quilt, and began to lug the machine to the table. SueAnn cleared away the crossword, and as I started toward the parlor, Beau stood. His face matched his hair as he came forward and, without making eye contact, put his arms out for the machine.

I nearly refused his help. But then the machine's weight disappeared, and Beau, cradling it as if he knew how precious it was, walked it to the table and set it down. Still seated across the table from the rest of us, SueAnn narrowed her eyes.

"Hmm." Mrs. Clark circled my mother's machine. Her curls didn't budge as she leaned over. "It looks a bit scratched up."

"Where?" I leaned forward to inspect it. The machine was perfect.

Mrs. Clark slid her fingers over the machine's solid black arm, then fiddled with the balance wheel.

*How much?* It was all I thought about these last few days.

"What do you think, Mrs. C?" Beau asked. "It sure looks nice." Mrs. Clark and I both looked up. For a moment, Mrs. Clark seemed taken aback. Then her face shifted into a sorry smile—a show for Beau, I was sure.

"Well, it isn't the newest model, is it?" Her sugary-sweet voice—the one that made me want to either run or hit her—was back.

I gave her an equally fake smile. "Only a few years old. It's never had any problems."

"I think I could come up with"—the smile flickered as she appraised me—"five dollars?"

I stepped backward. I'd expected her to try to cheat me. To so many, our incarceration was a bargaining chip. But five? My neck and ears heated.

"Here, let me get my purse," she said. Something about the triumphant look in her eyes made me speak.

"Well, I'll have to see what my sister thinks, of course," I said. Mrs. Clark's brow darkened as she turned back to me. "It's as much hers as it is mine."

Mrs. Clark pursed her lips. "That's a very heavy machine to drag all the way back to your house."

"Oh, that's okay." I hesitated, but I had nothing to lose. "Mrs. Hampshire also wants to see the machine, and she's on my way home." Mrs. Clark's eyes narrowed to sharp slants. "Thank you for your time." I picked up the quilt and bundled it around the machine.

"Wait." Mrs. Clark bit her lip and dug the knuckles of both hands into her hips.

I kept my face as blank as possible. "Yes?"

"I don't want you to have to carry it all that way. And I just . . . I just feel so much for your situation." The voice was back. "I think Mr. Clark would probably let me spend up to . . . say, fifteen?"

It was the offer I'd expected, but I took a chance. I turned and slightly lifted the machine.

"Or maybe twenty!" Mrs. Clark said.

I paused. It was just over half what Okaasan had paid. Better than I'd hoped.

"Yes, twenty." Mrs. Clark pulled her purse open and thrust a bill at me. "Here."

I looked from the crisp bill to her heart-shaped face. There wasn't a trace of saccharine sympathy on it anymore. It burned with resentment, as if *I* were taking advantage of her.

This was for the farm, I reminded myself. I took the bill, folded it neatly, and put it in my skirt pocket.

I turned to pull my quilt off the machine. Beau stood there, his soft blue eyes finally meeting mine. What he wanted to say, I didn't know. SueAnn sighed pointedly.

"Well," said Mrs. Clark, "I know you have packing to do."

"Right." I snapped my gaze away from Beau. I bundled the quilt under my arm and walked past Mrs. Clark, not stopping till I was out the door.

# CHAPTER 54

# A GOODBYE

Twenty dollars! The most I'd heard of our neighbors getting for a sewing machine was fifteen. And that had been for a brand-new Singer. As I plodded down the drive, wagon rattling behind me, I tried to focus on the money and not on the fact that Mrs. Clark now owned Okaasan's prized possession.

Behind me, the door crashed open, and a voice called, "Sam!" I turned. Beau stood on the porch, his jacket slung over his round shoulders. The door slammed behind him. "I—I just wanted to ask when . . . you leave."

I hesitated. It had been so long since we'd talked. Whatever friendship once existed had been neglected. Like the wagon I pulled, it had rusted. Only there wasn't any oil that could fix it.

Then again, in the Clarks' house, he'd . . . tried. "Two days," I said.

"Oh." He crossed his arms over his ribs.

I waited. When he said nothing, I turned back to the wagon. He let me walk four steps before blurting, "Sam, I'm sorry."

I stopped. Rain still fell, making the air musty.

"Sam, I said I'm sorry. About my dad. About . . . me."

I spun to face Beau. His hands were whiter than usual—almost blue. "You should be," I whispered.

Beau's head fell forward.

"I needed you." My neck and shoulders were tight. There was so much I'd been keeping back, so much I held inside. "At school, no one talked to me. They treated me like a spy."

Beau nodded. Rain glittered in his shellacked hair.

"Everyone knew that you knew me best—and *you* treated me like I was guilty."

"I shouldn't have." Water rolled down Beau's cheeks, but I couldn't tell if it was rain or tears.

"And when Kiki and I needed you most—" I gripped the wagon so hard it hurt.

"I . . . I'm sorry," Beau whispered.

I stood there, between the porch and Mrs. Clark's perfect white fence, and really looked at the boy who'd been my best friend. His head hung low, and his shoulders hunched, like a child waiting for the strap.

He wasn't the boy I'd thought I loved. He was weak, cowardly, not strong enough to be my friend when things got rough.

But he *was* the boy who'd believed I could win a photo contest. And for a time, he'd been my friend despite my race, and that was probably the bravest thing he'd ever done.

A thought occurred to me. "Beau, why aren't you in the band anymore?"

Beau looked up. His face was splotched and red. But his eyes were that clear blue that reminded me of water. "Dad." He sniffed. "He says it's a waste of time."

I frowned. "What do you think?"

Beau shrugged. "I miss it." His fingers twitched, as if they were pressing the valves on his instrument.

My index finger prickled—how many times had it itched for the click of a button, for the mechanical snap of the shutter? Quitting photography made me feel incomplete—muted. Was that how Beau felt now? "Don't give it up, Beau. Whatever your dad says, don't give up the things you love most."

Rain twinkled in the space between us. I didn't know if I had convinced Beau, but I recognized the words *I* needed to hear. I couldn't give up photography. It was my *voice*.

"I have to go," I said.

"Maybe," Beau stammered, "maybe I could come see you off . . ."

I shook my head. "It's okay, Beau." And it really was. I didn't need him—not anymore.

As I turned and rattled away, I took a deep, clean breath. *Goodbye, Beau*, I said silently. And my thoughts turned to someone who was everything Beau couldn't be.

# CHAPTER 55

# THE ACCOUNTING

*March 30*

"The time's come," Dad said. He sat on our last chair—a wobbly, paint-splattered stool no one had wanted—with a notebook in his lap. Charlie and Kiki stood at his sides, while Hiro and I stood across from them, standing closer than I would have dared only a few weeks ago. Pink-orange light streamed through the window, lighting Okaasan's faded wallpaper roses. It was strange—the kitchen was empty, the stove and icebox sold. Where they'd stood, the floor was darker than everywhere else. But somehow, with all of us filling the unheated, bare room, the kitchen felt brighter.

Dad opened to a new sheet in the notebook. On it, he scrawled a number. "This is what I have—everything I had saved plus everything I sold." Charlie looked at the number. "I wish it were more," Dad said. "But everyone's selling. If I asked for more, the buyers would just go elsewhere."

Charlie nodded. "You did good." He shuffled through his pocket and pulled out an envelope. "This is what I could get for the stuff *I* sold." He put the fat envelope on the notebook. "And there's this." He set a mason jar full of bills on the floor—his savings. The change at the bottom clanked.

"Are you sure?" I asked. We needed it. There was no question of that. But this would be the third time he'd postponed college.

Charlie shrugged. "Who knows how long we'll be gone. Even

when we get back, if things are like they are now, the chance of getting accepted . . ." His smile was bitter.

"Maybe someday," Hiro said.

"Maybe."

Dad hesitantly patted Charlie's forearm, then cleared his throat. Together they counted—Charlie tallying the money in the jar, Dad calculating the envelope's contents. Finally, Dad printed the two sums under his first scrawl. His mouth turned down. "Not enough."

"I've got some, too," I said. My hand brushed Hiro's as I pulled the twenty-dollar bill from my pocket.

"You got that much for Okaasan's machine?" Charlie asked. I grinned.

"I—I do, too," said Kiki. She pulled Okaasan's pocketbook—the silky one she had only used for church and town—from the folds of her dress. She didn't meet our eyes as she pulled a thick wad of bills from inside.

Dad and Charlie stared. "How—" Charlie asked, but I shot him a look.

"I shouldn't have kept it to myself," Kiki said, blushing. I beamed at her.

Dad counted Kiki's cash and wrote the sum down. We held our breath as he added it all together.

Charlie was the first to realize—he sighed.

Eighty-six. We were eighty-six dollars short.

Dad's pencil hovered over the notebook as he rechecked his calculations. He put the pencil down. The room went still.

Then Dad . . . smiled. It was a sad smile, one that tore at my heart. But it reached his eyes, and for once his brow unfurrowed. "We did all that we could," he said. Kiki, Charlie, and I looked at each other. But Dad didn't yell or turn desperate. "It was a long shot," he said. "You did well." He bent to pick up some bills that had fallen to the floor.

Next to me, Hiro cleared his throat. "Mr. Sakamoto?"

"Yes?" Dad shuffled the bills into a neat stack.

"I have some money. That Tacoma man bought out most of the Merc."

I touched Hiro's hand, shaking my head. Across from me, Charlie grimaced, as if refusing cost him actual pain. "You keep what's yours, Hiro. You'll need it."

Hiro frowned. "This isn't just out of the blue. I've been thinking about this all week. I *want* to do this."

With all the money piled together, Dad stood. His face contorted. Saying no was even harder for him than for Charlie. "I promised your father I'd take care of *you*. I cannot take your money." Dad swallowed. His face stilled. His decision was made. "This is *my* failure."

Hiro looked around the room, his eyes searching for someone to agree with him. "But—"

We all shook our heads, and Dad stuffed the money into the wallet Charlie had handed him. Kiki started to walk out of the room.

"Wait." Hiro's voice rang through the cold kitchen. "Look, Mr. McClatchy took more from me than any of you." His voice trembled. "I have wished and wished there was something I could do to get some kind of justice. This is a way." He glared at Dad. "I mean, can you think of any other way?" He glowered at each of us, daring us to answer.

We shifted uncomfortably, eyeing one another.

Hiro folded his arms. "Then you must take it. You cannot take this bit of justice from me."

Dad frowned. "Hiro, even if we pay the final mortgage, there will be taxes. If we are gone more than a few months, we may lose the land anyway."

Hiro didn't flinch. "To the government. But not to McClatchy. If he wants the land, he'll have to buy it at auction. Right?"

Dad rubbed his face with his palm. "That's right," Charlie said. He took a step toward me and Hiro.

Hiro nodded. "Then that's what we're going to do."

None of us wanted to stay home, so we all went to McClatchy's General together, only stopping to pick up Mr. Allred. Dad had asked him to come as a witness. Hiro pulled the truck in front of the wide white store.

We were still getting out of the car when Mr. McClatchy stormed out, flanked by the little clerk and a couple of shoppers.

"You're not welcome here." He dug his fists into his sides.

"We're not here to shop," Dad said. My insides pulsed with something between pride and fear as we formed a line on the asphalt, almost exactly where Mr. Tanaka had stood during the boycott. Next to me, Mr. Allred rolled the papers Dad had given him into a cylinder. I examined his sloped shoulders, his thin hair and wire-rimmed glasses. Could he really keep McClatchy in line?

"Then why are you here?" McClatchy stared down at us, his eyes like two dark raisins punched into bread dough.

Dad stepped up and held out the fat, torn envelope. His hands did not tremble.

McClatchy kept his hands on his hips. "What is that?"

"My last payment," Dad said, stepping forward and pushing it into McClatchy's unwilling hands.

McClatchy opened the envelope slowly. He thumbed through the bills—the twenties, the tens, the fives, and the ones.

"It's all there," Mr. Allred said.

McClatchy gave Mr. Allred a calculating look. "Oh yeah?" Something about the way his mouth curled reminded me of Mack.

"He's paid in full," Mr. Allred said. "I'm here to witness it." He unrolled the papers Dad had given him and pulled a pen from his inside pocket.

McClatchy's eyes widened as he took in the papers. "Hold up! It's not due yet."

"But," Mr. Allred said, "it's payable at any time before the due date."

"I won't take it. I just won't take it." McClatchy's voice rose. Several patrons stared.

Mr. Allred waited, as if watching a toddler's tantrum. Behind McClatchy, Beau slouched in the slightly open door.

Hiro, standing next to me, glanced between me and Beau. I shifted, brushing the back of my hand against his.

"They're leaving!" McClatchy said. "What's the point? They'll never pay the taxes. They'll lose it anyway, and this payment, too." He faced Mr. Allred, but it was Dad who answered.

"We can't know what the future holds." Dad spread his hands, palms to the sky, as if releasing a dove.

Behind him, Charlie took a deep breath, swelling his chest, squaring his shoulders. Anyone who didn't know him might have thought the tension was getting to him. But I knew it was exactly the opposite.

McClatchy stared at Dad, as if seeing him for the first time. "If you can't pay the taxes, it'll just go to the government. You want to give it to them? The ones locking you up?" His mouth twisted, and he bent down, so his head was the same level as Dad's. "Look, maybe we can make some sort of arrangement. An extension, say. Then you can hold on to this." He held the envelope toward Dad.

Dad shook his head.

"You don't know where you're going. You might need this money." McClatchy thrust the envelope at Dad.

Dad backed away. "I intend to see this through." Dad's voice was low and clear. "I want it squared away before we go."

McClatchy's jaw worked as he stared at us, then at his patrons, some now loitering on the decking, others peeking through the store windows. Kiki trembled next to me, but she pulled her shoulders back.

"Sign here, Elroy," said Mr. Allred, holding out the paper and his pen.

McClatchy's eyes narrowed, and for a moment all was silent. Then, teeth bared, he took Mr. Allred's pen and scrawled his name across the line. He threw the pen on the asphalt. "You steal this money?" He shook the envelope in Dad's face. "Like you're stealing *my land*? You come here and steal our jobs, our kids' educations . . ."

Dad's face was stony. "I am not the thief here," he said. "All the Japanese families you cheated, what you did to Mr. Tanaka and Mr. Omura and all those people who lost their jobs at the brickyard . . . Well, at least you won't get *our* farm free and clear. You'll have to put up cash, just like anyone else."

McClatchy's eyes bulged. "I should've let that Clyde kid loose," he said in a hoarse whisper. "I should've let those boys take your son, should've let them *string him up* like they wanted." His voice grew louder. "I should've let them give you what you've been asking for since you got here, you *uppity, ugly* . . ."

Mr. Allred cleared his throat. "Let's go," he whispered, just loud enough for us to hear above McClatchy's stream of profanity.

Hiro put one hand on Charlie's arm, taking mine in the other. As he pulled us backward, toward the car, I caught several white faces gawking at McClatchy's tantrum. The shutter in my mind burst open and clapped shut, capturing a mental snapshot of their disgust.

"Get in the car," Hiro muttered as Kiki, Dad, and Mr. Allred followed.

"Allred!" McClatchy spluttered, barreling down into the road after us. Behind him, Beau's eyes were wide. "You yellow traitor. You think I'm just going to give up my granddad's land?"

Mr. Allred, now standing next to the truck, paused and turned.

He pushed his spectacles up. "Elroy," he said, "there's not a thing you can do."

McClatchy stared as if he'd been slapped. But he didn't move as we got in Hiro's truck. Behind him, Beau's eyes met mine. I could have sworn he smiled.

Charlie, Mr. Allred, and Dad had piled into the back of the truck. I sat between Hiro and Kiki in the cab. As Hiro coaxed the truck into gear and backed up, I let out the breath I'd been holding.

"It worked!" I whispered. I wanted to yell, to crow, to dance-stamp. Hiro and Kiki grinned. I leaned back against the seat, feeling fiery and full.

The electric buzz of our victory propelled us through our afternoon of packing. Charlie, Kiki, and I swapped memories, cataloging moments that, strung together like pearls, made up our lives in this home. And at the heart of all the stories was Okaasan.

But as evening wore on and rooms emptied, we quieted. The reality hit. This was our last night here. Dawn would mean goodbye.

In the gloam of dusk, I picked my way to the orchard and retrieved the tin of photos. When I snuck inside, Charlie and Dad had already moved my suitcase from my room to the parlor. As they wrestled with a giant trunk, I laid my suitcase on its side and flicked the buckle. I shuffled through my sweaters till I found Hiro's white envelope and pulled it out.

I opened both the tin and the envelope. The sharp corners and clean edges of the photos I'd taken contrasted with Okaasan's worn prints. And mine were different in style, from both the Japanese snapshots and Mr. Simmons's portraits.

Yet there was something so right in them lying next to each other. Like the memories we'd shared while packing, the collection told our story. It wasn't a perfect story—maybe not even a pretty story. But it was ours, and it was documented.

A shadow fell over the contents of my suitcase. I peeked up.

"That tin—those are Okaasan's photos?" Dad asked.

"Yes," I whispered. My fingers felt slow and stiff as I tried to close the exposed envelope.

"And those?" Dad pointed.

The room seemed to constrict. Even with Charlie bustling in and out the open front door, the air felt overly hot. For a moment, I considered lying. But—even if Dad believed me—that wouldn't fix things. Because I knew now that—just as I'd told Beau—I couldn't give this up. But I also couldn't betray my father.

It was time to be myself in front of the person with whom it was hardest.

I held the packet out to Dad. He gazed at me before taking the envelope in his work-worn hands.

"I know you don't want me to break the rules," I said, my voice trembling as he opened the paper flap. "And I know it's risky . . ."

Dad contemplated each photograph slowly, as if trying to comprehend a difficult problem. His eyebrows twitched when he came to the photo of Hiro. "But, Dad, didn't you take a huge risk when you bought the farm?" I didn't know where I got the courage to ask. "Aren't some risks worth taking?"

Dad shuffled the picture of Hiro to the back of the stack. I gulped. He'd come to the photo I'd taken of him on his farm.

Dad spent several seconds staring. The room was silent. Charlie watched us from the opening to the entry.

"These . . ." Dad's Adam's apple rose and fell. "They're very good, Sam."

My ears buzzed, and my skin tingled. Had Dad really said those words? It seemed surreal. But when I looked at Dad, he was staring at me, and in his slightly sad, proud gaze I felt . . . seen.

"I'm bringing them tomorrow," I said.

Dad nodded. "I'm glad."

Dad went back to packing, but I took my time, looking over the photos of the last few months. They showed what people had done to us, but—I picked up the photo of Hiro—also how we'd kept going.

# CHAPTER 56

# EVACUATION

## *March 31*

My bags were stuffed full. Even still, we'd left boxes piled in our bedrooms. We'd packed up Okaasan's urn, but the empty butsudan sat on the hearth. Would it be here when—if—we got back?

Mr. Allred had offered to take us to the ferry, Hiro included. But Hiro showed up earlier than we'd expected. He set two suitcases on the worn wood porch. Their buttery-soft leather and shining brass buckles, so out of place on our porch, made me think of Mr. Tanaka. Unlike him, at least we got to go together.

"Sam," Hiro said, peering behind me into the house. "Can I talk to you before we go?"

I closed the door behind me, ignoring Kiki's quizzical look. "Is here okay?"

Hiro nodded and knelt down next to one of his cases. He popped the buckle open and pulled out a handkerchief-wrapped bundle. "I don't know what will happen when we get wherever we're going. And I don't want you to get in trouble. But I want you to have this." He handed it to me.

I peeled away the corners of the fabric. There, shining in the middle of the patterned cloth, sat the Leica, along with six rolls of film.

"I asked Mr. Simmons for the film last night," he said. "Tried to pay him, but he wouldn't let me."

I took one roll in my hand, folding my fingers over its perfect weight. "So kind of him." I swallowed. "But I can't take the camera. It's your father's."

"He'd want you to have it," Hiro said. "Someone needs to document what's happening."

*Document.* The word felt dangerous . . . And powerful. "But who would publish—"

Hiro shook his head. "We might not be able to do anything with the pictures right now. But they're important. And someday . . ."

I shivered, but not from the cold and not from fear. Like a shutter flashing open and allowing in light, something clicked. Photography didn't just give *me* a voice. It spoke for all of us. Taking pictures created proof of what was done to us—and of the strength with which we countered. It was exactly what Mr. Tanaka would want from me.

I nodded. "Okay . . . Only I wish your dad was going with us."

Hiro swallowed. "I'll keep trying—wherever we end up."

"I'll help you."

Hiro's eyes met mine. "I know." A sad smile crossed his face. "Dad's suitcase has a valuables compartment. I'll put the camera and film in there. That way if it gets found, they won't think it's yours. But . . . it is."

I looked deep into Hiro's maple eyes. The crinkles at the corners seemed wise rather than laughing. "I can't ask that of you," I whispered.

Hiro smiled. "Oh, Sam. Didn't I already tell you? It's my privilege."

I took the Leica around the house, snapping photos of empty rooms, Okaasan's curtains, and her special knots. I shot a portrait of each member of my family: Charlie, who even now posed like a "college man"; Dad, whose lined face was both worn and proud; and Kiki, her eyes still full of fire as we prepared to submit. Then I ran to the edge of Japantown, where Mr. Tanaka's sign still hung, and took the photo I'd wanted nearly four months ago.

Finally, I finished the roll with a second portrait of Hiro. I stared at him through the lens, allowing myself time to really see him. He stared back, and instead of feeling vulnerable, I felt comforted, familiar. Known.

Hiro repacked the camera, along with the film. I imagined the shots I'd taken someday joining the tin of Okaasan's photos. The thought made me smile.

# BENEATH THE WIDE SILK SKY

There wasn't room for all of us in the cab of Mr. Allred's truck, so Charlie, Hiro, and I sat in the back with the luggage. I was glad for the chance to be outside. I said silent goodbyes to the house, the blue door, and Okaasan's persimmon tree. I tried to memorize the salty tang of Linley's air, the sound of the killdeer in the trees, even the way the dilapidated road bumped beneath us.

As we passed the Merc, Hiro's expression turned grim. A gang of boys swarmed round the store.

"Mack." Charlie pointed. Mack leaned against the store, his baseball bat over his shoulder. He smirked as he caught our stares. Pointing at Charlie, he raised his bat.

*Crash!* Mack brought the bat down, shattering the front right window.

A few boys jeered, but most rushed into the store. Before we were out of sight, several emerged, holding as much as they could carry. One held the beautiful porcelain doll by her hair, whipping her like a lasso above his head.

I touched Hiro's arm. "I'm so sorry."

"I sold most of it." Hiro set his jaw and stared forward. "They won't get much."

As we drove up to the harbor, I saw the ferry, still even in the waves. It was massive—much too large for the number of Japanese on our island—and crisscrossed with ropes and pulleys. Mr. Allred drove us as close as he could, but the area around the gates was packed. Lines of soldiers stood in uniform, some holding clipboards, most holding rifles. Parallel lines of Japanese families waited, orderly and dignified. Dressed in their best clothes, their valises and trunks clutched tight, they might have been setting off on trips, except that no one smiled, and all of them—men, women, and children—had labels pinned to their coats.

On the far side of the gates, held off by a pair of soldiers, a group of white men and women jeered. But others had come as friends, helping families carry their luggage, bouncing crying children, giving tearful hugs goodbye.

Jean had come. Charlie jumped out of the truck before it came to a complete stop, and she hurried down the hill to meet him.

"I wish I could do more, Matsuo," Mr. Allred said after we'd gathered our things from the truck. "Please just write if we can ever help with anything. We're here, and we'll be watching over your farm."

Dad shook his head and clasped Mr. Allred's hand. "We already owe you, John."

"Sam?" I turned. Ruth and her mother had come up behind us. Ruth's cheeks were pink, and her eyes were bright.

"We wanted to say goodbye," said Mrs. Allred. "There wasn't room in the car, but we wanted to see you off."

"Thank you," my father said. "I appreciate that."

"I wrote you a letter," Ruth said, holding out a thin cream envelope. There was a roughness to her voice, and she blinked, but she didn't cry.

I swallowed, and before I could get too shy, I leaned forward and pulled her into a hug. Her honey curls mixed with my jet-black hair. "Thank you," I said. The two words weren't enough. How could I possibly explain how much her kindness—and her friendship—had meant? But I'd try, I promised myself, as we let go and I stepped back. Writing her would be the first thing I'd do when we got wherever we were going.

The Allreds walked alongside us, helping us carry our bags, as we made our way toward the line inside the gate—the adults and Kiki first, then Ruth, Hiro, and me. Charlie and Jean came last, silently holding hands.

The line snaked off the pavement and onto the beach. Sand sucked at my boots as we hauled our things to the end of the queue.

"Name?" a soldier asked Dad. He carried a clipboard and had a rifle slung over his shoulder.

"Sakamoto." Dad pointed at Hiro. "And Tanaka—he's with us." There was a forcefulness to the way he said it, and I was grateful.

The soldier nodded. "I'll make a note."

The soldier had Dad spell our names for him as he found them in his register. Then he made out a tag for each of our bags, as well as one to wear. "Leave it on," he said. "It's mandatory."

Mrs. Yamaguchi and Mrs. Omura were several families ahead. Mrs. Omura tried to keep the older Yamaguchi kids corralled, while Mrs. Yamaguchi struggled to hold both her bags and little Kenji, who wailed in her arms.

"I'm going to help," Kiki said quietly. She took up her luggage, begging pardon as she walked ahead.

When she reached Mrs. Yamaguchi, Kiki set her bags down. She held her hands out to Kenji, and Mrs. Yamaguchi—flustered and relieved—handed him off.

"Well," Dad said, a strange look on his face.

Kiki whispered something to Kenji, then twirled, making Kenji's shiny bowl cut fan out as his cries turned to happy shrieks.

Dad caught my gaze. "She's going to be okay, isn't she?"

"She's going to be fine."

We waited and waited, till the sun rose high and hot. Finally, a soldier called out orders, telling all non-Japanese that they needed to leave. The Allreds shook our hands one more time, and Ruth pulled me into one more quick hug as she whispered goodbye.

All around us, friends embraced and cried. But Charlie and Jean did neither, only looked at each other with that same deep, mysterious look I'd seen the night Kiki was hurt. Then Jean's hand slipped out of Charlie's, and she made her way back up to the gate, finally merging into the crowd and disappearing.

"Up the ramp," a soldier ordered. Jostling but hushed, my neighborhood—including my schoolmates, the elderly, children, and even a newborn in her mother's arms—surged up the ramp.

The ramp swayed slightly under my feet, and my stomach clenched. This was it. The bridge away from all I'd known and loved, the bridge to a blank and terrifying chapter. We'd thought this day impossible in the country we loved. And yet, here we were.

People quietly shuffled and bumped onto the deck of the ferry. The clean tang of ocean air cleared my head. I wanted to capture this moment. We weren't sure where we were going. But it would be away from the ocean. And I wanted to memorize this smell.

It didn't take long for all of Japantown to get on the ferry. The soldiers followed us, some stationing themselves around the deck, others gathering in the center of the boat. Dad found a chair next to Mrs. Yamaguchi. Hiro, Charlie, Kiki, and I made our way to the stern of the boat. After a short wait, a deep whistle blew. My heart lurched with the ferry.

As the vessel groaned, I surveyed my island. The bare cliffs stood tall, distinct from the emerald forest. The rocky beach glistened, jewellike. Above, gulls mourned.

It felt as if I were being pulled apart. They could take my body from this place, but my heart—how could I pull my heart from my home?

"Why did I think I wanted to leave?" Charlie wiped the ocean's spray from his face. Kiki inched close and put her arm around his back.

The sight quieted some of the ache in my heart. At least we were together. I reached out for Hiro's hand.

As the cliffs shrank, then disappeared, the sun rested on my shoulders, melting into my ribs, seeping into my spine. I stared out at the open water. It undulated, wide and vast, matched only by the sky above. Though calm on the surface, ripples of froth hinted at the power below.

*Like Okaasan*, I thought. Gentle and uncomplaining, she was the force that kept our family linked. Without her, we'd been lost for a while, tossed and driven, separate. But now . . .

I looked at Kiki, her small arm not quite reaching across Charlie's shoulders. His head tilted toward her. We were a family again. And somehow it felt as if Okaasan had been with us all along.

We couldn't change everything. We'd lost our home. We didn't know where we were going. There were some things about which nothing could be done. *Shikata ga nai* . . .

*And yet* . . .

We were safe. I had Hiro's hand in mine. And wherever we were going, we were together . . . beneath the wide silk sky.

# AUTHOR'S NOTE

During World War II, 120,000 persons of Japanese ancestry were forcibly removed from their homes and incarcerated in American prison camps. Two-thirds of the prisoners were American-born US citizens. Half were children.

The camps were constructed in remote, desolate locations, where prisoners lived up to four years in substandard housing, often with inadequate nutrition. Some prisoners died due to insufficient medical care. Several were killed by military guards. Almost all lost their homes, lands, and businesses.

At the time, 93 percent of Americans polled supported the forced evacuation of Japanese immigrants. In the case of Japanese Americans who were born in the United States and held US citizenship, 59 percent of those polled still supported their forced evacuation. Toward the end of the war, 13 percent of Americans polled favored "killing all the Japanese."

My great-grandparents, grandparents, great-aunts, and great-uncles were among those removed from their homes on the West Coast. They were sent first to temporary "assembly centers," including a racetrack where they lived in horse stalls, and then to a permanent prison camp at Heart Mountain, Wyoming. My father was born in the camp hospital.

In the 1980s, the Commission on Wartime Relocation and Internment of Civilians found that the internment was "motivated largely by racial prejudice, wartime hysteria, and a failure of political leadership." Historians also recognize the role economic rivalry played, motivating Caucasian farmers to lobby for the removal of Japanese farmers, whom they saw as competition.

Yet there were also people who acted as allies to Japanese Americans. Some neighbors spoke against mass incarceration. Some offered to store things or help settle affairs. A few even maintained farms or businesses until their Japanese American friends returned.

In this book, I mention one real-life ally. Sam's hero, Dorothea Lange, was a documentary photographer and photojournalist. In 1942, Lange was hired by the US government to make a record of the evacuation. Though she opposed mass incarceration, she took the commission because she believed a "true record" was necessary.

Military commanders soon found that Lange's gritty and powerful photos reflected her opposition. They seized her photos for the duration of the war. Others were hired to take glossier, "happier" pictures that eased the public's conscience. For years, Lange's photos were impounded, forcibly kept from public view during the war, and then quietly slipped into the National Archives without notice.

But decades later, Lange's work was rediscovered, and on a visit to the Smithsonian, my relatives saw a photograph Lange had taken. It portrayed my great-grandfather on the eve of the family's removal. A collection of Lange's photos of the evacuation has now been published. Her record is also available to the public through the National Archives.

Japanese Americans fought to create their own records, as well. While cameras were banned and confiscated, an imprisoned photographer named Tōyō Miyatake brought a lens into the Manzanar prison camp. He then had a wooden camera constructed and film smuggled in so that he could secretly take photos of camp life. At the Topaz camp, Dave Tatsuno carried around a video camera disguised in a shoebox. And other Japanese Americans also found ways to photodocument the incarceration, particularly in the later years when restrictions were lifted. These photos are now important evidence of how a society can hurt its own. More importantly, they are a record of the lives individuals continued to build, even when stripped of their rights.

Unfortunately, racism, hysteria, failing political leadership, and economic competition all still exist in our society today. I chose to write about the time before the internment because in a way we're always at a point *before* injustice. The question of how we will act, and of how we will define our society, is always before us. Are we a people willing to commit great injustices out of greed and fear? Are we a people who quietly let injustice happen around us? Or do we speak up? Do we act?

This book is my exploration of those questions. Samantha Sakamoto chooses to document her experience, finding her voice even as she faces certain incarceration. In doing so, I hope she reflects the courage and perseverance characteristic of the many Japanese Americans interned during WWII—and with which we still must fight to live up to the American experiment and its ideals.

# ACKNOWLEDGMENTS

First and foremost, I want to thank my grandparents, aunties, and uncles. Long before I had any thought of writing a novel, I felt a persistent need to better understand my family's World War II experience. My deepest gratitude and love go to the family members who shared their stories, and lifelong examples, with me. Additionally, I want to particularly thank Jeanette Misaka for her help with the book.

While writing is often portrayed as a solitary endeavor, one of the greatest gifts of this project is the people it has brought into my life. Thank you to Sarah Alva, Stacy Codner, Apryl K. B. Lopez, Miranda Renaé, and Julie Whipple for their many contributions. If the only results of this project were our friendships, it would be worth it.

I feel fortunate to have worked with the creative writing professors at Lesley University on the first drafts of this book. Thank you especially to David Elliott, Anita Riggio, and my thesis advisor, Chris Lynch.

I also want to acknowledge Dennis Packard, Byron Daynes, and Don Norton for helping me with much of the research that went into this book. And I count Carol Lynch Williams as a beloved mentor.

I'm indebted to Emily Hinchey and Allison Shiozawa Miles for their thoughtful feedback, and to Melissa Inouye for her input (and for being the Mr. Tanaka in my life). Thank you also to

Daniel Inouye for his help with the Japanese language and cultural elements.

I am grateful to Caryn Wiseman for believing in the book and helping me improve it. Thank you also to Allison Nolen for her help with the story and the language.

Many thanks to the team at Scholastic. I am especially grateful to Lisa Sandell for her always gracious yet incisive feedback.

There is no one in the world to whom I owe more than Jeanne Bryan Inouye. Thank you, Mom, for reading this manuscript more times than anyone else. And to Dillon Kazuyuki Inouye, my father, who somehow guessed I'd end up in the children's lit world decades before I did, there's so much of this book that comes from you.

Finally, to Robert Huey, thank you for your love and support. All the best things in my life are possible because of you.

# ABOUT THE AUTHOR

Emily Inouye Huey is the daughter, granddaughter, and great-granddaughter of Japanese Americans incarcerated during World War II. Her family was evacuated from their homes and farms in California and Washington. Her grandparents met and married in Wyoming's Heart Mountain Relocation Center, and her father was born in the camp hospital. When the war ended, the family was sent to Utah, where they started over and where Emily still lives, now with her husband and four children.

She holds an MFA in creative writing from Lesley University and teaches at Salt Lake Community College. You can visit her at emilyhuey.com or on Instagram at @emily_inouye_huey.